"The perfect beach read. *Out of the Clear Blue Sky* provides the kind of heartwarming tale of hard-fought growth, crazy family, and welcoming community that will linger with you long after the final page."

—#1 *New York Times* bestselling author Lisa Gardner

"Reading a Kristan Higgins novel is like spending time with a dear friend, one who understands your soul, captivates your senses . . . and every now and then makes you snort with laughter. Higgins never disappoints! If you're looking for a novel with heart and humor, look no further than *Out of the Clear Blue Sky.* With her trademark wit, Higgins tackles tough issues, and does so with sensitivity and heart. *Out of the Clear Blue Sky* is everything I love in women's fiction—smart, hilarious, and brimming with hope."

—Lori Nelson Spielman, *New York Times* bestselling author of *The Star-Crossed Sisters of Tuscany*

"Your big summer read has arrived! Book after book, Kristan Higgins is a can't-miss author who always serves up stories that are fresh, relevant, and deeply involving."

—Susan Wiggs, #1 *New York Times* bestselling author

"From the first page, I was deeply invested in Lillie's plight and desperate to keep turning pages. Kristin Higgins nails it with this laugh-oud-loud, pitch-perfect, heartfelt novel about a woman's life upended and the unexpected ways she finds her way forward. Full of hope, positive messages, and humor, *Out of the Clear Blue Sky* is the perfect book for summer, or anytime!"

—Elyssa Friedland, author of *Last Summer at the Golden Hotel*

"A fantastic journey with a brave, delightful, and mischievous heroine who will keep you laughing and rooting for her from page one. I did not want this book to end!"

—Jane L. Rosen, author of *Eliza Starts a Rumor*

"With a blend of humor and poignancy reminiscent of Nora Ephron's *Heartburn* . . . [*Out of the Clear Blue Sky* is] a beautifully told blend of grief, hope, and humor that showcases Higgins at her best."

—*Kirkus Reviews* (starred review)

"Higgins has created an accomplished protagonist with strong values, a good heart, and an enviable network of friends. Everyone in the community is on her side; take that, ex-husband! This will be satisfying for readers who like to see a strong woman thrive during times of trial."

—*Library Journal*

"Higgins is known for her emotionally potent novels about characters whose lives are in transition. . . . A bighearted treat for relationship-fiction readers." —*Booklist*

"An emotional, funny tale of second chances."

—*Woman's World*

Praise for
Pack Up the Moon

"*New York Times* bestselling author Kristan Higgins tells a heartwarming—and heartbreaking—story about young love, loss, and the lingering effects of grief. . . . A story about resilience and everlasting love, this stunningly written tale is a true tearjerker." —*Good Morning America*

"Kristan Higgins is beloved for her rich, heartwarming sagas—which her latest novel delivers." —*Woman's World*

"A gorgeous study of love, life, and grief, this book broke my heart—and then stitched me back together again. Kristan Higgins is a masterful storyteller."
—*New York Times* bestselling author Colleen Oakley

"A moving and life-affirming portrait of grief that's sure to bring the tears." —*Kirkus Reviews* (starred review)

"Higgins is a master of snappy dialogue, and her characters are authentic and relatable—a must for this type of novel. The heart of the story is tragic, but just like real life, there's humor hidden in the darkest moments. This warm, big-hearted story about grief, family, and the redemptive power of love will appeal to fans of Katherine Center and Jennifer Weiner." —*Booklist* (starred review)

"Perfect pacing and plotting lift Higgins's masterly latest. This is going to break (and restore) plenty of hearts."
—*Publishers Weekly* (starred review)

"Higgins has crafted one of the most beautiful love stories I ever read. It will make you cry but also leave you breathless and aching for a love like Joshua and Lauren's."
—Bookreporter

Praise for

Always the Last to Know

"A thoroughly entertaining exploration of families' complexities—from bitter disappointment to quiet strengths."
—*People*, Pick of the Week

"Filled with hilarious honesty and heartwarming moments. . . . A moving portrait of a family putting their differences aside in favor of love." —*Woman's World*

"This sparkling story is perfect summer reading."
—*Publishers Weekly*

Praise for
Life and Other Inconveniences

"Deeply touching, real, and raw, but infused with the love and hope that make life possible, despite everything."
—Abbi Waxman, author of *The Bookish Life of Nina Hill*

"Master storyteller Kristan Higgins deftly balances humor and heart in this latest tale of a young woman navigating her relationship with a dying grandmother who long ago abandoned her when she needed her most . . . another must-read from Higgins, who has long been an auto-buy for me."
—Colleen Oakley, author of *Before I Go*
and *Close Enough to Touch*

"Higgins is a mastermind of family dynamics in this poignant novel about two different generations of women struggling to find common ground. I couldn't put it down!"
—Emily Liebert, author of *Some Women* and *Pretty Revenge*

"Higgins brings hope and humor to intensely personal dramas and makes them everyone's story."
—#1 *New York Times* bestselling author Robyn Carr

"Readers will be riveted as the well-drawn characters uncover one another's hidden depths and heal old wounds."
—*Publishers Weekly* (starred review)

Praise for

Good Luck with That

"Masterfully told, *Good Luck with That* is a story with which every woman will identify. We all deal with body image, self-esteem, and acceptance of love at one time or another. Bravo, Kristan Higgins, bravo!"

—#1 *New York Times* bestselling author Debbie Macomber

"Kristan Higgins is at the top of her game, stirring the emotions of every woman with the poignant reality of her characters."

—#1 *New York Times* bestselling author Robyn Carr

"Wholly original and heartfelt, written with grace and sensitivity, *Good Luck with That* is an irresistible tale of love, friendship, and self-acceptance—and the way body image can sabotage all three."

—Lori Nelson Spielman, *New York Times* bestselling author of *The Life List*

"I LOVED *Good Luck with That*! It's hilarious, heartbreaking, surprising, and so true to life."

—Nancy Thayer, *New York Times* bestselling author of *A Nantucket Wedding*

"Higgins writes with her trademark heart, humor, and emotion, addressing the serious and somber subject of body image. . . . Highly recommended."

—*Library Journal* (starred review)

BERKLEY BOOKS BY KRISTAN HIGGINS

Good Luck with That
Life and Other Inconveniences
Always the Last to Know
Pack Up the Moon
Out of the Clear Blue Sky

For a list of Kristan's other novels,
please visit kristanhiggins.com.

Out of the
Clear Blue Sky

Kristan Higgins

BERKLEY • NEW YORK

BERKLEY
An imprint of Penguin Random House LLC
penguinrandomhouse.com

Copyright © 2022 by Kristan Higgins
Readers Guide copyright © 2022 by Kristan Higgins
Excerpt from *A Little Ray of Sunshine* copyright © 2023 by Kristan Higgins
Penguin Random House supports copyright. Copyright fuels creativity, encourages
diverse voices, promotes free speech, and creates a vibrant culture. Thank you for buying
an authorized edition of this book and for complying with copyright laws by not
reproducing, scanning, or distributing any part of it in any form without permission.
You are supporting writers and allowing Penguin Random House to continue to
publish books for every reader.

BERKLEY and the BERKLEY & B colophon are registered trademarks of
Penguin Random House LLC.

ISBN: 9780593335352

Berkley hardcover edition / June 2022
Berkley trade paperback edition / June 2022
Berkley mass-market edition / April 2023

Printed in the United States of America
1   3   5   7   9   10   8   6   4   2

This book is dedicated to my aunt, Teresa Kristan, the best and bravest. The biggest heart, the smartest mouth and quite an inspiration, too, whether you like it or not, dear Tess. Love you.

Lillie

Six months ago, if you had asked me what I thought I'd be doing today, the answer would *not* have been transporting a drugged skunk to the house where my soon-to-be ex-husband lived with his much-younger fiancée.

Yet here I was.

And today, for the first time in a long time, I felt happy as I bounced down the dirt road in my father's pickup truck, my cute little cargo snug and snoring in the back atop a pile of blankets, sleeping the sleep of Benadryl.

If you live in the wilds of Cape Cod, as I do, you know about skunks. They're everywhere—on the beaches, on the pond shores, in the woods, especially at dusk, or waddling past the house in the middle of the night, heavy with funk. When we were little, my older sister, Hannah, and I would lie still in our room and catch a whiff of that smell and instantly start giggling into our pillows, trying not to laugh and startle it. Back before Hannah left, that is. From time to time, my dad, who had also grown up here, would have to trap one if it made its home under our shed, before it had babies. We always used the catch-and-release traps. And since I was his shadow, I learned to do the same.

This morning, my mission clear, I walked from my house, which is tucked into a hill overlooking Herring Pond, one of the chain of glacier-formed kettle ponds on the ocean side of Wellfleet. I went down the steep, winding path of stone stairs we'd put in fifteen years ago, down the little path past the dock we'd rebuilt when we first moved in, and over to the sandy shore, accessible only to those who knew where to find it.

There was the trap, and there was my sweet little skunk, sound asleep, its little sides rising and falling, a slight snore escaping its pointy little snout. Adorable. Flower, I'd call her. I felt a little guilty for what I was about to subject it to. It wouldn't get hurt. Brad was so not the type to do anything other than jump on a chair and scream. I couldn't see Melissa bashing in a skunk's head and possibly getting her perfect clothes messy.

The daughter . . . she might like the chaos. She was practically a teenager, after all. And my sources told me she also hated Brad, and possibly Melissa.

Today, Bradley Thayer Fairchild, my husband of nineteen and a half years, was at my sister's office, making wedding plans with his child bride, sixteen years younger than he is. My sister, Hannah, is a wedding planner. The bride, or *that slut*, as I call her, was closer in age to our son than to Brad. Harassment was warranted.

The court views divorce as the dissolution of a business arrangement. It is a bloodless legal process that refuses to consider fairness, or hurt, or responsibility. It ignores the blazing trash fire of your life, in other words, and doesn't want to hear about what's fair or just.

Enter the skunk.

Brad and Melissa deserved some chaos after ripping up my life, my son's life, our family and our future. I pictured them coming home to their perfect, vast, expensive house and discovering this cute little critter in their all-white home. The screams!

Flower would stamp her tiny front feet, then turn, twitch

her tail upward, and spray, which, in this fantasy, would go directly onto one of their perfect white sofas, into the beautiful Persian carpets. Every rainy day, the smell would haunt them, no matter how hard they cleaned, or rather, how much they paid someone to clean. Even Melissa's $500 Jo Malone luxury candles wouldn't cover skunk, and with every whiff, they'd think of yours truly. Because who else would do something like this? They could call the cops, but I had babysat half the force and gone to school with the other half. Plus, I was leaving no clues.

It felt good to smile.

I wasn't always a half-crazy harpy bent on revenge. A few months ago, I was just probably the nicest, most normal person you could find. A certified nurse-midwife, delivering babies, soothing worried moms-to-be, taking blood pressure and teaching childbirth classes. I was the adoring mother of a wonderful young man, the loving wife to Bradley T. Fairchild, PhD, and the devoted daughter-in-law to his parents.

Now, our son had just left for his freshman year of college (in Montana, the wretch), and Brad had dumped me for a thirty-year-old widow who loved money, herself and middle-aged men, and I was transporting a skunk to their six-thousand-square-foot architectural monstrosity on the other side of Wellfleet.

You'd have thought that at least they wouldn't settle in my hometown. You would have been wrong.

Melissa. The name was a hissed curse in my mouth.

My sister had informed me that today was the first and lengthiest wedding consultation. Hannah, who owes me several decades of sisterly favors, is the most sought-after wedding planner on the Cape and islands. She was also my spy.

How would I get in the house with my furry black-and-white friend, you ask? Melissa's house—Stella Maris, because of course it had a name—had both a hidden key and a code that might not have been changed since I showed

Melissa the house last January. My in-laws were the Fairchilds of Fairchild Properties, and they'd been in Bali last winter. Vanessa had called—could I be an angel and show a house for them? Of course I could! Anything to help Vanessa, my beloved mother-in-law, more like a mom than my own mother. Seven months later, the new owner of that house would be marrying my husband. They'd gotten engaged three weeks after Brad moved out, which was also the day our son had left for the University of Montana.

You can't make this stuff up, right?

When Brad and I had gotten married twenty years ago, I was just about to graduate from Emmanuel College, and he was finishing his PhD at Boston University. We met on Boston Common when he ran past, sweaty, blond and gorgeous, and told me my ice cream cone looked amazing. (It was.) Eight months later, I found out I was pregnant— miraculous, given my medical history—and Brad and I were married in a hasty but tasteful wedding at the Hampshire House, tab picked up by my in-laws, who were utterly delighted that I was expecting.

This wedding—of my forty-six-year-old husband and his barely-thirty-year-old bride—was another animal. The kind my sister specialized in—archways made of orchids, bands flown in from Austin, dinners that cost $500 a plate, wine shipped in from vineyards and, if rumor was true, Bruno Mars dropping in for a quick solo.

Let's say it stung. Let's say it ripped my broken heart out of my chest and ground it on the sharpest shells and let the seagulls pick at it. Maybe I should've caught two skunks. Or a wolf. A great white shark. Then again, there was Melissa's kid to consider. Wouldn't want *her* to be eaten. I'm not a monster.

Obviously, though, I stalked Melissa on social media. She was filthy rich and loved showing the world how the one percent lived. There was nothing she enjoyed more than photo shoots starring herself, occasionally her kid, but also the apartment she had lived in with Husband #1 in

New York City. The vacations they'd taken—Thailand, London, Madrid, Kenya. Over the past six months, her feed had been filled with shots of the mansion on the water here on the Cape. Melissa just *adored* furnishing with the work of local artists. She posted a walk-through tour, like she was Oprah. The BMW she'd just bought herself, played down in a humblebrag. *Felt so strange, buying a $90K car, but want the highest safety rating for my Ophelia! Tried to make up for the guilt by giving money to the local food pantry. #RandomActsOfKindness #BMW #Tweens #Cape-Cod #SmallTownLife #SafestCar #Donate #EndHunger*

And now, she was *thrilled* to be working with Hannah Chapman Events to design her dream wedding! Would we like to see her vision board? Well, here it was!

So.

Divorce is especially painful when you didn't know your marriage was floundering. Splitting up is one thing, right? You grow apart, you're perpetually dissatisfied with each other, you agree that you'd both be happier unmarried. Happened all the time.

That was not the case with Brad and me. A couple of days before Brad told me he'd found love elsewhere, we'd had sex. Really good sex—the kind you could have when your only child was out of the house. Five days later, I was informed that he needed to infuse joy into his life, which meant dumping me.

During the four months since I found out Brad was leaving me for someone else, I swear I'd been running a fever. I hadn't had a good night's sleep since May 12, which wasn't helping my "woman on the verge" feeling.

But right now, I didn't care. I was just so dang proud of catching a skunk.

I turned off Route 6 and took a right to go into Wellfleet proper. On Main Street, I slowed down, waving to Bertie, who owned the general store, and Sarah, who owned the package store. At the Congregational church, I saw Reverend White, who lifted his hand at me as he crossed the street. I flipped him off and he nodded kindly. The good reverend, who had baptized me, was performing Bralissa's wedding. Word had it she'd just donated ten grand to fix the church's bell tower.

Beth, who had been my friend since kindergarten, was catering the wedding. She and her siblings owned the Wellfleet Ice House, the best restaurant in town, possibly on all of the Cape. She told me she'd do her best to spit in Brad's food. Again . . . a spy for me. And we Cape Codders accepted the dynamic—outsiders pumping money into the local economy was just how it was.

I drove slowly, fearful of jostling Flower. Past the shops and restaurants, which would all profit off of Melissa's money, no doubt; past the beautiful memorial garden where she'd probably already donated money; past Preservation Hall, the fish market, the library. There was the tiny bookstore, Open Book, possibly the only business in town that wouldn't benefit from Melissa's money, since I'd bet my right thumb Melissa was not a reader.

The roads became curvy and confusing, but I knew my way. Of course I did. I knew every street, dirt road and path from here to Provincetown. I had ridden my bike on every road in Wellfleet, from Route 6 to the secret dirt roads on Lieutenant Island. When Dylan was a baby, I'd take him for car rides late at night when he couldn't settle down. So of course I knew about the little road to nowhere that was adjacent to Melissa's house. Their alarm system didn't have cameras (yet, though this might change their minds on that issue). It was just the type that notified the police that someone was trying to get in. Someone who didn't know the alarm code, that was.

The truck bounced over a bump, and I glanced in the rearview to see that my skunk was still covered. She was.

I thought back again to that call last January, the coldest, quietest, grayest time of year on Cape Cod. Vanessa, my then-beloved mother-in-law, had said, "Darling, I hate to ask since it's such short notice, but we're obviously in Bali, and Norma"—their Realtor in the Cape office of Fairchild Properties—"is having her knee replaced. Would you mind showing a house or two? We have a new client who seems promising."

"I'd be happy to," I said. Not for the first time, I wondered why they never asked Brad. Both of us had flexible hours—Brad was a therapist in solo practice—but only I got the tap. Probably because I was better with people. It was fine. I didn't mind. "How's Bali?"

"Oh, darling, it's paradise! I wish you and Brad had come with us!"

"Well, another time, maybe," I said. "Once Dylan's in college, we'll have more time." A lump had risen in my throat at the idea that my son would be leaving.

"Of course. Well, next year, we'll have to go somewhere special. Our treat! Hopefully, it'll help with the . . . well, the loneliness. I know what it's like to have only one child, after all. It's awful when they first leave. But you do get used to it, and if you're lucky, he marries a wonderful girl and you become closer than ever."

"Thanks, Mom," I said, because she loved when I called her that (and because I got to secretly stick it to my own mother, who had the same maternal instincts as a lizard that eats her own eggs). "It's so nice of you, and we would love it," I said, smiling. Many times in the past, we'd gone on vacation with my in-laws, with our son, to places we would never have been able to afford on our own.

I had obediently called the client. "Hi, I'm Liliana Silva with Fairchild Properties. I understand you're looking for a place up here?"

"Oh, yes! Thank you so much for calling me back." She had a nice, low-pitched voice, and though her area code was 212, she didn't have a New York accent.

"Are you familiar with the area?" I asked.

"A little bit," she said. "We rented a house up there last summer in Truro, but Wellfleet seems a little more . . . civilized."

I laughed. "It's true." Wellfleet had a bustling Main Street, a wonderful old movie theater, restaurants that were open year-round. Truro was wilder and had less to offer tourists.

"It seems like a good place to raise a child," Melissa said.

"It is," I said. "Our school system is fantastic. How old is your child?"

"She's twelve," Melissa said.

"Such a fun age. My son is eighteen. I'd be happy to show you around. Have you looked online at any particular listings?"

"A little bit. I haven't seen anything perfect just yet."

"Tell me what you're looking for."

There was a silence. "Something . . . open. Lots of light. Maybe a water view?"

That would cost millions. No wonder my in-laws wanted someone to talk to her. "And your price range . . . ?"

"Well . . . to be honest, if it's the right house, I don't have one. I've been blessed with financial security."

That must be nice, I thought. "We have some lovely properties. Describe your dream house, and let me see what we can do."

I could hear the smile in her voice as she answered. "Oh, gosh. Well, big enough, because I like to entertain. Lots of windows, somewhere quiet and safe. It's time to get out of the city. We need a change, and a small town just sounds so lovely right now."

"And your partner?" I asked. "Any preferences on their part?"

"Sadly, I'm a widow," she said.

"Oh, no. I'm so sorry." Raising a twelve-year-old alone . . . gosh.

"Thank you," she said. "That's very kind." There was a pause. "Another reason for a change."

"You won't regret it," I said. "I'm a fifth-generation Cape Codder, and I couldn't imagine living anywhere else. What's your daughter's name?"

"Ophelia."

I winced. Who names their kid after the doomed innocent who commits suicide in *Hamlet*? Rich people, that's who. "Such a pretty name."

"Thank you!" There was genuine warmth in her voice. "What's your son's name?"

"Dylan," I said, as ever feeling a rush of pride and love (and panic, because he was a senior in high school and life as I knew it was ending).

"And he's been happy on the Cape? With school and, um . . . opportunities?"

I understood the code. *Are you hicks? Because I'm from New York.* "Very happy. The kids from Nauset High get into the full range of schools, from Harvard and Stanford to the Air Force Academy." It was true. Our school system rocked.

"Wonderful! I plan to come up this weekend. Would that be okay?"

"That would be perfect." Wanda, my boss and friend, would be on call at the hospital. "It's pretty quiet up here, and there's nothing like the winter beach. It's so pure and majestic. Can I take you to lunch first?"

"Thank you, Liliana!" she said. "That's so kind of you!"

"Call me Lillie," I told her. "And it's my pleasure."

Thus began my doom.

She came up, without her child, who was with a friend that weekend, and we met at the Ice House, Beth's restaurant, which was one of the few places open year-round. Melissa Finch was very pretty, *much* younger than I had expected. "I can't believe you have a twelve-year-old!" I exclaimed. "You don't look a day past twenty-five!"

She smiled. "Actually, Ophelia isn't my biological daughter. She came from a troubled background, and Dennis—my late husband—well, we just couldn't say no."

"How lucky for you and her both."

Melissa had been born in the Midwest, went to school in Connecticut and landed in New York City. "I was planning on going to medical school," she said, "but Ophelia came into our lives and I needed to devote all my time to her." The answer sounded as if she'd given it a hundred times.

"There's nothing like being a stay-at-home mother," I said, though I'd worked part-time all through Dylan's childhood. But Brad had juggled his schedule, and it was only on the rare occasion that we'd ever needed someone other than ourselves to take care of him.

"But now you work in real estate?" she asked.

"Actually, I'm a certified nurse-midwife," I said. "My in-laws are the Fairchilds in Fairchild Properties."

"Does your husband work in the business?"

"No, he's a therapist. But sometimes I show houses or stage them. Family, you know."

"Of course. Now that Ophelia is a little older, I'm thinking about doing something myself." She sipped her seltzer water. "I've even considered becoming a therapist, but I'm also looking into becoming a yoga teacher. Kind of the same thing, right?"

"Mm." I admit that I had to smother a snort. I mean, sure, everyone loved yoga. I took yoga classes with Beth. My mother's wife and Hannah did yoga together twice a week. My *father*, a crusty scallop fisherman, had to do yoga when he hurt his back last year. The Cape was glutted with yoga studios and yoga on the beach and yoga at dawn and yoga at sunset. Sure, it was wonderful. That being said, if I'd told Brad he and yoga teachers were kind of the same thing, he'd be furious and insulted. He took that PhD of his very seriously.

"Brad has a doctorate in psychology," I said. "I'm sure he'd love to talk to you." Insert the sound of my heavy sigh in hindsight.

But in that moment, I thought she was lovely. Her beauty was breathtaking—she wasn't just pretty, she was perfect, and it all looked natural. Her hair was long and blond, and her eyes were a pale, pure green. Beautiful, subtle makeup of the kind I could never pull off with my chubby cheeks (and lack of patience). Expensive, tasteful jewelry, a cashmere dress in ivory with a funky belt and high leather boots. I wasn't sure I'd ever been this close to a person who was so beautiful, so . . . smooth. Her voice, her manners, the way she talked and listened . . . she was the epitome of grace and class, old money and education, and I wanted her to like me.

We talked about the pros and cons of having an only child, the beauty of the Cape light, the natural glory of the sea and shore. Then I paid the check on the Fairchild credit card with a 30 percent tip for Jake, Beth's nephew, who'd waited on us.

I showed her two pretty good houses first, as was the Fairchild strategy . . . two almost-great places, then the big kablammy. We started with a lovely place on Lieutenant Island, which was stunning, but subject to accessibility . . . the bridge was underwater twice a day.

"Some folks don't mind," I said. "The views are incredible, but you would need a vehicle that can handle the tides. Sometimes, it's too high even for a truck, so maybe with an adolescent, it's not the best choice."

She agreed. The next one was an architectural tree house of sorts, one of a kind, weird and beautiful, listed at $2.3 million. But it "only" had three bedrooms, a too-small kitchen and just a glimpse of the bay.

Ah, rich people. That being said, the sunsets on the bay were incredible, and if she could afford it, why not? It was nice to picture her daughter running around at low tide, throwing a stick to a dog, maybe.

The final house was a modern monstrosity of glass and cedar on Griffins Island Road with an unfettered view of Cape Cod Bay and the sky. The driveway was marked by two stone pillars and an engraved granite slab that proclaimed the house's name: Stella Maris, star of the sea.

As we pulled into the crushed-shell driveway, the sun was setting, and God had graced us with a gorgeous winter sunset of violent red, pink and purple. As soon as I saw

Melissa's face, I knew it was the place for her. Sure, it was over the top, and to me, a bit grotesque. I preferred cozy to . . . vast.

Stella Maris had a two-story, vaulted living room with a massive stone fireplace. A library had French doors to a private deck and custom-made shelves with a ladder and under-shelf lighting. There was a huge chef's kitchen with dozens of drawers and cupboards, three sinks, a six-burner Wolf stove, wine fridge, vodka freezer, marble island with six stools and butler's pantry with two more sinks and another dishwasher. There were five bedrooms, each with their own full bathroom and private deck, each with views of the water and surrounding pine wilderness. The dining room would seat twenty easily, with another smaller screened-in dining room for nice weather. The basement sported a home theater and bar with an area for games.

The lawn was landscaped with pine trees and hydrangeas, a rose bower and half a dozen mature, flowering trees that would, I told Melissa, be stunning in just a few more months. There was an infinity pool in dark granite, a hot tub, a cabana, an outdoor shower and a subtly placed building covered in ivy that housed the sauna, a meditation room and a changing room. Just outside that was an exterior plunge pool of icy salt water. The vast lawn stretched right down to four stairs that led straight into the bay.

"At high tide, you can take a kayak or sailboat right off here," I said. "At low tide, you and Ophelia can go dig your own clams."

Melissa Spencer Finch paid a hundred thousand dollars above the hefty asking price, "just in case someone else falls in love with it." She paid in full, in cash. Within three weeks, she and Ophelia had moved—I saw the trucks as they passed Wellfleet OB/GYN. Since my in-laws were still abroad, I called Melissa for the official welcome, recommended some local vendors for handyman work, decorating and housekeeping, and invited her to dinner with Brad and me at the Mews, one of Provincetown's best restaurants.

The evening of that dinner, I felt proud of Brad and me as a couple. Me, the local, an earthy midwife who loved to garden and knew everyone, proud daughter of a Portuguese fisherman; Brad, the more erudite, preppy PhD from Beacon Hill. He studied the wine list as if it were a lost gospel and ordered a bottle of ridiculously expensive wine (since his parents' company would be paying) and listened to Melissa and me chat.

Was there a local florist open year-round? According to her, a house without fresh flowers wasn't a home, something I agreed with (though the flowers in my house were from my own garden). Did I know of any French tutors, since she wanted Ophelia to continue her lessons and become fluent? My mother's wife was from France, and I'd put them in touch. Did I know any wine vendors to help her stock her wine cellar? I did—Beth was a second-level sommelier. Were there any parenting groups, because she didn't know a soul other than Brad and me? I told her I'd call some people I knew who had kids Ophelia's age.

"You're so wonderful, Lillie," she said, her green eyes so pretty and clear. "It was my lucky day when I met you. I just know we'll be friends."

In the space of a few weeks, she and Brad were sleeping together, he decided he no longer loved me and that it was imperative for him to discover joy.

I think you can see why I kidnapped the skunk.

CHAPTER 1

Lillie

Let's spin back a few months.

Brad had never had great timing. Some examples . . . He booked a weekend for us to New Orleans for September 1. A massive hurricane hit two days before. A decade later, he planned a vacation to Puerto Rico for the last week of October, and New England had a nor'easter that crushed the power grid and grounded all planes for a week the day we were supposed to take off.

When he was twenty, his grandfather died and left him a drafty, never-renovated, single-family brownstone in Greenpoint, Brooklyn, a part of New York that no one had really heard of before. Brad, not telling his parents, wanting to be his own man, sold it immediately for $350,000. (The house is worth upwards of $4 million today . . . I check Zillow from time to time.) He invested the real estate sale money in the dot-com bubble four months before it burst and lost every penny he'd earned on the sale.

Brad would leave for the airport early enough, but he'd pick the wrong bridge to cross—if he chose the Sagamore, there'd be an accident. If he picked the Bourne, there'd be construction. If he went to the bathroom during one of

Dylan's games, our son would sack the quarterback or make a leaping interception and run the ball in for a touchdown.

He proposed to me as I was vomiting up lunch the day I learned I was pregnant. Literally, as I was on my knees in front of the toilet, gacking, he sat on the edge of the tub and said, "Will you marry me, Lillie?" I had to puke twice more before I could answer.

And then, the night before our son graduated from high school, he told me he was leaving me, mere seconds after I told him I had booked us a trip to Europe come October.

I should've known something was up. Brad never arranged our date nights, but that night he had announced he was taking me out to dinner. To Pepe's in Provincetown, even, one of my favorites, especially because of their incredible coconut cake.

"Wow!" I said. Pepe's was usually reserved for special occasions, like birthdays or anniversaries. "What a nice surprise!"

And, you know, how *lovely*. Maybe Brad was doing this to celebrate our eighteen years, four months, two weeks and three days of parenthood. Dylan Gustavo Fairchild, named for a poet and my grandpa, was our near-perfect son, a wonderful human and the sun, moon and stars to us. Maybe Brad was feeling sentimental, too. Maybe he wanted to talk about our boy and thank me, something he had done at every one of Dylan's birthdays over the years, which never failed to make me tear up.

Maybe he sensed that I was a little terrified of what life would be like without our boy living with us.

How *thoughtful*. And talk about perfect timing! I'd originally been waiting till after graduation to tell my husband about the big surprise. As a reward for raising a child into adulthood and sending him off to college—and to have something exciting and different to look forward to—I'd booked us a trip. In April, sensing Brad was getting a case of the blues (as I was), I'd decided we should take a vacation, just the two of us, something we hadn't done since our honeymoon, aside from the very occasional weekend away. I spent hours and hours on travel sites, looking for the best hotels, restaurants, cheap flights, special offers, upgrade possibilities.

Venice for three days, a train ride into the Swiss mountains, where we'd stay at a beautiful hotel on a lake, then five days in Paris, where Brad had always wanted to go. A trip to begin this new chapter of our lives and take the sting of our son's absence away.

Dylan would be out with his friends tonight, so he wouldn't miss us. He was the very best of kids—a football player who viewed his body as a temple and all that. Drinking and drugs could seriously screw up his place at the University of Montana. Also, the dangers of drinking, drugs, unprotected sex (and saturated fats) had been drilled into him since his conception. His mommy was a healthcare professional, after all.

When I got home from work that night, I shaved my legs and washed my hair, conditioned it so I wouldn't break the hairbrush—I took after my Portuguese ancestors with thick, coarse black hair. Last year, I'd found a few white strands, too, but hey. Well-earned, right? After I dried off and put on some lipstick and mascara, I decided I was gorgeous and Brad was a lucky man. Then again, he was damn good looking, too, just a little gray in his blond hair, a neatly trimmed beard, his aqua-blue eyes framed by glasses. He had movie star eyes, Beth liked to tell me. Almost too blue to be real.

I put on a cute summer dress and pulled my long hair into a side ponytail. Earrings, perfume, strappy sandals. Texted my patient Ciara, who was at thirty-eight weeks and felt like the baby had dropped. How are you feeling, goddess? Anything changed?

No, but she just punched me pretty good in the side, and I saw her knuckles, Lillie! So amazing!

You're growing a human, I texted back. YOU are amazing. Have a great night, and call me with any changes.

Being a midwife was like being someone's best friend for an entire year, from the first obstetrical visit— sometimes before, if they come to you for fertility or other issues—to the three-month follow-up. The thrill, the responsibility, the *honor* of guiding the mama through her pregnancy, birth and postnatal care, not to mention any other female issues she might have in her lifetime . . . it was like nothing else. Ciara was a primipara—this was her first pregnancy—and she was in awe of the whole process, as she should be.

Smiling, I went into the front hall, where my husband was waiting. "You look gorgeous," I said, kissing him on the cheek.

"Thanks," he said, looking up from his phone. "Take a sweater in case it gets chilly."

"Good idea." He was right . . . spring nights could be wicked cold on the Cape, and P-town, the narrowest part of our little peninsula, always had a breeze off the water. I grabbed a blue sweater from my bureau.

As we closed the front door behind us, I stopped to check the swallows that had made a home against the beam and ceiling of our porch. They'd been delightfully noisy the past few days, especially when Mama Bird came to feed them.

"Hello, babies," I said, peeking at their little bald heads. From the nearby lilac, the mama bird chirped, reassuring them that I was good people.

"Let's go, Lillie," Brad said, waiting at the top of the stairs that led to our driveway. He didn't love the birds the way I did, and he often startled when coming in, since Mama Swallow was territorial. Me, on the other hand . . . I was a bird lover. I'd grown up in this very house, on this land, and I could identify every bird that graced us by their call and markings. Swallows were favorites of mine, swooping on the water, tails spread in their graceful arc. Plus, they were lucky. They represented a happy home . . .

and, if you were feeling morbid, the soul of someone who died. My vovô, I liked to think, because I had adored my grandfather, and he was the one who'd built this house back in the fifties.

"Bye, babies. Sleep tight," I said, then followed my husband down the walk.

In the car, I texted Dylan that we were going to Pepe's for dinner and I hoped he was having fun. Ended it with a heart emoji, because I couldn't help myself.

"He says to have fun and bring him a slice of coconut cake," I said after the phone buzzed with a response. Soon, I wouldn't be able to do those little things for my son. "It's going to be so weird without him."

"Yeah," said Brad. "But it's also a new start for all of us."

"It is," I said, but the familiar lump rose in my throat. My little boy, now six foot three. High school had flown past in a blur of driving to and from Nauset High School, parent-teacher conferences, projects and proofreading his papers. I'd spent thousands of hours sitting on the bleachers, watching him at first stand on the sidelines, then become a starter on the football team. He grew seven inches in three years. He had a girlfriend and was on the honor roll most semesters. He was, and always had been, a wonderful son, good-natured and hardworking and funny, and my heart had been aching since September, when the clock began ticking.

Brad was quiet, too. I reached over and patted his leg, and he glanced at me with a quick smile that didn't reach his eyes. Yes. He was feeling it, too.

Five more weeks before Dylan left for football camp. Five weeks left of the life I'd known these past two decades, happier than I could have imagined. Dylan's birth when I was barely twenty-three, easy and routine and miraculous. Buying our house on Herring Pond from my dad, ensuring that it stayed in the family, and working for years on its renovation. Getting my certified nurse-midwife degree online (from Georgetown!). I worked part-time until Dylan was sixteen and no longer needed me to drive him around, which I missed more than I'd expected.

Every single day from his birth onward had been based around taking care of him, whether it was walking the floor the first three months of his life, or making him a steak after school during his growth spurt. Talking with him in the car when he still sat in the back seat, hearing things that he wouldn't admit at the dinner table . . . a girl he liked, a bad dream he'd had. Teaching him to drive . . . the time when he'd finally mastered parallel parking the night before his test, and had leaped out of the car to hug me—one of the last spontaneous hugs I'd had from him. Oh, he hugged me every day. Just . . . you know. In an obligatory way.

In five weeks, I wouldn't even see him every day. I might not *talk* to him every day. If he was sick, I couldn't help. If he broke his leg, I wouldn't be there.

But that's what you want as a parent. For your kids to grow into independent, self-sufficient adults. If you do your parenting job right, you're guaranteed heartbreak when the fledgling flies off and leaves you behind. I sent a thought of sympathy to the mama swallow.

I reminded myself that I was also a wife, a daughter, a friend, a sister. A midwife. A woman about to go to Europe for the first time ever. It would be good to reconnect with Brad, too, because this past year had been so focused on our boy. The last trip we'd taken had been three years ago, when we drove cross-country. Seeing Yellowstone was the reason Dylan was going to school in Montana.

Maybe we could swing a special vacation every year or so, just Brad and me. And sure, Dylan could come if he was on break. We could rent out our house for the month of July and that would pay for the trip. Many adventures still waited for us, I told myself firmly. The best years were still ahead. Traveling, our son in this final phase of childhood, then becoming a man, and hopefully a husband and father. Many adventures, for sure.

We turned off Route 6 and headed down 6A, past the

Days' Cottages, each one named after a different flower. When Dylan was little, we'd read every plaque with great enthusiasm—Daisy! Aster! Zinnia! Cosmos! When had that stopped? That constant surge of nostalgia made my throat tighten for the umpteenth time that day.

When Brad turned onto Commercial Street, Provincetown's main street, I automatically checked out the gardens, which were in full spring glory—lilacs and peonies, clematis and irises. My own garden didn't get full sun, being in the woods, so these were a visual feast. There was my mother's house. Beatrice, my stepmother, was out in the garden, a big straw hat on her head adorned with a jaunty red scarf. Even in the dirt, she looked glamorous and European. I lifted my hand, but she didn't see me, which was fine.

As we came into the center of town to park, pedestrians and bicyclists meandered on the street. Already so busy, and it wasn't even Memorial Day. We inched along, smelling the good smells of the dozens of restaurants and cafés. A gorgeous night in the prettiest town ever.

It was a point of pride to be the daughter of a Portuguese fisherman, and I always felt so welcomed in this town (except by my mother, that is). I knew the other fishermen by name, knew the harbormaster, knew the longtime bartender at the Governor Bradford, knew just about every scruffy townie leaving the dock. And everyone knew I was Pedro Silva's daughter. The Portuguese fishing industry was still alive and well—my father had retired a couple of years ago, but we still went to the Blessing of the Fleet and the Portuguese Festival each year. Dad, never one to sit still, went out a few times a week with Ben Hallowell, who'd bought the *Goody Chapman* from him.

We parked on the wharf, Brad grumbling about the price as usual, got out and weaved our way down the street through the other pedestrians. When was the last time I'd been to P-town just to stroll? Too long ago. I linked my arm through Brad's, but we had to part ways when the sidewalk narrowed (or stopped altogether).

At Pepe's, our table was waiting, a snug little booth toward the front of the restaurant. "Can we have a table with a water view?" I asked the server.

"I requested this one," Brad said. "It's more private, and it'll get chilly when the sun goes down."

"True. This is great. Thanks, honey."

We looked at the menus and ordered. Brad got a martini, which was new for him . . . he'd started being interested in "mixology" at some point this winter. I ordered a glass of white wine, acknowledging silently that I'd be the one to drive home. Brad was a lightweight, despite his somewhat pretentious grilling of the waitress over gin types and how many dashes of bitters he wanted. That's what marriage was about, wasn't it? Putting up with little irritants for the big picture of security and contentment?

I was dying to tell him about the trip—Venice! The Alps! Paris!—but he seemed intent on memorizing the wine and drinks list.

"Any speaking engagements this summer, hon?" I asked, knowing he loved to talk about his pet project. It worked. He brightened right up.

About two years ago, Brad decided that being a talk therapist wasn't enough. He decided to write a self-help book about living your best life, which he entitled *Living Your Best Life*. Not the most original title, and, if I'm being honest, not the most original content, either. *Breathe. Live mindfully. Eat healthfully. Take walks. Keep a gratitude journal.* Nothing you couldn't find in the 3.52 *billion* hits Google brought up when I'd checked the phrase. But he liked it, so he went with it.

When every agent and publisher rejected or ignored it, Brad went the route of self-publishing, sat back and waited for Oprah to call. She did not. He finagled a spot on NECN (one of the producers and I had gone to high school together, and I asked if she could put him in touch with the person who booked guests). The *Cape Cod Times* had graciously done a feature on his book and him. Alas, sales were almost nonexistent. It wasn't exactly a surprise—he knew nothing about indie publishing, after all—but I tried to be encouraging. I even bought a few copies from time to time and gave them to my pregnant ladies as gifts. Brad would mention an "uptick in sales," and I never had the heart to tell him that it was me.

Tonight, the question got his nose out of the wine list. "Thanks for asking," he said with more enthusiasm than he'd shown all day. "I'm working on a new marketing plan. I think it'll get some solid national attention, and I'm planning a blogging tour. Maybe even some signings." He lifted his eyebrows.

"That's great, hon," I said, though he'd said this three or four times in the past. This spring, for example, he'd started an Instagram account and taken a lot of pictures of himself on the beach or kayaking or staring over the ocean, hair ruffling, #LivingYourBestLife #BuyTheBook #ChangeYourLife #amreading #amliving #bestlife. No pictures of Dylan or me, but he said he wanted to respect our privacy, and this was only for the book.

I ordered the seafood puttanesca, and Brad went with the pasta. "No steak?" I asked, because he usually ordered red meat when we were out.

"I'm thinking of going vegetarian," he said. "Better for me. My thoughts are clearer, and I have more energy."

I smiled. "Says the king of bacon cheeseburgers. Didn't you eat two the other night?"

He rolled his eyes. "Maybe I did, Lillie. Typical of you to keep score."

"I just . . . Never mind." He'd been prickly lately, probably because of Dylan.

"Dylan got his roommate, did he tell you?" I said, and no, our son had not, so I filled Brad in. The kid was from Maine, had four sisters, seemed perfectly nice and was also a football player. I told him about the classes Dylan was taking—mostly core requirements, but he'd also chosen Fiction in the Twentieth Century, which made me happy, since I loved to read. I told Brad about my newest client, who was expecting twins.

Our food came, and I inhaled the sauce before tasting it. "God, they should make this smell into perfume," I said. "People would chase me down in the streets just to sniff me."

No reaction. Not the greatest date night we'd ever had. I wanted him in a better mood before I told him about the big trip. He seemed both a little bored and a little irritated, which in turn irritated me. I was doing 90 percent of the work here, after all. "Tell me more about the marketing plan," I said.

He considered his words carefully, tilting his head to one side. "It's so important, living your authentic life," he said. "Sometimes, it can take years to even find your truth, you know? People are so burdened by society's expectations and dated norms."

"Mm," I said, taking another bite of food. "I get it." I didn't, but I liked that he was talking with such animation.

"We all need a continued sense of purpose and passion. Joy, even. How many times this week have you felt joy, Lillie?"

"Oh. Um . . . I don't know. I feel joy right now, being here with you, eating this good food." I smiled.

His face showed his disappointment. I wasn't sure why, but it was the wrong answer.

When the waitress came to ask if we wanted dessert, Brad said no. "I'll have the coconut cake," I said, because speaking of joy . . . "We'll split it," I added, since we always did. One of our marital habits—Brad always pretended he didn't want dessert, then shared mine. Denial.

"No, no. All for you," Brad said, and for a second, I could've sworn he glanced at my midsection. He himself was lean. I was not.

Brad was nursing a second glass of malbec. That was funny . . . I'd *never* seen him order red wine, not even with steak. He said it gave him headaches, but here he was, sniffing it like he was a bloodhound, swirling it, savoring it. Before I said something snarky, I decided this was the moment.

"Honey, I have something to tell you," I said. I took a breath and tried to get into the romantic mood. The candlelight made Brad look even more handsome. His blond hair, still fairly full, that WASPy, almost delicate bone structure. His amazing cerulean eyes. He looked younger, the gift of candlelight. I hoped I looked equally beautiful. "It's pretty exciting."

"Really? I have something to tell you, too," he said. "Also exciting. But go ahead."

I paused for dramatic effect. "We're going to Europe! I booked us a trip!"

Brad's face didn't change. He didn't smile. He barely blinked.

"Oh," he said. "Uh . . . when?"

"October seventeenth. Venice, then a train ride up into the Alps for a few days, and then . . . wait for it . . . Paris! Surprise!"

Brad didn't say anything.

"Honey?" I asked.

"Yes. Um . . . well."

Not the reaction I was hoping for. Brad *loved* traveling. "Aren't you excited?" I asked. "You don't seem excited."

He drained his wine. "Actually, Lillie, I . . . uh . . . I was thinking it's time we . . . divorced."

"Here's your coconut cake," said the waitress, a pretty girl with dark hair. "Two forks, just in case."

"Thank you!" I said. "Dig in, honey, before I lay waste to this whole thing."

"This is hard for me," he said. "It wasn't an easy decision, but I'm sure."

"About what?" God. The cake melted in your mouth. Melted.

"Did you hear me? What I just said?"

"Did you hear *me*? We're going to Europe!"

He looked away sharply. "No. We're not. I want a divorce, Lillie. That's why I took you here. To discuss our future at this natural split in the path."

I snorted. "Oh, please. We're not getting divorced." God, this cake was *so* good.

"I'm serious. Please listen and don't infantilize me, Lillie."

"Brad. Honey. Is this because Dylan's graduating? It's normal to feel blue. But we're happy. Not like everyone else." There *had* been a rash of divorces among our crowd lately, and suddenly my skin felt a little too tight. "We've been talking about how fun being empty nesters will be." Hadn't we? No, we had. Just not recently.

"I've met someone."

"You know, this trip is going to be *perfect*," I said. "Change of scenery, new places, new food, different languages all around us. You can practice your French! Our son is going to college in Montana, and we've both been melancholy. I've looked at so many pictures of Venice, I *already* feel better."

Wait . . . what was that he'd just said? It wasn't about Europe. I felt a flush starting in my chest, creeping up my neck.

I took a sip of water. Glanced around the restaurant. There was our pretty waitress, listing off the specials at another table. A gorgeous young couple had just walked in, holding hands. Newlyweds, I thought, judging by the way they gazed at each other. Yep. He'd just picked up her hand and kissed the ring finger, where a gold band gleamed. Sweet.

"Lillie?" Brad said.

"We're going to Europe," I said again, more loudly this time. "We deserve it."

"Are you even listening to me?" he said.

"Are you listening to *me*?" I snapped. "We're not getting a divorce! Are you crazy?" Heads were starting to turn. I lowered my voice. "Look. I don't think . . . You didn't mean what you said, honey. I know it's a strange time, and it's natural to do some soul-searching, but we're in this together. It's going to be great! We've been talking about all the things we want to do." I smiled. *Yeah. Keep smiling, Lillie.* "And we *will* do them." That last line came out as a command.

He didn't look at me. "I haven't been happy in some time, and . . . well, as I just said, I've met someone."

There was a buzzing sound in my ears. "No, you haven't."

"I have, and we're in love."

"Oh, go fuck yourself." The words were supposed to come off as funny, as pals saying that to each other, knowing they were just goofing around. Instead, it came out as, well . . . a curse. The newlyweds glanced our way, concerned.

"I'm sorry this hurts you, but we're in love," Brad repeated.

"No, you're not. Nope. You're not in love. You love *me*, your wife of twenty years, I might add. Two decades, Brad."

"Nineteen years. And I want a divorce," he repeated in his soft therapist voice. "We've been growing apart, and this is a natural separating point. But we'll always be Dylan's parents."

"Is this about your stupid book?" I regretted the words immediately.

He refolded his napkin with sharp movements. "No."

"Brad," I said. "I'm sorry. The book is wonderful. But . . . you don't want a *divorce*. We have a great life! We have so much to look forward to." I smiled firmly and took another bite of cake to prove it. *See? Coconut cake! Our life is great!*

"You haven't been that great a wife, to be honest," he said, and my jaw fell open, a chunk of white cake falling out and splotching onto the table.

I covered it with my napkin. "I'm sorry, what?"

"You're so obsessed with work. And Dylan. And now

you're suddenly obsessed with Venice? There's no room for me."

"Are you serious?" My voice was rising. "I'm a *great* wife! We have a wonderful marriage, Brad!" Everyone was listening, and I didn't blame them. *Yes. Let them listen and weigh in on what a ridiculous idea this is.*

He sighed, gently, kindly, the therapist seeing his patient acknowledge a hard truth. Was he acting? It felt like he was acting. "I just haven't been feeling a lot of joy. And, Lillie, I *want* joy in my life."

"I . . . What does that even mean? We have a healthy, wonderful son, we have a beautiful home, and all of our parents are alive and well. We're healthy and still pretty young and we're going to Europe. There's your joy right there!"

"I just feel dead inside."

"No, you don't. This is idiotic."

"Lillie?" said a voice, and there was Samantha, one of my clients, whose baby I had delivered last fall. "Hi! Sorry to interrupt, but I just had to say hello."

"Sam!" I said, switching into nurse-midwife mode. "How are you? How's Luca?"

"Oh, he's beautiful," she said, pulling out her phone.

I looked at the pictures of a fat-cheeked, drooling angel. She'd done an amazing job in labor, even though it was her first. No screaming, no drama, just totally in tune with her body and nature, humming through the pain, her husband murmuring gentle words of encouragement. Three pushes, if I recalled (which I always did). "He's gorgeous. You were such a champ. Everything good otherwise?"

"Yes! We're trying for another, so hopefully we'll be seeing you again. You remember Paul?" She gestured to her smiling husband.

"Of course. Hi, Paul," I said. "Enjoy your evening, and kiss that little sweetheart for me."

"We will!" Samantha said, and they went to their table.

For a second, I wondered if I had imagined the conversation between Brad and me, like a weird hallucination. I smiled at him just in case.

"See?" he said. "A perfect example. We're talking about our *marriage*, and you drop everything to fawn all over them. That's how unimportant you've made me. I've been sidelined by your career, and I can't put up with your constant invalidation."

"What was I supposed to do, Brad? I pulled a baby out of her vagina! Should I have told her to shut up because my husband is acting like an idiot?" My Portuguese was rising, as my father used to say proudly whenever I got mad.

"You always put me down. You crush my dreams."

"What dreams have I crushed? Name one!" I snapped. "Brad. On Valentine's Day, you told me you were the luckiest man in the world because you had me. Remember? You handwrote three *paragraphs* about how wonderful I am. That was a beautiful card, and you meant every word." I swallowed. Eyed the cake.

"I was still hoping our marriage could be salvaged," he said. "But I'm afraid it can't be. I deserve to be happy."

I sat back, my head falling against the back of the booth with a clunk. "Brad—"

"I actually prefer Bradley," he said.

And there it was. *Bradley.*

He *was* seeing another woman, oh, yes he was. If *Bradley* wasn't a sign, I didn't know what was.

Memories sliced into my brain like jagged glass. This past winter or spring, Brad had suddenly started working out with a vengeance—he ran occasionally and swam in Herring Pond during the summer, but that was it. Somewhere in March, however, he joined a gym and started asking Dylan about the football team's workouts and muscle groups and ketoacidosis. I didn't complain. Brad had always been slim, but seeing a little bulk on his arms, a little hint of a washboard . . . it was nice. I naively thought maybe he was doing it, at least in part, for me.

Then there were the clothes. Brad had always been

preppy—with the last name of Fairchild, part of the Boston Brahmin, growing up on Beacon Hill, would you expect anything less? Always tidy, always neat, always a little boring, style-wise.

But one day he'd come home with bags and bags from some of the shops here in Provincetown, which was the male fashion capital of New England. Suddenly, he was wearing European-cut floral-printed shirts and slim-fit pants, low leather boots and vintage jeans that cost triple what regular jeans did. I'd just about choked when I saw the credit card bill. He'd even bought a little straw hat. But hey. Our son was going away to school. He wanted to feel young. I understood.

Sex, which had always been fairly frequent and heartily enjoyable, had tapered off. When I'd asked him if everything was okay—when was that? April? It had been a rainy night, I remembered that—he told me he was just sad about Dylan leaving. And I'd believed him.

The mixology. Bradley. The *malbec*.

Brad was arrogant at times. He never said it outright, but he'd thought he'd make more money as a therapist, be a little more . . . special. His parents were so flush and successful, dominating the high-end real estate industry in Boston and here on the Cape. Despite what you see on TV, therapists—at least, nonpsychiatrists—didn't make a huge income, unless you were Dr. Phil or Esther Perel . . . or wrote a bestselling book. Brad always insisted he was in the profession to help people, but the money bothered him.

A thought occurred to me. "How can you be in love with someone else when we had sex four nights ago?"

He sighed. "I was feeling a little sad that our life together was coming to an end. It was a sentimental mistake."

"A mistake? A *mistake*, Brad?" Oh, the Portuguese had risen now, yes indeed.

"I'm sorry if this hurts you, but I'm sure."

Suddenly, my plate was in my hands, and I was squishing the coconut cake on his head. "How dare you, Brad Fairchild! How dare you!"

"Jesus, Lillie!" he shouted, but I was already leaving. My breath was tearing in and out as if there wasn't enough air in here. I pushed past the startled servers, out onto Commercial Street. Furious tears blurred my eyes.

He had *cheated* on me. He was having an *affair*. I was going to need an *STD* panel. I didn't get to finish my *cake*.

My God. My God.

Brad caught up to me. I smelled his cologne (new, goddamn it!) before I saw him. He grabbed my elbow to stop me.

"Of course you had to make a scene," he said, brushing a glob of cake out of his hair. "I thought we could talk like adults, but apparently not."

"Don't you lecture me!" I shouted, bringing the pedestrian flow to a halt. "You're having an *affair*! Twenty years of marriage, twenty years of me having your back and loving you and raising our son and being fantastic to your parents, and you're cheating on me! And you dump this on me the night before our son's graduation? How *dare* you!"

"Preach it, sister," said a woman. "Let him have it."

"You are a class-A turd, mister," said a very beautiful shirtless young man.

"Nice, Lillie," Brad said, the condescending prick. "You always did love melodrama." He looked at the gathering crowd. "We've been growing apart for years," he said.

This was happening. This was really happening. My marriage was dying in front of a dozen strangers. My mother was going to feast on this. What about Dylan? What about our *son*?

My anger went out like a match in the wind.

I didn't want a divorce. I *loved* being married. I loved our little family. I loved our *life*. Could he just . . . just end it? With no input from me whatsoever? Was that even legal? Two people had to consent to marriage. Shouldn't two people also have to consent to divorce?

What could I do? I started walking to the car as fast as I could, dodging the tourists like a ninja, outpacing Brad. Thank God I'd grabbed my purse when I left the restaurant. Brad could call an Uber or Cape Cab. He sure as hell wasn't getting a ride from me.

Was my dad around? Should I drive down the wharf and check the boats? Should I circle around and head for Mom's? Ha. When had she ever been a comfort or support? No. I shouldn't talk to anyone right now. Maybe this wasn't really happening. Maybe it was a joke, or a momentary lapse on Brad's part. Maybe he had a brain tumor, and so he was sick and didn't know what he was saying.

I pulled out of the lot and inched down Commercial Street. Past the intersection where the cop jauntily directed traffic; past the Portuguese bakery run by my fourth cousins, where we bought malassadas every time we came here with Dylan; past the clothing shops where Brad had blown two months' income. Couples were everywhere—Provincetown was a romantic place.

Not for me. Not tonight. My husband wanted *joy*, and apparently not from me.

The filho da puta.

My brain was in shock, the poor thing, and a high-pitched whine was all I could hear.

When I got home, Dylan's car wasn't there. Good. I went up to our bedroom—mine now—and ripped off my clothes, got in the shower and let the water get so hot it burned. Scrubbed my skin with the scrunchie as hard as I could, because I felt filthy. Contaminated.

He was leaving me. *He* was *leaving* me. If I was honest, I'd always thought he'd won out in this deal of ours. He was (had been) a good enough husband, but I was an incredible wife. I made our home what it was. I created our family life, arranged our social life, organized our holidays, kept Brad in the loop about Dylan, because Dylan told me more. I *listened* to Brad, far more than he listened to me, because, as he'd once said, "I can only hear so many birth stories, Lillie."

I'd never said, *I can only stand so many client stories, Brad.* Never said, *Your book is unsuccessful because it doesn't have an original sentence in the entire thing.* I always told him how proud I was of him. I thanked him for working so hard, shouldering people's troubles, helping them find the right path. And now he was having an affair.

An hour later, as I sat on my bed in my pajamas, I heard a car come into the driveway and Brad's voice. The Uber. Brad slammed the front door to make sure I knew he was angry at having to get a ride. When I heard him stomp down the stairs to the guest bedroom off the kitchen, I came out and went into the living room.

Our home looked so sad. Was that possible? That our house, which was such a huge part of our family, our history, our holidays, our *marriage*, knew that our family was crumbling?

The mother swallow was chattering to her babies, clicking and squeaking at them. As it got darker, she quieted. I went outside to look in on them—she was there, her black eyes looking at me, snuggled in with her babies. Then, in a flutter of wings, her mate arrived, and they both settled in. After a minute, I went back inside and sat on the couch, unsure if this was how people sat. My body didn't feel like my own.

Some time later, Dylan's car turned into the driveway. I always waited up for him. Of course I did.

He came in with a rush and a thump, incapable of being quiet. Dylan, the best thing I'd ever do, so tall, so good-looking, the best of the Fairchilds and Silvas. He had my father's unruly hair, but it was blond, like Brad's. My dark eyes and some ancestor's long lashes. Once upon a time, I'd held that little boy there against my shoulder, tucked him on my hip, never wanted to put him down.

"Sorry I'm late," he said. "Pippa had a flat tire, and she

didn't know how to put the spare on, so I helped her. Grandpa will be wicked proud."

"Yes. He sure will be." My father showed his love by teaching important life skills, which meant that there was little Dylan and I could not fix or figure out.

"How was your dinner?"

"Ah . . . good. Yeah. Crap. I forgot your cake, honey."

"No worries! I'll get some before I leave home. Well, I'm whipped and should go to bed."

"Okay. Sleep tight."

"You too, Mom."

I stood up and hugged him, and he patted my back in an obligatory way. Then he went upstairs, his big feet thumping, and closed his bedroom door.

CHAPTER 2

Lillie

Less than twenty-four hours after my husband told me he was leaving me to pursue *joy*, our son graduated from high school. Brad and I sat next to each other, my body stiff and hard. "This doesn't mean we're not a family," he whispered. "We still have our wonderful son, and of course I'll always care about you."

I didn't respond, too busy having an out-of-body experience. *He's leaving me. They're both leaving me. My husband cheated. My baby is an adult. Oh, God, my husband doesn't love me anymore. I have to cancel the trip to Europe. Should I go alone? I can't afford it if I'm divorced! Dylan, why Montana? Why, you little ingrate? Who cares how beautiful it is out there? God, I love you so much! Shit, I'm going to be a laughingstock, a cliché, the abandoned wife. Oh, doesn't Rami look so nice, he was always such a cute child. Brad is in love with someone else, and I didn't even notice.*

Was this real, or just a really long, detailed dream? This *was* Nauset High's gym. Why couldn't graduation be outside? It was gorgeous out. *Dad is looking at you. Snap out of it. Whose cologne is that? Jesus, it's my husband's.*

"Here we go," Dad said. "They're on the E's. Finally."

"James . . . Gabriel . . . Edwards," the vice-principal recited in that slow, portentous way, each syllable thudding against the hearts of the parents. "Portia . . . Grace . . . Effinger." A beautiful girl, Portia. "Gabriella . . . Maria . . . Calderón . . . Espinosa."

He was next. My boy. My only child. My whole world.

"Dylan . . . Gustavo . . . Fairchild."

Time stopped. My dad gave a piercing whistle; my sister, Hannah, yelled, "Yeah, Dylan!" and the Moms (as I called my mother and her wife) clapped. Dylan grinned in our direction, then walked across the stage and shook hands with the principal. He turned and smiled for the photo that would soon hang on the living room wall. My beautiful, beautiful boy. The lump in my throat had turned to a shard of glass.

"Milo . . . Jude . . . Feinstein."

A sob came out of me, and my dad put his arm around me and squeezed.

Yesterday I had been happy. Today, I barely remembered what that word meant.

"Snap of out it," hissed Brad.

I turned my head slowly to look at him. "Shall I tell your parents at dinner?" I whispered back.

His face went white. "We agreed to wait." Yes, he'd sent me a text from the guest room this morning, saying it would be for the best if we didn't tell our son today and ruin graduation. Too bad I hadn't been given the same consideration. "But fix your face before someone says something."

"Shut your mouth, Brad," I hissed.

My dad gave me a weird look, but he was deaf in the ear closest to me and had missed it. Probably.

After the ceremony, someone—Diana, maybe, whose daughter, Jamie, had been Dylan's friend since third grade—took a picture of the three of us; the three of us with the Fairchilds (our last picture together? Ever?); the three of us with the Moms; the three of us with Dad, who'd refused to have a photo with Mom for the past thirty years. The three of us with Hannah. *The three of us. The three of us. The three of us.*

That was dead now.

Did I smile? Did I cry? Could anyone hear me screaming, or was that just inside my head?

Thank God Diana asked me to return the favor of taking photos, so I smiled and said, "Okay, everyone, one, two, three!" seven or eight times.

"This is a big day for you, too, sweetheart," Vanessa said, putting her arm around me. "What a wonderful mother you are."

"Absolutely," Brad's father, Charles, added. "Now, don't be sad. He'll always be your son." Brad, like Dylan, was an only child.

What would my in-laws say if they knew? Would they think less of me? Had they sensed this was coming? Would my sister roll her eyes? Would Beatrice tell me it was because I wasn't thin enough and I should eat more like a Frenchwoman? Would my mother say she'd always assumed we'd get a divorce?

My dad . . . he would *kill* Brad. That was a comforting thought.

"Hi, Mrs. Fairchild!" called Hayley, one of my favorites of Dylan's friends.

"Hello, honey," I said sweetly. I had never officially changed my name, but kids didn't care about stuff like that. I'd always answered to it. Until now. "It's actually Ms. Silva, but you can call me Lillie, now that you're a high school graduate."

She smiled and said, "Okay, Lillie!"

"Have fun in Boston, sweetheart," I said, because I knew she'd be going to school there.

"Mrs. Fairchild," said another girl. Cammie, that was her name. "I'm going to Endicott for a nursing degree. Maybe I could intern with you one summer?"

"Of course," I said. "Call me anytime."

I congratulated the dozens of kids I knew . . . kids Dylan had known since he was eighteen months old and we'd started going to story hour at our library. Boys who'd played football with him. Kids who'd slept at our house, who'd come to Halloween and cookie baking parties, kids whose houses he'd slept at. Kids who'd eaten in my kitchen, who'd sat in my back seat on drives home, kids I'd cheered on at games and meets and plays. They were all leaving for college or the military or vocational programs. Maybe a few would stay home and find jobs in landscaping or food service or fishing or some other local business, but here in the painfully bright afternoon, it seemed like every child I'd ever known was leaving, and the world was crumbling under my feet.

The longer we were at the graduation, the more unreal it felt. Brad couldn't . . . he wasn't . . . *leaving* me, right? Not when we were standing together with other families, other parents. An affair. An *affair*! But why? Why would he risk our life together? It was such a good life.

For the last time as parents of a student, we left Nauset Regional High School and headed back to Wellfleet for dinner at Winslow's. I rode with my father. We were silent on the short trip, but that was fairly normal for us. "He's a good kid," my father said eventually. Dad was a man of few words.

"Yes."

"Montana."

"I know."

We got to the restaurant, Dylan practically drowning in senior citizens—his four grandparents plus step-grandmother; my sister, who was forty-five but acted like she was eighty . . . the kind of woman who made tea in a teapot every day and poured it into a matching cup with saucer as her well-behaved cat looked on fondly. And me, flanked by Dylan on one side, my dad on the other. Dylan was all smiles, giving each grandparent some special attention, a hug, a word. The price of being an only child, all these elders focused on just him, but something Dylan had always carried with grace and kindness.

He would've been such a great brother. A different and very familiar pain, one sharper and more pure, slid through my heart.

"It seems like yesterday that you brought him home from the hospital," said Vanessa, reaching across the table to squeeze my hand.

My eyes filled with tears. I had always loved Vanessa, and she me. That phrase—*the daughter I never had*—she meant it. Mom was telling the waitress that the tab should come to her, not anyone else, and Charles was fighting her on it with good humor. Let them. I appreciated it. They were wealthy, after all, and Brad and I were just okay. We could have paid for dinner, but the Moms and the Fairchilds were rich.

Women who get divorced usually suffer financially. That was a known fact.

"Lillie?" asked the waitress. I'd delivered her twins a few years ago.

I switched into midwife role. "Hey, Emma, how are you? How are the babies?"

"Doing great and getting big. Congratulations on Dylan." She smiled. "What would you like to drink?"

"Um . . . a vodka martini. Straight up." It was a lot stronger than what I usually drank. So be it.

The drinks came out quickly, and Charles made a toast to Dylan.

The entire time, there was a narrator in my head. *This is the last family dinner you'll ever have. You may never see Vanessa and Charles again. Brad is screwing someone else. Who, by the way? Who, damn it?*

"Son," Brad said, standing up. "I'd like to say a few words, too." He waited till everyone quieted. "Dylan, I'm so excited for you as you take this new path on your journey.

Life *is* a journey, and it's up to you to make every single footstep meaningful and important and filled with joy."

Oh, that word again! I drowned out my hiss with a slug of vodka. Hopefully, Brad would also move far, far away. Maybe Dylan would change his mind about Montana if he knew his father was leaving his mother. But no, I wasn't supposed to want that kind of thing. I *didn't* want it, even though, sure, I wanted it.

Dylan caught my eye and smiled, his eyebrow raising just a little.

"Mom?" Dylan asked.

"Yes, honey?"

"Do you want to say anything?"

I hadn't planned on it, but I stood up anyway. "Dylan . . ." My eyes flooded. "I have no advice to give you, sweetheart. You're already a kind and responsible young man, funny and hardworking. I'm so proud of you. I love you more than anything, and I'll . . . I'm so excited for you, baby."

His eyes filled with tears, too. He stood up, all six foot three of him, and hugged me. I felt a little sob from him, and whispered, "It's going to be great, honey. You'll love it out there."

It's what we say, we mothers, even when our hearts are cracking.

There were enough people there, enough noise (thanks to Beatrice and my mother, who always had to show the world what a *fun* and *gorgeous* couple they were through stories and loud laughter). Hannah told a tale about one of her grotesque weddings—she was an event planner for extremely wealthy people, and her last wedding had apparently required an elephant. It was probably an interesting story, but I couldn't tell. Charles started talking about his own college days, when men weren't allowed into women's dorms, and how he'd serenaded Vanessa under her sorority house window.

"Maybe you'll be like us, son," he said to Dylan. "Meet

your future wife in college. Your parents did the same thing, so it runs in the family!"

Brad said nothing. I ate a piece of bread to soak up some of the vodka. Beatrice began talking about her first and second husbands, and no one noticed my weirdness.

"You'll be fine," Vanessa said, reaching over to squeeze my hand, and I jumped. Did she know? "Once you know he's settled in, you'll be just fine."

Ah. She was talking about Dylan. I wanted to fall into her arms and sob. Unlike my own mother, Vanessa *noticed* me. She had loved me from the moment I walked through her door on Beacon Hill, was *thrilled* when I got knocked up, adored her only grandson and praised me for raising him so well.

We talked at least twice a week, had lunch often, cooked together during the holidays. Once or twice, she'd treated me to a spa weekend with her in Vermont. She was so *proud* of me and loved hearing stories of labor and delivery. My own mother couldn't listen to me talk about work for more than a minute before saying I should have gone to medical school and become a doctor. Mom treated Dylan like a delightful puppy, then grew bored after half an hour.

Vanessa wouldn't be my mother-in-law anymore. I was about to lose half of the family I had now. My vision grayed.

Dylan was the first to finish dinner. The rest of his night would be spent at Project Graduation, where they locked the kids in the school gym for the night so they wouldn't drink or do drugs or have sex. There would be pizza and music, movies, all that. He thanked us all, kissed his elders like the kindhearted boy he was. Brad said "Have a great time!" in an overly jocular tone, ignoring the fact that he would soon destroy his son's family, home life, holidays. Things would never be the same because Brad wanted *joy*.

I got up and hugged my boy. "Have a great time, honey," I said. "I love you." He hugged me tighter for a second, then left, taking my heart with him.

I sat back down and looked at Brad. He smiled at me, and I scratched my nose with my middle finger. The smile on his face was immediately replaced with a sulk. Good.

Brad and I didn't speak on the way home from the restaurant. "I guess I'll stay down in the guest room until I leave," he said when we got home. "Unless you want me in the studio"—we'd converted my grandfather's old toolshed into a tiny, perfect guest space about ten years ago—"but Dylan likes to hang out there with his friends."

"When are we going to tell our son about your infidelity, by the way?" I asked.

Brad sat down on the couch and tilted his head in his shrink mode, his brows coming together. "Yes. About that. I've been thinking about what would be best for him."

"Not cheating on his mother leaps to mind."

"I think we should let him have these last few weeks be as normal as possible," Brad said. "Once he's settled at college, we can FaceTime him and say we've grown apart. He'll understand. It's already happened with half his friends."

"Brad . . ." My voice broke, and the fury wobbled for a moment as all the good times Brad and I had had flashed through my mind. Dating. Our honeymoon in the Maldives, a gift from his parents, me newly pregnant, him smitten. The way he'd cried when Dylan was born. The joyful and fun toddler years, rebuilding this house inch by inch. We'd laughed together, cooked together, always held hands when we walked, locked eyes in mutual love and pride for our son.

I cleared my throat. "Brad," I said, already hating myself for what I was about to say. "This is very hard for me to accept. We have such a beautiful family life. I think it's worth saving." Not that I didn't want to stab him in his sleep, mind you.

He closed his eyes for a second, then sighed. "It's been over for years, Lillie. This is just a formality. You've changed, and so have I. We want different things."

"That's not true. I want the same thing we signed on for twenty years ago. A family. Security. Love. A partner."

"Interesting that you're just now noticing that we don't have that anymore," he said.

"Don't have what?"

"A partnership. Not really."

"Since when? When did all of this happen?" I asked, wiping my eyes.

"Lillie." He clasped his hands loosely between his knees and leaned forward a little. "You haven't supported my dreams. You don't *listen* to me. You've been cruel. You're as much at fault for this divorce as I am."

"What? No, I'm not!" I screeched. "How can you say that? I took extra shifts so you could spend more time writing your book. I love hearing about your clients. And cruel? When, Brad? Name one time."

He tilted his head. "It's subtle. Passive-aggressive, much like your mother."

Ooh. A low blow. "Name a time. One time."

"Well, just last night, you called my book stupid."

"I was in shock! You'd just told me you'd met someone, and I was stunned!"

"Are you really telling me you haven't noticed the distance between us?"

"We say 'I love you' every single day. We have sex, like, two or three times a week. I cook you fantastic meals—"

"You'd make those even without me," he said.

"—and I do your laundry—"

"You don't iron my shirts."

"You insist on doing that yourself. Brad, come on! We've been partners and raised our son and made this home beautiful and cozy. And God knows, I'm good to your parents. This is our family, Brad. Don't shatter it."

He sighed again. "But you don't *see* me, Lillie. I haven't felt joy with you in a long time."

"Really? Not when we went kayaking last month and saw the loon? Not when we went to have dinner in Boston and took that walk on the Common? What about Christmas, when you said you were the happiest man in the world? That sounds like joy, goddamn it!"

"I was trying to convince myself," he said.

"You're lying." He was. I knew it as well as I knew my own name.

"And there you go again. Not *hearing* me. Dismissing me."

The absolute worst thing about being married to a therapist was their gaslighting skills. They could twist anything to make you think it was your problem, your reaction, your childhood that was the issue, not *them*. They could justify anything. Taking responsibility was not in Brad's wheelhouse.

"I'm drained," Brad said. "Good night." He stood up and headed for the stairs. "And, Lillie . . ." For one second, I thought he was going to say he was sorry, a terrible joke, really, but my *face* . . . priceless! "This is for the best. You'll see."

I went into the bedroom and closed the door, and barely made it to the bed. Tears leaked out of my eyes and down my temples, wetting my hair. How was this happening to us? To *us*?

I cried until I was exhausted, ugly sobs wrenching out of me, utter dismay and anger and, for some reason, shame. I had lost my husband. Another woman had slid in between us, and I hadn't even noticed.

The sound of the ocean, just over the ridge of the kettle pond chain, roared, and the leaves rustled a poor reassurance. A whip-poor-will sang, and I tried to let the sounds drown out the shrill hissing in my head.

This time, though, the magic of my home didn't do the trick, and sleep didn't find me.

⌒

Brad was gone the next morning when I got up. His office was in a pretty Victorian house in East Orleans (owned by his parents, of course). He shared the space with several other therapists, each of them in their own little suite. As son of the building's owner, Brad had the nicest space—the library in the back, overlooking a flower garden of my own making.

Brad's office bespoke a certain attitude that wasn't quite matched by his financial or professional success. Stacy Benson, one of his office mates, was the renowned one, to be honest. She handled troubled and traumatized children, had appeared on CNN and was often a speaker at national conferences. Jorge was the marriage whisperer, and one of the couples he had counseled worked for Netflix, and a show was in the works, which had made Brad incredibly jealous. Jorge was young, extremely handsome and excellent at his job. It had taken weeks of patience to get through Brad's sulk about that "blow to my professional dignity," whatever that meant.

There was also Ellen, a seventysomething hypnotherapist who helped people with chronic pain and addiction. She had a Scottish accent and two degrees from Oxford and was absolutely warm and lovely, the grandmother we all deserved. Four times a year, she gave hypnobirthing classes at Wellfleet OB/GYN with my full blessing—gentle, encouraging meditations for women in labor that worked wonders at helping my mamas feel calm and empowered.

Brad's corner of the market, now that I thought of it, was middle-aged men, unhappy with their lives, looking back at the roads not taken, the lives they might have had. While Stacy, Ellen and Jorge had a steady stream of new clients (and even waiting lists), I'd seen Brad's work calendar. He got to work at eight thirty, took two hours for lunch every single day, saying it was because to be a *really* good therapist (a pointed reference to his office mates), a person had to give himself some time for reflection, not just "assembly line your clients." He was usually home by five thirty.

But he still had the biggest office, if not the biggest practice.

Six years ago, for Brad's fortieth birthday, I'd redecorated his office as a surprise while he and his father were on a fly-fishing trip in Canada. Brad had been going through that same phase his man-child clients struggled with, and told me he hated his office, that it felt claustrophobic and suffocating. He was tired of being a therapist and had been talking about writing a book.

So I took that time to overhaul his office. I loved doing that stuff, don't get me wrong. Brad and I finally had some discretionary money, and I spent a couple thousand so he could have the office of his dreams. I thought it might give him a new lease on his profession.

Before, it had been a cozy room painted dark blue with a Victorian couch, patterned wing chair, Persian carpet and paintings of the Cape shores. But, sensing Brad wanted to seem more sophisticated and cerebral, I made it over with soft gray walls and a long, elegant couch from Pottery Barn (which was not as comfy as the old blue velvet Victorian). I bought three modern, slightly weird Danish chairs and had a desk built (begrudgingly but meticulously) by my father. New lamps, window shades instead of curtains, a low glass coffee table. I reorganized his bookshelves so there was room for a vase here, a sculpture there. A soft blue rug replaced the faded red-and-blue Persian (Stacy appropriated that, as well as the old sofa). Abstract paintings from a couple of avant-garde Cape artists. A gorgeous black-and-white photo of Brad, Dylan and me for his new desk.

He had been overwhelmed. "I feel like a new man," he said, and the phrase had, at the time, made me so *happy*, dumbass that I was. "It really suits the real me, Lillie. Thank you. I can't wait to get started on my book here."

Should my marital antennae have twitched back then? The book, the "real me," this "new man"? Should I have sensed his growing discontent? Did he have a point about my attention being too much on Dylan and work?

Regarding Dylan, please, could a mother ever pay too much attention to raising a child? As for work, well, I *did* love my job, and my job didn't have regular office hours.

Babies didn't care if it was 3:00 a.m. Miscarriages happened at 7:00 p.m. on a Saturday. Being a midwife was creating an entire relationship with your clients, not just drawing blood or listening to the baby's heartbeat. Besides, Brad took calls from clients, too . . . though it was true I got a lot more calls than he did. Was he jealous of that fact? That I was needed more often than he was?

I didn't want to go into work today. Truth was, I did feel sick. My head ached, my stomach was acid. While all our pregnant mamas gave birth at Hyannis Hospital, my boss and friend, Wanda Owens, MD, OB/GYN, had an office here in Wellfleet, right next to Outer Cape Health Services, a family practice staffed with nice docs, APRNs and PAs. I texted Wanda and Carol, our receptionist and medical assistant, and asked how full the schedule was and if I could come in a few hours late.

Sure! Wanda texted back, ever cheerful. A little maternal hangover after graduation?

Carol texted, too. Menopause? Welcome to my world. Can't sleep, can't stay awake, have been having hot flashes for 25 years.

Thanks, Wanda, I texted back. Carol, sorry to disappoint you, but I'm still ovulating. But as soon as I have my first hot flash, I'll call you.

Despite my acidic stomach, I made myself another cup of coffee and went onto the screened-in porch.

If Brad kept up this nonsense . . . could he touch this house? The house where I'd grown up, where our *son* had grown up?

Dad had sold it to us for a rock-bottom price seventeen years ago and bought a perfect, tiny condo in North Truro. He wanted to be closer to the *Goody Chapman*, his true love, or so he said. I was pretty sure he just wanted Dylan and me back on the Cape (he had never warmed up to Brad, who had knocked up his daughter and didn't even know how to shuck an oyster, let alone pilot a fishing boat). We'd been living in an apartment the Fairchilds had found for us, which we never could have afforded on our salaries.

When we bought it, the house on Herring Pond was creaky and leaky, with poor insulation and the original furnace from 1952, bad windows and a roof that was growing all sorts of botany. But it was also a house with waterfront access to and full view of a kettle pond in Wellfleet. The kettle ponds, formed by melting glaciers ten thousand years ago, fell within the National Seashore protected lands. In other words, there could be no new building.

My dad's parents, who viewed a new blanket as a ridiculous expense when the old one only had four holes, had built it on the cheap, and Dad never did anything to update it, either. When Brad, Dylan and I moved in, there was a kitchen, living room, two bedrooms and one bathroom. The cellar was damp and smelly, filled with tools and fishing gear waiting to be repaired, because Vovô, like Dad, had also been a fisherman. Knotty pine everywhere and the faint smell of mold and mustiness, a smell I loved, since it meant home, far more than our swanky apartment in Boston.

The kettle ponds were accessible only by a maze of very long, twisting dirt roads flanked by pine, maple and oak trees. I'd grown up in these woods, learned to swim in these ponds—Higgins and Gull, Herring and Horseleech. I fished, canoed, wandered through the woods my entire childhood. The first time Brad came home to meet my dad, he'd been dazzled by the quiet magic of the area, being a city boy himself.

For a year or two, Brad and I just saved our money and adored our boy. I worked just enough to keep my license, and only night shifts. My in-laws paid me to work for Fairchild Properties, redoing their rudimentary website, starting them on social media, making a new logo for their twenty-fifth year in business, so I earned a little on the side, too.

Dad came for dinner every Wednesday, and Hannah would babysit if Brad and I wanted to see a movie, which was a splurge for us back then. Mom and Beatrice would drop by if forced—they both preferred that I visit them with the baby. Mom said the house gave her PTSD, always one to pee on my parade. After all, I obviously *loved* the house. Her grandson lived in this house. Her marriage hadn't been violent or hateful or dramatic. Brad would roll his eyes and analyze her for me in bed later and tell me she had narcissistic tendencies with a borderline sociopathy, and I loved him for it.

We renovated it bit by bit, pouring our hearts and souls into the house. We made a winding stone staircase down to the pond, heaving the rocks, setting them firmly in the fertile ground. We turned the cellar into a fully habitable floor with kitchen, dining area, screened-in porch. We built an addition off the kitchen for a guest room with full bath (Brad's current hideout). We cut down a few trees to widen the view of the pond. A few years later, we refurbished the middle floor, adding a bathroom to our bedroom and putting in a powder room off the front hall. We knocked down the walls around the chimney so that the stones ran right up to the attic, which we insulated, Sheetrocked and made into Dylan's room. A balcony overlooked the living room, and we made a tiny little library around the chimney, the shelves crammed with books, with room for one chair. *My hidey spot,* Dylan used to say.

I say *we*, but now, standing in the house that was a part of my soul, I realized it was me. Sure, Brad had been a solid provider all those years I worked part-time. But I was the one who saw what could be. Brad used to be proud of me for that. I put in gardens and made a courtyard, and we turned the shed into the studio apartment with the idea that we could stay there after Dylan graduated and rent the main house for some extra money. Rentals were in high demand on the Cape, especially a house with private access to a kettle pond.

I couldn't imagine living anywhere else. Our hidden little house had a purity so deep on winter nights you could practically hear God breathing. In the summer, the birds sang constantly, and the occasional fox or coyote trotted past, and always you could hear the ocean just beyond the ridge.

It was the most perfect place on earth.

How could Brad be leaving *this*? The home where his son had been raised, the home that held thousands and thousands of happy memories. What would he do at Christmas? We *always* had Christmas Eve here—Dad, Hannah and the Fairchilds, a friend or two, the night happy and crowded and full of good smells. What would we do this Christmas? Would it just be Dylan and me?

I broke out in a sweat.

I didn't even know who this other woman was. Did I know her? How old was she? Would he have more children? I was having a panic attack, it seemed. *Breathe in, hold it, exhale.* I knew the drill. I *taught* the drill. It wasn't working today.

I'd been a wife for nearly half my life. How could Brad just strip me of that title?

Heart pounding, I texted Dylan. **Hope you had fun last night! How are you doing?** I needed to touch base, to remind myself that I was still a mother, even if my days as a wife were numbered.

He didn't answer immediately. As was true with all mothers, I pictured him in a car wreck / hospital / ditch, then told myself he was probably making out with Lydia, his girlfriend, and hopefully not impregnating her.

Finally, the dots waved, and I sagged in relief. **Doing great! Thx! Be back for supper.**

My son was safe. He would be home this evening. I still had him . . . for five more weeks. Four weeks and four days, actually.

I wandered through the house, constantly checking my phone for something, though I wasn't even sure what that was. Cell reception was awful out here—one bar on a good day—so we used the Wi-Fi for communicating.

In the bathroom, I looked at myself in the mirror—a forty-one-year-old woman with frizzy black hair and, to-day, circles under her eyes. Thought about calling someone—Beth, who'd been my best friend since third grade. But she was happily married, and for some reason, this stopped me. Wanda, but she was covering for me at work, obviously. Vanessa, who would surely be furious with her son for this nonsense.

So I didn't call anyone. I just waited.

I would divorce him. Of course I would. I was a strong woman with standards, goddamn it, and this was a line in the sand I would not cross. I would not tolerate this. I was a badass, and he would rue the day he left me.

Unless he was really, *really* sorry.

Nope! No. I should be more like Susan Sarandon in *Thelma and Louise*. The tough one. No hesitation, no doubts, just strength. Then again, she drove off a cliff.

You can fix this, said Geena Davis. She was the dopey one in the movie, right? But sweet. Also, she got to sleep with a young Brad Pitt. *This is worth saving!* she said, flashing her dimples. *You can win him back!*

You would take that lying, cheating, weak excuse of a man back? Susan Sarandon asked.

Shit. Would I? At this moment, numb with shock, rage and terror, the answer was yes. My entire life was about to change without my consent, and I loved my life. This split-ting apart felt like . . . like emotional rape. My future, my family, taken away against my will.

I could erase one day of Brad saying everything he'd said, because we had two *decades* of a good marriage. Nineteen years of good days. It wasn't perfect, of course, but it was *good*. It was solid. We were parents of the same child. We loved each other. Right?

Time to cook. I checked the fridge—there was sea bass, courtesy of my dad, who'd given it to me last night at the restaurant. Only my father would hand off fish at a party. But he'd caught it that day, he said. I had some shrimp and mussels. I'd make caldeirada, a Portuguese fish stew, and a loaf of fresh bread to go with it.

Brad would rue the day he left my cooking, that was for sure. I'd never made a bad meal in my *life*. Onions from last year's garden. Garlic, minced fine, making my fingertips smell like heaven. Tomatoes from the farmers' market. Thyme from my own garden, so sweet smelling. Butter, of course. Olive oil, smoked paprika, red potatoes. Wine for the broth. I let it simmer, then covered it and turned off the flame. By the time I got home, the house would smell incredible.

To the office I went, on autopilot during the drive, because all of a sudden, I was there.

"Feeling better?" Wanda asked as I came in.

"Yep." I smiled at her, then looked away quickly. She was very good at reading people. "Who've we got today, Carol?"

"Stephanie James. Terrible hot flashes. We compared notes. She hasn't hit the chin hair stage yet, but when she does, she's going to look like a nanny goat. What do you think, Lillie? Electrolysis or laser?" She jutted her chin at me so I could inspect, a pleasure I'd have to put off till later.

"And who else?" I asked.

"Rena Blake. And Annie Blanco."

"Before you get to work, look at this picture," Wanda said. She pulled out her phone. "Your godchild. I may be biased, but isn't she beautiful?"

"Oh, wow. Wow!" Leila, Wanda's daughter, was *incredibly* beautiful—her dad was from South Sudan, and she'd inherited his deep, rich, nearly black skin color. She'd also gotten Addo's height, but her face was Wanda all over, and the result was a stunningly beautiful girl. In this photo, she was wearing an orange dress, and she had it, all right, that innate knowledge of photography and angles, light and posing. She'd just signed with Ford, at only fifteen, but had already booked New York Fashion Week, as long as she stayed on the honor roll. She and Dylan had played together when they were little, and Wanda had been very glad he'd watched out for her in high school.

"They grow up so fast," I said, tears in my voice. I'd been there when Wanda gave birth. Seemed like yesterday.

"We want to pop over with something for Dylan before he leaves, okay? You know Leila worships him."

"Good thing we arranged their marriage when she was born," I said.

"We'll have beautiful grandchildren," Wanda said. "Check your calendar. The six of us haven't gotten together in ages."

"Remind Leila that her godmother misses our sleepovers," I said, handing the phone back.

"Girl, be careful what you wish for. Now that Miss Model is with Ford and is making her own money, she's getting an attitude."

"See? You're tired. She can come live with me, and you can visit anytime." I was only half joking.

"Only if I get Dylan," Wanda said. "Especially now that he's grown and all the hard work is done." She smiled and went into an exam room, and I did the same.

For the next few hours, I was Lillie Silva, BSN, RN, CNM, a woman who knew what to do and say, who could lose herself in her work.

Stephanie, who was indeed in the sweaty grip of menopause, had tried black cohosh, dong quai, and yoga for her hot flashes. "Lillie, I have to change my pajamas in the middle of the night, I'm so sweaty. I'm going to kill myself if these don't stop," she said.

"Oh, don't do that," I said with a smile. "I'm glad you tried the other stuff, but let's go next level. Paxil, ten milligrams. It's a subtherapeutic dose, and a lot of women say it's a miracle drug."

"Then give me the miracle," Stephanie said. "Oh, Lillie, thank *God* there's something."

I tapped the script into the computer to Steph's pharmacy. "Call me in a few days and tell me how it's going."

Rena and her husband were next, and my heart ached for them. She was a lovely forty-two-year-old woman trying to get pregnant for the first time. Unfortunately, she hadn't been aware of how much fertility drops each year after thirty and had put it off to focus on her career. James, her husband, had normal sperm count and motility. We'd tried Clomid to no avail. Intrauterine insemination, where sperm was injected right into her uterus, hadn't worked. Ultrasounds and hysteroscopy had shown nothing abnormal. In vitro was probably next.

Sure enough, they asked, then held hands as I talked about the process of in vitro, the cost, the chances. It wouldn't be easy or fast . . . fertility drugs, egg retrieval, sperm analysis, blood work, the hope that the sperm would combine with the egg to start a healthy embryo. Their faces fell a little with each fact.

"What are the odds that we'd end up pregnant, say, within a year?" James asked.

I took a deep breath. I hated questions that involved statistics. I myself had bucked those odds, after all. "Obviously, I don't know. Everyone is different. But my best guess, based on the data, based on the number of eggs we can retrieve, maybe . . . ten percent?"

There was a moment of silence. "Yeah," Rena said. "That's what we read on the internet."

"Listen," I said. "I know how important having a baby is to you. If you want to try this, I'm right there with you, all the way."

"Thanks, Lillie," Rena said. She and her husband exchanged glances. "But we've talked about this. Those aren't great odds, so we're gonna try foster-to-adoption and not put this old body through any more torture."

"There are a lot of older kids out there who need parents," James said. "They don't have to have our genes to be our kids."

Tears flooded my eyes. "I agree," I said. "I think that's wonderful. I'll send you a list of some agencies other clients have worked with." I stood up and hugged them both. Rena sobbed once, and I tightened my grip. I understood the pain of not having your body cooperate with what should have been a natural process.

But I had Dylan, at least.

Annie Blanco, age twenty-four, was seventeen weeks pregnant. "I want natural childbirth," she said. "No drugs."

I smiled. "That's what we always aim for."

"You delivered my sister's baby last year. Laura Peters? A boy?"

"Oh, yes! She did such a great job."

"That's what I want, too. No pain, just breathing."

I smiled again. "Well, there will be pain, I can just about promise you that. But it can be absolutely manageable. This is what your body was built for, after all. Unless there's a reason to intervene, we won't."

"Awesome."

I asked her about her diet, recommended prenatal yoga and some guided meditation for pregnant women, told her to get plenty of exercise. "Um . . . is it still okay to have sex?" she asked. She was a newlywed, and she blushed as she asked.

"Oh, absolutely," I said. "Sex won't hurt the baby. Feeling friskier these days?"

"Yeah," she admitted, turning pinker.

"It's the hormones. Totally natural. I bet your husband isn't complaining."

"He's not," she said, laughing.

I took out the fetal doppler and listened to the baby's heartbeat. Annie's eyes filled. "I love that sound," she whispered.

"She can hear your heartbeat, too," I said.

"Really? Sure, that makes sense. Oh." The tears spilled over, and I held the doppler there a minute longer.

Pregnancy was truly miraculous.

When she was cleaned up from the gel and dressed again, we scheduled her next appointment. She hugged me before leaving.

At least I'll have this, I thought. When Dylan was 2,662 miles away, I'd still have my job. The best job in the world.

The last patient of the day was a walk-in. "She won't tell me why she's here," Carol said, clearly irked. "She wants to talk to a doctor or nurse. I guess I'm not good enough for her."

"Don't take it personally, Carol," I said. I poked my head into the waiting room. "Hi," I said. "I'm Lillie Silva, the nurse-midwife. Come on in."

The girl—young woman—was blond, tanned and silent. "Hop on the scale," I said, and she obliged. We went into an exam room. Each one was a different color of a soothing shade—gentle gray, sage green, slate blue—with abstract paintings on the walls and a mobile hanging from the ceiling. Hey. If you had to put your feet in the stirrups, you may as well have a pretty room for it. Another of my redecorating projects.

"What can I do for you, Bonnie?" I asked. "Cute name, by the way."

"It's fake," she said.

"Okay." This happened—clients came in for Plan B after a night of unprotected sex to prevent conception, or needed a pregnancy test, or wanted to go on birth control. "How can I help you today?" She wasn't much older than Dylan, but I didn't know her. A summer person, maybe, or someone who had driven here for anonymity's sake.

"I need to get tested for STDs," she said, her eyes filling with tears. "My boyfriend cheated on me and then dumped me." She sobbed once, and my heart clenched for her.

I squeezed her shoulder. "I'm sorry. That's so hard."

"It is! I really feel like my heart is breaking in half!"

I handed her a box of tissues—the good kind, with lotion, not the scratchy kind. It's the little things, and we had a lot of tears in this office, happy, sad, terrified. "A few questions first. Did you use birth control, and if so, what kind?"

They had used condoms (thank God). I went through the

slew of questions, holding her hand when she cried. Sent her to pee in a cup, did a cheek swab, drew some blood. We had a quick HIV test here, so it would only take twenty minutes or so to get results. Then I told her to put on an exam robe (they were cotton . . . again, the little things), and had her put her feet in the stirrups. Her legs were shaking, poor baby.

In went the prewarmed speculum, and I did my thing. "Everything looks completely normal," I said. "Go ahead and sit up. It'll take about five days for us to get the results back. Okay if I leave a voice message on your phone?"

"Sure. Do you think I have anything?" she asked, her voice shaking. "I had that vaccine. For HPV."

"Excellent. I can't guarantee anything, but your odds are definitely lower because you used condoms. Every time, right?"

"Right. The last thing I wanted to do was get pregnant."

"Smart girl." I put my hand on her shoulder. "Try not to worry until you have something to worry about, okay? Everything is treatable."

"Except herpes. Herpes is forever."

"But still treatable." My phone dinged with a text from Carol. HIV test negative. "No HIV," I said.

"Thank God!" She closed her eyes with relief.

"I'll leave you to get dressed. If you need to talk, call us, okay? The service will put you through if it's after hours."

"Thanks, Lillie," she said.

"You'll be okay, sweetheart."

"My name is Emily, by the way," she said with a little duck of her head.

"Nice meeting you, Emily."

It was only after she left and I was getting ready to go home that I realized . . . shit . . . oh, God. I needed one of these panels, too. I could have herpes. Chlamydia. Gonorrhea. HIV!

My knees buckled, and I collapsed into a chair.

"Wanda?" I called, my voice weak.

She heard me anyway. "What's up, babe? I'm just about to . . . Jesus, what happened? You're white as a ghost! Are you okay?"

"Close the door," I whispered, and she did. Carol wouldn't break HIPAA, but she'd interrogate me if she knew. She was already obsessed with me hitting menopause.

"What's going on, Lils?" she asked, taking my hand. "You're shaking."

"Brad cheated on me, and I need . . . I need . . ." I started crying.

"No. No!" Wanda *loved* Brad. Many were the times we'd go out, Wanda and Addo, Brad and me, laughing over dinner, sharing stories. They'd even gone to one of Brad's book signings, two of three people to show up, me being the other one. "I will murder him, Lillie! How? Why? Why? You guys are so *good* together!" She started to cry. "God, I'm sorry! But I can't believe this! Addo and I try to be like you two, hand to God! Oh, Lillie!"

She hugged me, and I told her what I knew, my head swimming. I barely knew anything, after all. And then, after a second long hug, my own tears now soaked into the paper of the exam table as Wanda did for me what I'd just done for Emily.

It was utterly humiliating. But at least my HIV test was negative, and I'd know the rest in a few days.

Back at home, I poured myself a huge glass of Portuguese vinho verde from my dad's third cousin back in the old country, chugged it, and poured another. Checked on dinner and put the proofed bread in the oven.

Dylan and Brad got home at the same time about a half hour later; I heard their tires crunching on the shells of our driveway. Brad said something to him and Dylan laughed easily. They came down into the kitchen.

"Hey, guys," I said. "How are you?" *Guess what Mommy did today, Dylan? She got an STD panel because Daddy's penis was in someone else!*

Dylan came over and gave me the lean-in hug of a teen-aged male. "Smells good in here, Mom."

"Thanks, honey." I forced myself to look at Brad. "Wine?" I asked.

"Thank you, Lillie," he said smoothly. "I'd love a glass."

"I'll take a beer, Mom," Dylan said.

"Hilarious," I said. Did I sound normal? Maybe I did.

The guys went onto the porch, and I poured Brad a glass of wine and topped mine off, needing a buzz tonight. Another thing I should've noted—Brad's wine vocabulary. He was suddenly using words like *harmonious* and *balanced* and *lingering*. Before that, we'd separated wine into two classes: red and white, usually from Portugal, because of Silverio, the aforementioned third cousin.

I looked at our glasses of golden wine and spit in Brad's. Swirled the wine around, then joined them on the porch. Dylan was sprawled on the couch, looking at his phone. Brad was in one of the cushioned chairs. I sat in the other, glancing at him to see when he sipped. *Enjoy the saliva, asshat.*

"Nice lingering on the palate, don't you think?" I asked.

"Yes, actually." He took another sip, holding it in his mouth. Some wine connoisseur.

Our son put his phone away. "So what's new with you guys, other than your kid is done with high school?"

I looked at Brad.

"I've got some great marketing plans for my book," he said. "I hired a new publicist, and she has some really innovative ideas."

Was *that* the other woman? A publicist?

"Cool," Dylan said, carefully not looking at me. We held the same opinion of Brad's book . . . lame, but since we loved the author, we pretended.

Had loved the author.

"Mom? Any slimy, blood-soaked birthing stories you want to share?"

I smiled, feeling a flare of love for my boy in the tundra of my heart. "No . . . I just saw some patients for checkups.

Sorry to disappoint." I paused, staring at Brad. "Ran a couple STD panels. Gonorrhea, herpes, syphilis, chlamydia. You know. Sores on the labia, in the vagina, that sort of thing."

His face twitched, then flushed an unappealing shade of brick.

"Thanks for sharing," Dylan said. "I feel so much closer to you now."

I looked back at my son. "You are the son of a midwife, Dyllie. You know more about the female anatomy than most women."

"Such a gift," he said, grinning.

And so we sat there, Brad's betrayal swimming beneath us like a great white shark. When the timer dinged for the bread, I went into the kitchen, pulled out the round loaf and inhaled the rosemary I'd topped it with, then served up the stew in the big, heavy multicolored bowls we had. Once again, I added a little bodily fluid to Brad's portion.

Then we ate together. It seemed so *normal*. Brad asked about the football coach at the University of Montana, and Dylan answered. I asked Dylan when he wanted to drive to Hyannis to get his college stuff. Brad said he'd like to take Dylan to Martha's Vineyard for a day (was that where she lived?). I said I'd like a day of ocean kayaking, going from Boat Meadow in Eastham all the way to Coast Guard Beach through the tidal rivers.

Dylan amiably agreed to everything, blissfully unaware that these family meals were numbered. Brad had me over a barrel, didn't he? He knew I didn't want to ruin what time we had left. Knew I wanted to give my son this last beautiful summer before college.

The bastard.

CHAPTER 3

Lillie

We need to talk," Brad said a week or so after graduation.

Fortunately, since that first dinner together after graduation, I'd been asked to cover a couple of overnight shifts at the hospital. It was so hard to feign normalcy when Dylan was around, and when he wasn't, I was tight with rage. Brad and I hadn't been alone in the house since the morning after graduation.

But tonight, Dylan was out, and Brad cornered me on the porch. "Let's part ways amicably," he continued. "If we go to a mediator, things will move faster."

Part ways? These fucking euphemisms. "I think we should try counseling," I said.

"It's too late for that."

"I meant counseling for how to 'part ways amicably.'" I made air quotes. "I'm sure Jorge can help us." It was a knife between his ribs, and he took the bait.

"We don't need Jorge. We have me. I'm much more experienced than he is."

"I wonder why Netflix didn't call you, then."

His fair skin flushed. Bull's-eye. "Can we be adults about this?"

"I don't know. You're the one pretending to be a hipster twentysomething. You're the one who broke our vows. Who's breaking our family without regard for anyone else."

"There were many beautiful things about our marriage," he said. "And I thank you for them. But I'm just not happy anymore, and I deserve to be happy."

"What about my happiness?"

"That's up to you. I can't give that to you."

"But your mistress can give it to *you*?"

"Life is a journey," he said. "Cliché, but true. And our journeys are simply taking different paths now. I feel so much joy at the idea of a fresh start, and I'm sorry you don't, but you will, Lillie. You'll have joy again, too."

Oh, the condescending ass. "Stop using that word. You sound like an idiot." I swallowed as he took a sip of his *malbec.* "Seriously, Brad. Be normal for one minute. Don't you care that you're breaking my heart?"

"Of course I care," Brad said. "But honestly, this has nothing to do with you. It's about my journey."

"How can you say that? This is our *marriage.* You never said you were unhappy! You never mentioned anything being wrong. We *were* happy."

"You didn't sense my deep discontent?"

"I did not, because you weren't deeply discontented. And if you were, it's normal to go through those times. Our son is leaving for college. Of course we've had other things on our minds. You're taking our family and tossing it in the trash. Our whole future. Have you thought about this? All the things you'll miss? Christmas? Family dinners?"

"I never really felt welcomed by your family, honestly."

"Because they saw you for the superficial asshole you are, probably. I'm the only one stupid enough to have loved you."

"So much hostility," he chided. "These things happen. It's no one's fault."

"No, Brad, it *is* your fault! You said nothing about the deep discontentment. You've been seeing another woman behind my back. You've cheated on me and lied to me, you've been gaslighting me, and I have done absolutely nothing wrong!"

"Calm down," he said, because women love hearing that. "Your anger is one of the reasons I think I needed more j—happiness in my life."

"I'm allowed to be angry, Brad! How long has this been going on?"

"How long," he sang, "has this been going on?"

I laughed unexpectedly. Brad had a great memory for song lyrics. We used to play Name That Tune on long car rides. He was killer at that game. My heart did crack then. We'd never do those things again. We had such an easy rhythm, so many traditions and funny little inside jokes. Maybe, as we sat there in the ensuing silence, he was thinking about those things, too.

"Anyway," I said eventually, "answer the question. How long have you been having an affair? Who is she? I'm going to find out, so you might as well tell me." We were down to three weeks and two days before Dylan left for school.

He sighed. "It's not an affair. It's love." He paused. "Ironically, you introduced us."

My head jerked back. "What?"

"Melissa," he said. "Who bought Stella Maris."

What the hell was Stella Maris? At my blank look, he said, "Melissa Finch. She bought the house on Griffins Island Road last winter."

"The . . . the . . . widow with the kid?"

"Yes." He smiled.

"Oh, my God."

"She's so smart and talented. Wait till you get to know her better."

"I'm not going to get to know her better, Brad!"

"I've already told you I prefer Bradley," he said. "I would appreciate it if you could respect my wishes."

Who *was* this guy? Where was my husband?

As for Melissa Finch, I had *liked* her. I'd introduced her around! I'd suggested she join the council on the arts and had introduced her to two families who had kids her daughter's age. I had just seen her last week in the general store, and she'd been so *nice*. While she was sleeping with my husband!

That was one stone-cold killer. My God. She hadn't even blushed.

"When did this start?" I asked, my voice like gravel.

He sighed. "Does it matter?"

"Yes."

"I suppose it was . . . late February, early March."

She had moved here at the end of *January*. They sure hadn't wasted any time. Wow. It had taken him mere weeks to set fire to his wedding vows and our life.

"Look," he said, and his voice was tight and irritated. "It's done, Lillie. You and I are getting a divorce whether you like it or not, and it can go smoothly, or we can go to court and you can spend a lot of money on a lawyer. I'll let you have the house, I suppose."

"Big of you." We owed quite a bit on the house, after all the renovations. Quite a bit. Would I get our debt, too?

"Let's be kind to each other," he said. "We can get along as Dylan's parents, because we'll always have him to bind us. When the hurt fades, you're really going to like Melissa. You already do, you said it yourself last winter."

"That's before I knew she was stealing my husband," I said.

He sighed, sadly, patiently. "You can't steal a person," he said.

"What does her kid think?"

"We're forging a solid relationship, and Ophelia is her niece, actually."

So he'd met the child. I had, too, when I brought them flowers as a housewarming gift. She'd been a bit stone-faced, but she was twelve. It came with the territory.

"Can you please answer my very reasonable question about mediation?" Brad asked.

"Let me think about it." I hadn't done any real research yet, and I would have to, I supposed. "Have you told your parents?"

He looked away. "Not yet."

"They'll be so ashamed of you. Disgusted, really."

His face grew red, but his expression was almost haughty. "They'll want their son to find his joy and lead a life full of hope and self-care."

"They'll want their son to honor the vows he made before them and God, and they will be horrified that you're an adulterer."

"Maybe," he said. "I can't live my life based on some archaic view of society."

I left the porch before I punched him in the face.

I only knew one attorney well . . . my mother. But free legal advice was free, and she was nothing if not blunt. So I drove up to Provincetown the next day and sat in her stunning, cold white kitchen, which she and Beatrice had redone last year. She made me coffee from what appeared to be a small jet engine, based on its complexity, and listened as I told her the news.

"Can't say I'm surprised," she said, setting her cup down on the white marble island top. "I never liked Brad. So pretentious. Then again, that probably appealed to you, Liliana."

Two seconds in, and already she was twisting the knife. It was her special gift. "He wants to do mediation."

"That's the best way," she said. She paused. "Do *not* let him take the house or make you sell it. Don't move out, either."

Funny. She couldn't wait to flee that house when I was a kid.

"That's the most important thing to me," I said. "And Dylan's education."

"Oh, you haven't paid for that yet?" she asked.

Death by a thousand paper cuts. "No, Mom. But we have saved. Just not the whole amount yet."

"Really? Hannah could probably help you. She makes a wonderful living." Mom also made a wonderful living *and* had inherited a hefty sum when her father died years ago, but she had never offered to help with her only grandchild's college expenses, and I couldn't bring myself to ask.

"I'm fine, Mom. Financially. We don't need help. We just . . . we're just normal, Mom. We'll pay it as it comes."

She looked at her manicure, admiring the light pink polish. "If you say so. Anyway, mediation is the fastest, easiest and cheapest. Make sure you look at his pension and retirement funds. Is he hiding money?"

"No. I don't think so. I handle the money."

"Good." She looked out the window at her garden. "Do you have anything of value? Jewelry, art, furniture?"

"Just the house, mostly. Some paintings I bought for his office."

"Those count as gifts, then. Too bad, since you probably overpaid for them." She looked at the ceiling. "I'm not a divorce attorney, but there are a few things that are just de rigueur. Get your own credit card and bank account, and make sure he's not spending money you don't know about," she said. "Freeze your joint accounts and tell your financial adviser you're divorcing, if you have one, that is. If Brad has anything that might be valuable, take a photo of it and get it appraised."

"Like what?" I asked.

"Baseball cards? That hideous old hutch in your den? I don't know, Liliana. You're the wife. Oh, and try to get money from him that's not in the form of alimony. You won't get taxed that way. Get him off your insurance plan." She took a sip of coffee from her antique Limoges teacup— no "World's Best Grandma" mug for her. "Good for you, Lillie! I'm proud of you."

"Why? I don't want this. I want to stay married."

She snorted. "Why?"

"Because I was emotionally scarred when my own parents divorced. Because I value family as the foundation of—"

"Are we done? Do you want something to eat?" she said, glancing at her watch. "You'll have to make it yourself. Oh, you and Dylan should come for dinner. Saturday night, seven o'clock. Hannah's coming, too, of course."

Yes. Hannah *adored* Mom and Beatrice. Actually, she adored Beatrice. No one adored my mom.

"We're not available," I said.

"Try to wear something nice for a change," she said, ignoring me. "Now, I have work to do. Off you go."

I'd already been dismissed. Mom walked out of the kitchen, heels tapping.

For the next three weeks, Brad played up the role of devoted father, friend and all-around great guy. If Dylan was around, he smiled, joked, cleaned up the kitchen, asked me if my left tire was still losing air. We ate dinner together. On Wednesdays, the day my dad came over to eat, Brad pretended he had a late client and hid in his office, since he'd always been slightly fearful of my father. Or he visited *Melissa*.

Meanwhile, Dylan and I spent a lot of time together, fishing or kayaking, walking in the woods. I tried to press these moments into my heart—the perfect stillness of Herring Pond as we stood up to our waists in it, the minnows swimming around us in the clear water. Kayaking into the waves at Coast Guard Beach, my son reaching out to steady my boat.

I tried not to tell him how much I'd miss him. Parenting is a 90 percent–10 percent relationship. Dylan was following his life's trajectory, which was arcing upward and away, and all I could do was watch and wish him the best.

They don't tell you how agonizing it is to have raised your child well. To have made yourself superfluous, while your child never stops being your beating heart.

He was ready. Ready to leave home, and ready to leave

his parents. Football would guarantee him friends, and the coach texted him daily for reports of Dylan's workout and food intake.

Melissa was closer to Dylan's age than to Brad's. What if our son loved having a rich stepmother? What if she bought him a sports car? What if he spent Christmas with them, or they flew out to Yellowstone to see him without me?

This is what insanity was. Trying to answer the unanswerable.

Thank God I had work. Wanda was the only obstetrician with offices on the Outer Cape, and we handled just about every pregnant woman from Orleans to Provincetown. But this summer, when I saw a pregnant mama, I was awash in memories of my one healthy pregnancy . . . and the one I lost. Postpartum clients reminded me of my own days as a young mother. When my client Zoe miscarried at fourteen weeks, I held her close, crying with her, rocking her, thinking of my own little girl, so still and white in my arms. I always cried when a patient miscarried. But this time, I had to go to my car to cry, a wracking howling grief that had to be hidden from Carol and Wanda. Maybe I needed antidepressants. Maybe I should see a therapist (pause for bitter laughter).

The need to talk to Vanessa burned in my chest, and yet I couldn't bring myself to do it. My mother and Wanda were the only ones who knew. Mom had probably forgotten already. Dad . . . he wouldn't be able to hide his fury, and Dylan would find out within seconds if Dad knew, because Brad would be cowering in a corner, whimpering. Rightly so. Who could make a body disappear better than a fisherman?

I spent my nights in our—my—bedroom, which had a little office alcove, poring over our finances, trying to make a budget with half the income our life was based on. There were blogs and websites and information about women like me—Chump Lady, *Divorce Mag*, Betrayed Women's Club.

I read articles about how to tell your college student his parents were divorcing. In person, they all said, but I just couldn't do that to my son before he left.

I felt like I was teetering on the edge of a breakdown. "Push, that's right, you're doing so well, Grace!" *I need to spend less on groceries. Should I become a Costco member? I should list Brad's stupid book as an asset so I can get half of his piddling royalties just to piss him off.* "His head is crowning! This is the most intense part, Grace. Deep breaths, no pushing, okay? You're almost there. You're doing amazing work."

I felt like two people. No, three. The supportive midwife, the loving mother and the raging harpy who wanted to set fire to everything. My dreams were terrifying and bleak. Dylan's plane crashed last year, and I was only now getting the news. Brad said he wanted to make up, but Melissa had just bought our house, and she'd be living with us. The *Goody Chapman* caught fire, and Dad and I moved to Alabama.

I'd never been so tired in my life.

One morning, when Brad was allegedly working and Dylan was out, Vanessa burst into my house. "Oh, Lillie! I'm stunned! I can't believe he'd do this to you!"

She wrapped me in her arms, and the tears started flowing for both of us. "Come, let's sit down," she said. "I'll make coffee." Because yes, she knew where everything was, unlike my own mother.

She got a box of tissues and plopped it on the table in front of me, then stood by the sink, wiping her own tears until the coffee was ready. Then she poured us each a cup, black for her, cream for me, and sat down across from me. "Dylan's car isn't there. He's out?" she asked.

"Yes." Dylan was with his girlfriend and then would be going to his job at PJ's, a drive-up seafood place with the best fried clams anywhere.

"Brad called us last night and told us everything," she said. "I couldn't sleep a wink, so this morning, I got in my car and came right here. Oh, Lillie. We had no idea things were so bad! Tell me the truth. What's been going on, honey? How are you? You must be devastated."

Oh, how *wonderful* to talk to someone who cared. "I . . . I think I'm in shock," I said. "One day he was happy, the next day he's talking about adventures and journeys and growing apart, and I had no clue. He cheated on me, Vanessa! He cheated on me!" I started sobbing.

"Oh, honey." She squeezed my hand. "The wife is always the last to know, they say," she said, dabbing her eyes. "We're so ashamed of him. This is not how he was brought up. I almost wonder if he's having a nervous breakdown. Do you know what he said to us? That he deserves 'joy.'" She made finger quotes. "What exactly does that mean? And doesn't having a healthy son and a loving wife bring you joy?"

"Exactly," I said, my mouth wobbling.

"I mean, really. There's divorce, and then there's this," she said.

"To the best of my knowledge, we were fine, Vanessa. We were better than fine. We were happy and content and . . . happy."

"He said you've been drifting apart for at least four years, since Dylan started high school."

"I—That's not true. I mean, yes, life was busier with Dylan and football and all that, but if you'd have asked me a month ago if I had a good marriage, I would have said I had a *great* marriage. I really thought that."

"Maybe he has a brain tumor," she said, echoing my own thoughts. She leaned forward to lay her hand on mine, and the smell of her perfume, the caring in her voice . . . it meant the world to me. "We will not support this in the least. He says she's an aspiring *yoga* teacher! For heaven's sake!"

Ah, the Boston Brahmin. I thanked God Melissa wasn't a heart surgeon out of Harvard. "I appreciate you more than I can say," I murmured.

For an hour, we talked about Brad, me, Dylan and *that woman*. We decided this was a midlife crisis in every cliché way imaginable, from Brad's new glasses and clothes to working out.

"She's only thirty." Sixteen years younger than Brad. "She would've been twelve when Dylan was born. Twelve! She could have been his babysitter."

"Dear God. Well, we see it all the time, darling. Curtis Endicott just married a forty-year-old! He's seventy-two! She's younger than his *daughters*. At least Patrice died and didn't have to see her husband making a fool of himself."

"I don't know what to do," I confessed. "I want our family to stay intact, but I don't know that I can ever forgive him, even if he wanted to work things out."

"Of course you would forgive him, darling," she said soothingly. "Many spouses have dealt with infidelity and even become stronger for it."

I wondered if she was speaking from experience. "Is Charles on the Cape, too?" I asked.

"No, he had meetings all day," she said. "Well. I'm going to drive to Brad's office and give him a piece of my mind. I was too in shock last night to speak, but he's about to endure the wrath of his mother, and you know how he's always been with that."

She stood up and hugged me again, and for a minute, it felt like all would be put right by this woman, my champion and friend. "Let's have dinner tonight, just you, Dylan and me, shall we? Make a reservation somewhere fabulous. The Red Inn, perhaps? I'll call you very soon. Don't worry, sweetheart. We'll get this straightened out."

Oh, I loved her. She understood and was on my side, in a way I would never get from my own mother. Off she went in her Audi, and I sat back down, feeling better than I had since May 12. I called the Red Inn, and they told me they were now booking in October, so I called Victor's instead. Their food was just as good, *and* they had a table for three at six thirty.

～

I went to work and did my thing, but I was itching to hear from Vanessa. Maybe Brad had fallen apart in the face of maternal disapproval. Maybe he'd come back home this evening, sternly led by his mother, apologize and tell me how wonderful I was, that yes, it was a midlife crisis and he was an idiot.

I did a routine checkup on Tiana, who was expecting her fourth child in six years and was a goddess in the delivery room. "Can you tell me the gender?" she asked.

"You don't want to wait for an appointment when Trey's here?" I asked.

"He's watching the girls," she said, "and I can't stand the suspense."

"You got it," I said, smearing goo over her tummy.

I turned on the machine, pressed the controller against her gorgeous belly. A second later, I had her answer. "It's a boy!" I said, and she burst into tears of joy.

"I'd be just as happy with a girl, but oh, Lillie! A little boy! You know how that feels! Let me call Trey. He'll be thrilled."

Get ready to have your heart broken in eighteen years, I thought darkly. *Be grateful you have daughters. Raise your son so he doesn't cheat on his wife.*

As Tiana talked to her husband, I checked my phone. Nothing from Vanessa.

When five o'clock came, I still hadn't heard from her, and a tingle of anxiety weakened my knees. I'd ridden my bike to work, and I took my time on the trip home, breathing in the scent of the fallen pine needles and rambling roses that twisted and climbed the trees in the MacGregors' yard. The sky was perfectly clear and dazzlingly blue. Deep breaths, no tears. I had my health. I had my son.

Vanessa didn't contact me. I called Victor's and apologized, and they kindly said it was no problem, they had plenty of people waiting.

Finally, at seven forty-five, she texted. Had to go back to Boston unexpectedly. Brad and I talked. More later. Sorry about dinner.

That was not a good sign. That was not a white knight on horseback. That didn't sound like the wrath of a mother.

The next day, Vanessa emailed me to say she was so very sorry, but she and Charles had decided not to take sides, even if they didn't approve of the way in which Brad was conducting himself. He was their son, and I would always be the mother of their grandson, but it would be best if they didn't get involved.

Vanessa, who had swooped in when I lost my daughter, who had known just what to do, bringing over homemade mac and cheese, sending Brad and Dylan out for the day, letting me cry unfettered. Vanessa, who told me a thousand times that I was a remarkable mother. Who thanked me for making such a beautiful life for her son and grandson. The woman who had taught me firsthand what motherhood should be like.

She was ditching me, too. It almost hurt more than Brad.

CHAPTER 4

Melissa

Missy Jolene Cumbo was thirteen when she realized her looks were going to take her places—specifically, out of Wakeford, Ohio, tucked in the Appalachian Mountains, spitting distance from West Virginia, and the second poorest town in the state.

The gym teacher, Mr. Lambert, had brushed up against her, and she'd felt something odd . . . his *erection*, she realized. Ew! But also, like, interesting? Mr. Brent, the history teacher, called on her, and she thought there was a difference in his voice. Like, he totally wanted to hear what she had to say, even though she got Cs in his class. Leesa, the so-called smartest girl in their class, gave her a filthy look as Missy was getting her backpack out of her locker, then whispered something to Nicolette, and they laughed, glancing at her, then laughed some more.

Jealousy? Interesting! She'd never had any use for Leesa and Nicolette, since they thought they were all that, but their mean laughter told her something.

Later that week, she went to the Dollar General to test her newfound power, and there it was. Shane Lewis's daddy gave her a long gaze, then jerked his eyes away when he realized it was her, same age as Shane. She got a gross smile from the pervy guy in the pickup, who was drinking beer in the bed of his rusty truck. *Dirty old men,* she thought, but with a little hint of pride, too.

She walked home and went straight into the bathroom, closed the door and wedged the board under the handle, since the lock had been broken all her life. She stared in the mirror. Missy-Jo might come from a long line of hillbilly white trash, as her father proudly proclaimed them, and she wasn't exactly book smart, but that mirror was *telling* her something. She was pretty! She was . . . hang on a sec . . . oh my *word*! She was *beautiful*! She had always known she was prettier than Mama, and (sorry, sis) prettier than Kaitlyn, but thunderation! All of a sudden, pretty had gone and grown into *gorgeous*. Holy heck.

The face in the mirror had high, defined cheekbones— she'd lost that baby fat in the past year or so; clear, pale green eyes; naturally blond hair (a little dingy, but she could work with it); and a full, Kardashian kind of mouth (the Cumbos might have their electricity shut off a few times a year for not paying the bills, but they sure as heck had cable).

Suddenly, the world held new possibilities. Even at thirteen, Missy-Jo knew she wasn't going to stay in this loser town. Wakeford wasn't even a real town, just an unincorporated blob, filled with moldy trailers and rickety farmhouses, rusting cars, stray dogs, a garage that was open when the mechanic was sober and the Dollar General store. Missy-Jo had never left Ohio. The furthest she'd ever been was Portsmouth, and only because she'd broken her arm when she was nine.

Anyone with half a brain would want to get out of there. Very few did.

But she would.

Maybe she could be a supermodel! But dag nab it, she'd have to be *discovered*, and who in their right mind would come to Loserville to look for top models? Shoot. Maybe if she was somewhere else, like . . . like . . . Dayton or something, she could get discovered in a mall, have photos taken and whatnot. But dang, she was only five foot six and a half, and she'd pretty much stopped growing. Even so, she made her sister take pictures of her and sent them to some of them fancy New York agencies, but she never even heard back. Rude.

That left college as the means of her escape. She wasn't great at school, but then again, no one tried real hard to inspire the students. They were too busy breaking up fights and telling kids not to deal drugs or have sex in the building. Mama and Daddy would disapprove of her leaving, so she kept her plans to herself.

First step in Missy's plan—chastity. She wasn't going to get knocked up by some pimply teenage boy whose best prospect was *maybe* becoming a tractor repairman. No, thanks!

Second step—no drinking, no drugs, no smoking. Heroin was a huge problem in these parts, and most of the kids she knew already drank. Kaitlyn came home smelling like booze half the time, and she was only twelve. Missy-Jo told her to quit it, but Katie said it was only beer, and besides, she never listened to anybody.

Third step—get through high school without flunking a single class. The bar was not that high in Wakeford. She could probably be an honors student just by finishing homework and passing it in.

Fourth step—get a rocking body. She wasn't fat, but looking at her parents and their sizable bellies, her mother's wide hips and her father's double chin, she couldn't count on genetics. She started running, which was a great excuse to get out of the house. She would've joined the high school track team, but there wasn't one, so she ran on her own. Started an exercise routine to the best of her ability, doing fifty push-ups and fifty sit-ups as soon as she rolled out of bed, another set at bedtime.

"What are you doin'?" Kaitlyn asked from the other side of the room they shared, watching her with a look of disdain.

"Takin' care of myself, that's what," she said. "You should think about it. Stop drinking, Katie. You're gonna wind up just like Daddy."

Kaitlyn rolled her eyes and left the room to hang out with her no-good friends. Missy knew her sister was sneaking cigarettes. A shame she didn't have any plans for her own future. Missy loved her sister, but she couldn't fix what didn't want to be fixed.

Missy found a book on yoga at a tag sale and started trying that in the basement, the only place in the shabby house where there was enough space—Mama was a bit of a hoarder. Soon enough, her muscles were taking on definition and her ass was firm and high.

Next step—learn how to act and look rich. There were magazines for style advice. She learned how to apply makeup bought from the Dollar General. She found an Emily Post etiquette book in the church basement one Sunday morning, stuffed it under her shirt and took it home. Studied how to set a table, cross her legs, make easy conversation. At the library, where there was Wi-Fi, she watched makeup tutorials—natural glow, enhancing green eyes, contouring, lip stains. She was a natural. No crazy cat eyes for her, no clumpy mascara or ridiculous fake eyelashes, no tan from a can.

Next step—fix her accent. Ohio Appalachian wasn't going to cut it for what she had planned. She watched network news and adjusted her speech to sound more generic and less hillbilly. No more *y'all*, no more *fixin' to*, no more *done did*, no more dropping syllables and leaving off the g. She bought a Word of the Day calendar and memorized each new word, tried them out in sentences. In English class, she pored over sentence structure and figured out past tenses. Her schoolmates made fun of her, and her mother liked to tell her, "Y' ain't no Princess Diana."

High school inched past, and Missy-Jo positioned herself for greater things. She waited until she had applied to four colleges to tell her parents.

This caused an uproar from the family . . . all of them: her parents, aunts and uncles, cousins, grandparents. Her mom worked as a nursing assistant at the old folks' home, changing diapers and giving bed baths for seven dollars an hour. Her father had been on disability for years, courtesy of an alleged back injury attained while unloading a truck over at the Walmart in Waverly. He spent his days drinking beer in front of Turner Classics. *Not* being educated was an odd point of pride. "Not a single person in this here family ever even left the county," her father said. "What makes you think you're better 'n them?"

"*I* din't have to go to no college," her mother said, waving her cigarette in the air. "Your *daddy* din't have to go to no college, and we're just fine."

"Are you, though?" Missy-Jo, now seventeen, asked, gesturing around the kitchen, the chipped laminate countertops, the peeling linoleum. "This was your dream?"

"Don't sass me, young lady. You get fed around here, dontcha? Shut your mouth and show some respect. Gettin' too big for your britches, you are. That fancy-ass accent ain't foolin' no one."

There wasn't a lot of love demonstrated in the Cumbo household. Missy-Jo didn't think homesickness would be an issue. The TV shows she watched showed a different way of parenting—*Modern Family*, *Malcolm in the Middle*, *The Walking Dead*. (How many times did Rick save his son's life, huh?) Those parents loved their children. They *encouraged* them. They wanted the best for them. Mama and Daddy . . . not so much.

Kaitlyn was the only one Missy would regret leaving. But while Missy couldn't wait to leave, Kaitlyn wanted no such thing. "It's *beautiful* around here," she'd say. "It's home. Why'd you wanna go anywhere else?"

"Because *everywhere* else is better than this, Katie! Can't you see that?"

But by then, Katie had been swallowed into the druggie kids, and nothing Missy said could make her see the error of her ways. By the time Missy hit her senior year, she knew Kaitlyn would be trapped here, nothing good in her future.

On her eighteenth birthday, Missy-Jo went to the county courthouse and changed her name to Melissa Grace Spencer (as in Diana, just to get back at her mother). Missy could be a nickname for Melissa, after all, and it pinged her heart to give it up completely. It had been Kaitlyn's first word. But Missy-Jo was not a name that would help her, and just like that, she felt like she was moving up in the world. Melissa Grace Spencer sounded like someone with *class*.

There was obviously no college fund, so Melissa cast about for a scholarship and work-study program. She found one at Kansas Wesleyan University, a Christian school that was impressed with her college essay—"Bettering Myself through the Lord" (tell the people what they want to hear, folks). It worked. And didn't she do that? She believed in God, of course, and that He would absolutely want her to get out of this Podunk town. The Lord's hand guided those nice people at Kansas Wesleyan to give her a beautiful financial aid package.

At the end of August, Missy-Jo, now Melissa, packed up the beater car she'd bought with her earnings from babysitting and working at the Dollar General for the past five years. Her parents gave her listless hugs and speculated on how long she'd last before she dropped out.

She hugged Kaitlyn, whose eyes were glassy from weed. "Don't get pregnant," Melissa said.

"Live your own life, Missy," Kaitlyn said, scratching at the scab over her most recent tattoo. "Don't be worryin' about me. Love you."

Melissa called home twice a month, but she didn't go back. Why would she? Salina, Kansas, home of her college, was practically a *metropolis* (word of the day!) with restaurants and boutiques and art galleries. Cafés even, where people would sit and sip and order six-dollar coffees.

During Melissa's sophomore year, Kaitlyn called to say

she was pregnant. "Is that safe?" Melissa asked. "Are you . . . you know, still using?"

"No! Give me some goddamn credit, Missy Jolene Cumbo. I'm not *usin'*. Jesus. You're supposed to be happy for me."

Happy? Her sister had been arrested three times as a juvenile, once as an adult—shoplifting, vandalism, DUI, trespassing. The last arrest had been when she broke into someone's house, shot up and passed out. The family had found Kaitlyn unconscious on the eight-year-old daughter's bed, the syringe still in her arm. She was only eighteen.

When the baby was born, Melissa drove the fourteen hours to the hospital to see her sister and niece. Blond hair, same as Kaitlyn and Melissa; rosebud mouth. "Inn't she beautiful?" Kaitlyn asked. "Name's Harminee. Spellin' it different to be special. Harminee Fawn."

Well, that would just about guarantee the baby would become a stripper, Melissa thought. *Harmony* was a beautiful name. Harminee, though? Gosh.

Kaitlyn managed to stay sober for ten months after Harminee was born. After she was found high on meth with the baby crying in her crib, Harminee's paternal grandparents got custody, as the father was in jail. It was probably better that way, Melissa thought. Her sister was on a road that was hard to get off, and hopefully the baby would be safe with the grandparents. She tried not to think about it.

Her junior year, Melissa fell sort of in love with a fellow student at Kansas Wesleyan, and they stayed together for the rest of college. Unfortunately, Tom was studying to be a middle school teacher, and she was so *not* going to become a teacher's wife. "We just want different things," she told him as he cried the week before graduation. "I want a bigger life."

"What does that even mean?" he'd sobbed.

Money, she thought but didn't say. Money, elegance, prestige, art openings and charity event sponsorships, vacations. She'd never even seen the ocean. Never been on an airplane or a boat. She wasn't going to stay in the *heart-land*. Tom had been a nice boyfriend, and she'd lost her virginity to him (using the pill and two condoms). She knew she'd need some sexual experience to get where she wanted to go. He'd served a purpose, was a good kisser, let her feel what the fuss over sex was about. It was nice to be adored, and she did feel a little bad when she dumped him.

Melissa graduated with a degree in health sciences, focus on exercise and training. Her plan was to leverage that for a job with some famous athletes. Marry a football star, maybe, or a basketball player (they made more and played longer, but did she want to be married to someone who was six foot eleven?). She researched teams and sent out emails. *Soon,* she thought. Soon her real life would begin. Her job would be a stepping-stone. It wasn't what she wanted to *do*, though what that was, she couldn't exactly pinpoint. She was good at exercise. She liked feeling healthy and fit and beautiful. Otherwise, her goal was to . . . well, to have everything she wanted.

Her parents came to graduation and complained about everything. "We din't even know it was you," her father said. "Melissa Something Spencer? Last I knew, my daughter was Missy-Jo Cumbo. I ain't got no daughter named Melissa."

Melissa sighed. "I'm still your daughter, Daddy," she said.

They talked about Kaitlyn and Harminee; Kaitlyn was in rehab again, hoping to get custody back. Harminee's father had left jail, joined the military, and was stationed in Korea. His parents were happy to take care of the baby. Melissa's own parents babysat once in a while so they could have a break.

There wasn't much discussion about Melissa herself, though. Her parents were dubious about her ability to get a job, told her she'd wasted her money "becoming a liberal" and wanted her to move back and "help out."

She declined. Hugged them goodbye, telling herself

she'd probably never have to see them again, then went for an eight-mile run to cleanse her energy of their negativity, followed by meditation and yin yoga. Salina had a yoga studio, and she worked there, cleaning up and scheduling the classes, getting free studio time as a perk. Her faith in God morphed into faith in the universe. Same thing, more or less, she thought. Plus, it made her seem more worldly.

She stayed in Salina while waiting to get responses from the sports teams she'd contacted. Once they saw her, she was sure she'd get a job. The universe would provide. Her looks had only improved since her early teens, and she knew she was *very* beautiful now. She was well-spoken and good at making conversation. (Thanks, Emily Post!) For the time being, she got a job at a bar, which helped her learn about wine and spirits, another tool in her toolbox. She was a natural flirt and made excellent tips. She and three fellow graduates from Kansas Wesleyan rented an apartment, and it was all quite nice, really.

Except Melissa was bound for greater things. She felt that in her bones.

But eight months after graduation, she hadn't heard back from a single team, even with polite follow-up emails. Maybe her plan was flawed. And yet, it couldn't be! She *would* get where she wanted to go. She always did. She was special; she just knew it. She hadn't put in all this work, these eight and a half years of focus, for nothing.

She'd been researching elite gyms in LA to see if anyone might hire her, giving her proximity to the stars, when she got an email for a medical conference. It was because of a website she'd visited during her Anatomy and Physiology class. She'd gotten on their mailing list and had never bothered to unsubscribe.

Two months from now, the email said, there was a conference for orthopedic surgeons, and there was still space available.

Her hand moved to delete it, but stopped midair.

Doctors, especially surgeons, were also wealthy and, unlike professional athletes, had many more years of earning.

Huh.

To Google she went. Orthopedic surgeons were among the top earners of all surgeons, she learned, especially if they owned a surgical center or had invented some new tool or perfected an artificial joint.

Melissa had studied medicine, in a way. The human body was the human body, right? She had a lot in common with these surgeons, probably.

Melissa looked up the conference, which was in New Orleans, a city renowned for its beauty and food. She called the registration number. "Hello," she said, lowering her voice a bit. "I'm considering attending the conference in March."

"Wonderful!" said the man on the other end. "Are you a doctor or a vendor?"

"A doctor."

"An orthopedic surgeon, obviously?"

She thought fast. She was twenty-two years old, almost twenty-three, and she looked younger, thanks to her skin care regimen. "Yes, but I'm still in my residency." Thank you, *Grey's Anatomy*!

"Fantastic. This conference will be so helpful."

"Is there a hotel you'd recommend?" she asked. "Where some other doctors might be staying? You know, so I can pick their brains."

"There are several. What are you looking for?"

"Five stars, please. Something with a nice bar."

"The Roosevelt, in that case," he said. "It's gorgeous. Can I register you for the conference, Dr., uh . . . sorry, I didn't catch your name."

Melissa hung up. Looked at her savings account. She'd always hoarded her money; she'd had to hide it back home so her sister wouldn't steal it for drugs, and she had the same attitude now—if you don't see it, you won't spend it. How many times had she declined going to the movies or out for drinks, or flying to Florida for spring break? Every time, that was how many, unless Tom had been paying. With two jobs all through college, and the two she had now, she had $8,000 put away. Even so, the convention was *expensive*. Good gracious.

This email hadn't come for no reason, Melissa firmly believed. It was the universe answering her! This conference, this *investment*, was just as important as leaving Wakeford.

She googled "the Roosevelt New Orleans," and her mouth opened at the grandeur, the *elegance* of it all. Gosh golly, she'd be staying there! Walking down that grand hallway, looking up at those chandeliers, sitting in that incredibly sophisticated bar! Yes. Destiny itself thrilled through her veins. This was it. *This* was her path.

She booked a room for the dates of the conference with two extra days beforehand so she could get the lay of the land. Then she surveyed her wardrobe. The conference was in two months, so she had time to prepare.

She stripped naked and looked at herself in the mirror.

Perfect. She worked at it, for one, and for two, the good Lord had blessed her with this bone structure, these green eyes, this blond hair (enhanced at a salon every four months), these perfect breasts, these long legs. Time to put those blessings to work, and do a little research.

For the next few weeks, she was glued to her computer, researching the most common orthopedic problems, the most challenging surgical techniques, the latest developments in artificial joints. She would not come across as a girl on the hunt for a sugar daddy, no way.

She ordered high-heeled beige shoes with bright red soles (Christian Louboutin knockoffs from China, but would a man be able to tell?). On her day off, she drove 170 miles to the nearest Nordstrom. Sitting down at the Dior makeup counter, she asked the young man to make her look "more sophisticated and a little older." He got to work, telling her about using contour, eye shadow, finding a signature red lipstick. She bought every product the clerk used, and then found four body-hugging dresses, two that were work chic and two that were evening fabulous, all of which would show off her figure without making her look trashy. A brown leather pencil skirt and a sleeveless ivory mock turtleneck sweater in the finest cashmere. She'd never had anything cashmere in her life, and she loved how it felt against her skin. A tight pair of on-trend jeans and a classic white button-down shirt. Last, Melissa splurged on a pair of simple, dead-sexy Manolo Blahnik black suede pumps for the day. They felt like heaven, and the price tag didn't even bother her. She *deserved* these shoes.

In the figure-hugging red dress and fabulous shoes, with the Dior makeup enhancing her beauty just enough, the girl in the mirror looked like the woman Melissa wanted to be. She wasn't book smart, she acknowledged that. She *was* people smart, though.

And she knew that for this venture—to bag a doctor as a husband—she had to look rich and classy, not just pretty. Surgeons didn't marry underemployed personal trainers.

On the appointed day, she made the fourteen-hour drive down to New Orleans, parked in the cheapest lot she could find, then summoned a luxury car from Lyft to take her to the Roosevelt.

Oh, gosh. The hotel was *dazzling*—the columns, the potted palm trees, the intricate tile floor and the gentle, plentiful light that washed everything in gold. It was all so beautiful that champagne seemed to bubble through her entire body. She *belonged* in places like this.

She checked in at reception, asked if there was a shuttle to the convention center, learned that there was and went to her room. The most beautiful room she had ever seen. A king-sized bed! A minibar! Oh, my gosh, look at this bathroom. Free shampoo and body wash and lotion, oh, my goodness gracious!

She ordered room service (expensive!) and stayed in, strategizing, reading up on orthopedic surgeries, hospitals throughout America, things a medical student would know about.

At eight the following morning, she walked confidently through the lobby in her tight black dress, sexy as hell but conservative, in that it wasn't too short and the neckline was modest. Gold hoop earrings, a knockoff Cartier watch, the Manolos, and a pre-owned Prada bag she had gotten off eBay. A woman needed an impressive handbag. She wore her hair in a neat bun with a few wisps left out.

"Good morning," she said as she got onto the bus. "Who's excited for today?" It broke the ice. Five men, two women. "Since we're all staying at the same hotel, let's introduce ourselves," she said. "I take it everyone's a doctor?"

There was one drug rep. She crossed him off her mental list. There was an APRN (off the list as well). The two women would be of no use, which left three men, one who looked to be about seventy, the other who had a wedding ring on his left hand. Still, he was a contender, and quite handsome to boot. But the last man, though not as good-looking, had salt-and-pepper hair and a gleam of interest in his eye. "Dennis Finch," he said, shaking her hand. His grip was firm; his hands were soft.

"Melissa Spencer," she said. "I hope everyone is planning to enjoy the city while we're here. We can't just sit in seminars all day, not in New Orleans, right?" Thus followed restaurant recommendations, the best place for beignets (some kind of donut) and nonmedical chatter that Melissa could handle and guide with ease.

When they got to the convention center, the driver opened the bus door. Dennis lingered, offering his hand to Melissa as she got out. "I can't believe you're wearing those shoes for a conference," he said, gazing at her legs. "The orthopedic surgeon in me says not to."

"What does the man in you say?" she said, lifting an eyebrow.

"He says thanks," Dennis answered with a chuckle.

They went to the entrance, where someone was scanning

badges. "Shoot," she said, pretending to look through her purse. "I can't believe it, but I left mine at the Roosevelt."

The guy let her through.

"You don't look old enough to be a doctor," Dennis said.

"I actually just passed the MCATs, Dennis," she said, having done her research, "and I gave myself a couple years off before starting med school. I did a little physical therapy before this." She didn't want him to think she was *too* young, after all. "I know I want to be an orthopedic surgeon, though. I thought it might be wise to get the lay of the land from this perspective, rather than when I'm an exhausted and overcaffeinated resident."

"Smart woman. How old are you?"

"Twenty-eight," she lied, adding five years to her age. Young enough but old enough. "Where do you live and practice, Dennis?"

"New York. I'm at NYU Langone, but I'm also a partner in a private surgical center."

"I've been reading about those. Cutting through the red tape and all that."

"Exactly. Where did you go to undergrad, Melissa?"

"Wesleyan," she said. She'd learned to drop Kansas from the name.

"Ah, Connecticut. The gentlest state."

"It is, isn't it?" she said, though she wasn't exactly sure where Connecticut was. Up north somewhere. New England? She did know, however, that Wesleyan was almost an Ivy League school, so all the better. "Tell me about your experience, Dennis. Are you where you hoped you'd be professionally? Has NYU been good to you?"

"Absolutely, but I'll give you some advice. Invent something if you're an orthopedic surgeon. Get a patent on a new device. That's where the real money is."

"Really? Well, for now, I just want to help people get out of pain. Oh, gosh, that sounds so smarmy! Forgive me!" She gave a self-deprecating laugh, brought her well-manicured hand to her lips.

"Not at all! Shall we walk around together?" Dennis offered.

She accepted. He asked if she was free for dinner that night. She was. Eight o'clock? Perfect. She parted ways with him midday when he was about to go into a conference about the latest developments in hip replacements.

"There's a seminar I'm dying to see," she said. "But I'll meet you in the lobby at quarter till?"

"Sounds perfect."

She leaned in and pressed her cheek against his, hoping he'd smell her Chanel perfume—she'd talked the lady at Nordstrom into giving her a tiny sample. "I'm looking forward to it." Then she pulled back. "Oh, gosh. You're not married, are you?"

He held up his empty left hand. "Divorced this past year."

"I'm sorry to hear that. Well . . ." She paused and laughed. "Well, I'm actually pretty happy to hear it. Enjoy the rest of your day! See you tonight." Then she walked away, feeling his eyes on her yoga-perfect ass.

They had dinner at a swanky place in the French Quarter, and she ordered a dry martini, Hendrick's, twist of lemon, please. All went to plan—she charmed him, flattered him, asked him about himself and his life. Two children, one about to finish high school, the other just graduated from college and headed for the Peace Corps. Perfect. No pesky little kids, then. At the hotel, she paused in front of her room.

"I had a wonderful time, Dennis. How lucky that we were staying at the same place!"

"Can I see you again tomorrow?" he asked.

She pretended to be surprised. "Really? I'd love that!" She kissed him on the cheek, opened her door and gave a little wave. Sex on the first night? Nuh-uh.

They had dinner again the next night. She hedged about medical school, saying she hadn't made a decision yet. "What was your MCAT score?" he asked.

"Five twenty-two," she said, batting her eyelashes. Research, people. Research.

"Wow! Beauty and brains. With that score, you could go anywhere. NYU is one of the best out there."

"NYU is actually one of my top choices. Columbia, too, of course." *Please, God, don't let him ask anything else.* "I'm planning a visit to the city in the next month or so."

"Come see me." He put his hand on her leg, and she let it stay.

"Maybe I will." She smiled and took a sip of her cocktail. "No. Scratch that. I definitely will."

She flew out three weeks later, her first time on an airplane. On her third day in the city, a "fire" burned her "loft" in New Orleans, and she lost everything. Dennis insisted on paying for a hotel for her (five stars, "bespoke," whatever that meant, with fitness center and spa). She treated him to a massage there with the last of her savings, then took him up to her room.

Long story short, she became Melissa Grace Spencer Finch six months later at city hall. Oh, yes. The universe provided. She avoided a prenup with tales of her "abusive" childhood and fear of abandonment—her father, the successful businessman, had also been a drinker and a hitter. Her mother turned a blind eye and lost herself in the country club world of booze and tennis. Tragically, her sister struggled with addiction. "That's it. My sad little family."

"I'm your family now," Dennis declared, fully embracing his role as white knight. "I'll never leave you."

Men. So easily managed.

Melissa stepped into her new lifestyle as if she'd been in training to be a Real Housewife of New York all her life . . . which she had, at least since the age of thirteen. She hired a private etiquette coach to be sure she was up to date on her social graces (and paid cash from the allowance Dennis gave her, so he wouldn't know). She shopped in SoHo (Neiman's was so old-lady) and bought the best clothes—always classy, interesting and yes, always sexy. La Perla underwear,

Chanel makeup, designer shoes and handbags. She only bought one pair of gold hoop earrings, demure and classic, and murmured to Dennis, "I think it's tacky for a woman to buy her own jewelry. That's a husband's job." Her jewelry box filled up quite quickly after that.

She "put off" medical school so she could focus on making them a home . . . Dennis had been living in a boxy two-bedroom apartment in StuyTown.

"It's such a bachelor pad," she said, laughing, although it was the nicest place she'd ever set foot in. "You're a married man, a successful doctor, a business owner and a wonderful father. You deserve a real home, honey."

Within a month of their marriage, they owned (jointly!) a gorgeous place near Gramercy Park, the kind of apartment Melissa had seen only in magazines and on TV. She hired a decorator, the same one used by Kerry Washington! She followed enough influencers on Instagram that she knew what to buy and where (she'd begun studying New York stores the day after the conference). She took a cooking class and watched Ina Garten religiously.

She didn't know Dennis's net worth, but she did know the first Mrs. Finch was comfortably kept on alimony, and Dennis hadn't (yet) put a limit on Melissa's spending. He was *wonderfully* rich, not so much from being an orthopedic surgeon, which would have been rich by her Ohio standards. But he was next level, thanks to him and his three partners owning an entire surgical center. Direct pay. In other words, every nickel went to them, not the hospital or insurance company, she learned. They had just opened another center in Westchester County! Even more money would roll in.

"Baby, I'm so proud of you," she said over the coq au vin she'd made for their dinner. She poured him more wine ($400 a bottle!). "You're such a good provider. Even though I'm a total feminist, there's something . . . I don't know . . . *primal* about my man taking such good care of me."

They had sex on the dining room table. Yes. She understood men quite well.

That was another thing. Dennis Finch would never be able to say he never got any at home, nuh-uh. She read a few books, listened to a few podcasts, bought a few toys and outfits. Dennis, being in his early fifties, was on a mission to prove he was the world's greatest lover and oh so virile, and both of them were very content.

His kids were not happy, he said, but she didn't care. Amanda was eighteen, Nick twenty-two (just a year younger than Melissa, but Dennis thought she was twenty-nine). "They'll warm up to you," Dennis said. Melissa knew better, but hey. Let the man cling to his fantasy. "You're the most wonderful thing in the world. I haven't been this happy in years."

Dennis didn't mind her "deferment" from school, and why would he? She still googled articles about orthopedics, and tried to look knowledgeable when he discussed his work.

She threw dinner parties and charmed his partners, if not their wives. She could see exactly what they thought of her . . . and she could see exactly what their husbands were thinking when she touched their arms or laughed at their jokes or said, "No, don't you dare come into my kitchen! You sit there and relax. You've earned it."

Yeah, the wives all hated her. Oh, well.

The universe had put Dennis Finch, MD, in that van for a reason. He needed someone to take care of him, make him look good, assure him that he was still vital and masculine and young. And here she was, spending his money, living the life she deserved.

After a year, Dennis said he wanted a baby. In addition to acquiring a woman a generation younger, Dennis types needed to prove their sperm could still swim.

Melissa pretended to go off birth control, but she was *not* going to get pregnant. *Hell* no, though she well understood the financial benefit of having a child with a rich man. But she'd dodged the prenup, and the apartment was in her name, too. Pregnancy? Ick. All those physical ailments women loved to describe—nausea, heartburn, hair loss, fatigue, bloating, weight gain—and that was just the pregnancy! Then came the agony of labor, which every mother she'd ever met loved to discuss in horrifying detail. The contractions. The gush of fluid soaking their carpet/clothing/car. The agony, the writhing, the *screaming*—or, even more irritating, the serenity, the earth-mother moments of woman-power and holiness.

No thanks. It still left you with a soft pooched-out stomach, stretch marks, drooping milky breasts and a saggy vagina, which you'd later feel compelled to fix at great cost through a Park Avenue plastic surgeon.

Then the baby itself. Crying, helpless, vulnerable, its devices and carriers and toys filling up your once pristine home. The sleepless nights. The fall in favor as the father's attention shifted to his baby. Once, you were his porn-star, spoiled sex kitten wife . . . now, you were whining for him to please take the baby so you could get a nap.

There was no way she'd become a slave to a tiny baby, exhausted and obsessed and boring as hell. She didn't want *anyone* to be more important to her than her own darn self. So each month, she sighed and got teary-eyed and said, "Not yet, honey. Oh, heck, what if I *can't* have a baby? Will you still love me?"

"Babe! Of course I will!"

She pretended to sag with gratitude. "Oh, thank heavens, because I love you so much, Dennis. As for the baby, I guess the universe wants us to focus on each other." That shut him up for a while.

Her days were spent fussing around the apartment (a cleaning lady came twice a week). She did the cooking, always something delicious, knowing that a man liked his woman to be domestic . . . at least, Dennis's type did. The bed was made to perfection each day, and she had an icy cold martini for him ten minutes after he walked through the door. She went to spin class and yoga and the gym religiously, and on weekends, she and Dennis would take a run in Central Park and see a play (on Broadway!) or go out for dinner at places that prided themselves on tiny portions and Michelin stars.

Life was so good.

Did she love him? Sort of. He was perfect for her purposes. He was . . . well, he was fine. He was good in bed and had given her an Amex Black card. She couldn't ask for more. Even if he did divorce her down the line, she owned half of this apartment. She'd always have something in the bank.

As for friends, Melissa had drinks and coffee here and there with women from spin class or yoga, but she knew her job was Dennis . . . and that women had a sixth sense about other women. Her past couldn't get out, obviously, so she kept things friendly and shallow. She got a mani-pedi every week, waxes and facials and highlights and massages. She took a flower-arranging class and signed her and Dennis up for a couples cooking class. They joined a coed volleyball league, and Dennis crowed with delight when she spiked a ball for a point. (Thanks, Kansas Wesleyan!) She was careful to miss a few shots, pouting adorably and letting him encourage her.

One weekend, Dennis had his fraternity brothers over before they left for a fishing trip in Montana. They stayed in to watch a baseball game, and she fawned over the four men, bringing them homemade chicken wings and seven-layer dip and chocolate chip cookies fresh from the oven. She refilled their bourbons, dropping a kiss on her husband's cheek, then made herself absent so "you boys can have your time together."

But she eavesdropped on them, that's for sure.

"My God, you're living the dream, Den," Jim (or John) said. "She cooks, too." Uproarious laughter followed, and Melissa smiled, content. Men loved her. They always had.

She was living the dream, too. She had everything. Life was perfect.

Until her sister called.

CHAPTER 5

Lillie

What no one tells you is that there will be a last time you ever carry your child. A last time you tuck them in. A last time they run into your arms off the school bus.

All through his infancy, Dylan was attached to me, almost literally. I nursed him, and he was fussy, so I carried him almost constantly, patting his back, humming to him, breathing in his delicious baby scent. He didn't walk till he was fourteen months old, and I loved that, because I got to carry him that much longer. I took him for hikes in a backpack, his little knees hitting my ribs. I carried him on my shoulders, him clinging to fistfuls of my hair. I loved every minute.

He was an affectionate boy full of drooly kisses and cuddles. He was generous with his hugs, from Paul at the post office to Christine, our librarian. And especially with me. Every night when I read him bedtime stories, his sweet little head would rest against my shoulder, and he'd idly stroke my arm, smelling like Dove soap and baby shampoo.

Driving in the car was like a tranquilizer dart for Dylan . . . even bumping down our long dirt road wouldn't wake him up, and I'd park the car, get out and unbuckle him, then lift his sweaty little body into my arms to carry him inside and just sit on the couch with him in my arms, heart against heart.

And then one day, he no longer needed that. The bedtime stories stopped when he was about ten and wanted to read to himself. The last time I attempted to carry him from the car, he woke up and said, "It's okay, Mom. I'm awake." He never needed that again.

Had someone told me "This is the last time you'll get to carry your son," I would have paid more attention. I would have held him as long as I could.

They don't tell you that your son will stop kissing you with sweet innocence, and those smooches will be replaced with an obligatory peck. They don't tell you that he won't want a piggyback ride ever again. That you can't hold his hand anymore. That those goofy, physical games of chasing and tickling and mock wrestling will end one day. Permanently.

All those natural, easy, physical gestures of love stop when your son hits puberty and is abruptly aware of his body . . . and yours. He doesn't want to hug you the same way, finding your physicality perhaps a little . . . icky . . . that realization that Mom has boobs, that Mom's stomach is soft, that Mom and Dad have sex, that Mom gets her period.

The snuggles stop. This child, the deepest love of your life, won't ever stroke your arm again. You'll never get to lie in bed next to him for a bedtime chat, those little talks he used to beg for. No more tuck-ins. No more comforting after a bad dream. The physical distance between the two of you is vast . . . it's not just that he'll only come so close for the briefest second, but also the simple fact that he isn't that little boy anymore. He's a young man, a fully grown male with feet that smell like death and razor stubble on his once petal-soft cheeks.

Dylan was a wonderful son, don't get me wrong. I loved that he talked to me, dropped a kiss on my head every morning and before he went upstairs for the night. I thrilled at the chance to be useful . . . to fold his laundry once in a while, to pick up the right protein powder for his shakes.

But I was in mourning just the same.

The minutes rushed and slid precariously toward that dreaded day in August. But the truth was, he'd been leaving me for years. They don't tell you that. They don't tell you that this person—this person you grew inside your body, this person you pushed into the world with superhuman strength and joy, this infant you nursed, the toddler who proclaimed you his best friend, who drew you pictures and picked you dandelions, who leaned against you and fell asleep on you and threw up on you and needed you to bathe him and hold him on the potty and brush his teeth . . . that this person would go away, and in his place would be a young man who didn't tell you about his life, who did his own laundry, who didn't ask you to read his papers anymore. Who just didn't need you anymore.

All because you did a good job. All because your entire life for the past eighteen years was to make him an adult who was independent and kind and self-sufficient, and goddamn it, you did it, and what were you left with?

His absence.

Of *course* I was proud of my son. Of *course* I wanted him to be a man, not a snowflake who needed his mommy to get through the day. The clashing mix of pride and sorrow, when you want so much to be able to go back in time for so many reasons, to when you were sure of your life because this child *was* your life. If there was one thing I had never doubted in my life, it was that I was a good mother, all the way through.

But God, I missed my boy.

That's what they don't tell you. That you would leap out of your chair or pull your car over if your phone chimed, in case it was a text from him. That you would lie on his bed when he was out and smell his pillow that last summer before he left. That the sound of his voice actually brought tears to your eyes and an ache to your heart, and his casual "love you, too" was water in the desert.

It's the wretched contradiction of parenting. Once, you were their favorite human on the planet, and they were yours. For the rest of your life, your child will remain your heart . . . but it's not mutual. It's not supposed to be. Your importance is dwarfed by their friends. Romantic interests. Cool professors and great coaches. A spouse, someday, and kids of their own, and you . . . you got left behind at a certain exit on the highway of their life, and all you can do is look down the road after them and remember when you were so needed, so loved, so sure of your place in the world, because you were *Mommy*, and that was everything.

And for me, the person who was supposed to understand and share all of that, to comfort and reassure me . . . he was screwing a thirty-year-old who loved yoga and drove a car that cost more than I made in a year.

Living with a man who's cheating on you takes a toll. Trying to be pleasant for the sake of your child, and lying to that child—ditto. Feeling your heart crumble in your chest because your husband took away your future and forced you to live as a bleeding, silent witness to the last summer your family would be intact . . . it was nothing short of agony.

Which I endured for Dylan.

At work, it was fine—I was Lillie the Midwife, the nurse with the gentle hands, warming the ultrasound gel before squeezing it onto the lovely round tummies, handing tissues out for happy weepers, reassuring and full of wisdom for women of all ages.

But the second I left the office or hospital, my mind was buzzing with thought spirals. Even the *past* wasn't what I had thought, was it? I would now have to rethink, reframe, remember our past in an entirely different way. Brad wasn't just ruining the present and destroying my future—he was taking a sledgehammer to the twenty years we were together. After all, he'd proven himself more than capable of lying and hiding things. Was Melissa his first affair? All those times in the past nineteen years when we'd seemed happy and content . . . was he seeing someone else? That surprisingly horrible fight we had over how to load the dishwasher . . . was that a sign that he'd stopped loving me? How long had he been planning to leave me?

Every nice thing I'd done for him, I now resented. I had always been amused by his hypochondria but loved taking care of him—obviously, it's my career—covering him with soft blankets when he had a man-cold (or walking pneumonia, as he self-diagnosed). The breakfasts I'd made him every single weekday until this past spring, when he started with the green smoothies made of what was essentially compost and oat milk. Another sign he'd been cheating. Smoothies. Who wants to drink cucumber and kale for breakfast?

Like every married person, I'd put up with his unfixables . . . he could not for the life of him manage to see the smears of feces he left in the toilet, and nearly every day, I'd go into our bathroom, sigh and spray Clorox Clean-Up into the bowl and scrub. Before, it was just an irritant. Now, it seemed condescending and mean-spirited—he'd *literally* expected me to clean up his shit. His habit of leaving a dirty bowl on the counter above the dishwasher, just six inches from actually putting it away. The way he wouldn't scrape my car off in the winter, though I would always scrape off his. How he interrupted me constantly, then apologized for interrupting but continued speaking anyway, me always tolerating his unspoken belief that he thought he was smarter than I was.

I had bought every card and gift for our son and his parents, signing them from both of us. I was the one who knew the birthdays and anniversaries. We had a great relationship with Vanessa and Charles because of *me*, not him. I was the one who stayed in close touch, giving them updates on Dylan, inviting them to every significant event in his life from his baptism to football games. I helped at the family business; Brad did not. If his mother called his cell, their conversation would last ten minutes. If she called *me*, we'd talk for an hour. Back in the olden days, that was.

I hated him, and I hated myself for having loved him. He was so pretentious, so smug, so cruel in his new *namaste* philosophy . . . and yet, I fantasized about him begging me for forgiveness, for another chance, he'd spend the rest of his life proving that he'd made a terrible mistake. I wanted to stay married. I hated my husband, but I wanted my family intact.

Dylan and I drove to Hyannis to get all the things he'd need for his dorm room, and I held it together as he picked out his new comforter, extra-long sheets, towels, bathrobe, shower caddy. On the way home, he said, "I'll really miss you, Mom," and it was all I could do not to sob. Instead, I covered his hand with mine and said, "I'll miss you, too, honey. But this will be so much fun for you. It's a great adventure, going so far away, and I'm really proud that you're brave enough to do it. And of course, I'll visit."

Mothers lie. All I *really* wanted was for him to have a serious change of heart, take my father up on his offer to teach him how to be a scallop fisherman, buy the *Goody Chapman* back from Ben Hallowell and make it a Silva family boat once again. Or just crew for Ben. Or decide he wanted to be a nurse at Hyannis Hospital and marry Lydia, and in a few years, I'd sell them our house at a crazy low price, move into the studio and give them their privacy and work part-time when they had kids and needed me there to help. Lydia, who already loved me, would say how perfect it was to have me so close.

But he and Lydia broke up. Dylan said it was mutual, that it didn't make sense to have a long-distance relationship with someone he wouldn't see until Christmas.

Two weeks before our son left for college, Brad and I had our first appointment with a mediator. She was a calm, middle-aged woman with short gray hair, and she exuded intelligence. She waited for us to settle in (on opposite sides of the table, fittingly).

"I'm Elaine," she said, opening a notebook. "The first thing I ask my clients is, are you absolutely sure there's no chance of reconciliation?"

"I . . . I don't know," I said.

Brad put on his therapist sympathy face. "I'm sorry, Lillie. Too much damage has been done. It's been a dead marriage for years."

The urge to spit acid, like a velociraptor, was strong. "I have written proof that this is not true, Brad. But whatever. Have your midlife crisis with your Barbie doll."

"There it is. Your temper, for one. Your lack of true interest in my personal growth. You don't notice me anymore. I can't remember the last time you really *saw* me. You certainly don't care about my health, cooking with all that butter."

"So this is grounds for divorce? Too much butter?"

"You think you're a saint. So earth mother, delivering babies, caring for pregnant women. Admit it. You hate men."

"I do not hate men!" I screeched. "I only hate you."

"Okay," Elaine intervened. "I'm not a therapist, but I'd say he's firm in his decision to become divorced, Lillie. It only takes one partner to make that happen. So let's do what you originally said you wanted to—talk about dividing your assets."

"Do I get more since he lied and cheated and broke his vows?" I couldn't help asking.

"Interesting," he said. "You also broke yours. What about to love, honor and cherish?"

"I did that! When haven't I done that?"

"See, you're not even listening, even now. I just told you."

"So I should've kissed your ass more? Told you how brilliant you are, how strong and handsome and funny?"

"Yes," he said, almost sounding surprised. "Of course!"

"And when did you do that for me?"

He shook his head. "You didn't create space for me to say those things. You were too occupied elsewhere."

"So the fact that you didn't compliment and appreciate me is . . . my fault? Listen to yourself! *You* cheated on me! *You* had an affair! *I* am the injured party here!" I wiped my eyes with a fast slash of my hand, hating the fact that I was crying.

"Is one partner staying in the family home, or are you going to sell it?" Elaine said.

"That is *my* house," I hissed.

"It's worth well over a million dollars," Brad said, addressing Elaine. "I'm going to be generous and let her have it, but that financial sacrifice should definitely be reflected in the rest of our agreement."

"I agree," Elaine said. "What do you have in mind? Don't worry, Lillie, you get a turn, too."

For the forty-five minutes, we divided up our life as if we were trading Pokémon cards. He got the artwork from his office, since the paintings had been a gift (stupid me, spending all that money so his ego could have a boost). I got the house, the debt, the furniture except for the pieces of furniture that his parents had given us—my bureau, the one I'd used all of our marriage; the mirror in the front hall; the marble-topped coffee table. All the good stuff, in other words.

"I'd like my grandmother's engagement ring, too," he said.

"Fat chance. That's *my* engagement ring."

"Lillie, that has been in my family for three generations. It belongs on my future wife's finger."

My heart spasmed in shock and . . . grief. "You're *marrying* her? You met her in February! Dylan is going to be furious!"

"We'll see. I think he'll understand."

"Okay, okay, settle down," Elaine said. "An engagement ring is considered a gift as part of a contract. Brad, you gave it to Lillie in the hope she would marry you. She did. It's hers."

"Good, because I'm gonna need the money," I said. "I can sell it."

"Don't you dare!" Brad snapped. "At the very least, save it for our son!"

"So he can have the cursed ring of his divorced parents? Nah."

This is what happened during a divorce. Pettiness, hatred. An insatiable thirst for revenge.

"We've made good progress," Elaine said. "I'd like you to take a close look at your possessions—every little thing—and detail anything you want or need. See you next week."

In the parking lot (we'd come in separate cars), Brad turned to me. "Lillie, I wish you nothing but peace and light. I wish you joy in your new life, and I hope that we'll be friends. We'll always have our son, and we can be friends, you and Melissa and me."

"You're an idiot."

He said those things to infuriate me. He wished me peace and light and *poverty*, that's what. Suddenly, he needed half of our household items (or the money that it would cost to replace them). The Le Creuset Dutch oven I'd found on sale at Marshalls a few years ago. The ice cream maker. The new towels. The blender. The *pizza cutter*.

This is what you fight about while divorcing. This is when hatred would flare white-hot. He wanted the painting made by my *grandmother* and the KitchenAid mixer he had never so much as turned on. The Danish clock in the bedroom, which he'd *given* me for an anniversary present. "At least give me half of what it cost," he said. "You owe me that."

"No, I won't, and I don't," I said. "I'll sell it. Or smash it."

"You're being childish, Lillie. God! I'm so relieved to be leaving this toxic environment. As soon as Dylan leaves, I'll be free to pursue my joy."

"I'm going to slap you if you say 'joy' one more time," I said.

"Threat of violence," he said. "Maybe I should get a restraining order."

Dylan, at least, was happy and blissfully ignorant. The second we heard his car tires on the driveway, Brad and I leaped into our fake selves, competing for Favorite Parent. "How was the beach? Did you go swimming? Really? Another great white sighting? Did you see it? Are you hungry? Can I make you something?"

I reminded myself that at least I'd have this house . . . this empty house. Dylan would be home at Christmas. Maybe I could swing the debt if I rented it out all summer long, plus every weekend in May, September and October. The thought made my heart cramp . . . wealthy New Jerseyans messing up my kitchen, sleeping in Dylan's bed, sitting on my porch. Once, it had seemed like a smart option. Now, it seemed like another violation.

So there it was. My son was going to school thousands of miles away, and my husband was leaving me to live with a very wealthy woman almost a generation younger than he was, and I wasn't sure I could keep the house my grandfather had built.

Another thing about my type of divorce—a man finds a hot, limber yoga teacher, and while his peers might be shocked and momentarily disgusted, there's an element of . . . admiration. *Look at Brad! Look at where he lives now! Did you see his wife? He's a new man!*

That's not the cuckolded wife's experience. Once word got out, I'd go from being a nice Cape Cod girl who'd married up (yes, that was still a thing) to a woman dumped. A woman who couldn't "hang on to" her husband. A woman who *introduced* her husband to his lover. A woman without a son at home anymore, without a husband, who'd be dealing with the patriarchal notion that I was somehow flawed because Brad had left me.

If I could choose, I'd never see Bradley Fairchild again.

But of course, you can't erase the father of your only child. You can't forget the man who had tears in his eyes when he said his vows. He'd been my best friend. We'd overhauled this house and raised the best son in the world and laughed and talked and reassured each other for two decades.

Not telling anyone was killing me. Wanda and I had talked a few times after work, me crying, her soothing. But I had to wait for Dylan to get settled. Beth, who had been my best friend since third grade, wouldn't be able to not tell her husband, and Freddie was a notorious gossip. Besides, right now their restaurant was incredibly busy, as it always was in the summer.

I was going to grow old alone. These thoughts yanked me from sleep, sent my heart thudding erratically, caused tears to spill down my face before I was even fully awake. What if I fell out here? There were no neighbors close enough to hear me, and our house had two flights of stairs. In the rain or snow, the stairs to the pond were slippery and treacherous. I could picture it now . . . me going down to stare at Herring Pond to find some peace, slipping, the crack of my tibia as it broke, the tumble down the granite steps. I'd have to crawl with my limp and useless foot dangling. Or what if I broke my *femur*? That would be much worse! I could *bleed* to death if that happened! What if I broke my *skull* and gave myself a traumatic brain injury and had to go to a nursing home? What if, as I lay helpless at the base of the stone stairs, a bear ate me? Okay, we didn't have bears on the Cape, but what about coyotes?

And all the while, Brad and Melissa would be inhaling light and exhaling love, watching the sunset from one of the many decks of her house, drinking malbec.

Brad must pay.

It started one morning when Dylan offered to drive him to work. "I'd love that, son!" Brad sang merrily, and the two of them went off in male camaraderie, discussing if they should stop at Blue Willow Bakery or Hole in One for donuts. If he knew his father was screwing someone else, Dylan would have punched Brad in the face. But of course,

I had to be bigger than that and keep Brad's infidelity to myself until Dylan was in Montana.

My phone cheeped with a text. Wanda. Bring half-and-half to work or Carol and I may die, and you don't want that, do you?

I did not.

I had just been grocery shopping and had an unopened container of half-and-half in the fridge. I took it, grabbed my bag and went out to my car. Paused when I saw Brad's VW sitting there. Then, without much forethought, I opened the back door and poured a slosh of half-and-half on his car rug. Repeated the action on the other side. It would take a day or two to sour, sure, but that smell was hard to get out. I checked to see if I felt bad about that. Nope.

That night, I opened my laptop. Brad was one of those PhDs who *loved* those letters after his name. If someone called him *Mr.* Fairchild, he would immediately correct them. He always filled out forms with his title, so all his mail was addressed to Dr. Bradley Fairchild, PhD. (He entered his last name as *Fairchild, PhD.*) "That's *Dr.* Fairchild," he had told innumerable maître d's, AppleCare technicians, mechanics and teachers. Even Dylan's friends were chastised. If they said, "Thanks for letting me come over, Mr. Fairchild," he'd smile patiently and say, "That's *Dr.* Fairchild. I spent too many years in graduate school to be called mister, son! But you can call me Brad." Which they never did.

Hence, I stayed up till 4:00 a.m., logging in to Brad's online accounts and changing "Dr." to "Mr." (I briefly contemplated "Ms.," but figured it would be too obvious that I'd done it.) Amazon, Apple Music, his automatic signature on emails, his magazine subscriptions, his bank account, his alumnus listings at Boston University and Swarthmore, his listing on psychologytoday.com, his credit card. Every place I could access, and there were dozens. Sixty-eight, to be exact. This is what could happen if you let your wife handle the household finances and were dumb enough to use the same password for every account—Terriersbtfphd#1.

The Terriers were the mascot of Boston University. His initials. His degree. Every single account, the dumbass.

Sure enough, two mornings later . . . "Did you change something on my computer?"

"What? No. You have it with you all the time," I said, pouring myself some more coffee. "Why?"

"Well . . . they got my title wrong."

"What title?"

"The *doctor* title, Lillie. It used to be Dr. Fairchild. Now I'm listed as Mr. everywhere."

"Huh." I held up my cup to hide my smile.

Then came the ironing.

Oh, the *ironing*. Brad was fastidious in dressing and always had been, even when he'd been preppy instead of hipster. He didn't trust me to iron his shirts, saying I did it wrong (I hated ironing, so it was probably true). Fine by me. He *should* iron his own shirts.

But now, I wanted to . . . how to put this . . . leave my mark.

So I peed in a cup, diluted it with water, and poured it into the iron. It was subtle enough that he wouldn't notice it at first, not until the water evaporated and the urine remained.

"Dad," Dylan said one night at dinner. "Uh, no offense, but you smell like pee."

"What?" Brad said. "No, I don't!"

"I just walked past you, and you do." Our son shrugged, then sat down. "Oh, wow, Mom! Clams in garlic sauce! Thank you!"

"Amêijoas à bulhão pato," I said. "Be proud of your culture."

"I *don't* smell like urine," Brad said. He'd always been squeamish about using words like *pee* and *crap*, preferring the more medical-sounding words. Had he always been so prissy? Yes, I decided. He had.

"Did you have a little . . . leakage?" I asked, feigning concern. "I do smell something."

"I don't have leakage!" Brad got up from the table and stormed off into the guest room to sniff himself. (We'd told Dylan his snoring was too much for me.)

"It happens to men as they get older," I said to Dylan, knowing Brad could overhear. "It's probably not prostate cancer. Don't worry." A second later, I heard Brad tapping the keys of his laptop, doubtlessly googling "prostate cancer" and "leakage." I knew my husband, after all. And I knew how to punish him. I texted him. Urinary incontinence and leakage could be a sign of gonorrhea or chlamydia. Best get an STD panel.

I heard him yelp from the other room. "Sit down, Dylan," I said to my son, smiling. "Eat, honey." A second later, Brad texted back, I do NOT have an STD! And neither does she!!! But he'd get the test, I knew. Hey. I'd had to. It was only fair that he did, too.

I cleaned the toilet and tub drain with his toothbrush. The bathroom had never been so clean. I changed the passwords on our Netflix, HBO and Hulu accounts, since we didn't watch TV together anymore (but put the new password on Dylan's account so only Brad had the problem). I cut a small hole in the crotch of his new bathing suit, which was embarrassingly small (and ridiculously expensive). Melissa had not *just* waterfront property, but that infinity pool, sauna and hot tub as well.

In our den was a picture of Brad and Big Papi, the beloved Red Sox slugger, which Brad had paid $500 for on a trip to Fenway years ago (a necessary trip, he said, because he needed a break from our son's colic). Now, I took a tiny bit of bleach and rubbed it onto Brad's face, blurring it just enough so you couldn't tell who it was. I left Big Papi untouched, of course. My moral compass wasn't *that* bent.

I put Nair in Brad's body wash and waited for it to take effect, and sure enough, his eyebrows began to thin, and his arm hair was patchy within days. "Do you . . ." Brad began one morning, looking at his arms. He hesitated, then continued. "Is there a reason I might be losing hair on my arms and legs?" he asked, unable to resist the temptation of asking a nurse.

"Hm," I said. "Well, there are a lot of reasons. Alopecia universalis, which is basically inherited baldness. You know. Like your father. Could be anemia, an autoimmune disease or thyroid cancer, too. Or maybe it's your guilty conscience, eating away at your flesh."

His blue eyes narrowed. "You did this, didn't you?"

"What, Brad? I plucked you in your sleep? You're so neurotic."

Unfortunately, he did throw out his body wash and shampoo, replacing it with expensive, all-natural stuff that smelled like sage and patchouli.

As for Melissa, she was not left alone, either. I had her email address, since I'd shown her the house last winter. So I went to websites and logged in under her name, giving them her phone number and email and checking *yes* at every box that asked if I wanted text message updates and newsletter enrollments. Her inbox and phone would be full of offers for products to help with incontinence, body odor, and vaginal atrophy, odor and itching. I registered her for a support group for women with personality disorders. Gamblers Anonymous.

I also signed her up for a free trial of every dating website I could find, using her pictures from Instagram (she was so pretty, goddamn it), and clicked the heart button on the most egregious men out there. *Been sober for two days!* crowed George in Falmouth. *Sixty-eight years old, temporarily living with mother, not averse to having kids,* said Myron in Boston. *Love Jesus, football and my five kids,* said Beau. *Hunting enthusiast. Enjoy eating my kills.* Come, now. Melissa and Beau would be a match made in heaven. It was deeply satisfying.

But no matter what petty things I did for revenge, I couldn't get past the fact that until the night before our son's graduation, I had loved my husband, and somewhere along the line, he had stopped loving me.

CHAPTER 6

Lillie

Y ou're doing great, Molly," I murmured in the darkened birthing suite at the hospital. My client was lying in the birthing pool, floating on her back, eyes closed, her glorious stomach rolling with the contraction. She didn't answer, completely focused inward on the power of her body, humming as her muscles clenched. "Relax and breathe, nice and slow." Another low hum, and the contraction ended. "You look utterly gorgeous," I said honestly. "You're doing this so well."

She reached up and grabbed my hand, and I stroked her hair back from her head. Molly was single, having gone the sperm donor route at the age of thirty, not wanting to wait for a decline in fertility to have her first baby. Smart. Funny, to think that when she first told me that, I'd been a smug married, imagining how much harder she'd have it. Now, I sort of envied her. I would've saved myself a lot of money and heartache if I'd divorced Brad immediately after Dylan was born. Sure, he'd been a good enough dad, but these days, I wasn't in the mood to credit him with anything.

Molly's sister was en route, but traffic was wretched today, a Friday. Hopefully, she'd make it in time to see her niece being born. If not, well, nature didn't take well to direction, and babies waited for no one. Last week, a woman had given birth in the hospital parking lot. Sadly, I had not been the midwife on duty that day. Precipitous births could be wicked exciting.

The door opened, and the lights flickered on. Molly put her hand over her eyes.

"Lights off, please!" I snapped.

"Fine, fine." The lights went out again, and the dreaded Dr. Schneider poked her head in. "Still laboring? Damn. I thought she'd be done now. Is she pushing yet?" She had a loud voice that could be heard all the way to the nurses' station.

"She's progressing beautifully, Doctor," I said calmly.

"Are you in a lot of pain, poor baby?" she called over to Molly. I gritted my teeth. Dr. Schneider did not understand what it meant to empower the mother. "Poor maternal effort?" she said, lowering her voice so it could only be heard in half the hallway.

"The exact opposite," I said, keeping my tone firm and mild, though my eye twitched. "Amazing maternal effort."

"She's been here for four hours," the doctor said, as if that was a problem. "Did you break her water to get things moving along? How about a little Pitocin?"

Carline Schneider, MD, obstetrician and gynecologist, was a nemesis to CNMs everywhere. She was the kind of doctor who would order Pitocin to hurry things up or use the vacuum so she could be home by dinnertime. The kind who'd leave a patient when her shift ended, passing her off to someone else, rather than stay the extra half hour till the baby was born. Childless by choice, with the highest percentage of medical interventions at a place that prided itself on natural childbirth and healthy babies and mothers. How she had kept her job here was a mystery.

All the nurses and midwives (and other doctors, for that matter) hated her. She was the worst of the old-school obstetricians, lover of cesareans, the only one who still used forceps and used terms like "failure to progress" and "inhospitable womb" in front of patients. In her sixties, full of impatience for "you witches," completely dismissing the fact that every midwife at Hyannis Hospital had a bachelor's of science in nursing, neonatal intensive care nursing certification, master's in nursing with a specialization in midwifery, and certification as a nurse-midwife.

Every other doctor at the hospital, most especially Wanda, viewed CNMs as equals, respected our opinions and essentially turned labor over to us and the L&D nurses. They only came in to check on difficult labors or when medical intervention was absolutely necessary, or just because they had a special bond with the patient. Otherwise, they let us do our jobs. In addition to helping my own patients deliver here, I did a weekly twelve-hour shift at the hospital (or two, when money was tight).

I'd be doing a lot of extra shifts this fall, that was for sure, so I'd be seeing Carline more than ever. She lumped CNMs into a group of unnecessary healthcare providers, told patients that it would take longer with a midwife, "confused" us with lay midwives, who had dubious training, and doulas, some of whom had none. She micromanaged, interrupted, told women in the third stage of labor it wasn't too late for an epidural and clucked over women who took more than two hours to push a human out. Of course some women wanted or needed epidurals or nitrous oxide for pain control . . . but most came in hoping for a completely natural experience.

There are times when a medical intervention is absolutely necessary, of course. Multiples, breech presentation that we couldn't change, mother or baby in grave danger—all were situations that *needed* cesareans or a vacuum-assisted birth. But most times, women were completely capable of natural childbirth. Carline's patients had a 41 percent chance of C-sections, much higher than the national average. She generally viewed childbirth as Old Testament suffering, and herself as the scalpel-wielding savior.

"You're doing everything beautifully," I told Molly, pressing the waterproof fetal heart rate monitor against her belly. The ethereal, rushing sound of the baby's heart made Molly smile without opening her eyes. "Baby's heart rate is fantastic. I'll just chat with Dr. Schneider and be right back."

"Okay," she said.

I hated to leave her side, especially since she didn't have a partner, but she was calm. Her first baby, too. I was so proud of her. Another superwoman, letting her incredible body do its job.

"What is it, Carline?" I asked, knowing she preferred to be called Dr. Schneider.

"What's the problem here?" she asked, glancing at her watch.

"Nothing. There are absolutely no problems at the moment."

"If she's worn out, it might be time to section her."

"She's doing perfectly."

Dr. Schneider sighed. "I'd just rather do this now than have to come back in two hours. It's Friday, and my husband and I have plans."

"I need to get back to my patient," I said tightly, and closed the door in her face.

"Am I doing okay?" Molly asked, wincing as another contraction started.

"Are you kidding? You're the poster child for this. Deep breath, nice and slow." The contraction made her belly stiffen and list to the right. She rolled over in the pool and leaned her forearms against the side. I pressed down on her sacrum to relieve her back pain through the contraction. She took a deep breath and exhaled with a low note. "There you go," I said. "You're doing so well, Molly. Beautiful. Just beautiful."

God, I loved my job. For thousands of years, women had helped each other give birth. Some of the oldest practices in the world were still used—delivering on your hands and knees, not cutting the cord right away, letting the baby rest on the mama's chest before doing an assessment. We didn't need to yank babies away and weigh them or put in eye drops before the moms had a chance to look in wonder upon what they had done.

A healthy labor and delivery was nothing short of miraculous, every single time. I hated that some doctors (like Carline) still used the term "unremarkable vaginal delivery." It was a miracle, thank you very much.

"I'm here!" said a voice, and there was Bridget, her sister.

"Yay," said Molly, then took another huge breath.

"Hooray!" I said. "Wash up and come see your superhero sister." The water in the pool had some blood in it. Wouldn't be long now.

"Bed," Molly said, her voice urgent. "Now."

Ah, the one-word sentences. A sign that pushing was near. "You got it, queen," I said.

Bridget finished drying her hands and pulled on a gown, then rushed to her sister's side. "God, this is exciting," she said. "You're incredible, Molly."

Jane, one of my favorite nurses on the floor, came in— she had a sixth sense about when she was needed. We helped Molly out of the pool and onto the bed, which Bridget raised to a forty-five-degree angle. Molly closed her eyes and held her stomach, breathing deeply.

"Look at you," Jane said. "Won't be long now, honey." She leaned down to murmur in my ear. "Need me? We've got a footling breech down the hall, but Wanda's on it."

Oh, thank God. Babies coming feetfirst was tricky, and Wanda was the best OB here. "No, you go," I said to Jane. "Molly's got this."

Molly moaned.

"It's intense now, isn't it?" I said. "Your body knows what to do."

"Can I push?" she gasped. "I want to push. I have to push."

"You sure can," I said. "Grab your leg or the bar here, and on the next contraction, take a deep breath and go for it, exhaling as you push. Don't hold your breath." I checked between Molly's legs. The head was just starting to emerge. I got the mirror and positioned it so Molly could see.

"Oh, my God. There's a baby in there," she said, and Bridget laughed. I held a warm compress against her so the area would stretch more easily as the baby's head crowned.

The next contraction came, and Molly leaned forward and pushed with all her might, growling with the force of her effort. The baby's head came down another few centimeters.

"Great one!" I said. "Way to move that baby. Excellent job."

She pushed three more times, that wonderful, guttural sound coming out of her as she made herself a mother.

And here it came. "Molly, reach down and be the first one to touch your baby," I said, and she gave a sob and did so. Another contraction came, and she bore down.

"Beautiful, beautiful," I said. "Great job. Deep breath now. Relax every muscle you don't need." She did. She'd taken classes with Wanda, and it showed. We were seeing more and more unmedicated births, less tearing and shorter labors. "Okay, here comes another contraction, so work with it, Molly. That's right."

"Keep going, keep going, the head is coming, oh, my God!" her sister said, and yes indeed, the crown of the baby's head came out. Molly gave a squeak, her eyes wide, face pink with exertion.

"Holy jeesh!" she said.

"Okay, just relax now, Molly," I said. "I know you want to push, but just relax. Relax your legs, relax your jaw. Slow, deep breaths." The more slowly the baby came out, the less tearing there'd be. Her body would ease the head out.

This was the miracle. For nine months, Molly's body had protected and grown this baby, and today, her body would deliver that baby. For the mom, though, this was the hardest and most intense part—waiting for the head to be delivered. Molly made a keening noise with the next contraction.

"Little pants now, Molly, and your baby will ease right out." The black hair, covered in vernix, inched out more.

"Need an episiotomy?" Dr. Schneider stuck her head in the room.

I didn't bother to answer. "Molly, amazing work. Almost done now." Molly was whimpering, gripping the sheets in her fists. "I know, sweetheart. You're a champion. Just a few more minutes, and you'll be holding your baby."

Her sister was already crying. "You've got this, sis!"

The baby's head was coming, millimeter by millimeter. Lots of hair. When the forehead was visible, it was go time. "Whenever you're ready, Molly. Just one more push on the next contraction, and the head will be completely out." She pushed, silent, completely focused.

And then the baby's head slid slowly out, purply white, a swirl of dark hair, squished-up little angel face. "Oh, my God, oh, my God," Molly gasped.

I guided the baby's head, looked up at Molly and said, "One more, honey."

She pushed, and the infant slid into my hands, and I immediately slid her onto Molly's bare chest.

"Oh, my God!" Molly cried, sobbing. "Oh, baby, I love you. I love you so much, baby!" She was sobbing, kissing her daughter's head.

"Great job, Mama," I said, crying a little myself. You'd have to be made of stone not to tear up. I put a blanket over the baby, rubbing her back a little. She gave a healthy cry, then settled right back down against her mother's neck. Bridget was taking pictures, sobbing, touching her niece's head as the infant turned pink through the power of her own breath.

"How much does she weigh?" Carline asked, still standing in the doorway like a turd in the punch bowl.

"We'll find out soon enough," I said.

"Bridget! You have a niece!" Molly said through her

joyful tears. "Look at her. She's so *beautiful*." She looked at me with shining eyes. "Oh, Lillie, thank you."

"You did it all," I said. "I just caught her. You delivered her, and you were incredible."

"You were. You are," Bridget said. "Oh, my God, Molly! You did it!"

The placenta delivered intact. There was a tiny tear in the perineum, but it wouldn't need even one stitch.

"Rectal tear?" Carline asked.

"No." I felt Molly's belly, checking that the top of her uterus was where it should be. She had hardly any bleeding, and the baby was already rooting around for a snack. I slid the blood pressure cuff on Molly's arm and checked it: 117/72. Perfection.

Jane came back in. "Did I hear a *baby* in here?" she said in her customary postpartum greeting. "Oh, my goodness, look at that gorgeous little cutie-pie! She's beautiful! Do you have a name picked out?"

"Clara," Molly said, beaming up at her. "Clara Eloise Grady."

I smiled. I did like the classic names. So far this year, I'd met two Rivers, a Maxton and a Kerrett. (Kerrett? Come on, parents.)

With Jane there, I tossed my gloves, took off my gown and went to the door, where Dr. Schneider stood, frowning. "Can I help you with something, Carline?" I asked, pulling her by the arm into the hall and closing the door behind me.

She looked like she smelled a rotten fish. "How much fetal head molding is there?"

"None. She pushed for less than fifteen minutes. No tearing, no rupture, no PPH."

"*This* time. Don't curse yourself." She paused. "Is she going to eat the placenta or bury it in her front yard or whatever you earth mother witches do?"

"I would appreciate you laying off the negativity when I have a client in labor. ACOG recommended against routine episiotomies fifteen years ago," I said, hoping the mention of the governing body of ob-gyns would affect her, since my opinion wouldn't. "There was no reason for you to offer one, or even suggest it. It was almost like you were hoping something would go wrong."

"What? Why would you think that? You midwives— sorry, *nurse*-midwives—are so sensitive."

Do not mess with me, Carline. I am not in the mood these days. "You implied that she was too tired, in too much pain, not progressing fast enough, needed an episiotomy and had a rectal tear. None of those things was true. When I'm the midwife, I'll let you know if you're needed. Okay? Thank you."

Then I went back in and closed the door behind me. One look at Molly's blissful face, and the irritation with Dr. Schneider disappeared.

A healthy baby. A normal vaginal delivery without the need for intervention or medication.

Miraculous. Every single time.

⌒

Much to my surprise, I drove to Hannah's house after I left the hospital. It was six o'clock, Dylan was having his last night out with his friends before he left for college the day after tomorrow, and I didn't want to go home and steep in hatred. Might as well kill some time. Beth would know something was wrong. Plus, it was August. The Ice House would be packed.

I pulled into the driveway of Hannah Chapman Events. My sister lived on Wellfleet's Main Street in a beautiful old Victorian. The first floor was for her business; she and Thomasina, her cat, lived on the second and third floors, and had my entire adult life. She had a beautiful patio in the back, bursting with color. Love of gardening was one of the few things we shared.

Right after graduating from college, Hannah had moved back to the Cape and begun working for a florist, which confused everyone . . . she had degrees in economics and psychology from Bates College. Then, two years later, she bought the woman out, changed her last name to Chapman (Dad was horrified, but at least she took the name of his boat), and opened Hannah Chapman Events. She'd always been a great dresser, thanks to our stepmother, and now that sense of style was put to use in her business. Beatrice advised and helped, making them closer than ever, and when I came back to the Cape, newly married and pregnant, Hannah was fully ensconced in her work.

She quickly became the most sought-after wedding planner on the Cape and islands. Hannah didn't touch a wedding that didn't have a budget of at least six figures and often handled weddings that cost a *million* or more. Her professional life revolved around excess and materialism, high-maintenance brides and . . . well, greed. Showmanship. Wealth. All for a day (or a weekend).

My professional life revolved around bringing humans into the world and taking care of women's health. You can see we didn't have much in common.

But once, a long, long time ago, I had worshipped her.

The best part of my childhood was ages zero to eight, back when I was innocent and happy. Hannah and I would play outside, climbing trees, jumping off the tippy old dock into the cool, perfect water of Herring Pond. We were free-range kids, allowed to roam wherever we wanted. Every path, every trail and every tiny beach were ours. We were the princesses of the forest.

Hannah and I shared a bedroom; there were only two in the house back then. Our walls were knotty pine, as was common on the Cape, and the overall feeling inside was dark and cozy and safe (to me, anyway).

But outside . . . that was *paradise*. It was like we were the only ones in the world. Most of the other houses nearby were owned by summer people, so we were the only local kids around. Hannah taught me every bird, from blue herons to barn swallows. Deer stepped across our paths, foxes and coyotes scampered and skulked, little skunk families

trundled by, and it was everything a kid could ask for. My
sister wasn't quite as outdoorsy as I was, preferring books
to climbing trees, but she was a solid companion. Not as
fanciful as I was . . . I loved building fairy houses at the
bases of oak trees, pretending to ride horses down the
bumpy roads. By the time I was six, I could go off on my
own, as long as I didn't go near the water. I had to be
"within earshot," but otherwise I was free, which, to be
honest, was what my mother preferred. She was a lawyer
who consulted with other lawyers, constantly on the phone.

I knew Mom liked Hannah more . . . the lower-
maintenance child who didn't ask to sit on her lap. "Find
something to do, Lillie," she would say if I requested her
time, and the message was clear—unless arterial blood was
soaking my clothes, unless I was projectile vomiting or
running a fever of over 102, she had better things to do.
Back then, I assumed my mother loved me . . . sort of. Just
not the way my friends' mothers loved them. Beth's mother
would sit and chat with us at the kitchen table, offering us
coconut macaroons she made herself. Carlita's mother
couldn't walk past her without touching her hair or dropping a kiss on her head.

I remember watching in wonder as my friends ran into
their mothers' arms off the school bus, faces lit up with joy.
My mom was there, too, at the intersection of Collins and
Rose Roads, waiting in her car, tapping her finger on the
steering wheel. She never even unbuckled her seat belt, let
alone got out of the car for an embrace. "How was your
day?" she'd ask, but NPR would be on the radio, and I
learned to echo Hannah and say it had been fine (which it
generally was).

Our father was different. I only saw him for a couple of
hours a day, but his lined, harsh face would soften at the
sight of me, and even when I was eight, he still picked me
up. He wasn't much for talking, but his big rough hand
dropping on my head or a wink from across the kitchen
table made me feel so special. Some nights, he'd sit on the

edge of my bed or Hannah's and tell us that he'd seen a whale that day, or dolphins. He might give us a particularly pretty scallop shell he'd tucked in his pocket. His hands were scarred from a thousand little cuts—the price of shucking scallops every day. I'd trace the map of lines on his hand, glad he was home, proud to be the daughter of Pedro Cristóvão Silva, fourth-generation fisherman.

I also knew I was *his* favorite . . . at least in the sense that I was more like him. I was a true Silva. I could shuck a scallop at five, knew how to steer the boat out of the harbor at seven, and loved nothing more than tagging along with him and his crew when he let me. Hannah, on the other hand, got seasick and started gagging before we were even away from the wharf.

To her credit, Mom rarely lost her temper. She was just . . . irritable, and that irritation could rise till she gripped the kitchen counter and clenched her teeth and muttered to herself. The bedroom door might be sharply closed, her sign that we were not to disturb her.

I understood my parents didn't get along. Beth's parents hugged and kissed and teased each other, flirted with each other, complimented each other. It was as if "parents" meant something entirely different at her house. Dad worked long hard hours, gone before dawn, back for dinner, in bed by nine or earlier. Mom was always on the phone or in front of the computer.

When they were in a room together, tense irritability and dissatisfaction stewed and bubbled in the air. Mom was stylish in that quiet, WASPy way—reserved and elegant, her blond hair in a perfect, slightly asymmetrical bob, her makeup flawless. She wasn't a Cape Codder . . . she'd grown up in New Hampshire. They met when Mom was on vacation with her parents just after she graduated from law school. Dad was a good-looking guy, and maybe she was sticking it to her snobby parents, but she got a job at the district attorney's office in Barnstable and married him six months later. "He swept me off my feet," she said. "At the time, it seemed romantic. Then again, I was naive and ir-responsible."

Mom had a gift for twisting a blade you didn't know she carried. There was always the afterburn, as Hannah called it. "You look pretty," she might say to one of us. "What a nice change." Or, if she and Dad were going out, "Well, well, well. You don't smell like fish, Pedro. I didn't know it was possible."

Dinners were grim and fast: eat what was provided, clean up, go do your homework. When Hannah turned nine, Mom deemed her old enough to take care of me and started full-time at the DA's office. That was fine with me. That was better, in fact, because the minute Mom came home, the tension began. She'd always comment on what we *hadn't* done—if I had swept the floor, she'd ask why I hadn't emptied the trash. If Hannah had started dinner, she'd ask why the breakfast dishes were still in the sink. Then Dad would come home with HandsomeBoy, his faith-ful mutt who went out on the *Goody Chapman* with him. Mom would grimace and tell Dad to shower even though that was exactly what he did every single day.

Dad was a classic Cape Codder with a New England work ethic and a hatred for meaningless small talk. He was brief with his rare praise. "Good job" was about as eloquent as he got, and usually to Hannah, who had more proof of her worthiness—straight As, science fair awards, honors math.

But I never doubted his love for me. It was as constant as air. Mom . . . not so much. We were always her after-thoughts. Career, community, friends, then daughters. I don't think her marriage even made the list.

They fought constantly through body language and icy silences, irritable sighs and sharply closed cabinets. Weeks could pass without them speaking to each other. When they did hiss at each other, Hannah and I would turn on the radio or take out a game and huddle together between our beds, the familiar anxiety and slight fear when one of them raised their voice or their footsteps were too heavy. There was never any violence . . . just simmering tension, hanging over my sister and me like polluted fog.

It wasn't a surprise when they told us they were getting a divorce.

I was eight, Hannah twelve. We sat at the kitchen table after school, and Mom delivered the news in one sentence: "Your father and I are finally getting a divorce." Hannah and I exchanged a look of concern laced with relief. "It'll be fine," Mom said. "You'll adjust. Now go do your homework." Thus was the end of our heart-to-heart.

We both assumed Mom would stay here with us, even though this house had been Dad's and our grandparents' before that. Hannah speculated that Dad would buy a house nearby, and things would go on more or less unchanged. That night, in our shared room, we whispered about it. It would be better, we decided. Mom wouldn't be so irritated all the time, and Dad would probably buy us the puppy we'd been campaigning for, since HandsomeBoy was his.

"I know I should feel bad," Hannah said, "but I don't. Anything will be better than all this fuming. They don't even love each other. I bet they never did." I believed her . . . she was older and knew about relationships, having gone to the sixth-grade dance the week before.

I had a lump in my throat even with her reassuring words. I loved my father, and the specter of not seeing him every day . . . of missing the occasional bedtime talks, taking me through the woods to Newcomb Hollow Beach, scooping me up in his arms when the waves were rough, teaching me to fish. Who would bandage my scraped knees with such gruff tenderness?

I loved Mom, too, and admired her in that youthful way kids do. She was beautiful and respected, and while her affection was rare, it could make a person feel special. Kids love their mothers until they're taught not to, and mine wasn't exactly bad . . . she was just uninterested.

I said a prayer that Dad would move into the next house down the pond from us so I could still see him every day.

Therefore it was quite a shock when our parents informed us we could choose which parent we lived with. Oh, and also, Mom was moving in with her lover. Who was a woman.

No kid could grow up on Cape Cod and not understand what gay meant—Provincetown was one of the first places on the East Coast where being out was not only safe but celebrated, and it had been that way since long before Hannah and I were born. We grew up seeing gay couples, drag queens, trans people in everyday life. Provincetown was the brightest, most cheerful place in the world, rich with galleries and fabulous food, performers, gardens, art, music, parades. Three of my classmates had same-sex parents, and Filipe, my oldest cousin on Dad's side, was also known as Anna Conda, singing at the Crown & Anchor each weekend in the summer (a fact that won me points among my peers).

But our *mother*? Mom was gay? We had no idea.

"You'll love her," Mom said to our gaping faces. "Her name is Beatrice, and she's amazing." She saw our lack of enthusiasm and frowned. "It's really not a big deal. You'll want to be her friend the second you meet her."

"Don't tell them how to feel, Ann!" Dad barked. "They get to feel however they want." He frowned and looked at us. "You can stay here," he said in his gruff way. "This is your home."

"But I'm your *mother*," Mom said. "And wait till you see our house! It's right on the water on Commercial Street. You'll love it, and there are four bedrooms!" She so rarely tried to sell us on anything that it was weird, this . . . this pitch. "You won't have to share a room anymore, or even a bathroom . . . or live with the smell of mold." She cast a triumphant look at my father.

Provincetown? Provincetown was *fun*, but it wasn't home. It was busy and the houses practically touched, and in the summer, it was so crowded with tourists it took ages to get to MacMillan's Wharf, where the *Goody Chapman* docked.

"Think about it," Dad said. "Your decision, girls. Your friends are here. Your school is here. If you want to live with me, it won't be such a big change. That's all I'm saying."

"You can get a dog with Beatrice and me," Mom said.

"They can get a dog here, too," Dad growled. "They already have a dog." HandsomeBoy, who was lying next to him, thumped his tail in affirmation.

"I mean a real dog who doesn't smell like dead fish. One that you could hold. A Yorkie, maybe, the kind with the smooth fur, Hannah." Ooh. She was fighting dirty.

"Don't bribe them," Dad growled. "It's fuckin' unfair."

"Don't curse in front of the girls, Pedro," Mom said in her church voice. "It's vulgar. Girls *should* be with their mother. What are you going to do when Lillie gets her period or Hannah thinks she's pregnant? Hm?"

"I'm not getting pregnant!" Hannah blurted, turning beet red. "Mom!"

"You both should be raised by women," she said smugly. "Wait till you see the house, honey," she said to me. "It's so bright and sunny. And there are so many other kids to play with. A new school, so you can make new friends. And Beatrice will be your friend, too. She's like an aunt who loves to spoil you."

"Ann, don't you think you're laying it on a little thick?" Dad snapped. "They don't have to be friends with your *lover*, goddamn it."

Hannah and I looked at each other.

I started to cry. It usually stopped them from fighting. Not tonight, though.

"Now look what you've done," Mom said. "Come here, baby." She held out her arms to me, a rare gesture, let me assure you. Sucker that I was, I accepted after a brief hesitation, and crawled onto her lap.

"Girls," Dad said, then paused. "Just think about it. Whatever you want, that's okay with me. I love you no matter what."

"Do you, though, Pedro?" asked Mom, and I slid off her lap, unable to bear her cruel words. Dad *did* love us. He might not say it very often, but he did. "You're hardly ever here."

Hannah and I were informed that we would make our choice by the end of the week for court reasons. As is true in every divorce where there are kids involved, it was awful. We would have to choose between parents, and one of them would be angry or hurt or lonely or all of those things.

Hannah and I didn't talk that night. We just lay in bed, staring at the ceiling. At some point, I got in bed with her, and she put her arm around me, and after a long time listening to each other breathe, we fell asleep.

Mom turned on the full charm offensive. She took the next three days off—something I could not remember her ever doing unless we were going to New Hampshire to see Mimi and Papa—and wooed us. First, a big breakfast at a fancy new restaurant. She let me have chocolate chip pancakes with whipped cream. Then, the tour of the new house, minus the mysterious Beatrice.

The house *was* beautiful, that was for sure. Commercial Street is one of the prettiest streets in America, packed with old houses and mysterious crooked alleys, gardens that burst with blooms. The new house had been a teardown; the builder had bought a crooked, decaying old building, destroyed it and built this gem in its place. It was *so* glamorous—a cedar-shingled three-story house, traditional enough from the street, all windows and decks on the water side. The tiny front and side yards were packed with peonies and lilacs, and Mom had put a vase of flowers in every bedroom. The kitchen was modern and huge, and the sunshine almost hurt my eyes.

"Let's flip a coin and see who gets to pick her room first," Mom said, and I won the toss. My room would be—could be—overlooking the water. I could wake up and see Dad go out to sea. Yes, Mom said, of *course* I could paint it purple. Yes, that big bed *was* for just me. She let us jump on the beds and ooh and aah over the bathrooms. There was a cupola with a ladder to peek out. We splashed in the ocean, and then Mom took us shopping for clothes, a bribe even my eight-year-old self could see.

Still, I couldn't remember such a happy day with Mom. "Just us girls," she said. "It'll be like this all the time."

"Except for Beatrice," I said. Mom ignored me.

But when we got home that night, I knew I couldn't leave. The birds, the chipmunks I had worked so hard on taming, the blue heron that walked slowly along the edge of the pond . . . how could I leave this place?

And, if I moved to Provincetown, who would my father have? HandsomeBoy was a good dog, but Dad would be so lonely. Mom already had someone else, but Daddy would just fish and come home to a dark, empty house. So we would stay. Obviously, we'd stay. This was our home. We could visit Mom. It might even be fun.

"I don't care how fancy the new house is," I said to Hannah that night. "This is home."

She murmured in agreement, but she was almost asleep.

Which was why I was gobsmacked when, the night before we had to meet with the lawyers in Orleans, Hannah announced she'd be going with Mom.

"What? But you can't!" I yelped, bursting into tears. "We have to stay together!"

"Then come to Provincetown," she said in her calm way. "Don't you want to start over?"

"Don't you want to stay here?"

"Not really, Lillie. Here kind of sucks for me." She rolled over in her bed and looked at me, her face soft in the gentle glow from the night-light.

"What are you *talking* about?"

She looked at me almost sadly because I was so dumb. "You don't know what it's like to be ugly," she said.

"You're not ugly!"

"Yes, I am. Look at this nose. My whole face is weird." Okay, she did have a big nose. And she was very tall, already taller than Mom. "I have one friend, and she's been giving me the cold shoulder since September."

"What about me? *I'm* your friend!"

She sighed. "I know. But even if it's just a town away, Provincetown is . . . new. A fresh start."

Fresh start? I was aghast. I knew she didn't have a lot of friends at school, but that was because she didn't need them, not with me! She got good grades. Teachers liked her. We had *fun*, pretty much, though yeah, for the past couple of years she hadn't been as keen on playing our old games in the woods. "You can't leave, Hannah," I said, my voice thin and small.

"P-town will be better for me," she said. "Mom has a point about being with her. I can't see telling Dad I got my period and he needs to run to the general store and get me some maxi pads." She rolled onto her back and looked at our sloping ceiling. "Maybe it'll be easier, starting over where no one knows us."

"*I'm* not leaving," I said. "I could never leave!"

She gave me a kind look. "Well, then, we'll live apart." Her voice roughened with tears. "It's only fifteen minutes, Lils. Don't worry. We'll talk every day and see each other at least a couple times a week. We'll just have two houses now."

She was so serene about her decision. I was *furious*. I told her she was my *sister*, my *big* sister, and she was *abandoning* me and Daddy. She was going to live with a *stranger*! Our mother had been *cheating* on Dad! Didn't she have any *loyalty*? How could she *leave* this place?

Hannah was unmoved. "I'm sorry, Lillie," she said. "My mind is made up."

To be fair, back then, our home was dark and poorly insulated, filled with drafty windows and iffy electricity. You couldn't use the blow-dryer if the stove was on. The back steps were crumbling. We were always cold in the winter, as the furnace couldn't get the temperature above sixty-three, and Dad's solution was "put on another sweater." The modernity of my mother's new house, the light, the glamour of Provincetown had its appeal, sure.

But what about the woods and the pond and the breeze and the adventures? What about Daddy? There was no way I would go to Provincetown and stab my father in the heart.

Three weeks later, Hannah packed up her side of our room, hugged me and, with an excitement that felt like acid on an open wound, skipped out to our mother's SUV. "See you this weekend!" she called, and closed the car door on my childhood.

We never got it back, that sisterly bond. I think I was too young to forgive her, and as I got older, I stopped wanting to. Hannah did indeed love Beatrice, our glamorous stepmother. She learned how to dress, wear a "signature" lipstick, speak French. By the end of high school, she was unrecognizable to me, this imposingly tall, fashionable girl with an awesome haircut. And even though she returned from Bates College, she never really returned to me. The best I could say is that she loved my son. Otherwise, we had never—not once—spent any voluntary time just the two of us in the past thirty-three years. Which is a very long time.

So it was as much a surprise to me as it was to her when I climbed her porch steps, knocked on her antique oak-and-glass front door and asked to come in.

"Hey!" she said, rightfully surprised. She glanced at my scrubs and nurse's clogs. She herself was wearing a gray silk top and darker gray pants with snakeskin flats. "Just coming from work? Or going to?"

"From. So . . . Brad is leaving me for another woman."

Her eyes went comically wide. "Come in," she said.

I had been to my sister's workplace before—she had it open for the Christmas stroll each year and served mulled wine and French cookies, and sure, I stopped in. I didn't hate her, after all. We just had nothing in common as adults.

Her office was lovely—a front parlor where she met with her brides and grooms, the bookcases filled with glossy coffee-table books on floral design and wedding dresses, wedding cakes, wedding cultures. Her office overlooked the flower-filled courtyard in the back. Her assistant, Manuel, had a large, beautiful desk in the parlor and would greet people as they came in, make them tea or coffee or pour them champagne. So I heard. I'd never had a reason to visit her aside from the Christmas stroll, and I had never been invited over as a solo guest.

"Have a seat," she said. "Can I get you some water? Coffee or tea?"

"How about wine?" I suggested.

"I have that, too. One minute, please."

There was a silver vase on the coffee table, filled with creamy pink roses, white hydrangeas and bright pink ranunculus. Stunning. I sighed and looked around, hearing her fuss in the kitchen.

Hannah always treated me this way—like a pleasant acquaintance. We didn't talk about anything personal. To be fair, I'd given her the cold shoulder those six years she lived with Mom and Beatrice, or guilt-tripped her by sobbing and begging her to move back home. After she went to college, the window seemed to close on any chance of friendship. Later, we didn't even seem to think about it—me busy with a new baby, marriage and home, her completely occupied with her business of excess.

But as she often said, if she didn't do it, someone else would, and these weddings were a great infusion of money into the local economy. Which was true. Beth and the Ice House often catered Hannah's weddings and made a hefty profit. Her clients kept at least two florists in business, and the package stores adored her, bending over backward to get her guests the high-end stuff they demanded. She recommended local photographers, seamstresses, bakeries, chocolatiers, hotels. So Hannah was loved in the community, same as I was. Just in a very different way.

And then there was how we looked, dressed, decorated our homes. Hannah and I looked nothing alike. I was five foot three; she was six foot one. My clothing style was comfort based; hers was dress to kill. She knew how to put on makeup like a pro, and her straight black hair changed every few years, from bob to pixie to shaggy to sleek. My hair came down to my shoulders, was frizzy most days, curly some, and in a bun or ponytail most of the time.

Hannah was not conventionally attractive—she had a big nose and small eyes and her mouth was low on her face—but she was definitely elegant. Kind of an "Amy Winehouse in her better days" look. Strong boned. If she was Amy Winehouse, I was more of Carey Mulligan's less attractive sister—girl-next-door prettiness. Cute little nose, big eyes, chubby cheeks. All our lives, people had asked Hannah and me and our parents if one of us was adopted. Hannah was and always had been single (and may have been asexual or even gay, but if she ever had a lover, I had never met him/her/them). I had slept with only one man and zero women. A pity, now that I despised my husband.

Hannah's apartment was chic, sleek and comfortable (and chilly, I thought, all those shades of cool gray and stark white). My house was colorful, funky, often cluttered, and homey with worn couches that welcomed a nap and chairs frayed from Milo, our late great cat who had died in his sleep two years ago. Thomasina, Hannah's cat, would never be so rude.

Hannah came back in with a tray, two wineglasses, a bottle of white wine in a marble wine chiller, some crumbly cheese, grapes and crackers, as well as a tiny vase holding three roses in various shades of pink. She was very fancy, courtesy of Beatrice.

"From your garden?" I asked as she poured.

"Yes." She handed me a glass, sat down and crossed her legs. "How are you doing?"

"Shitty."

"Yeah. Of course."

I drank some wine. It was *really* good, all buttery and caramel and citrus.

"Do you want to . . . tell me about it?"

I sighed and sat back on the couch. Super comfy. Was it strange that we were in her office, rather than upstairs? Even though it looked like a very nice living room? "Um . . . it was the night before graduation," I said. "We went to Pepe's, and I surprised him with a vacation I'd booked. To Europe, to celebrate us having gotten Dylan off to college."

"Can you afford that?" she asked, our mother's girl. She closed her eyes. "I'm sorry. Go on."

"Well, we *could* afford it when we were a two-income family, Hannah. But no, and I did cancel it. Anyway," I said, my voice sharp, "he told me that he was in love with someone else. Has been for some time."

"My God. I never would have guessed he'd have the balls."

I felt a little twinge of affection. "Me neither. And anyway, he's moving in with her when Dylan leaves for college."

"The day after tomorrow?" she asked.

"Yep." Then something in me cracked, and I started crying, big ugly sobs. My hands went over my face, and I leaned forward against the pain.

"How horrible!" She leaned over and patted my knee, irritating me with that paltry gesture even as I grabbed a few tissues and blew my nose. *How about a hug, sis?* I wanted to ask. Then again, that would've been awkward. We weren't the hugging type. Even as kids, I'd been the emotional one. She'd been calm and wise, sometimes regretful, but otherwise the epitome of grace under pressure. No wonder she made a killer living at her job.

When I quieted down, a little embarrassed at my outburst, I suddenly realized I was starving. Shoveled some cheese onto a cracker and stuffed it in my mouth. Repeated twice as my sister watched. Did a palate cleanse with the wine.

"Do you know who she is?" Hannah asked.

"Yes. Actually, I *introduced* them, Hannah. Can you believe it? Melissa Finch. She bought a house from the Fairchilds last winter, and—What?"

Hannah looked stricken. "She . . . she just booked a wedding consultation with me."

My mouth fell open. "You're going to plan my husband's wedding, Hannah? Are you kidding me?"

"I—I didn't know who the groom was, I swear! Obviously, I didn't know," Hannah said. "We have an appointment for next week, but I . . . She just called to make sure I was free. Said she heard I was the best. And um . . . she paid me a deposit. Twenty grand."

I closed my eyes.

"I'll tell her I can't," Hannah said. "Of course I will. I'll cancel. She can use Rachel at Daylynn Designs. I'm so sorry, Lillie."

I exhaled a long breath. "Well, you didn't know." I picked up the bottle of wine and poured myself another glass. "Did you like her?"

Hannah looked away. She always did such a perfect, subtle cat's eye. It was a talent.

"You liked her," I said. It was an accusation.

"I didn't *know*, Lillie. I'll hate her from now on, okay?"

"Good. She's an amoral slut." Slut shaming. Me, a champion for women and their bodies. "Strike that. Brad is an amoral slut."

"I always thought you two were so . . . solid."

"Yeah, me too." I took another sip of wine.

"You've been sitting on this for all these weeks, Lils?"

"Mom knows."

"Mom?" She was rightfully stunned.

"Free legal advice."

"Ah. That makes sense." She drank some wine and ate a cracker with cheese, much more gracefully than I had. When she was done chewing, she wiped her mouth delicately, her red lipstick staying in place. Truly Beatrice's prodigy, as our stepmother, the former model, always looked camera ready. "What can I do, Lillie?"

A real sister, the kind you read about, the kind who knows you inside and out, would have offered to kill Brad.

To publicly humiliate him. She would wrap her arms around me and fiercely promise to take care of me, reassure me that I wouldn't be alone. She'd move in and sleep over for a month, and we'd drink wine and cry and laugh.

She was still waiting for an answer.

A thought occurred to me. "You know what? Take the job, planning their wedding. Be my spy."

She winced. "Oh. Um . . . I'm not sure I can do that."

"Okay. I understand. Great chat." I stood up. "Gotta go."

"Dylan came over this morning," she said. "To say goodbye. I gave him some money. I hope that's okay."

"Of course it is. You're his aunt."

"I'll . . . I'll be around, Lillie. If you need . . . well. Someone to talk to."

"Thanks."

She walked me to the door. "You know what?" she said. "I'll do it. I'll be your spy. I can't tank their wedding, but yeah, I can give you some details and stuff." She paused. "That is, if Brad wants me to handle this second wedding. He might not agree."

"Oh, I think he'll do whatever she wants," I said. "And thanks, Hannah."

"Of course."

She was a very nice stranger, my sister. We almost hugged, then drew back simultaneously. "See you around," I said.

"You bet."

With that, I got in my car and headed to the ocean side of town. To home, where I'd wait for my son to come home, wait for tomorrow, the last day our little family would ever be together.

CHAPTER 7

Lillie

The night before my son left for college, I cooked his favorite meal and favorite dessert. Then, after my son went to bed and my asshole husband went downstairs to text his bride-to-be, I fantasized that I would get a fatal disease, and *that* would teach them, those two males who were leaving me. Boy, would they feel horrible! Oh, yes! Imagine the guilt trip there! Plus, I wouldn't have to deal with anything, would I? I'd just die (peacefully, looking out over Herring Pond) in a blissful morphine fog and leave them to roil in guilt.

Or I'd move. I'd sell my house and move to Montana, not too far from Missoula, become a cook on a cattle ranch, learn how to ride horses and fall in love with a rugged cowboy who looked exactly like Idris Elba.

I didn't sleep at all that night. At 6:00 a.m., I got out of bed and made pancakes for Dylan, my tears hissing in the cast-iron pan.

Months ago, my son had asked that we not fly out to the University of Montana with him. "It'll be hard enough as it is, Mom," he'd said. "Plus, football camp starts the same day we move in, so I'd have to ditch you an hour after I got there."

I'd offered to do it anyway, saying I could make up his bed and unpack his stuff, hang his posters, all that. He'd kindly rejected the offer. Brad (who'd still been pretending to love me) held me as I cried that night in our bedroom. "Honey, I know it's hard," he said. "But it's a great sign that he's independent enough to do this himself."

Another punishment for having done a good job raising my son.

Today, Dylan's room was packed, and we'd already shipped four boxes of stuff to Montana. I'd bought every over-the-counter medicine, vitamin and supplement I could find in case of cold, flu, stomach bug, muscle aches, wound, infection, fever. Every comfort—heating pad, hot-water bottle, special neck pillow. Tons of Cape Cod reminders: a Wellfleet sign, a tunnel permit sticker (there was no tunnel; we just liked to torture the tourists as they sat in bridge traffic). A great white shark T-shirt, an oyster shell key chain in silver. I even sneaked in his favorite little stuffed animal from when he was tiny—Lambie, a Beanie Baby Dylan had slept with from birth to age thirteen. A soft throw blanket in manly gray with a maroon pillow to match the Montana Grizzlies colors. I bought a rug for his room, a cool lamp, some posters. A photo of my dad, Dylan and me on the beach; a photo of the view from our house in the fall; a picture of Milo, who had slept on Dyllie's bed all those years.

I wanted him to be surrounded by things he loved, things that would make him feel not so far away, things that would help him if he needed it. Things that would remind him how loved he was.

Dylan was quiet at breakfast. "Thanks for making these, Mom," he said, and I heard the nervousness in his voice.

"You're welcome, baby," I said.

"Well, we better go!" Brad announced cheerfully, coming in from the guest room. "We have to leave some time for traffic."

The car had been packed the night before. Dylan only needed his backpack. He thudded up the stairs and careened back down, then stood for a minute in the living room, looking out at the view. When he turned to face me, his eyes were wet.

"We'll FaceTime as much as you want," I said around the shard of glass in my throat. "It's a big change, honey, but you've got this. And you can come home whenever you need to."

Dylan nodded, then went outside. "I'm just gonna run down to the dock," he said, and took off.

"A new beginning for all of us," Brad said quietly.

"Shut the fuck up," I answered.

"So bitter," he said.

"You bet your ass I am." Our handsome son came running back up a second later, so athletic, so manly, and my heart cracked like glass. "Ready, honey?"

"I guess so," he said. "Yellowstone, here I come!"

He was quiet until the bridge. Once we crossed, though, he started talking about the weather in Missoula (surprisingly hot), how the team was going to get a guided tour of Yellowstone and camp out for two nights, how he hoped to see a grizzly bear and at least one or two moose.

"Just not up close," I said. Good God. My son was going to a state where people were *eaten* by *bears*. Yes, I had bought bear spray, but maybe I should get more? And what about moose? They killed more people than grizzlies! "Be careful if you see a moose," I had to say, because if I didn't, what if he was attacked by the rampaging beast and I had said nothing? "They're not very coordinated, so you can dodge around trees to avoid them."

"Good to know," Dylan said, laughing a little.

"Did you hear the story of how the wolves were reintroduced to Yellowstone?" Brad asked, even though we'd all listened to the podcast together last summer in the car. Nevertheless, he launched into the tale as if he'd lived it. Dylan didn't mind, making the appropriate noises here and there as I vacillated between hatred for my husband and love for my son.

Think of Dylan, I told myself. *The best thing you've ever done. No matter what, you raised him, and he's wonderful.*

We got to Logan airport way too soon. The one day of the entire century that there was no Boston traffic. Because we couldn't wait at the gate with him, we just pulled up at the curb for our goodbyes. Dylan bounded out, grabbed his backpack and set it on the sidewalk.

"Well," Brad said. "Good luck, son. I'm proud of you. Call us when you get there, okay?"

"I will," Dylan said. They hugged, slapping each other on the back, and Brad got in the car.

Then it was my turn. "Well," I said, my voice a little husky. "It's going to be fantastic, and you'll have the best time."

His eyes grew shiny. "Thanks, Mom," he said. Then he hugged me, a real hug this time, and I stifled a sob, because this brawny man-child in front of me—this little boy who had laughed so much, who once loved nothing more than making Play-Doh sculptures with me—was leaving, and nothing would ever be the same.

"I love you," I said, and my voice cracked a little.

"I know. I love you, too." He hugged me a little harder, then let me go. "I'll call you from Chicago."

"Okay, honey. Love you so much." I turned to the car, then turned back. "Dylan. You're gonna have the time of your life, honey."

"Thanks, Mommy."

Oh, God. He hadn't called me that in years.

Then he shouldered his bags and walked into the airport.

∽

Brad packed that same afternoon.

"I'll be living with Melissa," he said, as if I didn't know that already. Still, the words burned like acid. "I want you to know she and I are getting married as soon as possible. I'm sorry if that hurts you, but I can't be responsible for your feelings, as you know."

How I hated him.

Two weeks from now, we were due in court, and with that, our marriage would be over. Our family would be broken forever. No more Christmases, no holding hands in a waiting room as Dylan's future wife gave birth to our grandchild. No more the three of us, laughing as we played Scattergories at the kitchen table; no more glancing at Brad as my mother and Beatrice polished off another bottle of wine. I hated my husband, and yet I couldn't just pretend we'd never been happy, the way Brad seemed to be doing.

We'd finalized the settlement . . . I got the house, of course. But I also got the $337,000 we owed on it, thanks to twenty years of renovations. How I would pay that off, I had no idea. He, on the other hand, was marrying a woman who was richer than Bill Gates.

I leaned in the doorway of the guest room, determined to make this as uncomfortable for him as possible. He ignored me, carefully folding his new clothes, his new toiletries, his new workout gear, and putting them neatly into his suitcase. There was still an airline tag on it from the last time we'd used it—our anniversary a few years ago. We'd gone to beautiful Pittsburgh, because we got a flight for fifty-nine dollars, and we stayed in a nice hotel and ate delicious food and made love in the king-sized bed.

When had he changed? When had he stopped loving me? Why?

"Listen," he said, straightening. "I know we've discussed this, but I'd really like the engagement ring back. It's been in my family for three generations. I'll even pay you for it."

"Nope."

"Lillie. It was my great-grandmother's. It should stay in the Fairchild family."

"Still nope."

His face grew tight. "I'd like to give it to Melissa."

"Oh, okay, well, then, here." I pretended to take it off.

"Whoops! Actually . . . nope! It was given with the intent that I would marry you, which I did. It's mine."

He hissed in irritation. "At least give it to Dylan when he wants to get married."

"I'm actually gonna hock it," I said. "Or give it to a homeless person. I haven't decided. Maybe I'll throw it in the ocean, like Rose does in *Titanic*." That had always made Brad cry, the sap. (Why toss a priceless diamond, lady? Sell it and donate the money!)

"You're so petty," he said.

"You have no idea," I answered.

"I'm so relieved to be starting over with someone who embraces joy the way I do," he said, and my hand twitched to punch him. "The light in me sees the light in you, Lillie."

"Go fuck yourself."

"Melissa doesn't swear, by the way. One of the many things I love about her."

He shouldered his bag, picked up a knapsack and walked out of our house, backing his car neatly out of the driveway.

Since the day he told me he was cheating on me, he had never once said he was sorry.

I walked down to the dock, stripped off all my clothes and dove into the water. It was silky smooth and pure, and when I surfaced and looked at the darkening sky, I felt . . . cleaner. At least I wouldn't have to lie to my son anymore.

I stayed in the cool water, floating on my back, until my skin was pruney, and even then, it was some time before I went back into my empty house.

Time to get a dog.

CHAPTER 8

Melissa

Much to Melissa's surprise, about two years into their marriage, Dennis started to get . . . restless. Impatient. With *her*.

"I can't believe you're not bored," he snapped one night as she showed him the new sofa that had been delivered that day. "You don't have a job, you don't have a . . . a cause or a charity or whatever. You don't even have hobbies! You don't read anything other than magazines. You just go to the gym, take yoga classes, spend money and futz around here. I didn't think I was marrying someone whose goal was to be a housewife. You haven't even looked into adoption agencies."

She resisted the urge to roll her eyes. First of all, did he think this body didn't need upkeep? Secondly, yoga was a practice of self-awareness and calm. It was more than a hobby! Was she supposed to take up knitting? And thirdly, she didn't *want* a child, so she wasn't going to get pregnant or adopt a child. *Do the math, Dennis.* Instead she said, "Maybe we need to go in for fertility treatments."

"There's nothing wrong with *me*. I have two kids."

It was a warning shot across the bow, and it infuriated

her. Did she not earn her keep, gosh darn it? Didn't she give him porn-worthy sex? A delicious meal every night they didn't go out? Didn't she make him breakfast every day? Feign interest as he talked about the new doctor they'd hired? Throw the best grand opening party when they expanded the surgical center? Wasn't every man he knew completely jealous of him because his hot wife knew how to take care of a man in every possible way?

She said nothing for a moment, breathing deeply into her stomach. "You're right," she said, because it was the only answer he'd accept. "I've gotten a little lost. You swept me off my feet, and I do love our life. But you're right. I'll think about this. And I'll call a doctor to get checked out." She had to grit her teeth before forcing a smile. "There's nothing I'd like more than having your baby," she lied, kissing his cheek.

"Good," he said, then got up and went into the den.

Oh, no! Would she have to get pregnant?

She certainly couldn't go to medical school. She didn't want a job. She could be a yoga teacher, maybe . . . she'd done enough of it. A therapist, because that didn't involve anything besides listening to people, right? And she could have a swanky office, not dark and crowded like the one in *Couples Therapy* or *In Treatment*, but one with a view of Central Park, maybe. Now that would be cool.

Unfortunately, becoming a legitimate therapist would require quite a bit of school, Google told her. Dang it.

And then, as always, the universe intervened.

One night when Melissa was sitting in the bath, neck-deep in bubbles and drinking a glass of Antoine Jobard Meursault, pretending to be sore from her fictional gynecological exam, her phone rang.

Unknown number. She let it go to voice mail, then listened. "Hey, Missy, it's Kaitlyn. I need a favor. Call me back, 'kay?"

Her *sister*. Melissa had never told her parents she was married. They weren't the type to use the internet to track her down, but if they did, they'd want money, and she would die, having them invade her pristine, carefully curated life. She doubted they remembered her changed name, and if they did, it was a common enough name, Melissa Spencer. There were plenty of doctors, CEOs, authors, professors, real estate agents with the same name . . . they'd never be able to find her.

The only time Melissa reached out was to send cute outfits and gifts to Harminee (the name still made her wince) on the kid's birthday and at Christmas, wanting her to have something nice in her life. She never listed the return address . . . that was what Amazon was for, wasn't it?

But Melissa had given Katie her cell phone number. Her county had one of the highest per capita overdose deaths in the nation. If her sister died, Melissa would want to know. Kaitlyn may have been addicted to drugs and was a petty criminal, but once upon a time, the two of them had been close. More than close. They'd been best friends.

She got out of the tub, wrapped herself in her white bathrobe and peeked in on Dennis. He was watching a Yankees game, and the score was tied, which meant he'd be glued to the set till the last second of the game. Good. She couldn't risk him overhearing her. Back down the hallway she went, into the guest room and into the vast closet there where she kept her shoes, and called her sister back.

"Whaddup?"

"Kaitlyn? Is that you?"

"Yeah, hey, Missy-Jo. Listen. I'll get straight to the point," Kaitlyn said. "I'm heading to jail again, and I need some help."

"What?"

"Angela had a stroke, so they can't watch Harminee anymore."

"Angela . . . the one who's raising her? Her grandmother?"

"Can you give me a fuckin' break? Yeah, *raisin'* her,

watchin' her, whatever. Mama and Daddy said no because of Daddy's back, but you and me know *that's* bullshit."

The grammar made her cringe. Was that how she'd once sounded? Awful. "Who'll take care of Harminee, then?"

"Well, shit, Missy-Jo, I thought you were smart. Dintcha go to college?" There was a pause, and Melissa could hear her take a drag on a cigarette. "I want you to take her, dumbass."

"What?" She shook her head to clear it. Surely she hadn't heard right. "Can't . . . I mean, can't someone else watch her until you get out? Someone closer? What about Aunt Rena?" Melissa could hear the white trash creeping back into her voice. *Whubout Ant Rena?*

"Aunt Rena ain't right in the head, Missy. The social worker said immediate family's best. Look. I can't keep her. I gotta be clean for somethin' like two years before I can git her again, and I'm lookin' at five to ten. You're my sister. It should be you."

"I can't . . . That's crazy. I can't take her." She looked at her rows of shoes, so organized, so beautiful. A kid? No, thank you.

"She's seven," Kaitlyn said. "She's your niece, Missy Jolene Cumbo."

There was a threat in that sentence. While her parents were computer illiterate, Melissa was sure Kaitlyn could find her in about ten minutes. She'd always been cunning that way.

"Just let me think a minute," she said to her sister.

Her niece. Seven wasn't a baby. Seven was all-day school and lessons and maybe a nanny. She and Dennis were wealthy, after all. She could save Harminee and give the kid an escape from her all-too-certain future. Hadn't she prayed for the very same thing as a child? A rich aunt or godmother who'd swoop in and change everything?

Suddenly, the idea of rescuing a little girl sounded utterly amazing.

"Let me talk to my husband," she said. "I'll call you in a couple of days."

"So you'll do it? 'Cuz they need an answer."

"I can't say yes without him being on board."

"Get him on board, then. I'll call you tomorrow." Kaitlyn hung up.

Melissa went back into the den, where the Yankees game was just wrapping up. They'd won, so her husband was in a good mood. Fantastic.

"You should've seen the last inning!" he crowed. "García was on first, the pitch went wild, he stole second, then went to third, and the catcher tried to throw him out, but the Red Sox shortstop dropped the ball, and he stole home! It was beautiful!" He took in her robe, her damp hair. "Are you feeling better, sweetheart?" he asked, remembering that she had told him she'd had an exam today.

"A lot better, thank you." She paused. "Honey, I have some upsetting news." She took the remote and turned off the TV, noting that Dennis had gotten crumbs all over the new couch. Irritating. She summoned tears, a gift of hers, and looked back up at him, knowing her eyelash extensions caught the tears in a most beguiling way.

"Babe, what is it?" He really was a mensch (word of the day, and one she liked very much). She now had a Word of the Day app on her phone, having graduated from paper calendars, but she still took great pride in expanding her vocabulary.

"Well . . ." She took a shaky breath and blinked so the tears would fall. "It's my . . . sister."

His face was keen. "What happened, honey?" he asked. Good. He was using pet names again.

"Her addiction disorder has gotten severe, and my niece . . . my poor little niece needs a place to stay for a while. She has no one else but me, Dennis. My parents . . . well, you know about them."

She watched his face as the penny dropped. *What? A kid? Your niece? Live with us? I can be Daddy Warbucks?*

"Well, of *course* she can stay with us! Of course! Oh, honey, absolutely. Let's fly out this weekend. I should meet your parents anyway. Give your father a piece of my mind."

"No, no," Melissa said quickly. "I don't know how long this will take, honey, and my parents . . . they don't deserve to meet you." It hadn't really been a stretch when she told Dennis she'd grown up in an abusive household with codependent parents. She swallowed and looked out the window. "They don't even care what happens to their own granddaughter. They told my sister she'd be better off in foster care, and they refuse to give her any money." As if they had any.

"For their *grandchild*? Jesus. Coldhearted."

"You have no idea, honey. That's why . . . well, that's probably why I threw myself into making a home for you and me. I never had that growing up. When I fell in love with you, it was magical. It still is."

"Oh, honey." He pulled her into his arms and kissed her hair, and Melissa smiled. "Of course we'll bring your niece here. We'll take such good care of her, the poor kid."

"Dennis, I love you so much." She kissed him softly. "You are the best, kindest man in the world."

Tender lovemaking ensued, as Dennis was feeling heroic. Men were simple creatures.

Now she wouldn't have to get pregnant. Problem solved. Universe provides.

A few days later, Melissa flew to Columbus, Ohio, rented a luxury car and drove back to Wakeford, which hadn't changed a bit, unfortunately. It felt like a lifetime ago that she'd left at eighteen, but it had only been seven years. Pulling into the cracked driveway of her childhood home was far too familiar. It was going to take many cleansing breaths to put this behind her. Some very deep meditation.

"'Bout time," Mom said as she walked through the door. "I had to call outta work to take care of her. Nice of you to flounce in from wherever you're at."

"Lovely to see you again, too." She glanced in the living room, where her father sat in his recliner. "Hi, Dad."

"Hey." He didn't look away from Fox News.

"Some parents would be excited to see their oldest child after all this time," she said, irritation making her tap her perfect nails against her bag.

"Well, I don't have no daughter with your name, whatever the hell it is," Dad said.

"Miss High-and-Mighty, always too good for us," Mama added.

No compliments. No pride that she looked like a million bucks, dressed like Meghan Markle, was driving a Lexus SUV. No questions about what she did, where she lived, where she was taking their only grandchild. "Where's Harminee?" she asked.

"She's up in your old room, what did you expect?"

Up the stairs Melissa went. The house still smelled like tuna fish and beer. Lovely.

Her niece seemed much older than seven. She wore a dirty T-shirt with a pony on it and had snarled blond curls that looked as if they hadn't seen a comb since God was a baby.

"Hi, there. I'm your aunt," she said, saying it the way Dennis did—*ahnt* instead of *ant*. "My name's Melissa." No response. "I send you presents on your birthday?"

The girl gave her a wary look. She wasn't unpretty . . . the blond hair could be combed, and she could use an hour-long shower, probably. Harminee had blue eyes, a straight nose and resting bitch face.

"How are you doing, sweetie?" Melissa asked.

No answer. Well, boarding school was just a few years away.

"I'm going to take care of you until your mom gets better," Melissa said. Like *that* would ever happen. Kaitlyn had graduated from meth to heroin, she'd told Melissa. Not easy to kick.

"She's a addict," the kid said. Oof. That accent.

"Yes. Well. It's a disease, and we hope she can be cured." Melissa had read two articles on the plane about talking to kids about addiction. "I live in Manhattan," she said.

"Where's that at?"

For heaven's sake. Melissa forced a smile. "I think you'll like it, Harminee. It's a big, beautiful, shiny city with so many fun things to do." She paused. "How'd you like a new name?"

"What?"

"We can change your name. A new name for a new place."

"Really?" Finally, something that interested the child. "That'd be all right, I guess. How about . . . I dunno. Star? Or Dallas! How 'bout Dallas?"

Like mother, like daughter with the stripper names. "Oh, what about Ophelia?" Melissa suggested, as if she'd just thought of it. She'd been on Nameberry for days, looking for a name that wouldn't identify Harminee as white trash. "That's a gorgeous name. Very cool and mysterious. We can keep Harminee as your middle name." And change the spelling to Harmony and add Spencer, and then Finch. Ophelia Harmony Spencer Finch. Yes. That would fit right in with the New York elite.

Harminee had already said goodbye to her other grandparents (who might actually miss her, though Melissa wasn't getting any information from the kid). Kaitlyn was already serving her sentence for dealing heroin and cocaine.

If only Katie had followed her lead, Melissa thought. They could've escaped together.

After a few days of filling out the legal paperwork that made Melissa her niece's guardian and arranging for a social worker to oversee her transition in the city, they flew back to New York. Ophelia was unable to suppress her excitement at being on an airplane, then a car with a driver, then an *elevator*. Dennis welcomed her with a huge pile of gifts. It was love at first sight between the two of them.

Over the next few weeks, Melissa took Ophelia shopping for new clothes. Decorated her room with pastel polka-dot wallpaper (the child had wanted unicorns, poor thing . . . Melissa would teach her about style). An antique French double bed with a white duvet underneath a cascade of pink tulle, making the bed look like the most charming fort. A fluffy white rug, pink chandelier and carefully chosen throw pillows (not that Ophelia made the bed . . . not yet, anyway). Melissa bought her the prettiest dolls and stuffed animals, little trays and vases, a mobile. It was a dream room, the kind Missy-Jo Cumbo would not have been able to imagine. The girl had her own bathroom, with towels from Anthropologie and shampoo, shower gel and soap from Gilchrist & Soames.

Ophelia remained unimpressed and morose. It was clear she didn't much like Melissa. This was irritating, since Melissa was doing all the work of looking up schools and tutors and violin lessons and such. The child didn't want any of the meals Melissa cooked, just asked for macaroni and cheese from a box.

But when Dennis was around, life was like a Hallmark card. The child loved him, and he her. He told Ophelia gruesome stories from the OR, and Ophelia ate them up. "How much blood was there? Seriously? The bone was pokin' through the skin? Holy shit, Dennis!"

It was a little . . . annoying, the fact that the two had immediately bonded. Melissa had wanted a little mini-me who'd love shopping and manicures, or at least someone who was *grateful*. And Dennis! He'd never been that interesting, and now all he wanted to talk about was Ophelia. Heck, he'd even brought up fostering another kid! No, thank you!

Home, which Melissa had loved so much before, was now a place where her irritation bubbled. The sullen child was definitely putting a crimp in her life. She brought up a nanny. Dennis gave her an incredulous look.

"She already has abandonment issues, Mel!" God, she

hated when he called her that. "She doesn't need a nanny. She needs us."

Great.

Melissa found a good tutor for the rest of the spring and summer, because Ophelia could barely read. Elocution lessons to fix that white trash accent (Melissa wished *she'd* had a voice coach instead of having to learn it on her own). Ophelia was a solid little thing, so Melissa enrolled her in ballet and got rid of every bag of potato chips in the house, which made Dennis grumble, too.

But Melissa was firm. It became kind of fun, being totally in charge of someone else, and it scored many points with Dennis, his colleagues and friends, even his children, who came to meet Ophelia and were, Melissa had to admit, very kind. Amanda hugged Melissa the first time they met, and Nick gave Ophelia a piggyback ride in Central Park, the five of them laughing like a perfect blended family. Suddenly, other mothers in their circle were approaching Melissa, offering playdates and advice about schools.

"We should adopt her legally," Dennis whispered to Melissa in the kitchen one night. "We can provide a much better life."

"That would be my dream, too," she said. "Oh, Dennis. We're so blessed." Marriage troubles and talk about her lack of ambition or focus were a thing of the past.

At Dennis's urging, she called Kaitlyn at the women's prison and asked if they could adopt her. Katie wouldn't agree to it, despite the fact that she was now serving a seven-to-twelve-year sentence, thanks to punching a guard in the throat.

"She's *my* kid," Kaitlyn snarled. "You got her for now, but she's mine. And Jesus Christ, that name, Missy. Ophelia?" Her sister's accent turned the name ugly . . . Oh-feel-yuh.

"It's a Shakespearean name," Melissa said. "Better than what she had."

Kaitlyn hung up. Fine. Melissa was still in charge, no

matter what Kaitlyn thought. She'd had her chance, and she was in prison, so sit on that, Katie! Melissa was the mother now, no matter what Ophelia called her (Melissa, not even Auntie, which would show affection, at least). And, because she was the epitome (word of the day, even though she'd mispronounced it as eppi-tome) of grace, Melissa even let Ophelia call Kaitlyn every few weeks.

After a few months, Melissa thought she might love Ophelia. Wasn't love caring for someone else? Kaitlyn hadn't cared. She'd shot up, snorted, smoked, drank, whored and gone on crime sprees to support her habits. That sure as heck wasn't love. Poor Ophelia. Melissa would make everything better. She felt quite holy, in fact.

Melissa bought Ophelia pretty, expensive clothes, which was especially rewarding after Ophelia slimmed down. They took her out to dinner once a week, the three of them a happy little modern family. They hired an etiquette coach, and soon the ill-mannered child who only ordered chicken nuggets or pasta with butter knew how to use a fork and knife, European-style.

When fall came, they enrolled her in the Amory-West School, where tuition was $50,000 a year. It wasn't Chapin or Spence, but it still smacked of privilege. The principal assured them that Ophelia would get the attention she needed for academic, social and spiritual excellence (whatever that meant). Ballet, elocution, etiquette and French lessons kept Ophelia busy after school, and that was fine with Melissa. The girl would have everything she and Kaitlyn never did. Also, it kept her out of Melissa's hair.

Life fell into a pleasant routine. During the school day, Melissa's life was much as it had been before—gym, yoga studio, salon, shopping, planning dinner. But now she had a child to care for, and she found that she had a little more prestige. More respect. It seemed that the women who had disapproved of her for being a trophy wife now admired her for taking in her niece. She had lunch dates and was invited to be on committees. A group of mothers from Amory-West invited her to join their book club.

"God, you're too beautiful to be here with us crones," said Mirabelle, the hostess, sitting in her massive living room with a killer view of Central Park. "Honestly, how is your stomach that flat?" These were the kinds of compliments that women volleyed back and forth as a test, and Melissa played the game well.

"Oh, please," she said. "Look at you! I'd kill for your legs! I cannot *believe* you're thirty-eight!" A lie. Her own legs were perfect, for one, and for two, Mirabelle looked *fifty*-eight. Melissa told Helen how daring and adorable her pixie cut was (Melissa would never cut her hair, ever . . . men *loved* long hair). She told them how delightful and smart their little ones were (not that she ever really talked to them).

"Did you ever model?" asked Libby. "I swear to God, you're a ringer for Karlie Kloss."

"Marry me!" Melissa said, laughing. She scoffed when Tanisha cooed over her poreless skin. "You should've seen me in high school," she said. "My face looked like a half-chewed golf ball. *Your* skin . . . now that's perfection. I'm so pasty compared to you!"

And so she was accepted by (a) becoming a de facto mother, (b) pretending she wasn't beautiful or significantly younger and (c) acting like the most devoted wife in the world. She never flirted with anyone's spouse but her own, and boy, did the other women watch her. No, Melissa complimented their homes/children/outfits/jewelry and stayed just a little removed, dodging questions that were too probing.

Missy-Jo Cumbo was dead and buried. Much better to be a beautiful woman who'd been educated at Wesleyan, who threw fabulous dinner parties and had taken in her tragic little niece, selflessly putting off her dreams of . . . whatever.

Ophelia's accent faded, though she put it on when it was just her and Melissa, knowing it irritated her. She wouldn't practice violin, was terrible at art and was (let's be honest) a mediocre student at best, though she got As, just like all the other little monsters at Amory-West. You didn't pay fifty grand a year and not have your kid on the honor roll.

And then, three years after Ophelia had come to live with them, came a swerve Melissa hadn't prepared for.

Dennis died. Just like that.

He had been walking through the posh foyer of his Westchester surgical center, a half-eaten bagel in one hand. His receptionist said he stopped in his tracks, pressed his fingers to his head, said, "Jesus *Christ*," and fell to the floor like a bag of rocks.

He'd been fifty-seven years old.

Melissa sure hadn't seen that coming. Dennis had never been healthier, thanks to her cooking, especially since she made him lay off the junk food after Ophelia came. He played racquetball and went for the occasional run. Sometimes he even used the elliptical in the den.

No, it was a shock. A terrible shock. Her legs gave out when his partner Saul came over to tell her the news, and he had to help her to the couch. She cried without even trying. Dennis had given her so much. He'd been generous and kind and . . . well, generous. They'd been so happy these past three years. He'd been a wonderful father figure for Ophelia, who sobbed for a week straight, her cheeks red, nose raw. Shock carried them through the wake and funeral and after-lunch (at the Princeton Club, since Dennis was a member . . . quite lovely).

And then . . . then Melissa realized that some of her newlywed decisions had been extremely prescient (word of the day!). She had taken out a life insurance policy and, after they bought the apartment, mortgage insurance. Her life of poverty before Dennis had made her financially savvy, and she had planned carefully once the golden door was opened for her. She wasn't going to be one of those second wives who got nothing if Dennis died first (and he would, because he'd been twenty-nine years older than she was, though he never knew her real age).

Dennis didn't leave a will, which served Melissa quite well. Probate said she got the apartment, now fully paid for and worth somewhere in the realm of ten *million* dollars. Also, her lawyer informed her, because of the nonexistent will, Melissa got 50 percent of all his money and stock holdings, including his share of his orthopedic practice buyout, with Nick and Amanda dividing the other 50 percent.

His first wife . . . she got nothing.

Melissa was suddenly very, *very* wealthy. And, because she was *not* stupid, she invested most of that with a stodgy wealth management firm so it would keep earning her money. No spending spree (yet). She knew to take her time and reframe her life. From trophy wife to independently wealthy woman . . . not bad at all! (May you rest in peace, Dennis.) She would be a queen of New York. An important hostess, a charity maven, the head of many committees. Maybe she could get on the board of the Met and go to the gala and become friends with Rihanna! Wouldn't *that* make the other women in her circle jealous!

However, once the fuss over Dennis's death died down, Melissa's social status changed. She was a widow now. In other words, wife material. The book club and dinner invitations stopped. An older man had married Melissa, and she'd made him very happy. In other words, she could do it again. No taint of divorce, just a young, beautiful, wealthy widow. The quadruple threat.

⌒

One night a couple of months after Dennis's death, Melissa sat in their beautiful apartment and looked out at the city lights. She missed Dennis, the companionship, his good nature, the buffer with Ophelia. All the things they'd done together—Broadway shows, dinners out, charity events, running in the park, weekend brunches, even just watching a movie after Ophelia had gone to bed. Dennis had appreciated her, except for that short period when he was irritable and restless.

She missed being married.

A change was needed. She was only twenty-nine, a single mother, not that Ophelia would call her "Mom." She hadn't even given her a card on Mother's Day. Hadn't even drawn one. Dennis had given her flowers and perfume the past few years and signed the card from both of them. This year, the first without him, Ophelia hadn't done a thing.

New York, which had been so dazzling at first, was getting dull. Ophelia was silent and still cried at night as Melissa tried to make her feel better, stroking her mass of matted curls that no hairbrush could tame, trying not to let the child hear her sigh.

It was a real downer. And she was sitting on a *pile* of money. It might be time to move. Someplace where rich people lived, but also somewhere romantic. Palm Beach? Ugh. Florida's weather spared no one. Southern California, maybe? Except there were so many celebrities there, it would be hard to stand out. The Monterey Peninsula, where that TV show had been filmed? Maybe. California was intimidating, though. Earthquakes and wildfires, those whipping winds.

But the itch to move had taken root.

When summer vacation hit (her least favorite part of the year, with Ophelia flat-out refusing to go to sleepaway camp, no matter how posh), Melissa tried to book a house on Nantucket, where so many of the other families in their circle—their former circle—had homes. Unfortunately, there was nothing left, as all the really cool rental houses were solidly booked. Same with Martha's Vineyard.

Besides, those islands were glutted with the rich, important and famous, and the thought of bumping into Jennifer Lawrence or Michelle Obama made Melissa feel . . . ordinary. *She* wanted to be the star. *She* wanted to be the one people talked about. It had been the case for her six-year marriage in their wealthy little circle, and it had been so . . . *affirming* (word of the day!). Was it wrong to want that again? She didn't think so.

She found a lovely rental for a few weeks in August on Cape Cod, a place she had never been. The Outer Cape. It sounded so romantic . . . and it *was*. The wind gusted from every direction, howling in the chimney of their rented home. Melissa felt like she'd never seen a sunset before their first night there, watching the glorious colors linger for well over an hour after the sun sank into the sea. The ocean roared, and there were sharks, even! Seals popped up in the water, and a red fox trotted through their yard.

Even Ophelia couldn't pretend to be unhappy here.

Here, Melissa knew she'd stand out. She could be special in a way she couldn't in New York or Montecito. Her wealth, her good looks, her carefully modulated voice and bright white smile would make more of an impression here. On the Outer Cape, she'd be *seen*.

She'd buy a house—so affordable compared with those other places!—and maybe start a yoga studio. She'd give Ophelia a different kind of small-town life than the one they'd both had in Ohio, and a more relaxed, less competitive life than New York offered, because let's face it: The child didn't try too hard at anything.

And so she bought a house in Wellfleet, right there on the shore, dazzling and full of light; took Ophelia out of school and promised her a puppy. She took great pleasure in organizing the move . . . and also telling her former friends that she and Ophelia were tired of the grime and noise of the city, the *privilege* that put children so out of touch with the real world. Take that, book club that had stopped inviting her. Take that, orthopedists and their spouses who'd dropped her. Melissa felt as excited as she'd been that day long ago when the conference email had popped into her inbox.

The universe would take care of her. It always had.

All she needed now was a husband. And this time, *she*

would be in charge. No more flattery, no more doe-eyed gratitude. No. This time, *he* could worship *her*.

It was pathetically easy, and it happened even faster than she had imagined it would. The good old universe always had her back.

Maybe she had daddy issues, maybe she loved being in control of things, but she wanted another older man. Someone who would know how lucky he was. Someone who would be dazzled by not only her but her new lifestyle.

Men came in two categories, Melissa thought one day as she braced against the cold wind from her bedroom deck at Stella Maris. Cheaters, and non-cheaters. Non-cheaters were that rarest of mammals—the guy who'd met his wife, knew she was the one and never looked back. She'd known one couple like that—Dennis's partner Liv and her husband. Watching them had been like watching a documentary about a strange new species. They were the one couple in New York who'd seemed genuinely, safely in love.

And then there were the cheaters. Dennis, she imagined, had probably cheated on his ex-wife. Her father had cheated with that disgusting Loretta from the Dollar General (and got herpes as a parting gift). So many husbands in their circle back in the city had hit on her, asking for an afternoon at the W or Bryant Park Hotel.

Dennis had never cheated on her. Melissa knew this because she tracked him on his phone every single day, and he was always where he said he was. Besides, she made sure he didn't have reason to. In other words, she married money and earned every cent through frequent, dirty, porn-worthy sex (which she did enjoy) and being a Stepford wife. She hadn't realized how exhausting it had been—smiling, preening over him, complimenting him.

But it sure had been worth it, especially now, owning the most beautiful, expensive, expansive house in town, driving a new BMW, filling the house with white and blue furniture and subtle references to the ocean (the octopus coasters, the lobster throw pillow).

Dennis had been like college—working so hard for a goal. His death had been her graduation. Her *liberation*, even.

Melissa had been studying men since she was thirteen years old, had nabbed a rich husband with ease and managed to keep him more or less interested for *years* before his untimely death. If there were a degree in understanding men, she'd have a PhD. As for women, she understood that she was a threat to them, especially now. Oh, the women of Wellfleet she'd met so far had been pleasant. But there was an immediate wariness in addition to their interest—they were like a cat who hears an intruder in the garden, ears swiveling, whiskers twitching. There were surreptitious scans of her figure, especially in yoga class. They took note of her clothes, her jewelry, her car. When they found out she'd bought Stella Maris, their interest spiked. Stella Maris! That house had been on the market for months, thanks to its ridiculous price tag.

Who *was* this woman? They were dying to know, dying to categorize her.

Melissa just smiled and let them think whatever they wanted. From Ophelia's sixth-grade teacher to the interior decorator she'd hired to help furnish the house, she let them wonder.

People said money didn't buy happiness. People who said this didn't have money.

The first few weeks in the house with Ophelia were both trying and exhilarating. All the new things were like the best drugs on the planet—the furniture, the plates and glasses, the paintings, the rugs, the car . . . all bought from her own money. Gosh, it was the best! And no husband watching over her shoulder, tallying her receipts.

Even Ophelia's misery didn't touch Melissa's mood. The child still gave Melissa sullen glances and answered in grunts, no matter how wonderful this new change was.

Melissa pretended to relate, petting Ophelia's snarled hair and telling her she'd get over it, and did she want to fly over to Nantucket and go shopping? Ophelia just rolled over to face the wall of her beautiful new bedroom. Melissa had the decorator paint it pale blue (Ophelia had asked for purple, which was so *not* going to happen). It had a view (all the rooms did) and a queen-sized bed with the softest white sheets and comforter. Melissa filled Ophelia's bathroom with plush towels and delicious-smelling bath products from Nest—bamboo and jasmine body mist, body wash, body lotion, hand cream, scent diffuser, candles. She bought a special detangling conditioner and brush for Ophelia's difficult hair.

The kid had no right to be sulky. Still, Melissa knew she missed Dennis. And Melissa did, too, sort of. She missed regular sex. No matter how expensive the vibrator, it just wasn't the same. Ophelia needed a father figure. Melissa needed a man. A husband. She was far too classy to simply have a *lover*.

On a frigid February night, she left Ophelia with a babysitter, a nice high school girl named Sophie who'd been recommended by three people. Melissa was pleased to see the girl gaping at the house. "I've left you fifty dollars if you want to order food, Sophie," she said, smiling, loving her new role as beneficent (word of the day!) employer.

"Oh, wow! Thank you! That's more than enough, though."

"Well, keep the change, then. And twenty-five dollars an hour is enough? You're sure? Don't forget, I'm from New York. It doesn't seem like enough."

"Twenty-five dollars is amazing," said Sophie. "Seriously, call me anytime." She put her arm around Ophelia, who didn't protest.

"Okay, then." Melissa air-kissed Ophelia's hair, pretending not to notice when her niece pulled away, then walked toward the garage.

"Your mom is so beautiful," she heard the babysitter say.

"She's my *aunt*," Ophelia said.

"Oh. Well. Want to play a game?"

Sophie would be a wonderful babysitter, Melissa thought, especially with that amount of cash on the table, an easy enough child to care for, and this house to lounge around in. Maybe Melissa would give her some cast-off clothes or shoes. Make a real impression on the girl, because her Instagram account could use some teenage followers.

Melissa was not going to be one of those stuck-up rich people who treated the help like they were invisible, like those witches in New York who complained about the housekeeper right in front of her. Gosh, no. She'd be the nicest rich person this town had ever seen.

She got into her prewarmed car and drove off to the Ice House, where she'd had lunch with what's-her-name . . . Lucy? Lillie. Tonight, Lillie and her husband were officially welcoming her to Wellfleet. The restaurant was in the center of town, and she parked on the street right in front, then walked into the restaurant. She'd worn a new dress, a clingy black cashmere thing with a deep V neckline; a simple, perfect golden pearl pendant from Mikimoto; gold hoop earrings from Menē in her ears. A limited-edition Cartier wristwatch. Attico Anais pumps with a pop of hot-pink cutout leather and soft leather ties that wound around her ankles. Thigh-high sheer silk nylons. A creamy white cashmere coat, the same kind Meghan Markle had worn in last month's *Vanity Fair*. She'd given her straight hair a retro-Hollywood wave with a side part. Gucci matte red lipstick. Subtle eye shadow; eyelash extensions in a tasteful length, making her look blessed, not fake.

Going inside, Melissa immediately knew she was the best-dressed, best-looking woman here. She'd known that short, curvy, frizzy-haired what's-her-name wasn't in her league, but she felt triumphant just the same. Lillie. That was her name.

And there they were. Well, well, well.

He was *very* good-looking. Blond hair, a neat beard, tall and slender.

"Melissa, hello," Lillie said, giving her a hug. "This is my husband, Brad Fairchild."

"So nice to meet you," Melissa said smoothly. His eyes were *incredibly* blue. She offered her hand, and Brad Fairchild's face flushed. His pupils dilated and he held her hand firmly upon introductions and for just a second too long.

Wellfleet had just become a little more interesting.

And Lillie, the midwife or massage therapist or something, didn't even try, did she? Here she was, *knowingly* taking her husband out to dinner to meet Melissa, and she wore brown pants (pants!) and a roomy yellow sweater. She didn't even have earrings on, and her hair looked like she'd hung her head out the window all the way here, like a dog.

"So lovely of you to invite me for dinner, Lillie, Brad. Thank you. The move has been wonderful, just what Ophelia and I needed, but gosh, I think I need some adult friends around here." She smiled broadly with a little head tilt.

"It's our pleasure," Lillie said, leading the way to their table. Melissa followed, feeling Brad's eyes on her. She was glad she'd worn a clingy dress.

Throughout the dinner, Melissa answered questions and asked about their son (yawn). Lillie, smug and secure in her marriage, did what so many first wives did: She looked at Brad like he was on her . . . her bowling team or something. There was absolutely no chemistry between them. And when Brad mentioned his book, Lillie gave her a little smile and sipped her wine. Yes, the book sounded on the ridiculous side, but Melissa knew how to look fascinated. She'd had years of practice, after all, listening to Dennis praise himself.

Within fifteen minutes, Melissa knew she could see what Lillie didn't know.

Brad was afraid.

So many middle-aged men hit a certain landmark birthday and became abruptly terrified that their youth was behind them (because it was). They were suddenly invisible to college-age girls. The barista didn't flirt with them any-more, didn't even remember their names. Those youngsters they worked with and supervised were surpassing them. Their potbellies and reluctant erections were a sign that youth was coming to an end. Their children were grown, lives ahead of them, and these men were jealous . . . jealous that their kids had so many chances middle-aged men no longer had. What did they have to look forward to? An en-larged prostate and a brain aneurysm?

Dennis had been easy to get. Brad . . . it would be like a hot knife through soft butter.

First step, call him by his whole name, as if it's far too important to shorten.

Second step, awe and wonder at his accomplishments. "Oh, wow, a therapist. I've been thinking of getting my master's in counseling, believe it or not." Then, later, "I can't wait to read your book!" She took her phone out of her purse. "There. I just ordered it."

Third step (new for Melissa), befriend the wife. "Oh, Lillie, what an amazing job you have. Did you always want to be a nurse? Sorry, nurse-midwife?" It would be easier to evaluate Bradley if Lillie were friendly and unsuspecting.

Meanwhile, Bradley fell under her spell. He was quite handsome, well educated, and he looked at her as if she were a new planet, beautiful and fascinating, like nothing he had ever seen. All while Lillie sat there, blissfully ignorant.

There weren't a whole lot of men to choose from up here. She didn't want a laborer—her landscaper had been quite attractive, but he was too close to her age, and be-sides, he loved his wife and had six children. The second selectman had obviously been interested, but he was on his third wife, so no, thanks.

Brad—Bradley—was handsome in that pretty-boy, Ralph Lauren way. He had a soft voice that made her lean forward a little as he commended her on taking in her niece and asked her about life in New York. His hair was still fairly thick, and the gray made him look distinguished.

And his eyes . . . his eyes were nearly turquoise, and utterly unguarded.

How would he be in bed? It didn't matter. She could teach him.

Meanwhile, she made sure not to exclude Lillie.

Lillie had been quite nice to her. Had welcomed her with flowers when she and Ophelia moved in, as well as a home-made cake that Ophelia said was delicious (Melissa didn't do carbs, and certainly not desserts). Lillie had put her in touch with every person she could need, from the girl currently babysitting Ophelia to a cleaning service.

But that didn't matter. Bradley was a cheater waiting to happen. As he talked about his book, his education, slipping in mentions of his Beacon Hill childhood and boarding school days, Melissa knew he hadn't had a woman this interested in him in a long time. He asked her about herself, and she glossed over her interest in becoming a therapist (she was actually accruing quite a few Instagram followers and was leaning toward becoming an influencer).

"I thought you were opening a yoga studio," Lillie said.

"Well, I was, but there do seem to be a few around here. Do you practice yoga, Lillie?"

"Well, I take classes. And I do love it."

"Really!" Because you sure couldn't tell, looking at that round little body. "We should take a class together sometime, if you don't mind. You can tell me who the best teachers are. Go easy on me, okay? The most exercise I've done this year is unpack boxes." A lie, of course, but they laughed merrily.

Bradley (and Lillie, she supposed) wanted to know all about Ophelia, and Melissa spun her as a smart, brave kid who'd had a rough time of things, rather than the petulant, irritating, ungrateful tween she was. She told them Dennis had been the love of her life, and she was still grieving, of course. "I just keep putting one foot in front of the other, as they say," she said. "But really, my focus is on Ophelia.

Dennis was the only father she ever knew." More murmurs of sympathy and praise. This was fun!

By the time dessert was served (to Lillie), Bradley had invited her to visit his office so they could talk about the different types of therapists. Lillie finished her entire crème brûlée, set up a date for them to take yoga and told her she should join the Wellfleet Cultural Council, since Melissa had said how interested she was in the arts.

All the while, the poor chubby woman didn't realize her marriage was about to crash.

Bradley was distinguished by nature of his good looks, advanced degrees and wealthy parents. He stood to inherit a beautiful home on Beacon Hill, but from what Melissa could glean (which was a lot), they were solidly middle class. Rich parents were just extra. She didn't *need* his money. He would be so grateful to her as she freed him from a stale marriage and granted him the opportunity to be with her—sixteen years younger (practically the same age when compared to Dennis). A beautiful woman, independently wealthy, sexy as JLo but without all those divorces. Melissa didn't need to be a trophy wife. Now she could choose a man who interested *her*, who thought *she* was amazing. Someone who'd be *her* arm candy, but someone with class, too.

They would be *such* a great couple. The couple everyone would want to have over for dinner, the couple who could endow town projects and support local galleries and throw fundraisers at her *incredible* house. A prenup, of course. Unlike New York, Cape Cod was a place where Melissa would be someone of great importance.

Not bad for a hillbilly graduate from a little Christian college.

It was pathetically easy. She went to see him at his office two days later. He invited her to lunch, which lasted for four hours. Two nights later, she texted him and they met for lunch again. Oh, it was easy. "You look tired, Bradley," she said at the restaurant. "Is everything okay? I know we just became friends, but you seem a little . . . sad."

She led him down his already forged path of middle-aged discontentment, seeding in a few lines about how consuming Lillie's work must be, how it could be hard to be with a woman who was so focused on other women, who lost herself once she became a mother. Once they had sex, it was a done deal, and a month after they'd met, Bradley informed her he'd be leaving his wife when their son went to college.

Bing, bang, boom.

CHAPTER 9

Lillie

The thing about divorce is that it shatters your family. It breaks everything you thought you knew and affects everyone in your radius.

Two weeks after our son landed in Montana, Brad and I set up a Zoom call with Dylan. I let Brad do the talking, turning off the computer camera to wipe away tears so my son wouldn't see.

"Mom and I will always love each other," Brad lied, "and we have absolutely loved raising you. But our paths are diverging now, and we're finding our joy separately."

"What the *fuck* does that mean?" Dylan asked, also crying. After a few minutes of snarling at his father, he said, "Mom? What happened?"

I couldn't lie to my son. "Well . . . this has come as a total surprise to me, honey. But I'll be okay. I'm fine. I'm sorry, honey."

"*You* have nothing to be sorry for. Dad, I can't believe you're such an idiot! You'll never find anyone like Mom!"

"Now, son," Brad said. "People get divorced all the time. Your mother and I have had a great marriage, but it's simply time to start a new journey. We have different needs and hopes."

"Is there someone else, Dad? Is that it?"

It was gratifying to see Brad's face flush with shame. "Your mother and I have been growing apart for a while, Dylan. That's all."

Liar.

"You're an asshole, Dad," Dylan said, and left the call.

Since then, he'd called every day, sometimes crying to me on the phone because he couldn't believe what his father had done, sometimes barely speaking.

I understood. Our wonderful boy had been thrust into the ugly task of reenvisioning his father, his family, and home.

"I'm actually *glad* to be so far away," he said one night, his voice bitter. "I can't imagine home without Dad. And I hate him at the same time. I can't wrap my head around this, Mom! No more family game nights? What about Thanksgiving? What about Christmas?"

Oh, God. Dylan would probably have to split holidays. Or would he? He was eighteen. He could choose, right? "I don't know, sweetheart. I know it seems like a disaster right now, but we'll get through it."

"I don't *want* to get through it! Why did Dad leave you? Did you do something?"

I hadn't expected that, and felt a gut punch. "No! I just . . . No. I had no idea he wasn't happy."

"He sure seemed happy."

"I know."

"It's not fair!"

I closed my eyes, his voice tearing my heart in half. "I don't know what to tell you, honey."

"I'm sorry, Mom. I know this is worse for you."

My sweet, sweet boy. "You're allowed to feel angry and sad and anything else, Dylan. We're in this together, okay? You can always talk to me. You'll always be my first priority. That will never change."

Dylan hadn't called his father since the Zoom call, and

Brad didn't want to talk to Dylan when our son was angry. Brad wanted him to be *happy* about this. For a therapist, he had no clue about the human soul.

A few days after we dropped that bomb, I was heading home from Hyannis Hospital after a long night. The mama, who hadn't been my patient for prenatal care, had been stunned by the force of the contractions and begged for an epidural, which was fine . . . unmedicated birth was not appropriate in every case. After two hours of pushing, her baby boy had been born, healthy and robust, and she nursed him right away, smitten and amazed.

Thinking about them made going home to an empty house that much worse. For the first time in my life, I was lonely . . . and a little scared. With a sigh, I got in my car anyway and headed for Wellfleet.

About ten years ago, a guy had gone missing around the kettle ponds. A young man, Matthew Dudek, age thirty-four. His car was found parked on Old Hay Road, empty, no signs of foul play or struggle. His family, who lived in Peabody, had reported him missing when he didn't come home from the Cape. The police had gone all out, canvassing the houses of all of us who lived in the area. Volunteers—myself included—had done a grid search, lines of us walking carefully through the woods, looking for any trace of him . . . a backpack, a sneaker. They dragged the ponds twice and waited to see if his body would rise, as most drowned bodies do.

He was gone without a trace.

I cried so hard when they gave up the search. Maybe because I was a mother to a boy, maybe it was because it was so close to home, but I couldn't stop thinking about him. I didn't let Dylan, then eight, out of my sight for the next six months. From then on, every time I took a walk, I automatically looked for a sign of Matthew Dudek.

Now, it could be that he just ran away from his old life, because it wasn't like the terrain was rough around here. Could be he drowned and his body got stuck under the water. It was unlikely, but there'd been a similar case in Connecticut where a child's bones had been recovered from a lake after more than fifty years. It could be that Matthew Dudek walked to the ocean and drowned there, in which case his body might never be found. Could be he was an addict and overdosed out in the woods, and his remains were still out there but no police dog ever found him.

Living alone in my house for the first time in my life, I thought of Matthew far too much. My beloved woods seemed a little . . . sinister, and I could not let that happen.

On impulse, I pulled off at the next exit, got on Route 6 West, went back to Hyannis and headed for the Cape Cod Animal Shelter. It was time to look for my four-legged friend.

"Lillie?" came a voice as I went in.

"Poppy!" I said, instantly becoming my midwife self. "How are you? How are the girls?"

"I'm great! We're great," she said. "Want to see a picture?"

"You know I do." She pulled out her phone, and I was treated to pictures of her two little girls, both of whom I'd delivered.

"Gosh, they're beautiful," I said. My eyes were a little teary. They were four and two now, that sweet age when they can talk and express themselves but still think you're the best human on the planet.

"How are you, Lillie?"

"My husband left me for another woman," I said. Oops. Hadn't meant to tell the truth.

She looked at my face. "Holy crap," she said. "What an asshole."

"Thank you," I said.

"You here for a dog?"

Sounded good to me. "Maybe," I said.

"They're better than men anyway." She smiled.

"I believe you."

"Okay," Poppy said, "usually we do a lot of paperwork

and ask for references, but I know you and I trust you with my life. I actually *did* trust you with my life, and my babies' lives, so you get to cut to the front of the line. What are you looking for?"

"Oh . . . maybe a dog who can tolerate being alone for a good chunk of time? I can put in a dog door, but my hours are unpredictable."

"Totally understand. Come on in and see what we've got."

We went into the kennel part of the building, and Poppy described each dog to me. "This guy here is a pit bull, very sweet. Still a puppy, though, and they need 24/7 attention. This pretty girl has way too much energy . . . probably needs a family with kids, but you're a beautiful girl, aren't you?" She was—part border collie, part black Lab. "Don't worry, she'll go fast. Oh, okay! How about this big guy? He's part Dalmatian, as you can tell, part bloodhound, part Labrador, maybe part Great Dane. Super mutt, right, Zeus?"

Zeus was lying on the floor. He lifted his head to look at me, and on his nose were two spots, coming together to look like a heart. There was a big patch of black over his right eye, and my heart swelled. His tail thumped on the floor, and he seemed to smile, his doggy cheeks crinkling, but he didn't get up.

"He's a little lazy," Poppy said. "He sleeps about twenty hours a day, don't you, buddy? He might work for you. He's been here awhile because of his size. He weighs ninety pounds."

I had a vision of this rather gigantic dog lying on my big bed at home, or in front of the fireplace. Yeah. I wanted a pet of substance. Maybe I could train Zeus to protect me. It was a nice thought—Brad coming back, this dog with the heart on his nose savagely chewing off his arm.

That happy image sealed the deal. "I'll take him," I said. "If I can."

"You absolutely can," Poppy said. "That stupid husband of yours. Why are men like that?"

"How's yours, by the way?" I asked.

"Oh, he's wonderful," she said, her face melting at the thought of him. "He'll be so glad I ran into you." She opened the kennel, and Zeus leaped up, suddenly energized. I knelt, and he licked my face with great enthusiasm, his backside swaying with the force of his wags. His ears were silky and his muzzle was velvet.

We were in love.

Zeus was three years old; his head was as hard and square as a concrete block. His coat was silky and short, and I was fairly sure I could ride him, since he came up to my hip. That tail could leave welts, I thought as I let him into my car, but hey. Death by tail wags was not a bad way to go.

I stopped at Petco and bought an invisible fence system, a red leash and collar, dog food, dog treats, dog shampoo, a dog bed and a brush, which I tested on him, since they allowed doggies in the store. He crooned when I ran the brush down his back, and I couldn't help smiling.

"Sit, Zeus," I said, and he did! Brilliant dog! I took a picture, texted it to Dylan with the words You have a new brother. Meet Zeus. I got him today from the shelter and he's the new love of my life.

A second later, his answer came. Wow! He's awesome, Mom! Can't wait to meet him at Christmas!

Four long months away. But you know what? My son sounded delighted, and the dog was so cute, smiling away at everyone who passed, wagging and wagging. Today was my lucky (if expensive) day. But I knew Zeus would be worth it.

"Right, boy?" I asked, bending over.

He agreed, licking my face, and we went to the front of the store to pay for all his stuff.

∽

Three days later, Zeus lay sprawled on the couch, taking up most of it, his head in Beth's lap as she stroked his ears while I took a tray of stuffed clams out of the oven. She might have a five-star rating on Yelp, but she loved my food. Wanda was here as well—my two closest friends.

"Who's a beautiful boy?" Wanda crooned. "You are, Zeus. Yes, you are!" His tail thumped in agreement.

"God, it's so nice not to cook," Beth called. "Thanks for having us over. Do you mind passing me some clams? I'd do it myself, but I can't disturb this handsome guy."

"I understand," I said. "Plus, he just got a bath, so he's extra silky." I served the clams out with little plates and forks, refilled Beth's wineglass—Wanda was on call tonight—and topped off my own.

"How's Dylan?" Wanda asked.

"Struggling. Brad is insisting—" At that moment, the phone rang. I looked at it, my mood falling. "Speak of the devil, and the devil appears."

"Ooh, answer it," Beth said. "Put him on speaker. We want to hear his New Age language."

I obeyed. "What?" I demanded. He still had belongings here, and the divorce agreement said he had six months to come get them before I could set them on fire, or sell them, or give his precious leather jacket, bought after the "launch" of his book, to a homeless person.

"Lillie, hello. How *are* you?" he asked.

Wanda's face scrunched in horror at his sappy tone, and Beth mimicked throwing up.

"None of your business," I said. "What do you want?"

"Can you say something to Dylan? He's really shut down about Melissa."

"Yeah. Because she ruined our family. You and she killed our son's family. Of course he's shut down."

"You're not helping, Lillie," Brad said. "She's a kind woman."

Wanda raised her hands in incredulity while Beth silently gave him the finger.

"Brad, tell me, how does a kind woman justify stealing someone else's husband and causing a boy to lose respect for his father? She's a mother, isn't she? Wouldn't it bother her if someone ruined her daughter's family?"

"Ophelia is her niece," Brad said, unperturbed. "She took her in because Ophelia's mother has narcotics abuse disorder. Melissa is incredibly generous, and so good-hearted. Really, Lillie. You'll love her once you get to know her better."

Beth mimicked cocking a shotgun.

"No, Brad! I won't! I hate her."

"I'm sorry to hear that," my ex-husband said. "Hatred is so corrosive, and the only true victim is you. You could look at this a different way, Lillie. We could all be friends."

I muted myself. "See what I have to put up with? I think he has a brain tumor." I tapped the phone so he could hear me. "We're not gonna hang out and drink wine, Brad. She is an adulterous slut who ruined our marriage."

"Can any outsider really do that?" Brad speculated.

"Let me rephrase. *You* are an adulterous slut who ruined our marriage."

"Lillie. This anger won't serve you. It is what it is. I hope you can come to see that for yourself, and that we can all be friends someday. I want us to stay a family. It just looks different now."

"Save me, Jesus," Wanda muttered.

"I will never be your friend, and you are out of my family," I said. "I wish nothing but the worst for you. You hurt my son. You broke his heart. For the rest of your life, the mother of your only child will hate and resent you."

"I'm so sorry you feel that way," he said. "Maybe someday—"

I hung up.

"Unbelievable," Beth said.

"The worst part," I said, "is that somehow *I'm* the damaged goods here. The aging wife who couldn't keep her husband."

"It's true," Beth said. "You're pathetic, am I right, Wanda?"

"Well . . ." Wanda was my sweeter friend, obviously. She took another clam and ate it delicately. "These are amazing."

"The thing is," Beth said, "this happens all the time. The Temples? Kate just told me she's moving to Arizona and hasn't spoken to Robbie in *years*. And the Carsons. They've been married for forty-five years, and he left her for a Russian college student who works at Ben and Jerry's. You can't make this shit up. It's a pandemic. Zeus, my leg is numb, honey. Your head must weigh thirty pounds. Off you go." He obeyed sadly, gazed longingly at Wanda, who shook her head firmly, and reluctantly collapsed into his new doggy bed.

"Fill me in on what people are saying, you two," I said. "Between the two of you, you know everything."

"This is true," Wanda murmured. "I'm hearing a lot of sympathy for you, Lillie, a lot of shock. No one suspected your marriage was—"

"Fragile? Built on sand? A lie?" I suggested.

"Yeah," she said.

"They're getting around, Lils," Beth said. "Eating out at least a couple times a week. She's donating buckets of money and just employed, like, eight people to clean, cut the lawn, service the car, do handyman stuff, all that. Get this. Reverend White just asked her to serve on the vestry after she paid to have the bell tower repaired."

"Who looks after that poor kid when they're out buying friends?" I asked.

"Right now, Sophie Lynch, but rumor has it they're getting an au pair from France."

"I hope Brad sleeps with the au pair," I said. "No. I hope Melissa sleeps with the au pair."

Beth snorted and Wanda clinked her glass against mine.

"Seriously," I went on. "Why can't they move? Do they have to live in my hometown? Do they have to live, period? Can't there be, I don't know, a tidal wave that hits their house, and their house only, when Ophelia's in school? Or a shark attack when they're frisking in the water?"

"So this is your last glass of wine," Wanda said, "and you know shark attacks are extremely rare on the Cape."

"Brad hasn't turned off Find My Phone, so I can track him. I may slash their tires the next time they eat out."

Beth nodded. "Just make sure it's really dark, and wear a baseball cap. Security cameras are everywhere these days, you know?"

"Well, I have to get going," Wanda said, snagging one last clam. "Leila has a shoot tomorrow in Boston at the ass-crack of dawn, and Addo told me it's my turn. The good news is, the child will be able to pay for college. This modeling thing is crazy."

"Give her a kiss from me," I said. "Remind her that I loved her when she was a squishy-faced little baby, long before Gucci was calling."

Beth left, too, and I cleaned up the paltry mess. The quiet of the house pressed down on me. I could count on one hand how many times I'd been alone in this house before Brad left. He'd always hated visiting his parents without me, and taking Dylan camping or the like? Nah. Brad wasn't the outdoorsy type. That was more me.

I went upstairs to Dylan's room, Zeus following me. In a rare hour of domesticity, Dylan had cleaned his room the day before he left, so it was neat and tidy . . . and strange. But it still smelled like him. I lay on his bed, and the dog jumped up next to me and put his head on my stomach.

"You're a good boy, Zeus," I said, wiping a tear from my eyes. Christmas couldn't come soon enough. Dylan wasn't coming home for Thanksgiving—too far, too expensive, too short a break, too crazy to travel that weekend. A "cute girl" had invited him to come to her parents' home in Helena for that holiday, only two hours away. I was glad. I'd get her address and send them some bola de carne, which Dyllie loved. Meat-stuffed bread.

A rather large nose nudged my hand. This dog was already worth his weight in diamonds. "Who's a good boy?" I asked, and his tail wagged. "Yes. You are correct. It's you, Zeus."

I got up and wandered through the house some more. Should I paint it and change it up a bit? Should I get a room-mate? Because this being alone, even with a giant doggy, was tough. Especially picturing *them*, across town, gazing out at the stars and bay, cooing psycho-yoga-babble at each other.

The debt on this house was terrifying. I made about $80,000 a year, and Brad made about the same. We—I— had the mortgage *and* the home equity line of credit, which had paid for our renovations throughout the years and covered a portion of Dylan's tuition. I still had student loans. My car had 130,000 miles on it and was going strong, but soon, that would change.

I could sell this place for well over two million dollars. I didn't want to, but I could.

"We're not going anywhere, buddy," I told my dog. "We are staying right here." He pushed his nose against me and flopped down at my feet.

It was going to be a long night.

⌒

I had Friday off, so after I took Zeus for a lengthy walk all the way to the ocean and back, cleaned the house and made some fish stock, then drove to Provincetown. The harbor-master waved to me as I drove to where the fishermen parked. Sure enough, the *Goody Chapman* was out, but it was afternoon, and I could wait.

The working end of MacMillan's Wharf was one of my favorite places. Unlike my sister, I loved the smell of raw fish, diesel fuel and salt water. I loved knowing every boat in the fleet by its silhouette, loved the rough wood and tac-iturn fishermen and women. I loved the creak and groan of the boats when they moored, the clank of the ropes against masts, the noise and music of Provincetown coming in little gusts on the wind.

Today was that perfect Cape Cod day of the deepest blue sky you could imagine. Seagulls hovered and cried, gliding, waiting for someone to unload their catch or throw unused bait into the water. Tourists came to take pictures of the fleet, charmed to see how their expensive meals got from the ocean to their plates.

"Those people pay for the roof over your head," Dad used to tell Hannah and me. "Be respectful."

And so, when someone asked a question, I'd answer, an informal, unpaid tour guide, talking about the different kinds of boats, the fish they brought in, the Portuguese heritage in the fleet. Yes, I was the daughter of a captain. No, I wasn't a fisherman myself. Yes, I was Portuguese, and yes, I could recommend some great places to eat.

I sat on the rough edge of the wharf, my feet dangling over the side. When I was a kid, I'd jump in for a swim at high tide. Sometimes the tourists would throw us quarters, and we'd swim down and catch them—me, Maria, Dante, some of the other kids of the fleet. We'd gather without hesitation, play for a day, not see each other for a month, and pick right up where we'd left off, comfortable in the familiarity of a shared place, of being from here.

I missed those days.

Sunsets on the Cape lasted for hours, the sky becoming increasingly beautiful. The air turned almost liquid with golden light, and a person couldn't help feeling that . . . I don't know. That God loved them, because there were sunsets like this. Skies like this, with clouds and changing colors and the sounds of piping plovers, cormorants and gulls. How Dylan loved coming here, watching his grandfather bring the *Goody Chapman* home. How proud he was to be the grandson of a fisherman.

I heard the *Goody Chapman* before I saw her. She came around the breakwater, and there was Dad, standing at the wheel, just like old times, Ben Hallowell next to him, leaning on the gunwale. Ben was like a son to my father, I supposed. Even after the accident.

I stood at their slip. Ben tossed me a heavy rope, and I automatically looped it over the piling.

"Hey, Squash," my father said. Nothing like a childhood nickname to keep you humble. Dad had told me a thousand times that my head had been shaped like a squash when I was born, thanks to Mom's long and torturous labor. Molding was the medical term, but I kind of liked squash-head, personally.

"Hi, Daddy."

"Lillie," said Ben, jerking his chin at me.

"Hey, Ben."

He got off first, secured another line, then looked at me. This, I can assure you, was a rare event. His blue eyes slanted down at the outer corners, and his face was lined from twenty-five years at sea. He wore a T-shirt and the coveralls that all fishermen wore, and the effect was working-class hottie. Always had been. "Heard your husband left you," he said.

"Thanks for bringing it up." I tucked some hair behind my ear.

"He's an idiot," Ben said.

"Yes."

And that was that.

"Wanna grab dinnah?" Dad asked. "We're stahvin'." Yes, I had a Cape accent, too, but it was tempered with Mom's prep school / Vassar accent. Sometimes I played it up to annoy her.

"Sure," I said. They'd talk about scallops and weather, and it would kill time before I had to go home. I'd fed Zeus early. "Hey, Dad, I got a dog. Think you can put in a dog door this weekend?"

"Sure thing, hon."

Dad. He was the best. He hadn't seen Brad since the weasel had moved in with Melissa, but I had no doubt that my father would do a great job defending my honor and making Brad pee himself in terror. Dad had a gift that way. Since he hardly ever spoke, his yelling was quite . . . impactful.

I helped the guys off-load the catch and tidy up the boat.

Then we walked down the wharf to the intersection, where a cop directed traffic with some dance moves. We went into the Governor Bradford, a sticky, grubby place with pool tables and cheap beer and damn good food, one of the last townie strongholds.

"Do you have a reservation, sir?" asked a large, tattooed man at the door.

"Go fuck yourself," my dad said fondly. "How you doin', Danny?"

"Not bad, can't complain. Ben. Three of you tonight?"

"You remember my daughter," Dad said.

"Hey, pretty lady," Danny said.

"Hi, Danny," I said. It had been a while since I'd been here. Most of the time I ate in Provincetown with the Moms, and we usually went out to somewhere with six-page wine lists and tiny appetizers, or ate in. Always a tense affair, and always worse if Hannah was there, speaking French with Beatrice.

We ordered beers and sat in silence for a few minutes, sipping, watching the pool game in progress. Dad and Ben nodded hello to a few people.

"Having a bad day?" Dad asked finally.

"Every day is pretty bad this summer," I said.

"Ben, we can make a guy disappear, can't we?" Dad asked.

Ben, sitting across from me, grinned slightly, one side of his mouth moving, his eyes crinkling. "Sure can."

"Don't tempt me, guys," I said. "Though yes, I'd be a lot better off as a widow." It was definitely not the first time I'd had that thought, and it wouldn't be the last. Dead Brad would at least have left me some money through life insurance. Dead Brad could have remained untainted.

"So what happened?" Ben asked, surprising me. The four sentences he'd said to me so far were more than he'd said to me in the past twenty-five years.

"I'm sure my father has told you."

"Nope."

I looked at my father. "Not my news to share," he said with a shrug.

"He left me for another woman. Sixteen years younger. She's filthy rich. And blond. And very limber, he tells me, because she is a practitioner of yoga." I had nothing against yoga, but thinking of Melissa in twisty poses made me seethe. I just knew she was great at it. No falling out of poses for her.

"Wow," Ben said. "Sorry."

"Thanks. I thought we were happy, but we weren't, apparently. According to Brad, I was a shitty wife for years." I took a slug of my beer. "You left your wife, Ben. Tell me why men pull these stunts."

Ben and my father exchanged a look.

"Dad, you're *my* father. Don't do all this silent male 'is she crazy?' communication."

"I think I'll move in with you," Dad said. "You could use the company."

I mock shuddered. "That's why I got a dog, Dad. Besides, you and I lived together for ten years, just the two of us. That's enough, don't you think?"

"Happiest years of my life," he said, winking. "Then she had to go to college, Ben, get married and ruin my life."

"Kids. So ungrateful," Ben said.

"How's your daughter, by the way?" I asked.

He glanced at me, seemed to assess his answer, then took a swig of beer. "Fine."

You'd never know that Ben and I had known each other for, oh, thirty years, that he was Dad's surrogate son, that he'd eaten at our house at least once a week when I was a kid. Or that we'd been in a horrible accident together. That might have bonded some people. Not us.

Our food arrived, and I fell on my fried calamari like a ravenous shark, and we didn't talk much till we were done. Dad and I played a round of pool (I won), and Ben talked with some guys at the bar.

"Walk my daughter to her car," Dad instructed Ben.

"I'm gonna have another beer and talk to Danny. He owes me money."

"I don't need a chaperone in Provincetown, for God's sake," I said. It truly was one of the safest places in America.

"Walk my baby to her car, Ben."

"Okay. Thanks for the help today," Ben said.

"Bye, Daddy," I said. "Thanks for dinner."

"Thank Ben. He paid."

"Thanks, Ben. I don't need you to walk me to my car," I said. "It's not even a thousand feet away."

"I have my orders," he said.

"My father is still the captain, eh?"

"Absolutely."

It was more crowded now that darkness had fallen. Lots of happy people, lots of couples, gay and straight. Cars inched down Commercial Street, the cheerful neon of the Lobster Pot sign bathing everything in red light. Folks were sitting on the anchor, eating ice cream cones, or standing in line to get lobster rolls or hot dogs.

Once we got out on the wharf, the crowd cleared, as the recreational boats were in for the night. We passed the gangplanks for the whale-watching boats, the big wooden sailboat that took tourists out at sunset. There was the storefront where the *Whydah* museum had been. The *Whydah* was the only pirate ship ever recovered from the deep. A wicked-cool find. Dylan used to be terrified to go in there; they'd recovered some bones from the ship, and the image of them sitting in a fish tank had given him nightmares for months.

I wondered how he was sleeping these days. It was so hard not to know.

Then we were in fisherman's territory, and there was virtually no one, aside from the harbormaster inside his office.

My car was just beyond. "Thanks again," I said.

"No problem." Ben watched me open the door, as if

there might be a kidnapper lurking in the back. "By the way, she left me."

"Who?"

"Cara."

His wife. "Oh." Rumor had been that he'd cheated on her, which, given his tawdry escapades as a youth, was easy to believe.

"No cheating involved."

"Sorry, Ben. I thought . . . Well."

He gave a nod, then turned away.

Divorce bonding over.

As I drove back to Wellfleet, though, it was nice to think about someone else's marriage. Cara and Ben had been high school sweethearts, married in their early twenties, sometime after the accident. I wondered if she'd found someone else, too, or if she'd just gotten bored, or if Ben was a raging alcoholic or a bully. He didn't seem to be. *I'd* never seen him drunk, anyway.

In a way, it was comforting, knowing that someone else, someone who'd once been so in demand as Ben, could be left, too. That it wasn't just me. Besides, the idea of Ben suffering a little . . . it made a small, ugly spot on my heart flare with a malevolent glow. My father had never blamed Ben for what happened to me, for what he'd taken from me, accident or not. It bothered me that my father had never said a bad word against the man who'd caused me to lose a spleen and break so many bones and, worst of all, scar my uterus so badly that the poor thing couldn't hold my tiny daughter inside.

It wasn't fair to blame Ben for that. I did anyway.

CHAPTER 10

Lillie

When I was seventeen, I was already aware of Ben Hallowell. Not in a good way.

Ben was four years older than I was, which, at that time of life, made him practically a different generation. He was from Brewster, so we didn't go to elementary school together, and by the time I started at Nauset Regional High School, Ben had already graduated. But he had played soccer the year Nauset won the state championship, scoring both goals, and his fame still lingered in our hallways.

His father had been a fisherman, like mine, but Mr. Hallowell had died at sea, gone overboard Ben's senior year, and his body was never found. Suicide, maybe, or just bad weather and bad luck. Ben started crewing for my father after that. This made me a little bit of a celebrity in high school—yes, he'd had dinner at my house. Yes, I spoke to him from time to time. Yes, he worked for my dad.

But there was something I didn't trust about him. As my grandmother would have said, he had pulga atrás da orelha—"a flea behind his ear," meaning (for some unknown reason) that he looked . . . guilty. No, not guilty. More like he was plotting to do something illegal, and he couldn't wait to do it. A secret smile, those downward-slanting, dark blue eyes. "You just know he's an amazing kisser," Beth had whispered one night during a sleepover. Ben had come for dinner, and Beth had blushed and blushed. "You can tell."

"How?" I asked, still innocent thanks to my father's overprotective ways.

"He's . . . I don't know." Beth was more experienced, though she had not yet gone all the way with her boyfriend. "You can just tell he knows what to do. A bad boy in all the right ways."

"Oh." I had no idea what she meant, but yeah, I knew the stories. He had a past. Once, he allegedly broke into the high school at night and trashed the science lab. He'd had a fake ID when he was sixteen; he drove way too fast in his beater pickup. He always had weed, it was rumored, and this was long before it was legal in our state.

I knew women liked him, because I saw him in action. Ben Hallowell always had a sly smile for the female tourists who would walk out on MacMillan's Wharf, eager to catch a glimpse of a real fisherman. He'd flirt from the deck of my father's boat as they unloaded their catch. He might take off his shirt to thrill them, and he was lean and muscled and tan, a great advertisement for reasons to come to Cape Cod. Sometimes, the girls would wait for him to jump onto the dock, and they'd walk off to a bar or an alley and do God knows what.

He wasn't exactly good-looking—sandy-brown hair, a slightly crooked nose from a fistfight, and an upper lip that stuck out just a little over his bottom lip. To me, he always looked a little sulky, a little broody. But when he smiled, the pheromone storm could be felt for miles. Even I, a virgin, felt it, and knew without being told that he was off-limits for a number of reasons. He was too old for me. He'd gotten around plenty. He worked for my dad. He had a girlfriend.

But now that Beth had opened that Pandora's box of

imagination, I knew she was right. Ben Hallowell would be incredible in bed, doing things to you that you didn't know existed.

He was, of course, perfectly respectable around me. I was the daughter of his boss. He flirted with Hannah quite a bit when their paths crossed; they were the same age and had both worked at the Cooke's Seafood in Orleans for a couple of summers. There was an affection there, and Hannah flirted back, much to my surprise. Then again, Beatrice had probably taught her how. Hannah had become quite sophisticated, living with the Moms, and I resented it.

On the other hand, I was completely invisible to our resident hottie fisherman. When Ben came to our house for dinner every month or so, he would say "hi" and "thanks" and "bye." The flea-behind-the-ear feeling didn't dissipate, even with my father there. I often cooked dinner, simply because I loved to, even back then. Ben would eat the meal and talk to my father, barely glancing my way. He and Dad would talk about the ocean, the market for scallops, the *Goody Chapman*, the weather. If my dad left the room, Ben said nothing to me.

Ben's girlfriend, Cara, was studying to be a dental hygienist at Cape Cod Community College, or 4Cs, as we called it. Chances were high they'd get married, and soon . . . it was the Cape Cod way. You either stayed and worked in some kind of blue-collar or service job—fishing, construction, landscaping, hospitality and restaurants—or left for college, possibly to return, but most likely not.

There just wasn't a lot of work out here. The hospital was the area's biggest employer. The cost of living rose every year, and it was tough to make ends meet without a higher education or an inheritance or trust fund (and sure, we had those kids, too). If you stayed, you sucked it up and did your best to afford a little house . . . like Brad and I had.

Cara was beautiful and nice; Ben brought her to dinner once at Dad's request, and I immediately liked her. She asked questions about my school and hobbies, unlike either man at the table—even my father was surprised to learn I was taking AP Chem. Cara was tall with red hair, clear green eyes and pale, lightly freckled skin. I felt like a peasant compared with her—my childbearing hips and significant boobage; thick, frizzy black hair; and brown eyes. My mother and Beatrice tried to take me to the posh salons of Provincetown and make me over, but I wouldn't let them. (Unlike Hannah, I had my loyalties.) Obviously, I yearned to be beautiful, the way any teenage girl did, but I wasn't about to let my mother gloat about how pretty I was under "all that hair" or dress me in floaty summery frocks like the kind she wore on the weekends. Hannah had been bought and paid for, but not me.

During my junior year, I started looking at colleges. After years of taking care of my dad and myself, I thought I'd make a pretty good nurse. I'd helped a lot when Avó, my dad's mother, had cancer, and it had come naturally to me, making me feel proficient and useful. My plan was to go to school somewhere not too far away, then come back to the Cape and work here. I never wanted to live anywhere else. How could I? Once the Cape's salty fingers got ahold of you, you were addicted to the place.

So I studied hard, knowing I'd need a chunky scholarship. I had Beth as my best friend and a nice circle of other girls—Jennifer, Jessica, Justine and Ashley. I was never bullied or overly teased. A lot of my classmates came from wealthy families, and Nauset High's parking lot had plenty of Volvos, Range Rovers and BMWs. But there were plenty of beater cars, too, like the one I drove, my beloved Honda Civic with 250,000 miles on it. I was a solid student, As and Bs, just enough to separate me from the wicked-smart kids. I sang in the choir but didn't have solos. Played field hockey and made varsity, but big deal, right? Nothing special, nothing *not* special, if you know what I mean.

Until the end of my junior year of high school.

Like many torrid stories from one's youth, this one started with alcohol and ended at the hospital.

Chase Freeman was the resident god of the senior class, from an old Cape family with old Cape money, and they still lived in Eastham, as they had generation after generation. Chase's great-great-grandfather had been a whaling captain, and his house was now a small museum. Chase and his parents lived not far away from there, on a winding road that had views of the town cove and the salt marsh. Their home was Eastham's answer to the Kennedy compound down in Hyannis—a sprawling, gray-shingled house on a couple of acres, the lawn stretching out to a sharp drop-off to the marsh.

Old money and privilege; a name that would get a reservation at a great table just about any night of the week, even in high summer. Add to this that Chase's aunt was an actress of some renown and occasionally flew her nephew to California for a screening or as her date for an awards show. We had all seen him at the Golden Globes last year, looking handsome and confident as his aunt told E!'s red carpet correspondent that her nephew was her favorite person.

So he was draped in entitlement, good looks and security, with that access to fame gilding the lily. In the fall, Chase would attend Harvard like his parents before him. He played lacrosse, drove an Audi, wore Vineyard Vines bought from the flagship store on Martha's Vineyard. He'd eyed me in the hallways a time or two—I had grown a few inches since my freshman year and was now not short and thick, but almost average height and curvy in a way that shouted "Fertility!" In the past couple of months, I'd discovered that I was actually kind of pretty, especially once I'd discovered John Frieda's anti-frizz hair empire. My lips were full, my eyes were dark, I was a 36C, and suddenly boys went on high alert when I walked past.

This terrified and thrilled me. For one thing, I still loved nothing more than to walk in the woods and swim in the kettle ponds with Beth or HandsomeBoy. I had zero experience with boys, had never been kissed, had never met a boy

I *wanted* to kiss (or a girl, for that matter). I had absolutely no idea what to do when it came to romance, or even why people liked French kissing, because it sounded quite disgusting to me. This new male attention made me flushed and flustered, so I did what many girls did—I ignored it.

Boom. I may as well have draped myself in bacon and sprayed myself with new-car smell. It was a strange and abrupt change. After all those years of feeling abandoned by my sister, fairly invisible in school outside of my little circle, I was suddenly drunk with the power I had over boys. I started wearing V-necks. I stopped hating that I had a significant ass, because I had just learned that it was a *booty*, and Sir Mix-a-Lot told me that this was a good thing. There was a storm brewing on the horizon, and it was me.

And then, on May 16, the storm broke . . . just not in the way I'd imagined.

On May 16, Chase Freeman stepped out in front of me in the hall and asked my breasts if I'd like to come to a party at his house on Saturday. My breasts and I accepted. "What time?" I asked, as if this kind of invitation was normal in my life.

"Seven," he said, meeting my eyes with a smile.

"Great." Then I turned away and walked off to English class with Beth, willing my knees to keep working.

"Oh, my God," Beth whispered. "Lillie! Oh, my God!"

"You have to come with me," I said. "I have no idea what to do at a party, especially at Chase Freeman's house." Beth was wise about these things. She was further up the social ladder than I was and had been kissed at age fourteen, like a regular person. I needed her help.

She was glad to give it. I told my dad I was sleeping over at her house on Saturday, and he nodded and told me to have fun. As far as I could tell, I was the only girl in my class who wasn't allowed to go to parties.

But I wasn't going to pass this one up. It was the first time I lied to my father, and it would be the last, given how the evening turned out.

Beth and I spent three hours getting ready, trying on outfits, swapping shirts, doing our makeup, putting on perfume. Then we got in her car and headed for Chase's house.

"What am I supposed to do?" I asked. "I mean, he invited me. But it's a party, not a date, right?"

"Right," said Beth. "Be cool. Let *him* come to *you*. You don't want to seem too eager, but you want to be friendly at the same time, but not desperate or weird. Don't make that scrunched-up face you make when you're nervous."

"I make a scrunched-up face?" I asked.

She glanced at me. "You're doing it now." I looked in the visor mirror and saw that yes, I was, and we both started giggling like the teenage girls we were.

Beth parked in the long line of cars in front of Chase's house. We had waited an hour after the seven o'clock start time, per her advice. According to the buzz in the hallways of Nauset High, the Freeman parents were at their vacation place in Santa Monica, visiting the famous aunt. Music thumped and roared from the house, and purple-and-red lights flashed inside. There must've been a hundred people there.

Cue the ominous music.

"You made it, Lillie!" Chase himself opened the door. "I thought you were blowing me off." He leaned in and hugged me, and for a second I didn't know what to do. Then I hugged him back. Oh, God, he felt good. Muscled and warm. He was wearing *cologne*, and I didn't even hate it. "Hey, Beth," he added. "Get yourselves a beer or a drink or whatever. There's food, too."

We were abruptly shoved into the cliché of the unsupervised high school party. At first, Beth and I sipped beers. We ate some cookies. We went from room to room, unable to see the furniture because of the throngs of people.

Then someone offered us a joint. Beth nodded and demonstrated. I imitated her, and my God, the burn down my throat made me cough and hack till my eyes teared. Then, suddenly, I was floaty and *so* happy. Beth looked at me, and we started laughing at nothing. Dancing? Why not! In fact, *yes*, damn it!

Like all other nonsober people, we thought our moves were amazing. And lo and behold, "Baby Got Back" started playing, and Beth and I dissolved into helpless laughter. Time seemed to stretch, and I had flashes of wondering where I was. Was I home? Was I at my mom's? Did it matter? We were having so much fun, and everyone was smiling and laughing and having *such* a great time.

Someone pulled me against him on the makeshift dance floor. Chase! I danced with an uninhibited joy, feeling like a really good stripper, but with clothes on, which made me laugh and laugh. Then someone was leading me upstairs. Oh, it was Chase! Holy sheesh! I was *that* popular. We went into a big room painted dark blue with a lava lamp on the desk.

"You have a *lava* lamp?" I asked, crying with laughter. There was a big photo of Chase taking up half a wall, mid-catch or mid-throw at a lacrosse game. More hilarity—he had a *photo* of *himself* on the wall, and I collapsed on the bed.

You already know how this went. Chase joined me. He started kissing my neck, put his hand on my breast. Huh. Nice, I thought. I'd never been fondled by a boy before. "You're my first fondler," I said, setting off another stream of giggles. Chase waited patiently for my laughter to subside, then turned my face toward his and kissed me. Though it was quite wet and sloppy, it was also kind of tingly and nice and hot. We kissed for hours, or maybe minutes. I couldn't tell because of this slippery time thing.

Oh! His hand was under my skirt. Should I have worn jeans? Maybe. I should ask Beth if I should change. Where *was* Beth? Then his fingers slid into my underwear. It felt scary and . . . good. Should I say something? Or just lie here with the room spinning and let him make me feel good? Was I a slut, or was I normal? Was this what people did at our ages?

It was only when he stood, pulled off his shirt and unbuttoned his jeans that I realized we were about to have sex.

"Oh," I said, sitting up abruptly. "Uh . . . where's Bethie? How long have we been up here?" It felt like hours, time oozing like warm caramel.

"She's fine," Chase said. "Come on. Lay back down."

"Um . . . I don't want to have sex," I said, and my mind was a little surprised that my words were so clear. It was definitely true. I did not want to have sex, not like this, when I was stoned and at a party and . . . Well, shit. I was just too young. I'd just had my first kiss this night. I didn't want every first to happen in an hour. "Yeah. Sorry, Chase. I don't want to do anything else."

"Sure you do," he said. "You were making all sorts of noises a minute ago."

"Was that me?" I asked. *Get up, idiot,* the remote sober part of my brain instructed. *Get up right now and leave.* "I'm gonna go now. Thank you for this party. You have a lovely home." I laughed again, but it didn't feel as good as earlier.

"Don't leave," Chase said. His voice was gentle and low, coaxing, but his eyes . . . yeah, those weren't nice eyes.

"No, I need to go. Sorry."

If only I hadn't been stoned for the first time in my life. If only I hadn't had two beers on an empty stomach. I wouldn't have let this happen sober. I started to stand. Chase shoved me back down.

"Don't be a tease," he said, lying on top of me. "You know you like me. I can make you feel really good."

"Not tonight," I said. "Sorry." I was sobering up fast, but the room was still spinny. "Chase, please get off."

He didn't move. Kissed me again, shoving his tongue in my mouth.

"Please stop," I said, hearing the fear in my voice. He didn't. He ground his groin against me, groaning, and I was helpless and terrified and crying now. I was about to be raped, and it was my own stupid fault.

At least, that's what my teenage brain told me.

Chase pinned me down, holding my wrists above my head with one hand. He had big hands, I thought distantly. This was easy for him. This was . . . practiced. And, shit, he was strong. His other hand slipped to my bra and smoothly unfastened the front clasp. "Oh, yeah," he groaned, fondling my breast. "You're beautiful, Lillie."

"Chase, please, get off me," I begged. "I don't *want* this."

He squeezed my breast and kissed me again, licking my lips in a most disgusting way. I turned my head and pressed my lips together, stifling a sob.

He smiled. "Come on, baby. I'll be gentle if it's your first time. You want this. You're built for sex. And you can always tell people your cherry was popped by a Harvard man."

Those words turned my fear to fury. I wrenched my hand from Chase's grip and swung my fist, catching him hard in the face. Then I jerked my knee up as hard as I could and connected with his soft parts. He gave a high-pitched yell and rolled off, clutching his balls. In a distant part of my brain, I could hear my mother's voice. *If you're going to make stupid decisions, at least know where to kick.*

Chase wasn't done. He grabbed my arm and yanked me toward him, and I spit in his face and punched him again with my free hand, but it wasn't hard enough, so I grabbed his ear and twisted it ruthlessly. He swore and let go of my wrist, and I kicked him again, as hard as I could, in the shin. Grabbed a trophy from his nightstand and raised it over my head.

Stop, said my mother's voice. *Do not murder him.* Chase's eyes were wide with fear, and his hands were up in defense.

"How dare you, Chase Freeman!" I hissed. "I said *stop*, you piece of shit. I'm calling the cops!"

His expression changed from fear to something mean

and hard. "Like they'll believe that a drunk, stoned girl was raped when seventy-five people saw her dance like a whore and *willingly* come upstairs to my room."

I held the trophy up a second longer, then threw it on the floor. It broke.

"Get out of my house, Lillie. I'm the one who's been assaulted here. Maybe I'll call the cops on *you*."

"Fuck you," I said.

"No, *you* fuck me," he said, and his voice was sharp and cruel. He reached up and tried to grab me again, and the terror roared back. *Get out, get out, get out,* a voice was saying, and I was so certain he would win this time, and this time he *wouldn't* coax, he'd just rape me, and it would be brutal, and he'd stick a sock in my mouth and tie me up, and . . .

I wrenched back, fell on my butt and scrambled up. Then I was running out of his room, down the hall, down the stairs so fast my feet blurred. I slid down the last three steps but managed to keep my feet under me. "Looks like *someone* was having a good time," said a guy.

"Beth!" I yelled, but my voice was just a squeak.

Get out, get out, get out.

I burst outside, gasping and panting. There was a huddle of guys smoking weed in the driveway, blocking my path to the car. Chase's friends. They gaped at me, then laughed, and I turned and ran. No. I *flew* across the Freemans' wide lawn, toward the water, toward the town cove. I fell off the drop-off into the muck, the stiff reeds scratching and stabbing my legs. I was gasping for air and shaking hard.

Hide.

I crawled further into the tall reeds until I felt hidden in the marsh.

I covered my mouth, trying to quiet down, because I was gasp-sobbing. Then I looked down, and a little mewl of dismay escaped me. My shirt and bra were still undone . . . everyone had seen my breasts. My hands shook so hard it took me four tries to do up my bra. I buttoned my shirt and wrapped my arms around myself. Mud seeped into my skirt and panties, and there were dark smears of muck on my sleeves.

The anger was gone, and all that was left was fear. Fear, and utter disdain for myself.

How could I have been so *stupid*? How? Our health teachers had warned us about drugs and date rape and not leaving your friend alone at a party since *fourth grade*, yet here I was, sitting in the mud, hiding, shaking like a terrified Chihuahua, trying not to scream or cry.

I didn't have a cell phone. They were expensive, and we didn't have a lot of service anyway, not out by the kettle ponds. Dad had said maybe for Christmas.

I was alone here. But at least it was dark, and I was hidden. The air was cold and clear, and I remembered that I loved nature, and I would be okay, out here in the marsh, smelling the sea.

Then I heard voices. Chase and another guy, maybe two. A flashlight swept across the reeds and I froze.

"She ran across the yard," a male voice said.

"Well, if she calls the cops, I'm fucking dead. This will fuck up Harvard, too. My dad will kill me."

They were *looking* for me. Jesus God, they were *looking* for me. And what if they found me?

I froze. Even the shaking stopped, and my breath quieted. I put my hands into the mud and smeared my face with it, slowly, silently camouflaging myself so my skin wouldn't catch the beam of light. Thank God I was wearing black. My legs were already filthy with marsh muck.

I was a girl from the woods of Wellfleet. I knew how to be quiet. I told myself it was just like standing in the water of Herring Pond, being so, so still that a heron would walk right past you, that the fish would swim between your feet and nibble at your skin, that you were part of the landscape. I pretended that I was part of the marsh, invisible, safe.

"I don't see her," one of the other boys said. Camden from the lacrosse team, also a senior. "She probably caught a ride home. It's better this way. Everyone saw her slutting it up in there, Chase. Nothing happened. She left. Story over."

The flashlight beam swept past me again, and I closed my eyes.

Then it was dark again, and the boys' voices grew fainter. I stayed where I was. What were they going to do if they found me? What was my punishment going to be? The words *gang rape* floated in front of my eyes. *Slut. Easy. Whore. Drunk. Stoned.*

I sat there for hours, my knees pulled to my chest, afraid to leave in case I was seen. At some point, the voices moved outside. Engines started, kids laughed, cars drove off. I sat there, praying that Beth would come, that I'd hear her voice and could run to her and be safe again.

How could she have let me go off with Chase? Wasn't that the cardinal rule of parties? Never let your friend go off with a slimy rich boy.

But then I remembered that she didn't know. Sitting there, sobering up in the mud, I remembered the details. I had told her I was thirsty and had gone into the kitchen. I'd pulled a Coke out of a cooler, said hi to Jessica, who was making out with her boyfriend and didn't pause. Then I turned and found myself face-to-face with Chase, and he asked me to dance. We did, and after a little while, he said, "Want to see my room?" and I said yes.

I said *yes.*

Oh, God. It *was* my word against his. It was.

Then I heard Bethie's voice. "What time did Lillie leave?" she asked, and her words carried easily across the lawn. Thank God! I started to stand up, then froze mid-crouch.

"She didn't feel good." Chase's voice. "Bruce said she called someone and left. Dunno what time."

"Weird. She didn't even find me. Well, this was wicked fun, Chase! Thanks!"

No, Beth! No! It wasn't fun! It was horrible! I peeked

through the reeds, waiting for Chase to go inside. He didn't. He stood with his arms crossed, and then, as if he sensed my presence, turned his head toward me. I sank back down, fresh terror zinging through my limbs. I wanted to run out, run to my best friend, collapse in her arms and sob out my all-too-predictable story, but I didn't. I couldn't. It wasn't just fight or flight. It was fight, flight or freeze.

I froze. Then came the familiar roar of Beth's car starting, and it was too late for her to save me.

I waited there, achingly cold now, tears slipping down my cheeks, until Chase's house went dark. Then I waited more, praying to Saint Anthony of Padua, patron saint of Portugal and fishermen, that Chase wasn't standing in his dark house, waiting for me to show myself.

Finally, my legs numb from crouching, I crept out of the reeds. Onto the lawn of the house across the street from the Freemans', staying behind the trees, trying to be a shadow. I passed Chase's driveway, my heart pounding so hard I could feel it slamming against my ribs.

Then I ran. I ran down the twisting road as fast as I could, my breasts bouncing painfully. I *hated* my body now, hated it for not being faster, for being the kind of body that attracted male attention, the kind that couldn't handle weed or beer. I would go on a diet. I would become as slender as a willow. My chest would flatten and my ass would become small, and I'd dress in oversized clothes, I would never have another drink or do drugs, and this kind of terror and loss of control would *never* happen again. I would never be that stupid again.

It was probably less than an eighth of a mile to Route 6, but it felt like a marathon. Once on Route 6, I kept running, past the road where the Captain Freeman Museum sat like a smug, overweight senator. Past Governor Prence Road, which led to Fort Hill. Route 6 was a two-lane highway, and it wasn't very safe running in the little bike lane this late. Anytime a car passed, I jumped off the road, hiding in the bushes or behind a tree in someone's yard, afraid it would be Chase. All the houses were dark. Of course they were. I had no idea what time it was, but it was clearly well past midnight. Maybe even close to dawn. I didn't know.

I passed the tiny Eastham Tourist Information house, the gas station. Was it the residual beer and weed in my system that made it feel as if I'd been running for hours? I kept going, kept running, kept hiding. *Almost there. Almost there. Almost there.*

By the time I reached the police station, I was whipped. I stopped to catch my breath, my legs shaking, filthy. I wanted a shower. I wanted to burn these panties that Chase had touched. I wanted to scrub my skin with bleach.

I started toward the station, then stopped.

If I went in, they'd investigate. They'd call my father, because I was still a minor, and he'd know that I was not only stupid, but not to be trusted. The Moms would lecture me about how utterly naive I was, and then Beatrice would launch into a story of how beautifully she had lost her virginity at age seventeen. Hannah would be disgusted and pitying.

The police would ask Chase if . . . if what? What exactly had Chase done? He *hadn't* raped me. I'd gone to his room willingly. Made out with him willingly. Let him unbutton my shirt and stick his fingers in my panties. God! I shuddered in revulsion.

And then, I could imagine Chase saying, *she wanted to stop, so we stopped. She kind of panicked and ran down the stairs, and I didn't see her again.*

All of that was true. If I said I had to punch him and kick him in the nuts . . . it would be his word against mine. He could spin it, and I already knew he was good at spinning things. *She didn't feel good. Called someone and left.* Everyone in school would know that I'd freaked out because Chase got handsy with me. Would anyone believe me that he'd pinned me down and threatened me? That he'd kept me in his room against my will? *Dancing like a whore,* Chase had said. Even *I* thought I'd danced like a stripper. I'd been rather proud of that.

My father would be so disappointed.

My shoulders fell. I wasn't going to file a report. I couldn't walk in there like this, filthy, covered in mud, probably still stoned and drunk, without ramifications.

So I kept walking. Hannah was in college, way up in Maine. I could call my mother from the visitors center, where there were pay phones. She wouldn't tell my father, would she? But shit, she'd be disgusted with me, and smug, and maybe she *would* tell Dad, because it would be a way for her to hurt him. *Why didn't you check in with Lillie? Are you that dumb, Pedro? Our daughter was nearly raped, and it's because you trust her too much.*

But I couldn't walk home to Wellfleet. It was miles to go, and I was so, so tired. I didn't have to tell Mom the truth. I could lie. Or I could call Beth. Beth would keep my secret.

Just as I started to turn at the entrance, I heard a motor, a car slowing down. I bolted toward the building. The car followed me into the parking lot. Shit! It was Chase, I knew it. Oh, God, what would he do to me now?

"Lillie?"

I stopped and turned. It wasn't a car. It was a battered pickup truck I knew well. I should've recognized the sound of that rusty engine. It wasn't anything like Chase's purring sports car.

Ben Hallowell pulled to the curb and stopped his truck. Got out and took a long look at me. "You okay?" he asked.

"Um . . . uh . . . yes." I swallowed the sudden tears that rose in my throat. "But I could use a ride." My voice cracked.

"Sure. Get in." He opened the passenger door for me. It creaked horribly, and I jumped. Ben didn't say anything. For once, it didn't seem that he had pulga atrás da orelha. He knew me, he wouldn't hurt me and he'd take me home.

He got back in, waited till I was buckled, then turned the truck back onto Route 6, toward home. "Rough night?"

"Yeah."

"Did anyone hurt you?" He kept his eyes on the road.

"Um . . . not really. No."

He was quiet a minute. "Do you need to go to the hospital?"

"No. Just take me home. Thanks, Ben."

He nodded.

"If you could . . . not mention this to my father," I said.

He glanced at me. "Maybe *you* should mention this to him," he said, turning his eyes back to the road.

"Maybe." I leaned my head against the window and closed my eyes, the smell of the truck so much like my dad's—ocean and fish and coffee. It felt safe here, and a few tears leaked out. Soon, I'd be home, and I'd creep in and take a long shower, and this night would be a memory.

That's the last thing I remembered.

I woke up in the hospital three days later, minus a spleen, with a broken femur, broken collarbone, broken jaw, two broken ribs and a deep gash on my forehead. There'd been an accident, I was told. I was lucky to be alive. My abdomen had been pierced by a chunk of steel from the engine, resulting in the loss of my spleen, six inches of my intestine and the tearing of my uterus. They'd avoided a hysterectomy because of my age but couldn't rule that out in the future. "But we can talk about that once you've healed," the doctor said with a kind smile.

My father was there, holding my hand, watching my face as the doctor told me the damage. Neither of us cried. It hurt too much, and Dad . . . Dad wasn't a weeper. But he held my hand a little more firmly, then kissed it, making me feel unworthy.

This was the price of my stupidity at the party, I told myself. For not going into the police station and just calling my dad and owning what every teenager has to own someday—we were stupid, and we put ourselves in danger. I should've known better than to accept a ride from Ben Hallowell, who'd always driven too fast, who'd totaled a car in high school. Dad would've hugged me and banged on the Freemans' door and scared the life out of Chase.

Too late now. I lay in the uncomfortable hospital bed, sipping Ensure through a straw, trying not to breathe too deeply because of the pain that pierced and throbbed with unrelenting fire in my leg, my ribs, my jaw, my stomach.

Hannah came home from college to visit. The Moms came. Beth and her parents; Jessica, Jennifer, Justine and Ashley. I couldn't tell them what had happened at the party, because it hurt too much to talk. Beth told me Chase Freeman had brought my purse to school and given it to her. Everyone already knew Ben Hallowell had been at the wheel, that he'd given me a ride home.

There were flowers from my entire class, Beth's parents, a few teachers, the choir director, our neighbors down the road on Herring Pond.

Not a scratch on Ben. Not one scratch. My mother told me this with bitter triumph poisoning her voice. "That's always the way, isn't it? The driver walks away. Did you even bother to check if he was drunk, Liliana? Even if he was sober, that truck of his is a death trap. Why didn't you call a cab, for heaven's sake?"

He hadn't been drunk. The police did a Breathalyzer and a blood test, and he passed. But yeah, his truck was a piece of shit.

He came to see me a few days after I woke up, holding a mason jar full of daffodils. "I'm so sorry, Lillie," he said.

I nodded, then winced. The police had already told me the truck's alignment had been off, the tires were old, and one of them blew out. The truck had flown off the road, through the guardrail and into Blackfish Creek Marsh in Wellfleet. The tide was halfway out, the truck rolled, and when it stopped, my side had been partially underwater. Ben had pulled me out, possibly saving my life, possibly making the abdominal damage worse. A passerby called 911.

All I remembered was the smell of his truck, feeling safe.

Ben sat in the chair next to my bed and said nothing. As my mother had said, he hadn't broken a single bone. But she had been wrong about no scratch. There was a cut on his palm that had warranted some stitches.

The nurse came in and put some pain meds and antibiotics into my IV. I fell asleep. Ben was gone when I woke up, but the daffodils were in the jar on my windowsill.

Ben and I never spoke of it again. He only visited me that once, said that one sentence and never followed up again. My father didn't fire him, whereas my mother thought he should be serving time.

I didn't blame Ben Hallowell upon learning that my body would have a harder time fighting off viruses without my spleen there to help. I didn't blame him when I limped for a year thanks to my broken femur, or when the physical therapy made my leg burn and ache so fiercely that tears streamed down my face. I didn't blame him for the twenty pounds I lost with a jaw wired shut. When, a year after the accident, a hysterogram showed significant scarring in my uterus that would "likely" affect my ability to have children, I still didn't blame him.

But, oh, I blamed him when I lost my unborn daughter, when I held her and keened and felt my heart rip apart. My body could not hold her, and that was because of a stupid accident caused by a man who drove too fast and didn't take care of his truck. If not for that accident, I would have had a daughter. I knew that in my heart, and my doctor confirmed it. My uterus was just too battered to hold her.

The miscarriage changed me. In most other ways, it made me more tender, more loving, more sentimental.

Getting pregnant at age twenty-two . . . it was a miracle. Sure, it pushed the time frame of my life forward faster than I had planned, but I was *pregnant*. It sealed the deal between Brad and me, and his parents were over the moon, not even minding that we were having a shotgun wedding, more or less. Dylan seemed like God's compensation for that car accident and the year of pain that followed. Giving birth didn't hurt nearly as much as had been direly promised—I was in awe of what my body could do. Clearly,

I was a champion with these childbearing hips and juicy ovaries. And because Brad and I were utterly smitten with our baby, we wanted more. Dylan would be such a good big brother. By the age of two, he was so kind and adorable already.

Brad, an only child himself, wanted our son to have siblings. We'd have two girls, we fantasized, then another boy who'd worship Dylan as a demigod and be suitably adored by his sisters. Maybe the girls would be twins. Catia and Aline, with little Rafael a few years later.

When I got pregnant the second time, Dylan was three. Easiest thing in the world, right? But it was a very different pregnancy—with Dylan, I'd had only a little bit of heartburn toward the end, and my belly stuck out in front of me like the prow of a ship. From behind, you couldn't tell I was pregnant.

With this second pregnancy, I knew it was a girl, because I spread. I looked pregnant from my ankles to my eyes. "Looks like you sat on an air hose," my dad said fondly.

"Thanks, Pop," I said, rolling my eyes and depositing Dylan on his lap.

And yet I was nervous. Call it maternal instinct, but there was a strong foreboding in my heart. Something was wrong, I kept thinking. I was getting my master's to become a CNM at that time, learning about every aberration and chromosomal abnormality there was, wondering if my child would have cerebral palsy or Down syndrome or microcephaly.

The ultrasound showed a perfect baby girl. Every lab test told me I was fine. No diabetes, no high blood pressure, no anemia. Placenta in its rightful place, weight gain perfect, no signs of anything but clear blue skies ahead.

I pushed my fear aside, knowing it was normal to worry (though I hadn't with Dylan, so stunned and overjoyed at my good luck). I was exhausted (normal, again, showing that all my energy was going to the baby). I could see it in

Brad's eyes—he was so happy at the thought of a daughter. When Dylan asked why my tummy was so round, we told him.

"I be a big brudder!" he crowed, and Brad and I were so happy with his reaction, so delighted. Our perfect little family would grow.

And still, I counted the days, waiting for that magic week when viability would be reached. Nothing was medically wrong, and I kept reminding myself of all that I knew about pregnancies and birth, telling myself it would be okay.

But there's another thing midwives know, and it's that some mothers have a sixth sense about their babies, even in utero.

The dread lurked in the back of my heart.

At twenty-two weeks and four days, when I was sitting on the floor making a city out of blocks with Dylan, I got up to answer the phone and saw a splotch of watery red on the floor. For a second, I assumed it was ketchup—Dylan had had ketchup with his carrots at lunch, and somehow, he must have . . . Nope. No.

A sudden, knifelike pain pierced my abdomen, causing me to bend over, keening. "Mommy, what's wrong?" Dylan asked.

I forced myself to straighten up. "Nothing, honey. I'm fine."

Another rush of blood soaked my jeans, and I shuffled into the bathroom, holding my stomach. Called 911, then Brad, and told him to meet me at the hospital. Called Beth and told her to come get Dylan right now. I managed to put him in his car seat and drive down Black Pond Road to Route 6 so the paramedics could get to me faster.

My daughter was born in the back of the ambulance on Route 6 about fifteen minutes from the hospital. Tiny, perfect, beautiful, stillborn, shockingly white in a sea of blood.

I stayed in the hospital for six days—complete placental abruption, requiring an emergency hysterectomy and four units of blood. Brad brought Dylan to see me, and he was so sweet, so kind. "I'm sorry, Mommy," he said. "I love you." He had drawn a picture of the three of us, giant heads with eyes and smiles, long stick legs, all of us holding hands. My mother came and was uncharacteristically silent. Beatrice wept and held my hand, making me feel awkward. Hannah sent flowers and brought Dylan some presents to distract him and called me to say how sorry she was. And for the first time in my life, I saw my father cry as he sat at my bedside.

These things happen. Oh, they happen all the time. Everyone's life—especially every woman's life—is marked by something like this, it seems. Miscarriage, infertility, breast or ovarian or uterine cancer. It's so *personal* when our female parts fail us in some way. So hard not to think that we—that I—had caused this, should've known, should've done something. No matter what my doctors said, I knew. My hubris at thinking my scarred, weakened uterus could hold another baby. My greed in wanting another child when my first had been nothing short of a miracle.

Because she was born after twenty weeks' gestation, my daughter got a fetal death certificate, which meant she needed a name. We could have left that part blank, but it seemed so cruel not to name her. But we hadn't settled on one yet, and oh, the deep, aching pain of naming a child who was already gone. The tragedy of it all. The absolute, wrenching grief.

Grace Mariana Silva Fairchild. I could never bring myself to think of her by name. After all, she had never been called that in life . . . to me, she was just my poor little daughter.

Dylan was sad and so sweet for a few days after I came home. He knew "Mommy's tummy hurt," and there would be no sister for him. He brought me his stuffed animals to comfort me. A few days later, he said that he'd woken up from a dream where his baby sister was snuggled against him, and he cried because she went away.

Then, cruelly, he forgot about her, as toddlers do.

We had her cremated and took the achingly small box and scattered some of her ashes on Herring Pond. I buried the remainder in my garden and planted blue forget-me-nots in that spot.

We got screened by a few adoption agencies, but we never got a call, and honestly, affording it would've been a stretch. Foster parenting was fraught with the idea that a child could be taken away from us, and what would that do to Dylan? By the time he was seven or eight, we had withdrawn our applications and settled into the reality of being a family of three.

We knew we were lucky. Dylan was everything to us, and there were plenty of studies showing that only children had many advantages. I worked as a nurse part-time, and helped out with stagings or showings for my in-laws. Brad had a full load of patients. Our little house was coming together bit by bit, year by year. We were happy. Of course we were. It was a choice we had to make.

And still, I thought of my poor little baby every day. I'd held her there in the ambulance, and after my hysterectomy, they let me hold her again. I'd memorized her perfect face. Every year on the first of December, the day I'd lost her, Brad would bring me flowers, and I'd cry a little (or a lot), remembering the fear and love and grief so pure it was like a scalpel, slicing my heart in half.

But you keep going. The memory is there every day, but the days grow and multiply until it's years and years. Her story was so brief, and after a while, there was nothing new to say. She was branded on my heart, and she always would be. It became my private loss, spoken of no more. Brad had lost her, too, but he hadn't grown her inside him, felt every wriggle and kick; hadn't known my secret fear; hadn't seen all that blood or felt her tiny body slide out of me, even as I fought to keep her inside.

Maybe I became a better mother to Dylan because I knew how remarkable a healthy baby was. Maybe I appreciated life more. I know it made me a better midwife. Nevertheless, it made me feel feral and vicious to believe that her death made me a better person. Sometimes I dreamed that I was in that ambulance again, jolting myself awake with the wail that was torn from my soul when I couldn't stop her from leaving me.

I had a beautiful son, a happy marriage, a home that was part of me. I had my quirky, imperfect family, my wonderful dad. But every spring, when the forget-me-nots appeared, I missed my little girl in a way that still surprised me. That after five years, ten years, twelve, I could still sob, alone in the downstairs bathroom, for my lost little girl.

When Brad left, he'd left our daughter's remains, too. I wondered if he ever thought of her at all anymore.

But sometimes, on these nights when the house was so quiet, when Zeus lay next to me on the bed, I thought of her more than ever. I imagined her alive, now fifteen years old. At night, when the rain rushed in the gutters and the wind blew against the roof, I could even picture her face, a feminine version of Dylan's.

We would be best friends, my sweet girl and I. I wouldn't be alone here. She would be smart and kind and helpful. Her existence would've underscored the importance of a man treating a woman with honor, and Brad would never have cheated on me. Dylan would've chosen a school closer to the Cape—in Boston or Connecticut or New York—because he wouldn't have wanted to be far from his beloved sister.

Or, even if her father *had* cheated, and even if Dylan was still at the University of Montana, my daughter and I would become even closer. Popcorn and movie nights, walks around the kettle ponds, kayaking, cooking, baking, laughing. School events, her friends filling the house with the sound of their laughter, their youthful beauty and curiosity bringing life into this uncharacteristically silent house. I'd be too busy to deliver skunks. No. I'd want to be a good role model for her, not this crazy-ass woman fixated on her ex-husband's life. Vanessa would still be speaking to me, as she wouldn't have the heart to alienate her grand-daughter.

My daughter would be my closest ally, and I would be hers. We'd go to Provincetown this weekend to see her grandpa, and I'd buy her a treat. We'd get sandwiches from the Canteen and eat on the beach, watching the glorious September light turn the entire town gold. She'd lean her head against my shoulder and say, "You're my best friend, Mommy."

The longing . . . it never goes away. My little girl. How wonderful she would have been.

CHAPTER 11

Melissa

Hannah Chapman had no problem planning the wedding, despite the fact that her sister was Bradley's first wife. It just confirmed Melissa's belief that money could buy anything, even loyalty. Plus, it would send a strong message, wouldn't it? Even Lillie's *sister* supported this new marriage.

Melissa had done her research, and Hannah was the best. She'd consulted her before she knew about the sister connection, but this made things even more satiating (word of the day!). There had been a few stares at yoga when word got out, a cold shoulder at the market, but so what? Half of marriages ended in divorce. Melissa already had Brad saying things like "We've been growing apart for years" and "It was very amicable."

But God, she was sick of Bradley talking about Lillie! Dennis had never talked about *his* ex-wife. She knew Bradley's divorce was only ten days old, and he had to get it out of his system, but all his complaints of "Lillie never" and "Lillie always" and "When Lillie and I" . . . it was grating! Bradley (like most therapists Melissa had met) needed therapy more than anyone. *Get over her!* she wanted to say. *You're with me now! Erase her.*

Ophelia had zero interest in her new stepuncle/father. It was so different from Dennis, but Ophelia . . . whatever. It was just two or three more years till boarding school, anyway. Meanwhile, Bradley went overboard in his efforts with her, asking her about school, friends, books, talking over her silence or pretending her one-word answers were delightful.

Both Melissa and Brad loved posting to Instagram, and whenever possible, Bradley would always use #girldad. He'd always tag her, too, and Melissa's influencer status was growing. Ophelia was always a hit, though Melissa had to be careful not to let her know she was being photographed, or she'd get a stony stare. #LoveMyNiece #LegalGuardian #FosterParent #FosteringSavesLives #FosterKidsMatter #Niece #Auntie #Motherhood. It worked . . . Sandra Bullock followed her! (It wasn't blue-check verified, but even so!)

Stella Maris helped her numbers grow as well—she used the same professional organizers Gwyneth Paltrow had, and they tagged her closet! Not only that, a Real Housewife commented on the fact that they had the same purse!

And now, the wedding. Everyone on social media loved a wedding, *especially* one that was expensive and gorgeous, which Melissa's certainly would be. With Dennis, she had just needed the marriage certificate and the ring on her finger (which, yes, had been a diamond band). With Bradley, she would swing for the bleachers, and no one did that like Hannah Chapman Events, according to *Cape Cod Life*, the Knot and *Martha Stewart Weddings*.

Hannah had style, unlike her sister, Melissa thought as they sat in the parlor of her very charming and posh office. She wasn't pretty, and she was old (well . . . the same age as Bradley), but she knew how to dress. Perfect manicure, great haircut, fantastic lipstick. An arrangement of white orchids was in a low vase on the coffee table, and the place smelled fabulous, thanks to a pear-and-freesia-scented Jo Malone candle.

Hannah and Melissa could be friends, maybe. That was one of the only flaws in Melissa's new life. No friends. Not yet, anyway. Not that she'd ever really had anyone super close, but . . . well, there'd been her roommates back in Kansas, but she'd had to block them, since they obviously knew she hadn't gone to *that* Wesleyan. One woman at yoga seemed nice, and they'd had coffee once, but after Brad left Lillie, she'd stopped speaking to Melissa. Whatever.

Kaitlyn had been her friend, once. Before the drugs and drinking and slutting around. Once upon a time, they'd laughed together so hard their parents had yelled at them to settle down. If only Kaitlyn had tried harder, they could be living this life together.

What a strange thought. Melissa cleared her throat and squeezed Bradley's hand. The ring on her finger (which she'd insisted Bradley pay for, since she was giving him everything else) had been made here on the Cape, another way to make friends and influence people. A two-carat solitaire diamond flanked by two tapered-cut baguette diamonds. Flashy but classy. She'd already spent tens of thousands in town, at the galleries and shops, the wine store, the church. She'd have friends, especially after they came to the wedding of the century.

"So," Hannah said, pouring more tea into Melissa's cup, "now that you've told me about your love story"—she swallowed hard, but Melissa let it pass—"give me some adjectives of what you want your wedding to be."

"I just want it to be simple and personal, you know?" Melissa said. "But beautiful." This was a lie, and Hannah seemed to sense it.

"Simple, personal and beautiful, of course. This is *such* a special day," she said, not looking at Bradley. "We want it to reflect you as a couple, the things you love most, that reflect what's important to you." Another swallow. Bile? It didn't matter.

"Exactly, Hannah," Melissa said. "Personal, intimate and lovely. Right, babe?"

"Right, babe," Bradley echoed. "And, Hannah, again, thank you for being so professional about this."

"Of course," Hannah said. "This is my business, and I want you to have a stunning day."

Or at least cash the check, Melissa thought. Because she was going to spend *so* much on this wedding, and she was going to invite just about every resident of Wellfleet. Hannah charged 10 percent of the event budget plus a non-refundable $20,000 deposit, so she'd be making at least $200,000 on this little soiree. Melissa would make sure she earned it.

In the two weeks since Bradley had moved in with her, Melissa had already improved him. His beard was four days of perfect stubble and no longer gray. His glasses were now tortoiseshell Armani, replacing those silly Harry Potter gold rims. She was thinking he should get LASIK, but there wasn't time before the wedding. Highlights in his blond hair. Pants by Tom Ford, shirt by Burberry. She'd surprised him with a Jaguar convertible, and she had to admit, he was adjusting to his new life quite well.

The sex was damn good, too. He wanted to impress her, and it was so *wonderful*, him being the one to do all the work. He'd offer a massage, starting at her toes, spreading rose petals on the bed (corny, but he was trying). She knew he was making sure she didn't have any doubts about marrying an older man. So far, she did not. And if she had them later, that prenup was airtight.

Three hours later, much was decided, and Melissa had to give Hannah credit. This would be a wedding no one forgot. Ceremony on the lawn of Stella Maris with a string quartet from the Boston Symphony Orchestra. A dress appointment with Candice Wu for her *and* Ophelia (the flower girl, of course, not that she showed any interest). Bespoke floral design from Lilacs. Catering by MAX Ultimate Food out of Boston. Music by Memphis Train Revue, whose lead singer sounded like Aretha Franklin (they'd have to be flown in from Texas, but it was *her* wedding, and money was no object). Signs painted by a calligrapher on reclaimed wood pulled from the bottom of Lake Champlain.

"And how many guests are we thinking?" Hannah asked.

"We want to keep it small," Melissa said. "Intimate. A hundred and fifty? Two hundred? What do you think, honey?"

"Whatever you want, babe." His amazing turquoise eyes glowed at her. She'd have to park Ophelia in front of the TV when they got home so they could make love.

She looked back at Hannah. "I know we're asking a lot with the wedding being so soon, Hannah," she said, keeping her voice low and warm. "We appreciate your expertise so much."

"We do, Han," Bradley said. "We don't want to go on living together without a legal commitment and set a bad example for Ophelia."

"Like adultery would?" Hannah asked mildly.

Bradley said nothing, so Melissa gave him a sharp jab in the ribs. "That was unfair, Hannah," he said, his tone frosty. "We're using you because we want to support your business, but there are other wedding planners, you know."

Exactly. "I understand this may be hard for you," Melissa said. "If you'd prefer us to take our business elsewhere . . ."

"No, no," she said, flushing. "But you're both so compassionate, and Brad, you're a psychologist, of course. I'm sure you can understand that I feel a tiny bit disloyal. Lillie is my sister, after all, and Dylan is my nephew. I promise to be better at compartmentalizing from here on out."

"Oh, Dylan's fine with it," Bradley said. "I've asked him to be my best man."

"Can he come home from college during football season?" Hannah asked. Irritatingly, they started talking about the boy. Who had been quite rude, by the way. The one time Bradley passed the phone to her, Dylan hung up, as if divorces didn't happen every single day. He'd get over it. Melissa had been planning to give him a car, too, but not if he wasn't civil. Then again, he hadn't met her and experienced her personality and charm. She'd win him over. He was male, after all.

"Getting back to the wedding," Melissa said, forcing a smile. "We need a place for our wedding night before we fly to Paris. Any recommendations?"

"Of course! Lands End has a beautiful suite. I'll arrange for a car to take you. Would you prefer a limo, or an antique car?"

"Oh, an antique car," Brad said instantly.

"Honey? My dress in a grubby old car? I don't think so."

"We can get you a classic Bentley that's absolutely immaculate," Hannah said.

Ooh, a Bentley. "Okay. I trust you, Hannah. I'm sure there are a million things you'll think of that we haven't covered, but we do need to get back. Ophelia's French lesson ends at four, and we're already late."

She and Brad held hands walking out, and Melissa felt so happy. She couldn't *wait* for the wedding. She'd skip a maid of honor . . . it was classier to be alone, really. Oh, and she'd invite all the mothers from New York and see who came and/or what gifts they'd send. Should she register? Yes, she decided, even though she needed nothing. Maybe she'd tell people to donate to their favorite charity. But she kind of wanted gifts, even if she might not like them.

Most of their guests would be from here. Can't buy friends? Think again. There was a reason she'd already given more than a hundred grand to local causes, from wetland conservation to turtle rescue to drug rehab programs.

There was the flicker of Kaitlyn again. If she ever got out of jail and was still addicted, Melissa would send her to a really good rehab place, now that she had her own money and didn't have to hide Kaitlyn anymore. Maybe that would finally get Katie on the road to sobriety.

⌒

Ophelia was in a foul mood when they got to the French teacher's house. "You're late," she said, throwing her backpack into the car and flinging herself after it so hard the Beemer rocked.

"Sorry, honey," Brad said. "But guess what? You're going to get a special dress made for the wedding! Mommy wants you to be her flower girl!"

"She's not my *mommy*," Ophelia snarled. "And I'm too old to be a flower girl."

"Junior bridesmaid, then," Melissa said. "It'll be fun, you'll see." It was lucky that Ophelia was on the short side. Little kids were cuter in weddings, but they could steal the show, too. Ophelia would not. She'd have to tell Hannah to book a trial run for straightening Phee's hair, too. (She'd started calling her niece Phee since they'd moved to Wellfleet, feeling slightly closer to the girl in the new house.)

They pulled up to the pillared driveway of Stella Maris, and it was still a thrill. "Home, sweet home!" Brad said, and Melissa laughed. Tonight would be wonderful. She'd hired a cook, now that she didn't have to earn her keep as she had with Dennis, and Chef Paul had prepared coq au vin and roasted baby brussels sprouts with diced prosciutto (she chose the meals each week, and Paul did all the work). Melissa would get a lovely pinot noir from the wine cellar—Bradley needed to drink more than just malbec. They could have a glass while sitting on the deck, watching the sunset. So relaxing. So elegant. So *enviable*.

"Something smells weird," Ophelia said as they went in. "I hope it's not dinner."

It was a smell Melissa knew far too well. Skunk. Her father used to shoot them for fun when he was drunk. Even when they didn't spray, they smelled. Apparently, they were plentiful here on the Cape. She'd have to make sure Hannah took steps to keep them away on the wedding day.

"There's a skunk somewhere outside, Bradley, honey." She made wide, pleading eyes at him. "Do something."

"No worries, babe," he said. "Do we have any mothballs? The smell will make them leave."

"I have no idea," she said. "Let me text Lucia and see."

She went into the house, hands on her phone, and texted the housekeeper. Do we have mothballs? We need to chase a skunk away. She glanced around. "Gosh, it's worse in here. It must've walked right under the window." Or it might be under the deck. Shoot!

So much for sex followed by a nice evening sitting outside. Dang it! That was her favorite part of the day. Fine. They'd sit in the living room. Maybe she'd turn on the gas fire and send Ophelia to bed early (not that the child liked spending time with them).

Melissa went into the living room, where Ophelia was standing by the grand piano. Since Phee had dropped violin, Melissa was trying piano lessons. "Are you finally going to practice, Ophelia? That'd be a nice change. I would've loved piano lessons when I was your age. It makes an impression, knowing about music. It's very classy. You've already given up on the violin, but—"

"Shut up and don't move," Ophelia said.

"Ophelia! Don't talk to me like that, you—"

"There's a skunk under the piano."

Melissa froze. No. Not in her perfect house! "What should we do?" she whispered.

"I dunno. It's pretty cute, though." Ophelia glanced over her shoulder at Melissa. "Where's Teeny?"

Oh, God! Teeny, the Chihuahua Melissa had bought Ophelia just a few weeks ago. What if the skunk sprayed the sweet little dog? What if it got into a fight with her and killed poor Teeny? Wait. No. Teeny was closed in Ophelia's bedroom, because she tended to piddle when left alone (and

Melissa sure as heck didn't want the dog piddling anywhere else in the house).

Ophelia reached out toward the skunk.

"Don't touch it!" Melissa hissed.

"I think it's a baby."

Melissa inched over to Ophelia, making sure to stay behind her. It was *not* a baby. It was, in fact, as big as a large cat. "It's a rodent," she whispered. It was blinking at them both, tail down, looking a little surprised to be inside. Its claws were unpleasantly long. "Go to your room, Phee. It might bite you."

"Melissa. It won't bite me. At worst, it'll spray the room, so don't scare it. Besides, I like animals. Hi, honey." She squatted down. "Hi, baby skunk."

"Don't!" Melissa hissed.

"Babe, I found them! They were in the garage," Brad said, and he strode into the living room, all male pride at having found the mothballs. She threw out her hand and he lurched to a stop. "What's wrong?"

"It's right here!" Melissa whispered.

"The skunk?"

"Yes, the skunk! Lower your voice!"

The skunk took a few waddles toward Ophelia.

"Ophelia!" Brad hissed. "It could be rabid!"

"Oh, my God," Melissa whispered.

"It likes me," Phee said. "Right, baby skunk?"

"That's not a baby," Bradley said.

"Mr. Fairchild," Ophelia said, "make yourself useful and get a carrot or something."

Mr. Fairchild. God, the girl resisted everything! She'd called Dennis "Pop" after a few *days*, and poor Bradley was trying so hard. But the girl had a point. "Do it," Melissa ordered quietly, and he backed into the kitchen.

The skunk *did* seem to like Ophelia. "Lure it out of the house," Melissa whispered. "I'll go open the slider, and you lead it over—"

"I know what 'lure' means, Melissa," Ophelia said, not looking away from the skunk. It waddled a little closer.

"If that thing sprays in here, we'll never get the smell out," Melissa said.

"I *know*. Stop talking. You're scaring it. Don't listen to her, baby skunk. You're just fine."

For a second, Melissa almost liked Ophelia. Her confidence in this moment, her attitude, her steady gaze, her . . . her fearlessness.

Well. Melissa slowly glided toward the sliding glass doors that lined the entire back of the house and carefully, carefully opened one, then slid the screen door open. "Ready when you are," she whispered. The fug of the skunk was heavy in the air. Lucia was going to have to fix that tomorrow. Make that *tonight*.

"Aw! Look at your li'l nose," Ophelia said. "Are you so cute? You are."

All those years of elocution lessons, and still the twang was in her voice. Sometimes, Melissa thought she did it on purpose.

Brad came in holding a loaf of bread and a carrot.

"You gonna make it a sandwich?" Ophelia said, glancing over her shoulder. "Bring me the carrot."

"Is that what they eat?" Melissa asked.

"No, it's what *you* eat, and you're the one I'm trying to *lure* out of the house," Ophelia said.

"Don't be disrespectful to your mother—" Brad attempted.

"She's not my mother," Ophelia said in a singsong voice. "Try to get that through your head, Mr. PhD." She reached back, and Bradley inched forward and put the carrot in her hand. "Do you like carrots, honey?" she asked, offering the carrot. "Do you?"

"Now start backing away," Melissa whispered. "Toward me."

"Have you two ever heard the word 'micromanaging'?" Ophelia asked.

And then the skunk abruptly fell on its side.

"Is it dead?" Melissa whispered. "Did the rabies kill it?"

"You are as dumb as a box of hair, you know that?" Ophelia said. "It's breathing, isn't it?"

"What should we do?" Melissa asked, her anxiety spiking. She'd need to do some deep meditation after this. "It smells horrible even if it hasn't sprayed."

Ophelia thought a minute. "Get me a towel, Mr. Fairchild," she said.

"Okay," he whispered, and tiptoed out.

Great. One of her super-plush Turkish towels in mineral gray. A second later, Bradley returned with one and once again approached Ophelia. She took it, covered the skunk, and then made to pick it up.

"Don't!" Melissa said. "Let Bradley do it. He's the man. What if it bites you, Phee?"

"What if it bites *me*?" Bradley said. "I don't know anything about wild animals. Lillie was the one who dealt with—"

"Shush," Ophelia said. She slid her hands under the skunk and lifted it slowly. The critter didn't move. Phee took a step, then another, then another, coming closer and closer to the open door. "I'm just gonna walk down to the shore and leave it," she said. "If it's dying, we'll know soon enough, won't we?"

Melissa had to give her credit. She was so calm and mature. So much like Kaitlyn in so many ways, bad choices aside. Thank God the windows were closed, since it had been humid today, and Melissa preferred air-conditioning anyway. If the skunk sprayed, the damage would be mitigated (word of the day!).

Ophelia was getting closer. What if the skunk woke up and bit her? Melissa shot her fiancé a look. "You're letting a girl do a man's work," she whispered.

"Sexist," Ophelia murmured.

Bradley looked injured. "She's doing fine."

"What if it *is* rabid, Bradley?" Melissa hissed. "You're going to sacrifice a child's health because you're too scared to do anything?"

"Like I said," he whispered, "I don't know anything about wild animals. Lillie was the expert."

"For the love of Pete, Bradley! Be a man!"

"Fine." He tiptoed over—Ophelia was almost at the door. "Give it to me," he said. "I've got this."

"I'm fine, Mr. Fairchild," she said softly. "It's still breathing. Just stay put."

"I'll take it. Melissa's right. I don't want you to get hurt."

"No!" said Ophelia. "Just stay there and don't do nothin'."

"Anything," Melissa whispered.

"Ophelia, I'm almost your stepfather. Let me do this." He reached for the bundled skunk.

Ophelia rolled her eyes. "Fine. Go for it."

About dang time. He took the animal from Ophelia, gave Melissa a triumphant look that only a middle-aged white man could pull off and walked down the steps. Finally! Melissa pulled her phone out and started to text Lucia, one eye on Bradley.

And then the skunk woke up, poking its little head up. Phee was right . . . it *was* cute. "Shit!" Bradley yelled, and Melissa grabbed Ophelia, jerked her close and slid the door closed so hard it bounced.

Almost in slow motion, Brad bobbled the towel-wrapped skunk in his hands.

"Don't drop it!" Ophelia yelled, but the skunk wriggled, shrugging off the towel, turned its butt toward Bradley and did what nature told it to do.

Bradley screamed, clots of spray all over his face, and dropped the animal, which lifted its tail and sprayed again, this time hitting his Tom Ford pants. Then the skunk calmly scurried away.

"I think it's okay," Ophelia said, watching the animal's progress toward the water. "He didn't hurt it. Yep. It looks real healthy."

Bradley was wiping his eyes furiously. He ran up on the deck, but just before he got to the door, Melissa locked it. "Let me in!" he yelled. "I have to rinse my eyes!"

"Are you crazy? I'm not letting you in here! Use the hose!" she shouted back through the door.

"I need to get in the shower!"

"You're not coming in here, Bradley!"

"You sure picked yourself a stupid man," Ophelia said. Melissa looked at her. She was smiling.

Melissa felt her own lips pull up. "Not exactly great in an emergency."

Ophelia snorted.

"Melissa! Let me in!"

"Use the outdoor shower, dumbass!" Ophelia shouted. "Outdoor shower!"

Finally, Bradley understood and stumbled away to the enclosed cedar shower. They'd had sex in there the other day. Today, its use would not be so glamorous.

Melissa took out her phone. "Google, how do you get rid of skunk smell on a human?"

CHAPTER 12

Lillie

I t's just that I love sex," said my patient.

"Which is awesome," I said. "But four times a day is gonna take its toll." And oof, had it. Karen Henderson was in for the seventh time this year, a urinary tract infection *and* a yeast infection. "I recommend that you take a break until the yeast beast is cleared up."

"Do I have to?" she asked. "I have a date tonight, and I usually get ready by . . . you know. Relaxing myself." She grinned, and I smiled back. Where the woman found all her partners, I had no idea, since I'd been off the market for the past nineteen years. Maybe I'd hit her up for tips when the time came. If it came.

As a midwife, I saw women of all ages. Karen was in her fifties, postmenopausal and horny as hell. And while you didn't want to judge, you did have to be honest. "I love that you're enjoying yourself," I said. "And the hormone cream is definitely helping with the atrophy. But try to avoid penetration every time, Karen. You said you use a lot of toys, and while I'm sure that's fun, you've got to be careful. That's how the bacteria gets in."

"Killjoy," she said.

I smiled. "Have you tried the cranberry extract we talked about last time? It helps keep the bacteria from sticking to the wall of your bladder."

Karen sighed. "Yes, yes. And I pee after sex every time."

"Good. For now, you know the drill. Keflex, Monistat, Uristat if you need it, lots of fluids. I'd like you to try this probiotic, too. A lot of women swear by it to help the flora down there."

"You're the best, Lillie!" she said, jumping off the table. "Hey, can I get a speculum? You know, just to . . . check things?"

I hesitated. "Um . . . yeah. Sure. They're available online, but get one from a reputable medical supplier, okay?"

She wiggled her eyebrows at me, and I pulled off my gloves. "You know you want to tell me I'm a perv, Lillie," she said.

"Enjoy your weekend, Karen," I said, laughing. "Take care of yourself."

I left the exam room. "How's the sex addict?" Carol asked.

"Inside voice, please," I said. "Ask her yourself when she comes out." Karen did love to talk about her escapades, and Carol loved to listen. Match made in heaven (or hell, depending on your tolerance for oversharing).

"You have a message, by the way," Carol said. "On the office voice mail, not your direct line."

"Gotcha." I went into my office and listened.

"Hi, Lillie, it's Tasha. Everything's good, so don't worry." I smiled. I loved Tasha, who was a repeat client. She was eight months pregnant with her second baby, and everything was going great. "Listen, I was at the hospital for the birthing class, and I ran into a doctor who said something weird. She said that if I used you, I'd definitely have a lot more pain, and labor would take longer, maybe raising the risk to both me and the baby? Which I totally don't believe, but I figured you should know someone was trash-talking you. Carla Something? Colleen? I think her last name was Schneider. I told her I'd had a great experience the first time and was definitely using you, but I thought you should know. It was weird. Anyway, have a great evening, and I'll see you in two weeks! Bye!"

Carline Schneider, the evil obstetrician. "Are you kidding me?" I said, grabbing the phone to call her. Then I put it down. I'd talk to Wanda first to see how to handle this. Carline didn't take well to comments from "underlings," as she liked to call the nurses and midwives, CNAs and techs. Instead, I texted Tasha. Dr. Schneider does love a quick birth to get her home in time for a meal. Deleted that so I wouldn't get sued, just in case. Ah, Dr. Schneider, I wrote instead. Not a fan of midwives in my experience. Thanks for letting me know, and don't worry. We'll have every base covered for the big day.

Wanda was at the hospital. I stayed at the office as long as I could—we closed at five, though we'd do the occasional evening appointment (and of course, we'd go in for emergencies). For now, I did paperwork, still fuming about the idiot Carline. Some people had no business being in obstetrics. I couldn't imagine why she'd chosen that field instead of, I don't know, dentistry without painkillers. Unmedicated amputations. Hemorrhoid lancing. Wanda hated working with her, too, but Carline was the senior doctor in the Labor & Delivery Center.

I could not afford to attract Carline's ire. Literally could not afford it.

Brad would—

Nope. Brad would not. Once, Brad had listened to my tales from work, commenting, assessing. He'd told me Carline had passive-aggressive tendencies and a fear of her own inadequacy. "A little narcissism, some OCD, a God complex covering a deep insecurity of her own worth . . . the whole package."

Back when we were still sharing work stories. When I had someone who had my back. A sounding board, a sympathetic ear. Brad hadn't always been perfect, but marriage . . . I had loved being married.

Based on Melissa's and Brad's Instagram accounts, *they*

loved being engaged. So many pictures, so many hashtags. When I saw a photo of the three of them that Brad posted, and saw that he'd added #girldad, I cried. I did. Tears of rage and latent grief. He *had* been a girl dad. He had held our baby daughter and sobbed with me, and he'd been so incredibly kind in the months afterward. Now, this stranger's niece was apparently his daughter.

Soon, I told myself, I'd be past this. Soon, I'd be one of those women who'd say *I've never been happier* and mean it. Soon, thinking about my ex-husband, my son, the shattering of my family wouldn't be the only thing on my mind. Soon, I would fully embrace this independence and be completely solid in my new life.

It seemed impossible, but I wanted to believe it.

ᴄ~

With Hannah as my spy, I had already learned a great deal about Bralissa's wedding. It would cost somewhere in the neighborhood of $2 million. Two *million* dollars. For one day. Well, two days. There was a welcome party the night before, held at the Red Inn in Provincetown. The entire restaurant, closed for my ex-husband and his child bride. Hannah was coming over tonight to share more details. Information was power, after all.

But the two mil floored me. My finances, on the other hand . . . well, let's just say that I was never going to get out of debt, or I'd be a toothless, senile, humpbacked crone when I did. Or I'd have to work until I was eighty-three. Or win the lottery. Or marry someone rich. Or get nonfatally hit by a car, sue the driver and win. That one seemed like the most realistic option at this point.

I made a decent living, sure I did. But they don't call it Taxachusetts for nothing. It was the property taxes that killed me, since the house's location and fifteen years of renovation had boosted its worth to, ironically, $2 million. Son in college with my legal share being half: $15K. Annual mortgage and home equity line of credit: $30,000.

That left me with $10,000 a year for car, groceries, utilities, phone, internet, clothes, copays on Dylan's and my insurance, clothes and supplies for Dylan, Dylan's plane tickets home, etc. Brad didn't pay child support, because our son was eighteen. *Maybe* someday Brad would pay for some of Dylan's things, but right now, Dylan wasn't asking him, and neither was I. Add onto that vet bills (I did get pet insurance on Zeus, thank God, but they only covered emergency stuff).

So, you know . . . I was going to have to squeeze every dollar till it bled.

I got home, loved up Zeus by staring into his big eyes and kissing his heart-splotched nose and head, stroking his silky ears and running up and down the dirt driveway with him seven or eight times. Then I fed him, took a shower and cooked some snacks for Hannah and me. For the first time ever, my sister was deigning to visit me.

At seven thirty sharp, she knocked, dressed to kill as always, a stylish blue leather computer bag in one hand, a bottle of wine in the other.

"Hi," she said, giving me a quick once-over (pajama bottoms and a University of Montana Grizzlies T-shirt). "Oh, my God, you got a dog!"

"Hannah, this is Zeus. Zeus, my sister." He was already nosing her crotch. I watched, amused, as she tried to dodge his efforts. "Okay, Zeus, that's enough. Go lie down, boy."

He obeyed, flopping in front of the fireplace on his giant doggy bed.

"I'll just open that, then," I said, taking the wine from her.

"It's weird to be here without . . . Shit. Sorry."

"Without my husband? Child? Without a crowd?"

"Yep. All of those." She glanced at her fingernails, started to bite one, then stopped.

"Only the two of us," I said. "Seems like old times."

She didn't answer, just looked around the living room like she'd never been there. I went downstairs to the kitchen, uncorked the bottle—it was a nice sauvignon blanc—and put two glasses on a tray with a wine cooler and some sliced bolo do caco, a simple but delicious Portuguese bread made with flour, sweet potatoes, yeast and salt, still warm from the oven. I spread it with garlic butter and scallions, added it to the tray and carried it back upstairs.

"Wow," Hannah said. "You cook like Avó."

"Thank you," I said. I poured us the wine and put a sliced bolo on a plate and handed it to her. Hannah had never been too interested in learning from our grandmother. Then again, she could afford to eat out whenever she wanted. She'd given Dylan a lovely big check for graduation. That was nice, anyway.

We sat there a minute, her in the easy chair, me on the couch, the coffee table and tray of food and wine and thirty years of unspoken feelings separating us.

What would we have been like as sisters if she hadn't left? The eight-year-old me still missed her. The forty-one-year-old still resented her.

"So. Tell me everything," I said, taking a bite of the bread. Heaven.

She opened her laptop obediently and showed me her notes.

The hypocritical Reverend White would do the ceremony, thanks to the restored bell tower. I'd forgive him (someday). The special reception drink would be named the Stella Maris. *Enjoy our signature cocktail! Nolet's Reserve modern gin with makrut lime leaves, organic lemon slices and English hothouse cucumber!* This was in addition to a top-shelf full bar.

An arch on the beach made from Cape Cod driftwood just for them, entangled with roses and springtime wildflowers that would have to be shipped from New Zealand, given the fact that it was autumn here. The tent would be hung with enormous floral designs and special lighting. They'd hired the same photographer who had shot the Jonas-Chopra wedding.

"Seriously?" I said.

Hannah had the grace to roll her eyes.

There would be a raw bar, of course . . . it was Cape Cod, and every wedding had one. But *theirs* would have not just our famous Wellfleet oysters and clams, but also Maine lobster, wild Gulf shrimp, Alaskan king crab and otoro Atlantic bluefin tuna, whatever the hell that was. *Ten* types of passed hors d'oeuvres, all organic, including sushi made at the sushi station.

There'd be lobster bisque, a salad, five kinds of bread, biscuits and crackers, including gluten-free. Palate cleansers? Of course. Mint sorbet for the first course, apple and calvados sorbet for the second.

"What's calvados?" I asked.

"A type of brandy," Hannah said, taking another slice of bolo.

For dinner, Bralissa's wedding guests would be treated to a crab-stuffed filet mignon and lobster tail, or herbed sea bass curry with lemon rice and grape salad, or penne rigate with shaved brussels sprouts and Gorgonzola cheese, or summer squash with green zebra tomato lasagna with basil-pistachio pesto. Dessert would be a $10,000 five-tier cake shipped in from New York City, plus a Viennese table containing cream puffs, crème brûlées, miniature cheesecakes, tarte tatins, macarons in pale blue, and napoleons. A gourmet coffee bar staffed by the nice folks at Beanstock, serving espresso, cappuccino, and a custom blend made just for their wedding. Four kinds of red wines, six kinds of white, none of which sold for less than $600 a bottle, and, for the champagne toast, Dom Perignon Rosé from 1975, rolling in at $2,300 a bottle. A scotch and vodka tasting. A cigar sommelier.

"What is a cigar sommelier?" I asked.

"Exactly what it sounds like. Some guy pushing cigars that cost a hundred bucks a pop."

Later in the evening, a slew of gourmet sandwiches would be served in case the guests got peckish. A final champagne toast, then off went the happy couple in a blee-pin' Bentley.

I put her laptop down on the coffee table. "Wow."

"I know. I'm sorry. I would never have taken them on if you hadn't asked."

"You've done well for yourself," I said. It was supposed to be a compliment, but it didn't come out that way. "I mean, you know. You're a very good wedding planner."

"Thanks."

"No, I'm being sincere. You have . . . style."

"Well. Beatrice taught me a lot." Yes. Beatrice had been Hannah's Svengali, back when she was a teenager. "You know," she added, "Beatrice might be a great person for you to talk to these days. She's very kind. If you let her in, you'd know that."

"I have nothing against Beatrice."

"Right."

"I mean, I did, way back when."

"Why, Lillie? She was so nice to both of us."

"Um . . . because she was the other woman? Because she broke up our family? Because she hypnotized you and turned you into a different person?" Obviously, I was raw. What if Melissa hypnotized Dylan? My God! What if he loved her more than he loved me, the way Hannah loved Beatrice more than our mom? I grabbed a napkin and wiped my eyes.

"I needed to be a different person," Hannah said, her voice gentle. "Don't you remember?"

Zeus, tired of sleeping on his bed, jumped up onto the couch next to me to sleep there. He put his head in my lap and gazed up at me, his doggy eyes concerned.

"I mostly remember how much I missed you and how lonely I was," I said, tracing Zeus's spots. "Meanwhile, you were walking around their house with books on your head, speaking French and learning how to set a table for a five-course dinner."

She looked at me steadily. "I was bullied so badly at school here in Wellfleet. I was five foot ten at age twelve and had this face."

"What face? Your face?"

"Yes, Lillie! An ugly face. Big nose, weird forehead, small eyes. They called me—" She stopped. "It was a long time ago."

"I never thought you were ugly."

"You were the only one."

"Dad never did, either."

She sighed. "Well, you don't know what it was like. They called me . . ." She paused. "They called me the Virus. Said they didn't want to get too close in case my ugly was catching."

"What? You should've told me! I would've beaten them up for you, Hannah!"

"Yeah, well, you were eight."

"So? I was fierce!"

"You still are." She gave a small smile, but her sadness was undeniable.

"What else happened that I don't know about?" I asked.

"They'd trip me whenever they could. Shove my face down if I was getting a drink at the water fountain. I chipped my tooth when I was ten, remember?"

"No."

"Well. They'd do other things. Put stuff in my lunch."

"What stuff?"

"I don't know. Pencil shavings and dust. Once, Billy O'Hearn farted in my lunch box. I'd go to the bathroom, and Carrie-Ann Mortello would order me out and tell me to go to the boys' room. I had no one to sit with at lunch. That sort of thing."

My mouth hung open. "Why has it taken thirty years for you to tell me this?"

She shrugged. "I was embarrassed. It was . . . humiliating. And you . . . you loved me. I didn't want you to know you were the only one."

More tears surged into my eyes. "Oh, Hannah."

"Then this fairy godmother came into our lives, and I got the chance to go to a new school district and become someone else. The stepdaughter of a Chanel designer, two moms, the house on Commercial Street . . . I couldn't say no." She finished her wine. "Of course I felt bad about leaving you. I tried for us to stay friends, Lillie. I really did."

I sat back. "Well, we're not exactly enemies."

"But you never forgave me. And honestly, I don't blame you. I picked me over you. You're right. I left you."

I swallowed. "I never really knew things were so hard for you, Han."

"I know." She sighed. "Well. I should go. This wedding is happening in three weeks, and I have a lot to do. What else would you like to know?" She was back to Hannah Chapman, wedding planner.

"What time does the ceremony start?" I asked, putting away all the information Hannah had just told me. For now.

"Four. But listen, Lillie. You can't come. They've hired security, and they'll be passing out your picture."

"Wow. I guess I'm very scary. Glad I'll be on their minds, anyway."

"They called me a couple hours ago, asking for a biohazard cleaner for their house and lawn. There was a skunk in their house. Sprayed Brad right in the face."

I laughed. "Oh, that's *delightful*. Karma's watching, I guess." In the *face*! Huzzah! Well done, Flower!

Hannah looked amused, her version of uncontrollable giggles. "You wouldn't know how the skunk got in, would you?"

"Inside their house? Do they have a dog door?"

"No. And being the daughter of a lawyer, I noted that you didn't answer the question."

I looked away from her old-soul gaze and squashed my smile. "Well, I can't say I'm sorry to hear about this. Can you blame me?"

"I cannot. Well. I'll see you soon." She came in for a

hug, which was awkward, given our ten-inch height difference.

Still, it was nice. "Thanks, Hannah."

"Don't do anything that will get either of us sued, okay?"

"Okay."

She left, and I went to the window and watched her pull out of the driveway.

She *had* tried to keep things the same, pretending that my life hadn't been gutted. She went to that sunny, shiny new house, threw herself into the arms of our stepmother and didn't look back. It was far worse than my mother's desertion, because Hannah had always loved me. She had been my best friend. My only friend, really. It was only after I no longer had a big sister at home that I started meekly making friends with the girls in my class, the kids who rode the school bus with me. Until then, I'd never needed anyone else.

It had been so lonely, despite the chipmunks and turtles, the herons and seagulls. Without Hannah, our room felt too big, her empty, neatly made bed a constant reminder of her absence. Every other weekend she'd come home and seem a little surprised that she'd once lived here. "It seems smaller," she'd said, but she was having a growth spurt that made her taller than even Dad. Each Wednesday night she'd come for dinner, which was sustenance food—Dad wasn't much of a chef, so it was either from a can or a box, or his specialty—roasted carrots, potatoes and chicken cooked until it was practically jerky. Dessert was Oreos, the knockoff kind. Small wonder I became a good cook.

Contrast this with Mom's, where I was summoned Monday nights for dinner and where I spent every other weekend. "You can always change your mind and move here," Mom said at least twice per visit. She had painted "my" room purple—a lilac-hydrangea shade that I loved against my will. My bed was giant and covered in a fluffy white comforter with embroidered accent pillows. Where were those pillows the first eight years of my life, huh? Why couldn't I have had pretty pillows in Wellfleet?

Beatrice, who told me to call her Maman, seemed to expect that I, like Hannah, would be bowled over by her fabulosity. I was not. She was beautiful. Stunning, really . . . her father Ethiopian, her mother Norwegian. Her French accent made her sound elegant (to be fair, anything sounded elegant compared to what we spoke here in Massachusetts). She had modeled in her early years and then gotten a design degree. She and my mother made quite a striking pair, Mom tall, blond and blue-eyed like her Danish ancestors, Beatrice with her shaved head, glowing brown skin and green eyes. It was like living with Tyra Banks. You couldn't take your eyes off her.

"Lillie," she told me the first weekend I stayed with them. My name sounded like Lee-Lee from her lips. "You must find a signature lip color. It defines a woman's power and beauty, yes?"

"I'm eight," I said.

"It is never too early to start," she said. "Come! You may sit with me and try mine."

"No, thanks."

I didn't want to like anything about Mom and Hannah's new life. They had left me. My mother hadn't even put up a fuss, really, and didn't seem to miss me. She would simply sit back in her kitchen chair in the glaringly bright sunlight and point out the sparkling view, the flowers and the French food. Like Satan, she tried to steal my soul.

Between the party atmosphere, the wine, the food, the good looks, the superb conversation on things about which I knew nothing, I was lost. On the weekends I was forced to spend with them, I passed the time by throwing sticks or rocks into the bay, wooing seagulls with potato chips, hoping they'd crap on Beatrice's vintage Peugeot convertible, and waiting till I could go home.

Hannah drank up everything Beatrice had to teach—

how to dress, how to style her hair, how to care for her skin, eat less, walk more. By the time Hannah was sixteen, she could make boeuf à la mode and a fresh salad, could converse in French *and* Spanish, and I was a slumping teenager with oily skin and hairy arms, jealous and disgusted at the same time.

So that's how it was—Mom with her steely edges and razor-sharp insults, always telling me in one way or another that all this could be mine, too. It wasn't that she wanted me to live with her, not really. She just wanted to win another daughter so she could best my father.

But Hannah . . . Hannah had just tried to save herself. And she had.

Maybe, after all these years, it was time I started cutting Hannah some slack. She'd done what she had to do . . . and so had I.

I sighed and looked down at my notes.

Ceremony: Four o'clock, Saturday, October 14.

Thanks, sis.

CHAPTER 13

Melissa

Clear blue skies, seventy degrees and a wedding waiting to happen. The photographer snapped a few more pictures and muttered instructions to his assistants.

"Okay, Melissa," he said to her. "Chin down, eyes on me, gorgeous, gorgeous, you're *so* pretty, that's it!"

She smiled. She *was* so pretty. It was true. She dropped her gaze to her bouquet, knowing her fresh eyelash extensions would show beautifully.

"Now, over by the window, eyes straight ahead, yes, yes, you're sure you haven't modeled, my God, you make my job easy."

Oh, everything was *perfect*. Hannah had done an incredible job, Melissa had to hand it to her. Just looking out over the yard made her heart soar.

There were endless strands of bulbs across the vast green lawn (smelling like skunk no more, thank goodness!). Hannah was outside, talking to the crew of a half dozen people as they uplit a few trees and put out the three hundred luminarias that would be lit at dusk. The infinity pool was filled with small, floating glass bowls, each one holding a bobbing candle atop an orchid blossom. The centerpieces were cream and white roses, white hydrangeas, gardenias and orchids, all spilling out of beautiful Waterford Lismore Rose bowls. Above each table hung a stunning, huge flower arrangement with tiny fairy lights hidden within.

To the left of the vast yard, the ceremony area was set with chairs, the driftwood arch stunning under its cloak of flowers. Each row of seats had a bountiful floral arrangement, and it was utterly magical. The wedding favors were boxed and wrapped and set out by the exit—each guest would receive a one-of-a-kind Judith Stiles vase (she was a local potter, quite talented *and* the mother of a movie star, which would help Melissa's influencer status hugely, she hoped). In addition, guests would get a sampling of Chequessett Chocolate truffles, a bag of specially roasted coffee from Beanstock, a bottle of locally made Dry Line gin and a set of gorgeous, heavy Waterford candlesticks.

So far today, Melissa had done yoga at dawn, had a light breakfast, had a massage on the master bedroom deck (Bradley had had one, too, on another deck, since she wanted to surprise him at the First Look). The massage was followed by a soothing green tea and cucumber facial and hand treatment and a fresh mani-pedi. A light lunch, a mimosa, several bottles of Perrier mineral water. The hair and makeup stylists had arrived, and right now, she felt like a princess, sitting there in a white silk robe with her minions around her, the photographer moving through the room, his assistants holding up light reflectors.

She had been waiting all her life to feel this way.

"Isn't this fun?" she asked Ophelia, who was having her hair done as well.

"Not for me."

"Oh, Phee!" Melissa said, laughing lightly. The photographer took a string of photos, and Melissa turned slightly toward him while still looking at Ophelia. "Go ahead, admit you like being pampered."

"Can I call my mom today?"

"I thought she was your daughter," whispered the hairstylist, who was pulling on a few strands of Melissa's hair to texturize it.

"In my heart, she absolutely is," Melissa said, glancing up at the woman. Marie? Mary? Marny? Something like that.

"Can I?" asked Ophelia.

"Not today, honey." Melissa didn't want the negativity of her sister tainting the beautiful energy today. "You can call her tomorrow and give her all the details. She'll be dying to hear," she said, conscious of the eyes on her. "But today, just relax and enjoy, honeybun."

Now that Ophelia had brought Kaitlyn to the fore, Melissa couldn't help picturing a different scenario. One with her loving, sober sister, minus the hillbilly accent, minus the numerous tattoos, minus the attitude. Instead, Kaitlyn would be teary-eyed and hilarious, making everyone laugh. In this scenario, she had changed her name spelling to Caitlin, so much classier—and would be the maid of honor. Ophelia would be the happy junior bridesmaid.

It would've been nice to have a sister like that. Or a friend.

But she couldn't taint her big day by thinking sad thoughts. "It's time to put your dress on, honey," she said to Ophelia. "You'll look so gorgeous in it."

"Fine." Ophelia stood up. "But this is stupid," she said. "I barely know him. *You* barely know him. He's an idiot, and he's so fake. I can't stand him. He just told me to call him Dad, for crying out loud."

"He loves you," Melissa said. "Can someone take her to her room and help her with the dress? She won't be able to zip it alone."

Ophelia was removed to be dressed. Melissa took a cleansing breath and released it. This day was everything. Her sullen niece was not going to ruin it. No one was going to ruin it.

"Twenty minutes till First Look," Hannah said, sticking her head in the doorway.

"Thank you, Hannah," she said smoothly. "I'll be right

on time. Um . . . could you stay and help me get in my gown?"

"Of course. My pleasure."

Because honestly, the person Melissa knew best in this room was Hannah Chapman. There was that sister pang again. Hannah *felt* like her friend. For the past six weeks, even before Bradley's divorce was final, Melissa had talked more to Hannah than anyone, even Bradley. Hannah knew her favorite colors, foods, fabrics, desserts, flowers, vacation spots. She'd told Hannah about Dennis's "tragic passing" and why this day would be so important.

Because Melissa Grace Spencer Finch soon-to-be Fairchild was in control, living her *destiny*.

As Hannah zipped her up (and the photographer took more photos), Melissa had to ask. "How's your sister doing today? I hate thinking that she's upset or sad."

Hannah gave her a mysterious look. "I did call her this morning. She seems great, actually."

"Is she working today?"

"She said she was reading. She didn't mention her schedule."

Melissa had nothing against Lillie, of course. She wasn't out to hurt her or rub her face in all that she, Melissa, had. No, she wished Bradley's first wife the best, because that's what classy people did. Wished the losers luck and kept moving onward and upward. Even so, she was glad she'd thought of security guards.

She put on her simple necklace—a gold bezel-set two-carat diamond—and added her diamond drop earrings. Simple, but so stunning. Her hair was perfect, and she couldn't take her eyes off her reflection. *Click-click-click* went the camera.

Take it in, said the wedding advice. *Notice everything. You'll never get married again.*

If things went well with Bradley, that might even be true.

"It looks beautiful out there," Hannah said.

Melissa again glanced out her window, relishing the view,

the splendor. The tide was almost out, and there were people and dogs in the distance. Someone was clamming, which was so romantic and perfect for the moment. This place was *real*. Coming here had been the absolute right decision.

As for the guests, there were four of the New York mothers and their husbands here. Curiosity, Melissa knew, and possible jealousy. They were sipping champagne, all dressed to kill. As they should be for the wedding of the year! There were Vanessa and Charles Fairchild. Strange, to have in-laws this time around. At first, they'd been totally on Lillie's side, until Bradley had told them—when she was out of the room, of course—that if they ever wanted to see him again, they would have to accept and love Melissa. She'd helped with the wording, and it had gone perfectly. Then, when she came back in, she'd been so warm and welcoming. If they were still stiff and awkward, well, who really cared?

So many eyes on her, soaking in her style and good taste, her money, her power. Oh, and her love for Bradley, because she did love him. He fit the bill—older, handsome, educated. Not as impressive as an orthopedic surgeon, of course, but not bad, either.

"Stay right there," said one of the photographers. "That light is incredible on you. You look radiant."

"I've never been happier," she said. "Everything is so perfect, Hannah! I can't wait to get out there."

"I'll get Brad ready for the First Look. And you do look incredible."

A few moments later, Melissa floated down the stairs in front of the camera crew, the Swarovski crystals sparkling in the golden afternoon light. Out the front door, over to the First Look area. Where was Ophelia? Oh, for crying out loud. Lying in the hammock, biting a fingernail and getting all wrinkled. Melissa chose not to dwell.

Bradley stood on the lush front lawn between two brilliant red maple trees, his back to her. This was the moment! A photographer's assistant fluffed her dress so the train was perfect, and when the photographer said "Go," Melissa walked slowly up to Bradley. The camera whirred in a stream of clicks as Melissa tapped his shoulder. He turned around, covered his mouth with his hand, and tears filled his gorgeous blue eyes.

"My God, you're so beautiful," he said, and she laughed and posed, the gown tossing off the light. She kissed him, then turned to the makeup artist, who dabbed her lips with a bit more gloss as the photographer captured Bradley's tears.

"Let's get this wedding started," Hannah said when fifteen more minutes of First Look had passed. She handed Melissa the bouquet, a mass of white and blush blossoms, gave Ophelia her basket of flower petals, and went around the house to give the reverend the heads-up.

"I love you so much," Bradley whispered.

"Oh, darling, I love you, too," she said back. "See you at the altar."

"You're perfect. This day is perfect. Our life is perfect."

Enough with that word. "I know. Now go! Get up there!" She beamed at him, her slight irritation fading. After all, he knew his place. To adore her. Full stop.

Bradley went up to the arch and waited, alone except for Reverend White. Sadly, Dylan had refused to come for the wedding and be his best man, which would have been nice for Bradley, but you know what? It was better this way. No reminders of Lillie, except for her sister. And former in-laws. And every guest from Wellfleet.

It didn't matter. There was a new Mrs. Fairchild in town.

She peeked around the corner. Bradley was smiling at the crowd—one hundred and seventy-four guests.

And then, the string quartet began playing Mozart's "Ave verum corpus," a beautiful song, the meaning of which she didn't know, but the melody of which she loved.

"Ophelia, you're up," Melissa said, patting her shoulder. "Have fun, sweetheart!"

Ophelia rolled her eyes, clenched the basket in her hand and stomped toward Bradley.

One more fluff of her dress, one touch from the makeup artist. Then off she went, walking slowly, smiling with bliss in her heart, her entire soul soaring at the sight of all these people, all this admiration. It seemed like the entire world was watching. There was what's-her-name from the yoga studio. Mirabelle and Libby and their husbands from New York. Yes! Let them see her in her glory! They'd dropped her fast enough after Dennis died. The reverend's wife, the lesbians from the arts council, the first selectman. Everyone had their phones out, too. Oh, she hoped they'd use the hashtag she'd come up with—#HappilyEverFairchild. It was encouraged on all the programs and the three chalkboards they'd had custom painted.

There was Bradley, teary-eyed, handsome. A gentle breeze blew Melissa's tendrils, and the guests sat down. Melissa handed her bouquet to Ophelia and kissed her cheek, pretending that the child didn't pull away, then joined hands with Bradley.

Surely, this was the most beautiful moment anyone here would ever see.

"I love you," she whispered.

"I love you, too," he whispered back, and it was so romantic!

"Dearly beloved," Reverend White began. "We are gathered in this beautiful place to join this man and this woman in the holy bonds of matrimony."

Melissa felt herself sparkling. Sparkling!

Then she heard the murmur. Looking at the crowd, she put her hand to the back of her head to make sure her veil was in place. It was. Ophelia was gaping, open-mouthed, at something in the distance. *Everyone* was gaping.

Melissa turned. Brad turned. For a second, the image was too bizarre to process.

"What . . . what is that?" Melissa said, and the microphone picked up her words. People were standing now, taking pictures, murmuring in excitement.

Something—someone—was standing out on the mud

flats, not thirty yards from where Melissa stood. Someone freakishly tall and dressed in a long, black robe or dress or something. Its face was huge and gray, and dreadlocks flapped out behind it. The garment was shredded so that long rags of black fluttered in the breeze. It looked like one of Harry Potter's Dementors . . . or the angel of death.

Bradley's face was frozen in horror. He wasn't scared, was he? Should she be?

"Is that Lillie?" someone asked.

Oh, my *God*. "Bradley? Is that her?" Melissa said, her voice shrill.

"I—I don't know!" he said. "Hannah? Hannah!"

"On it," she said, hustling toward the shore. She stopped and murmured something to the caterer and kept going.

Oh, gosh *darn* it! Everyone was taking photos. They better not use her hashtag!

"Get security!" Melissa called, an edge of panic in her voice. "Get her out of here! She's *ruining* my wedding!" Her voice was too loud—crud, the microphone! Tears blurred her eyes, and her makeup would have to be touched up.

"I guess there's a slight delay, folks," said Reverend White. "Why don't you two sit down?" he suggested.

She didn't want to sit down! Her magnificent dress would wrinkle! But Bradley led her to the front row, where Ophelia sat, smirking.

"It isn't funny," Melissa hissed.

"You sure about that?" Ophelia said. "'Cuz I think it's awesome."

This couldn't be happening. It could not happen. Melissa started to cry, and Bradley put his arm around her. She shoved it off, furious. He should've known this would happen! Everything was going to be ruined now. No one would be talking about her!

She deserved so much more.

CHAPTER 14

Lillie

I watched as my sister approached in her bare feet, her rose-pink dress elegant. On the lawn, waiters were passing out champagne, and yes, the wedding seemed to be on hold. The breeze blew a little harder, and my dress flapped in a most gratifying manner.

"Hey," Hannah said.

"Hi," I answered.

"That is some mask."

"Thanks. Amazon." It really was an A-plus mask . . . latex, super creepy with its gaping, fibrous maw and too-big eye sockets.

I should probably see a therapist. Nevertheless, I *was* having a great time.

Hannah cocked her head. "How are you so tall? I'd pick up the hem of your dress, but I don't want to ruin the illusion."

"I'm standing on a bucket. I was clamming an hour ago."

"Did you make the dress yourself?"

"Goodwill with some alterations."

"Mm." Hannah stood for a second, looking out to the horizon. "Beautiful day, huh?"

"Weather-wise, yes."

"So . . . any chance you'll leave?" Hannah asked.

"Nope. Sorry if this hurts your business."

"I've already been paid. It might hurt yours, though. There are more than a few townies here. I'm not sure they want a Dementor delivering their babies."

"Eh. I think everyone will understand, and I'm beyond caring." My voice was calm. "Also, can they really prove it's me?"

"I have to give you credit, Lils. This is legal and everything. Not like the skunk."

"Skunk?" I said, but I was smiling under the mask.

"Okay, well, let's pretend I'm working very hard to convince you to leave." She put her hands on her hips.

"No one owns the ocean," I said.

"True enough."

"I just want to make sure I'm in every shot of the ceremony."

"Oh, you will be," Hannah said. "They'll photoshop you out, of course."

I shrugged. "It's worth it."

"Anything else I should know about?"

"There may be some music." I pulled a little speaker out of my pocket. "The guy at Verizon said it was the loudest one."

"I see. Got a playlist?"

"'Night on Bald Mountain,' 'Phantom of the Opera.' That organ song by Bach. I googled 'scariest songs.'"

Hannah glanced back at the wedding, where a sea of phones, as well as the famous photographer, were photographing me. "You gonna stay till the tide comes back in?"

"I'm not sure yet. As you say, it's a gorgeous day."

Hannah sighed. "Okay, I'm going to go back, exasperated but helpless to make you leave. I'll say you're a performance artist."

"Thanks, Han. Snag me some food for later."

My sister smiled reluctantly. "I'll see what I can do. Talk to you tomorrow, no doubt."

"You bet."

My sister turned, threw up her hands in fake frustration, and walked back, picked up her shoes and approached the unhappy couple.

Whatever she said, it worked. No one came out to arrest me, and even if they had, I knew and liked every cop on the force, especially the three I'd babysat way back when. I turned on the music—the theme from *Prometheus* was the first song up. Oh, yeah. Nice and loud.

That's how I watched my husband marry another woman. He glanced at me occasionally, probably glaring. I didn't move, just stood there like an evil witch, until the sun went down and the tide started to come in. Then, under cover of darkness, I got off my bucket, took off my mask, scooped up my clams and walked back to Great Island Trail and to my car, where I changed back into jeans and a T-shirt.

∽

A few hours later, I was relaxing at home with a nice glass of wine, garlicky clams in my tummy, feeling pretty damn smug. Aside from a little sunburn on my neck where the mask hadn't reached, I was happier than I had been in months. Zeus was lying on my feet, keeping them warm.

Dylan had texted me three times today, all cheerful stuff about football and classes, and a few pictures, too, trying to distract me. Such a good, kind boy. I called him, and miraculously, he was free. My heart squeezed hard at the sound of his voice. We talked about football practices, his writing class, the cute girl who lived on his floor, his roommate's horrible taste in music. And then . . .

"You okay, Mom?"

I knew what he was asking. "Yeah! I had a really nice day, actually. Dug some clams."

"I sure miss your cooking." He paused. "I meant about Dad's wedding."

"I know. I'm fine, honey. What about you?"

"Not so fine. I hope it rained."

"Unfortunately, no." We were quiet for a few seconds. "I can't wait for you to meet Zeus," I said. "You'll love him."

"I already do. Send me some more pictures, okay?"

"You bet."

"Okay. Well . . . take care, Mom. Love you."

"Love you, too, sweetheart. So much. Have a nice night, Dyllie."

"You too."

I clicked off with a bittersweet sigh. Took another sip of wine.

It was so different, living here without husband or son. Everywhere I looked, I saw how Brad and I had changed the house, taking it from a musty little cottage to a sunny, charming three-story home. I remembered Dylan at age five, peeking down at us from the balcony, grinning, spying on us when he should have been asleep. Slipping into bed after delivering a baby late on a winter night, the warmth and good smell of my husband, how his arm would drape over me. Cooking and laughing in our funky kitchen downstairs, eating at the table or on the porch. *Anyone* looking in would have seen our happiness.

You're damn right I ruined his wedding.

Around 1:00 a.m., Brad sent me an email, as I had known he would.

Do you know how upset you made Melissa??? YOU are going to have to pay the extra money so the photographer can fix our photos! I will send you the bill and take you to small claims court if you don't pay. Dylan would be ashamed of you! By the way, it doesn't even matter. Nothing could have, because I am with the woman of my dreams. I have never been happier, and incidentally, the sex is unbelievable.

He sure didn't sound happy, and he sure wasn't screwing his new wife, not from the keyboard.

I couldn't resist responding.

Why are you emailing me a nonsensical diatribe on your wedding night? I typed. You sound unbalanced. Maybe you should see a therapist.

I hit send with a flourish, then bent down to kiss the cute little heart on my dog's nose. He wagged his tail.

Today was the best day I'd had in months. Months. Today, I hadn't been a woman scorned. I'd been one of the Furies, a goddess of retribution and vengeance.

It was *wicked* fun.

CHAPTER 15

Lillie

Did you put a knife in my suitcase?" Brad barked over the phone the next afternoon when I was at work.

"What?" I said, genuinely shocked.

"I'm being held by TSA at Logan because you put a knife in my suitcase!" he yelled.

Wow. Hats off to the person who did that. My sister, maybe, in a gesture of loyalty? "What kind of knife?" I asked.

"A Swiss Army knife!"

"Are you feeling homicidal again?" I asked, hoping a TSA agent was listening in.

"No! Of course not! Now we're going to miss our flight."

Poor, *poor* thing. "I'm at work, Brad," I said. "Please don't call me unless there's an emergency involving our son." I hung up.

"Trouble in paradise?" Wanda asked, looking up from the computer.

"He's being detained at TSA and thinks it's my fault."

"Such a jerk." She paused. "Is it your fault?"

"No, but I kind of wish it was. Hey, did you check Heidi? She had some cramping."

"Yeah. We're keeping an eye on it, but I won't be surprised if she delivers at home again." Heidi had had her first baby on the beach; this was her fourth, and to say she was a champion pusher would be an understatement. Her last child had taken all of two contractions and one push. I'd just been glad the baby hadn't been born in the produce aisle, as Heidi had just been grocery shopping an hour before.

Speaking of groceries, I needed to drive down to Orleans to get some food. Cooking for one was hard. I hated throwing away food, so my father was eating a lot of leftovers these days.

But first, an errand. I took the long way to Orleans. In other words, I drove to Bralissa's house. Still no security cameras. Dummies. I mean, breaking and entering was almost nonexistent on Cape Cod, at least in these parts, but I had thought they'd take me into consideration. They had only the alarm, something Hannah had confirmed.

I may not have put a knife into Brad's suitcase—the thought of him being interrogated and, I hoped, cavity searched gave me a shudder of pleasure—but I was about to rain on their little slice of heaven (again).

Nikki Demeter, who owned the cleaning service that did Stella Maris, had given me the new code to the house. Her husband had left her, too, and now lived in North Carolina with his second wife and their newborn twins. I parked in my hidden spot and walked right up to the front door. No other cars in the driveway or garage. My intel (Louis, one of the security guards they'd hired for the wedding and who had ridden the school bus with me) had informed me that Ophelia was staying with Vanessa and Charles in Orleans.

The thought of the Fairchilds' house, where I'd once been so welcomed and loved, gave me a pang. I'd never go into Vanessa's kitchen again. Never sit on their porch and sip coffee. Charles would never welcome me with the words "There she is!" when I came into their house. Two years ago, when he'd had a heart attack, I was the one who talked to the doctors, oversaw his rehab and new diet. The one who'd given him a sponge bath on his third night in the hospital to spare him the indignity of being washed by a stranger.

Those two had been my family, but they sure had been able to drop me in an instant, hadn't they?

I walked down the slate path to Melissa and Brad's front door, punched in the code and went inside. I hadn't really taken a good look around when I let Flower out, too worried about being caught.

It was stunning. White everything, floor-to-ceiling windows, posh midcentury furniture. Beautiful artwork . . . I recognized some pieces from Left Bank Gallery and Long Pond Arts. Gerry and Elsbeth Smith, who owned Long Pond Arts, were happily married, and they'd been together for, what, forty years? They held hands so sweetly when they walked down Main Street.

I had thought that would've been Brad and me. Guess not. Already, there were pictures of Brad and Melissa displayed. My heart cramped. After all this, I would not have taken him back if he crawled on Legos, but seeing him in these frames with another woman . . . that was where I used to be.

I stopped in front of a picture of Brad and Dylan, and my heart cramped again. Brad must've kept it on his computer, because I'd never had it printed.

I'd taken that picture, the two of them standing in the golden light at Boat Meadow in Eastham five years ago, just before Dylan had started eighth grade. They looked so much alike. Dylan was just about as tall as Brad there, but skinny. Still my little boy who kissed me on the cheek without reservation and hugged me happily when he got off the school bus.

I hoped Brad missed our son. I hoped it clawed at his heart. But it sure didn't seem that way. Brad was on his way to France . . . if TSA had let him go, that was.

Here was one of him with Melissa and Ophelia, the

child scowling directly into the camera. I couldn't help smiling . . . but at the same time, jealousy flared. Brad had a stepdaughter or stepniece now. Our daughter never got to draw a breath, and yet Brad had a little girl in his life. I was all alone.

I turned and started. My intel had not warned me of a dog. A trembling, light brown Chihuahua in a Burberry plaid sweater sat looking at me. They must've hired a dog sitter. At least the dog wasn't crated all day. Was the dog sitter here? No. No cars, no bike in the driveway. It was possible a teenager had been dropped off, but Louis had said the house would be empty. Probably, the dog sitter came and went a couple of times a day.

The dog cocked its apricot-sized head and whined.

"Hi, honey," I said. "Don't be scared." Zeus could swallow that creature in one gulp. I hoped it stayed inside; foxes and coyotes would make short work of the bony little thing.

I approached the wee rat and picked it up. "Teeny," said her pink name tag. "Sorry you didn't get a better name," I said. "I would've called you . . . I don't know. Toffee." She was cute, with her bulging little eyes and tiny paws. I tucked her under my arm and continued my tour of the house.

All very tasteful, all very perfect. I'd take a house with some character to this *Architectural Digest* spread any day. How could Brad, who had sat in a fat recliner from Cardi's every night for the past twenty years, be comfortable in this sleek wooden number? Oh. Right. He was a pretentious dick. That's how.

Teeny was licking my hand. "Thanks, puppy," I said, petting her knobby head.

I went into the master bedroom. Soaring ceilings, huge windows with electric shades. Enormous bed with an upholstered cream-colored headboard, gorgeous blue duvet with a dozen accent pillows. Their bathroom was bigger than my kitchen. Soaking tub, giant shower with all sorts of bells and whistles, a huge double-sink vanity, toilet room, two closets.

Brad and I used to fondly share a sink at night, talking around our toothbrushes. He never had any qualms about bursting in to take a dump if I was in the shower. Now, Melissa would be spared such crudity.

Well, I had a job to do. I pulled the ziplock baggie out of my pocket, opened it and offered it to Teeny. After all, this wouldn't work if she ate it. Fortunately, she sniffed and turned away, chastising me with disappointed eyes. Good. I set her down, got on my hands and knees, then wriggled under their giant bed. Teeny observed me, then trotted to me and curled in a circle against my side, no bigger than a donut from Hole in One.

"Aw," I said. "You poor thing, having to live with these two. I hope Ophelia is nice, at least."

Then I did the job I'd come to do—took the shrimp out of the baggie. They'd had shrimp at the raw bar yesterday, so any guest could be blamed. I looked for a spot to hide it. Here. Right here, between the wall and the foot of the headboard.

I lay there, staring at the underside of the mattress, Teeny's little ribs rising and falling under my hand. This is where Brad slept now . . . well, not under the bed, presumably. Here, in this soulless, glorious room. Did he ever miss *our* room? Did he miss me? Right up until June, we'd always slept together like two spoons, an invisible, magnetic force drawing us to each other.

My eyes were tired and gritty. I still wasn't sleeping well. It was dim and peaceful under the bed here, and the warmth of the little dog at my side felt so good. I'd just close my eyes for a minute.

I woke up to the sound of voices. Teeny was still at my side, snoring softly.

Shit.

"Teeny?" A kid's voice. Ophelia, no doubt. "Teeny, where are you?"

"What do you want for dinner, darling?" Oh . . . crap. It was Vanessa. I thought they were staying at the Fairchilds' house! Well, apparently their plans had changed. My heart started thumping with guilt.

"I don't care," Ophelia said. "Anything's good with me." Her voice was friendly enough. "Teeny? Where are you?"

"Go," I whispered to the little dog, pushing her. "Go see Ophelia!"

The dog barked. "Sh!" I hissed, giving her tiny butt a gentle shove. "Go get supper! Suppertime!"

Teeny tilted her head at me and barked again.

"Now I hear you," said Ophelia. "Where are you, honey? You under the bed?" There was a slight twang in her voice.

Then I saw knees, then a face surrounded by tight blond curls. Teeny bounced into her arms the second before the kid saw me.

Neither of us moved. Teeny licked Ophelia's face.

"Hi," I whispered after a second.

"Who are you?" she whispered back.

"Um . . . the cleaning lady?"

"No, you're not."

"No, I'm not." Time for the truth, I guessed. "I'm Brad's ex-wife. I met you when you first moved in, remember? I brought flowers and cookies."

Her pale eyes widened. "Wow." Teeny's tail was wagging hard.

"Ophelia, honey, come into the kitchen and help me make a salad," called Vanessa. Ophelia grimaced.

"Salad. So boring," I said.

"You got that right." She didn't seem inclined to bust me, or to leave her spot.

"Um, so listen, Ophelia . . . I'm obviously not supposed to be here, and if Vanessa finds out, I'll be in a lot of trouble. Think you can keep this to yourself?"

Her eyes narrowed. "Whatcha doing under there?"

I tried to think of a good lie and came up empty. "I . . . I left a shrimp here." I pointed to the bed's foot. "In a few days, it'll stink to high heaven, just in time for your . . . for the newlyweds' homecoming."

She nodded slowly. "Hey. You're the one who put the skunk in our house, aren't you?"

"Skunk? What skunk?"

She smiled. "You are, aren't you? You hate them. My aunt and that boomer she married."

Boomer. I loved this child. "'Hate' is such a strong word. But yeah, he cheated on me and dumped me, so I'm a little . . . bitter."

"He's gross. He keeps calling himself a girl dad, like he's Ryan Reynolds or something. He even hashtagged it on Insta." Yes. I had seen that. "And he is so *not* my dad. I barely even know my real father. Dennis, I liked him, but he died. This guy . . . Mr. Fairchild, though, he's trash."

"That's true."

"They bought me Teeny as if that would make everything okay." Her twang seemed to infuse all the more disdain into her voice.

"Teeny *is* pretty cute," I said.

"Yeah. Except for this dumb sweater."

"Agreed." I paused. "I don't suppose you know anything about a Swiss Army knife in his suitcase."

"I don't even know what that is." She grinned. "I'm just a kid."

This child would go places.

"Ophelia? Are you talking to someone?" Vanessa's voice was closer now.

"I'm on the phone. Be right there," she called over her shoulder. "You're Dylan's mom, too, I guess?" There was worry in her eyes.

"Right." I hesitated. "He's a really good kid. He'll be nice to you."

"If they even stay married long enough for me to meet him."

Oh, yes, I liked this kid a lot. "Give me your phone," I said. "So you have my number in case you ever want to talk."

Her face softened. "Okay." She pulled it out of her back

pocket and handed it over, and I entered my info under Contacts.

"I'm giving myself a code name . . . Harriet. Like Harriet the Spy."

"Who's that?"

"You don't know Harriet the Spy? It's a book about a nosy kid in New York City. I bet Open Book has it in stock this very minute. I'll send it to you."

Ophelia smiled, and Teeny licked her chin.

"Well, you better git," she said. "I won't say anything, don't worry."

"Thanks. I appreciate that."

She watched as I wriggled out. I extended my hand. "Lillie," I said.

"Ophelia. I used to be named Harminee, but that's my middle name now."

"Pretty." I stood there another second, resisting the urge to hug her. It felt like she could use one. "Well. I'll see you again, I hope."

"Same here. Best if you go out that way." She jerked her chin at the sliding glass door, and I obeyed. Turned back and waved. She waved back, then made Teeny wave as well.

Seemed like I had a new friend.

CHAPTER 16

Lillie

I parked in the tiny driveway on Commercial Street, sighed and got out of the car.

"Oh, stop," Beth said. "Fix your face. At least the food will be good. Do you think Beatrice will have free stuff?" As a longtime Chanel employee, my stepmother got lots of makeup, skin care, perfume and clothing.

"Probably," I said. Chanel's largest size was 16, which they classified as extra-extra-extra-large. I refused to wear anything of theirs on principle. Also, I was more of a scrubs/jeans person, anyway, and I didn't usually wear makeup, so . . .

"I'll take anything," Beth said. "That suit she gave me a few years ago? I saw it online for more than a thousand bucks! Used!"

"Okay, calm down," I said. "I'm sure she'll give you something if you ask." Maybe I should be asking her for stuff I could sell to increase my income. It wasn't a bad idea.

Dinner at the Moms' was never pleasant, so I'd brought Beth along as a buffer. Like most people, Bethie adored my stepmother. I didn't hate Beatrice . . . I just didn't fawn all over her like everyone else. Sure, she was beautiful, charming and talented, spoke four languages and could have comfortably chatted with the Obamas (and probably had). Someone who *wasn't* in love with her was probably refreshing.

As for Mom . . . I had never understood her. If she loved Beatrice, it was in her own weird, passive-aggressive way. Why Beatrice had fallen for Mom was a mystery. Sure, Mom was also beautiful and smart, but kind? Not a word that ever leaped to mind. I remembered one time when I'd fallen out of a tree while playing, back before the divorce, and come in with bloody knees and scraped palms.

"What do you expect, Lillie?" she said. "If you're going to play outside like a feral squirrel, you're going to get hurt! Go wash up and put on some Band-Aids." There was no boo-boo kissing in our house, no sir.

Her sole purpose in life seemed to be winning, which made her a fantastic lawyer. It didn't seem to give her any real happiness, though. *Brittle* was the word that most often came to mind when I thought of her, which I tried not to do unless necessary. When I'd told her Brad and I were getting married, she said I was stupid. When I added that I was pregnant, she told me a child would tie me down. The house in Wellfleet—money pit. Being a nurse-midwife—"Why would you want to look at genitalia all day, Liliana?"

"You're late," she said as Beth and I walked in, proving my point.

"Hi, Mrs. Silva!" Beth said, as I had made her promise to do.

"It's Ms. Clifton and has been for thirty-three years," Mom said, raising an elegant, contemptuous eyebrow. She had changed her name to Silva when she married Dad, but snatched it back when she left him. Didn't change her name for Beatrice, whose last name was Laurent.

"Not your first cocktail?" said I.

"You and your puritanical sensibilities, Lillie. You get that from your father. It's so boring."

"Bonsoir, Lillie!" Beatrice said, coming in for her Chanel-scented kiss-kiss on either cheek. She wore white jeans and a cream-colored off-the-shoulder sweater that looked amazing against her skin. Leopard-print high heels. "Bonsoir, Elizabet." She left off the *th* sound, and Beth lapped it up.

"Comment ça va?" Beth asked, the only sentence she knew in French.

"Très bien, chérie. Regardez-vous, si belle!"

"Hi, Beatrice," I said. My sister was sitting on the couch, sipping wine. "Hi, Hannah. How are you?"

"Great. I had a lovely chat with my favorite nephew today."

"Aw, nice," I said.

"Such a good boy," Beatrice said. "It must be hard for him, his parents divorcing when he is far away."

"It's not easy when it's up close, either," I said. "As I know firsthand." Beatrice looked confused, then glanced away as the penny dropped.

"Lils," Hannah said. "It's been more than thirty years. I'm just gonna toss this out there, but maybe it's time to let go?"

"I'm fresh off the divorce wagon of suckiness, Hannah. I think it's acceptable that I get to bitch and moan a little. Why has no one made me a cocktail yet?"

"Gin and bitterness?" Beth asked.

"Sounds great."

She grinned and went into the kitchen like a good friend.

I sat down next to my sister. Like Beatrice, she was dressed beautifully, in a yellow silky top and a white skirt with tiny yellow triangles all over it. Perfect makeup.

Funny that she'd said the other day that she was ugly. Yes, her nose was long and crooked, but so was Meryl Streep's, right? No one called Meryl ugly. But I'd been thinking of our childhood days together, and while I mostly remembered my own contentment, there were flashes of Hannah's misery. Her hunched posture to hide her height. How she'd been a cheerleader for exactly one practice before quitting and weeping into her pillow. She'd had a boy-friend in college, but she'd never had a serious relationship since. I assumed it was by choice, since she projected confidence and success. Each year, she took a vacation in January, somewhere exotic like Kauai or Thailand. Unless Beatrice went along, she'd go alone, or on one of those women-only tours.

Could my übersuccessful, superclassy sister be lonely?

"Beatrice," I said as Beth came into the room and handed me a drink, "Beth was wondering if she could tour your closet, get some ideas for her wardrobe." I knew Beth would leave with an armful of castoffs. Beatrice was French. She didn't keep things that weren't perfect for her.

"Bien sûr! Elizabet, come, come! Perhaps you will do me this favor and take some of the things I must part with, yes? Hannah is so blissfully tall, the clothes do not fit her, and Lillie is delightfully petite. You, though, are the same size as I, so voilà!"

"Oh, *thank* you," Beth crooned. "I'd be delighted." She threw me a gleeful smile.

"Do you need any makeup? I have just been sent Chanel's new line . . ."

"This is better than Sephora," Beth said as they went up the stairs, Beatrice glancing back.

"Take your time up there," Mom said. "I have to talk to my daughters."

Was it my imagination, or was there an emphasis on the word *my*?

I took a sip of my drink. I wasn't puritanical. More of a lightweight. I drank wine, didn't I? Mom and Beatrice, though . . . a cocktail or three every night, a bottle of wine with dinner. Hannah seemed to keep up, but I had never seen my sister drunk, either. She was the very portrait of self-control.

Silence settled around the three of us. Hannah and I looked at each other. She shrugged.

"Well, there's no easy way to say this," Mom said.

"Beatrice and I are getting divorced, and she's moving back to France after Christmas. Sorry, Hannah."

My mouth dropped open. I glanced at my sister. Shit. Her face was white, and her red lipstick made her look like a stunned vampire.

"What . . . what happened, Mom?" I asked. "You've been married so long."

"So we're too old to divorce, then? Isn't that ageist, Liliana, or is divorce reserved for you and that idiot you married?" She rattled the ice cubes in her glass. "Any questions?"

"Yes! A thousand," I said. Hannah's eyes were wide. "What happened? You left Dad for her. She's fantastic. Did you cheat on her, too?"

My mother rolled her eyes. "Honestly, you're so provincial. Is that the only reason people divorce? It's simply time for us to part ways."

Brad had said the same thing, and *he* was cheating. I took Hannah's hand and squeezed it.

"Excuse me a minute," she said. She went upstairs. A door closed.

I looked at my mother. "Anything else you'd like to share?" I asked.

"No."

"Why is Beatrice going back to France? This is going to ruin Hannah."

"Well, maybe Hannah shouldn't have imprinted on Beatrice quite so hard. No one told her to crawl inside Beatrice's uterus and become a clone."

"She's not a clone, Mom! She's . . . she loves Beatrice. It's hard not to."

"*You* managed to avoid it. I need another drink. You?"

I'd barely touched mine. "I'm fine. I also love Beatrice. Just not in the same way."

"Right. You've had Vanessa Fairchild to worship for the past twenty years. How's that going?" She got up and went into the kitchen, and I looked down to see if there was a knife sticking out of my chest.

Beth came down the stairs with an armful of clothes and a Chanel bag swinging from her hands. "Your sister is in Beatrice's closet, sobbing her eyes out."

"They're getting a divorce," I said. "My mother and Beatrice."

"Oh, no!" She laid her bounty on a chair and glanced around the living room to make sure my mother wasn't here. "Can Beatrice get custody of you two?"

I gave a half-hearted laugh. "I'm gonna go upstairs and check on Hannah," I said. "Can you stay here with the dragon?"

"You bet. I'm sorry, Lillie." She gave me a quick hug. "Mrs. Silva, do you need anything in there?" She winked at me.

I hadn't been upstairs in years. They'd repainted, and the hallways were the color of melted butter. I went past the room I'd slept in on visits, past Hannah's room and Beatrice's office, and knocked on the master bedroom door, opening it a crack.

"Okay to come in?" I asked.

"Of course, of course," Beatrice said. The two were sitting on the side of the bed, arms around each other, so I sat on one of the white chairs next to the French doors that led to their deck. It was dark by now, and the lights of a few boats dotted the ocean. A sliver of a moon was just visible.

"I . . . I don't know what to say, Beatrice," I said. "I'm very sorry to hear about this."

Beatrice gave Hannah's shoulders a squeeze. "As I was telling Hannah, Lillie, my time here in this beautiful place is finished. I wish I had been able to tell you myself, but your mother, she insisted."

"Mom made her miserable. She can't take it anymore. Surprise, surprise," Hannah said, grabbing a tissue and blowing her nose. "You can live with me, Maman. You don't have to leave the Cape. You know I would love it. It would be a dream come true."

"Perhaps I will spend some time at your beautiful home, chérie," Beatrice said. "But there is an ache in my bones for my home. You girls must understand the desire to be close to the place where you were born, where you played."

I sure did. I'd based my whole life around living on Cape Cod.

"You can spend a month there and then come back," Hannah said. "Why leave the place where you've lived for thirty-three years? What about me?"

"I will visit you often," Beatrice said.

"How many times is often? Once a month? Once a year?" Hannah cried harder, and the sound broke my heart. I got up and sat on her other side, and Beatrice gave me a sad, sweet smile. I couldn't remember Hannah ever crying. She was so . . . so together. Now, with her mascara and eyeliner smeared, her lipstick worn off from biting her lips, the misery on her face, she looked utterly lost.

"We'll get through this, Hannah," I said, and she looked at me with wet eyes. "I know it's not the same for me as it is for you, but it'll be okay. You and Beatrice have a bond that can't be broken, right, Beatrice?"

"Vraiment," she said. "Absolutely. And the same is true with you, Lillie," she added kindly. "And Dylan, I feel he is my grandson."

"Thank you," I said. "You'll always be our family."

"But you'll stay through Christmas?" Hannah asked.

"Oui. That is my plan. So let us not cry, Hannah. Let us spend so much time together until then, and we can plan your first visit to my home."

"You've already bought a house?" she asked, sounding like a sulky teenager.

Beatrice nodded. "But I will need your help in furnishing it." Her face was a study in sadness and love for Hannah, and I abruptly regretted rejecting her so constantly all those years. The truth was, once I'd married Brad, I'd become a Fairchild. My mother was right. I'd had Vanessa as a mother, and Hannah had Beatrice.

"Dinner's ready," Beth called from downstairs.

"I have made confit de canard and a tarte tatin," Beatrice

said. "Your favorites, Hannah. And the cheese I bought at the market! You will be amazed."

"Just let me wash up," Hannah said. She got off the bed and went down the hall to her bedroom. Knowing Beatrice, I imagined it was fully stocked with high-end products that she'd bought just for my sister.

"I'll miss you," I told Beatrice. "You've always made my mother easier. And . . . well, you're a wonderful person."

"Merci, Lillie. I will miss you as well. But we have months left to enjoy each other's company, n'est-ce pas?" She linked her arm through mine, and we went downstairs, my stomach a whole stew of feelings.

ᴄ

A few days later, the inevitable happened. I saw Brad.

I was at the Wellfleet Marketplace, where the prices were high and the food was great. I'd just come from Tasha's delivery of a healthy baby boy, which, despite Carline's dire warnings, had gone beautifully. But I was wicked tired, since the baby had been born at 4:00 a.m. and I'd left the hospital at nine. I had no food in the house and didn't feel like fighting the throngs at Stop & Shop in Orleans. Wellfleet Marketplace was a store where you could get really good food, a book, a card, a candle, socks and wine. I figured I'd hit the deli for a massive grinder, grab some chocolate and wine and head home.

As I was perusing the red wine for the cheapest brand, I heard my ex-husband's voice. I froze, bottle in hand, something like fear gripping me in a wave of cold. Back from Paris, apparently. I hoped it had rained nonstop.

"Oh, you're more than welcome," Brad said in this new plummy tone. "We're so glad to help the community. Obviously, we care so much about the wetlands and promoting green technology."

Right. They lived in a six-thousand-square-foot house because it was good for the environment. But first things first—I didn't want to be seen. For no good reason, I felt suddenly ashamed. The discarded woman, ten pounds heavier, frizzy hair coming out of a ponytail, dressed in ratty jeans and a T-shirt that proclaimed my love of sharks. Granted, I'd had to go to the hospital at midnight and had grabbed the clothes closest to me, but . . . but Melissa wouldn't be caught dead looking ratty. Or chubby. Or with frizzy hair.

I slunk down to the deli counter and darted behind it. "Hey, Lillie," said Christopher, the owner's son. I'd babysat him as a teenager.

"Shh, honey," I said, though he was in his thirties now. I crouched down behind the meat case, clutching my wine bottle to my chest.

"Why are you hiding?" he whispered.

"My ex-husband is over there." I gestured. "I don't want to see him."

"Got it. Want to go in the—Hey, Mr. Fairchild, how's it going?"

I sat on the floor, pressing my back against the case as tightly as I could, knees to my chest. Christopher moved closer to me, offering me shelter. *Please don't let Brad see me,* I prayed.

"Hello, young man." Despite Brad having lived in Wellfleet for twenty years, he still barely knew a soul. "It's *Dr.* Fairchild, by the way. No problem, of course. It's just that PhDs don't grow on trees, huh huh huh." I rolled my eyes at the fake laugh. Such a pretentious ass.

"What can I get you today?" Christopher asked.

"Well, my wife and I are going to be grilling tonight. I don't suppose you have some Wagyu fillets, do you?"

"We sure do. They're thirty-nine ninety-nine each, though."

"Oh, money is no object when it comes to a great meal, right? Huh huh huh. I'll take four."

One hundred and sixty dollars' worth of beef for one meal. My jaw clenched.

"You got it," said Christopher. "You'll want to rub these with olive oil and salt a few hours before cooking them.

Make sure they're at room temperature before you throw them on the grill."

"Don't worry about that," Brad said. "My wife is an *amazing* cook. We do have a chef come in, but on special occasions, we like to cook ourselves." My teeth were clenched so hard they'd be dust soon. Stupid Brad. He just had to let the world know how *rich* he was now.

"Uh-huh," said Christopher. I heard the sound of the case opening, the cool air and smell of raw meat wrapping around me.

"Yeah, it's not a terrible life. Huh huh huh. And I'm not half-bad in the kitchen, either."

I was suddenly on my feet.

"Jesus!" Brad said, taking a step back. "Lillie! What are you doing there?"

"You're not half-bad in the kitchen?" I said, my voice possibly a tiny bit loud. "Really, Brad? Because when you were married to *me*, the best you could do was scrambled eggs!" I grabbed the fillet out of Christopher's hand and threw it at Brad. "Enjoy, Chef!"

The fillet, wet and red, hit him in the face, stuck a moment, then dropped. Brad caught it automatically. I took another one and pitched that, too, getting him in the head before it plopped on the floor. Red meat juice dripped down his face.

"How dare you?" he said. "Get control of yourself, Lillie, before I call the police!"

"Bite me," I said, reaching for a third fillet.

"Those are wicked expensive," Christopher murmured. "Keep that in mind."

I seemed to be making a scene. Cameras were out, waiting.

Shit. I put the fillet back in Christopher's hand. "Enjoy your dinner."

"You're paying for these!" Brad snapped, putting the chunk of meat he'd caught on the counter. "They're ruined now." With great, pained dignity, he took a handkerchief out of his pocket and wiped his face. He carried a handkerchief now, of course. It was patterned in blue and red checks and I bet it cost a bundle.

Christopher retrieved the fallen fillet, came back behind the counter and rinsed it while Brad and I glared at each other.

"I feel sorry for you," Brad whispered. "You're alone and pathetic."

"I feel sorry for *you*," I said, not whispering. "You're phony and materialistic. You're a kept man. A gigolo, and not a very good one at that."

"Okay, that's enough," Christopher said, handing me a plastic-wrapped package. "Two filet mignons, on the house, Lillie. You were the best babysitter I ever had." He grinned.

"Thanks, honey." I washed my meaty hands, took my eighty dollars' worth of meat and walked past Brad to the front of the store, head held high.

"How are you, Lillie?" asked Harlow Smith, who owned the bookstore. "You look wonderful."

A few other people said hello, told me I looked good, nice to see me, as I stood in line, waiting to pay for my wine. There was Luna, holding the daughter I'd helped come into this world, and she waved the baby's chubby hand at me. Because this was *my* town, and I'd earned my place here. My ex-husband was a mainland nobody as far as we townies were concerned. Carrie, a middle-aged woman who'd worked the checkout for as long as I could remember, put a chocolate bar in my bag with a wink.

"No charge," she said. "Your husband's an asshole."

"Ex-husband," I said, managing a smile.

It helped. But Brad knew where to hit, so to speak, and my heart was sore and angry just the same.

I walked across the street to the town hall parking lot. There, sitting at an empty picnic table in front of Hatch's Fish Market, was Ophelia. Her face perked up when she saw me.

"Hi!" she said, then blushed.

"Hi, Ophelia. How are you?"

"Good, I guess. Waiting for what's-his-name. He made me come with him. Hashtag girl-dad. Gross."

"It *is* gross." I sat down across from her. "How's it going?"

She shrugged.

"Sucky, then?"

"Kind of. I don't know. I miss my real . . . well, my other stepfather."

"You were going to say dad, weren't you?"

Tears filled her eyes. "He wasn't actually my dad. But it felt that way."

"I'm so sorry." I set my bag on the table. "What was he like?"

"He was just . . . nice. He was so excited when I came to live with them. We'd go out sometimes without Melissa, and he'd buy me a hot dog from a cart. Street meat, he called it. He told me about his patients and the grossest injuries and stuff. It was cool. He didn't care if my manners weren't perfect or if I didn't make my bed." She wiped her eyes.

"He sounds like a great guy," I said.

"Yeah."

"Then again, you seem like a great kid, so it makes sense that you'd get along."

"How do you know I'm a great kid?" she asked, adolescent sulk creeping into her voice.

"Well, you're your own person. That's obvious."

"How do you know?"

"Your hair, your clothes. You have style." She was wearing a pair of overalls over a black T-shirt, her nails were painted blue, and her hair was in two clumped ponytails, the curls making them look like shower scrunchies. "You have opinions, you're clearly smart and you're well-spoken. You have a lot going for you."

"Melissa just likes to tell me what I do wrong. And that jerk in there . . . he talks *at* me and never even listens when I try to say something, you know what I mean?"

"I absolutely do." I paused, sad for this kid, so at the

mercy of the whims of her self-centered aunt. "When I was a kid, my parents got a divorce, and my sister went to live with my mother. I stayed with my dad. It was hard, not being able to have the family I wanted."

Ophelia gave a reluctant nod. "My mom's an addict. I only met my bio-dad twice. My grandparents were taking care of me back in Ohio, but my grandma got sick. I got shipped off to Melissa, and the one great grown-up was Dennis, and then he died."

I covered her hand with mine. "I'm sorry, honey."

"I mean, it's stupid to complain. Melissa's loaded and I live in a big house and all that. It's pretty here, and I love some things about it. All the crabs and birds and stuff. The skies."

I smiled. "The skies are the best."

She gave me a tentative smile back. "Yeah. They are. Oh, crap, here comes Bridiot right now."

Bridiot. My heart swelled with love for Ophelia.

"You might not want to say that to his face," I said, glancing back at the grocery store. He was waiting to cross the street, bag in hand, and I was pleased to see a meat-juice stain on his shirt. "He loves to lecture."

"I know, I know. Respect your elders." She stood up. "Can't wait to see his latest Instagram post that'll tell the world how close we are." She sighed. "Well. Nice seeing you, Mrs. . . . um . . ."

"Lillie."

"Lillie." She blushed again.

"Call me anytime, Ophelia. We can get coffee or ice cream."

"I doubt they'd let me."

True. "Well. You have my number. Maybe if we just ran into each other again. I go to the library most Saturday mornings."

Her face lit up. "Okay, cool! Thanks. It was nice talking to you. Oh, I got the book, too! Thanks for that. I really liked it."

"You're welcome, sweetheart. Hope to see you around." I got up and went to my car, not willing to see my ex for the second time in an hour. As I drove toward home, I called my dad and invited him over for dinner. "Filet mignon, Daddy," I said.

"I'm actually at your house right now. Cleaned out your gutters," he said, and I smiled even as my eyes filled with tears. Dear old Dad. The one thing in my life that never changed. You wanted a girl dad, you had one right there. The real thing, and long before it was a hashtag.

CHAPTER 17

Melissa

Ever since they'd come back from France, Melissa had been feeling a bit peaked, as her mother used to say. She felt achy. Bloated. Premenstrual, even though she rarely had the kind of cramps and suffering other women detailed, which she credited to clean eating and yoga (and the pill). She'd probably caught something on the plane, which wasn't fair, since they'd flown Virgin Atlantic first-class. You'd think they could do better.

She looked at herself in the mirror of her bathroom. Bradley had left a big smeary fingerprint on it. She should just have him use a guest bathroom. That would preserve the romance of marriage, wouldn't it? Yes. She didn't need him watching her flossing or shaving her legs, and she didn't want to know that he had a huge bowel movement every morning, often requiring the plunger.

Wait. She squinted, then pulled out the extension mirror to the 10x magnification side. Was that a *pimple*? How could she have a pimple? She hadn't had a pimple since she was twelve!

It *was* a pimple. She grabbed her phone and called Shui

Spa in Provincetown. "Hello, this is Melissa Fairchild. I need an appointment urgently, I'm afraid. A facial."

"Melissa! How was the wedding?" cooed Ian, the receptionist.

"It was beautiful," she said, stifling the blood pressure surge that accompanied any memory of her wedding day. All the guests had talked and talked about *Lillie*, even though Hannah had smoothly informed them it was a performance artist, part of the quirky Cape Cod landscape. Everyone knew it was the evil first wife. "Ian, can you be my angel and get me in today? I'm also dying for a mineral soak."

"For you? Of course! Come in at two o'clock, okay? And I want to see pictures!"

The pictures of the ceremony were not ready yet, since they had to be *photoshopped* to erase Lillie.

The truth was, the wedding hadn't been perfect at *all*. Her reception gown had been so tight that her breasts hurt (but looked incredible; she had to give Candice credit). She hadn't even wanted the gorgeous food she'd paid for, but then again, every bride said they didn't eat much at their wedding. The cake was fantastic, though. She'd even had a second bite, which was so unlike her.

Oh, on the surface, it was still probably the most splendid wedding anyone would ever go to. The ceremony had lasted only fifteen minutes, after all, and Hannah had steered people to the patio for cocktails, where the "performance artist" wasn't so obvious.

But still.

Paris had been utterly magical, though, and Bradley had been a perfect husband. They ate and strolled. Paris *was* for lovers, and Bradley had finally mastered cunnilingus. How had Lillie borne it for twenty years? Oh. Right. She'd been a virgin when they met. Bradley had told Melissa. So Lillie didn't know any better.

Melissa brought gifts for Ophelia, Lucia the housekeeper, the yard service man whose name she couldn't remember and a few friends at yoga. Future friends, she thought. The presents would help. She'd even bought a beautiful bottle of perfume for Hannah.

But then they'd come home to an *awful* stench in their bedroom. One of the wedding guests had dropped a *shrimp* behind the bed, and the smell was so bad, Melissa had thrown up. Bradley had, too. Of course, Melissa had expected people to wander through the house, and she'd *wanted* them to see how splendid and tasteful and gorgeous it was. But for Pete's sake! You drop a shrimp and don't even notice it? Then the jet lag hit her hard, and she slept late for the next week, missing every early yoga class she'd booked.

That pimple. Could it have been from French food? All that cheese? But she'd been to Paris with Dennis twice and that had never happened.

Oh, well. Her aesthetician would take care of that. She probably just needed to change skin care products.

She went downstairs, and there was Bradley, sitting in the living room, Teeny on his lap, snoring. "Oh! You're home. Is everything all right, honey?" she asked.

He put Teeny aside, rose and came over to kiss her. It must've been her imagination, but she swore she could still smell skunk in this room. "I canceled my afternoon patients because I missed you too much," he said, hugging her against him. The pimple on her chin pressed against his shirt, and it throbbed. "Ophelia's still in school. Shall we take advantage of that and make love on the kitchen table?"

She almost rolled her eyes. Why did men think that a woman lying on a hard slab of wood was enjoyable? Dennis had loved that particular naughty scenario, too, going so far as to make her pretend to be a Spanish-speaking chef. But she didn't *have* to earn her keep anymore, did she? "I have an appointment I can't miss," she said, her tone frosty. "I wish you'd called to inform me of your whims"—word of the day!—"before you left." Yes. Let him remember who was in charge.

Brad's face fell. "You're right, babe. I'll call next time. And we can always hit the sheets later tonight."

Hit the sheets. For the love of Pete. Couldn't he just say *make love*? That being said, she *was* in the mood. Very much so. She glanced at her watch. She could manage a quickie.

"Come with me, lover," she said, leading him to the steam room. "I think I have time to rock your world."

Four hours later, the pimple having been gently extracted and injected with corticosteroid, Melissa felt *much* restored. A half hour in the Himalayan salt sauna, another half in the mineral tub, the shoulder massage that went along with the facial, plus a pedicure because someone had canceled . . . she hadn't felt so relaxed in a long time. Then the makeup artist had asked if she wanted him to make her gorgeous, so of course she said yes. It was always fun to see what someone else might do with her perfect face.

She walked up Bradford Street to her car. "I love your look," said a man who was holding hands with another man. "You look like a mature Taylor Swift."

Her smile, which had begun at the start of his compliment, fell. A *mature* Taylor Swift? Taylor Swift was *older* than she was!

In her BMW, she looked in the visor mirror. She looked fantastic. Perfect makeup. No wrinkles, thanks to preemptive Botox shots four times a year. But there were shadows under her eyes, visible even under the concealer. She was *thirty* years old. She shouldn't have shadows!

Suddenly, a wave of nausea rolled up from the pit of her stomach to her mouth, and she barely had time to open the door to vomit.

She wiped her mouth with a few tissues, rinsed and spit with the mineral water she always had in the car to make sure she was hydrated at all times. Gross! Her stomach, now empty, growled, and sure enough, she was suddenly starving. The smell of garlic in the air made her want to burst into a restaurant and stuff fried shrimp in her mouth. God, yes.

Fried food? She hadn't had fried food since she was fifteen.

What the heck was . . .

Oh.

Oh, no. No, no, no.

Sore breasts. That second bite of cake. The pimple. Puking. The presumed jet lag. And now, a craving.

Melissa could not be pregnant. She *never* missed taking the pill, and it was 99 percent effective. She was just premenstrual. "You *are* in your thirties now," she told her reflection. "Some things might be changing."

As she drove down the street, she noticed a drugstore. Should she stop? No. She'd get her period any minute now. The universe would take care of her. It always did.

⌒

The universe was taking its sweet time. Melissa did not get her period. Nor did she buy a pregnancy test, for fear Bradley or Ophelia or the household staff (Lucia every day, plus a band of cleaners twice a week) would find it. Also . . . pregnancy was impossible. The pill was 99 percent effective, wasn't it?

She waited. And waited.

Twelve days after her period had been due, she made an appointment with Wanda Owens, MD, who had a five-star rating on Google and Yelp. Right here in Wellfleet.

The office was a snug little building off Route 6. She pulled in and parked in the back, since her BMW was quite identifiable, then went inside. Of course, women went to the gynecologist for many reasons, not just a possible (and *very* unlikely) pregnancy. But even so, she wanted privacy. She was becoming a celebrity in this town, just as she'd hoped.

The waiting room wasn't quite what she was used to—those Park Avenue doctors in New York had waiting areas that looked like the lobby of a luxury hotel. But this one was cozy, she supposed. More like a living room than a doctor's office. Attractive enough club chairs, a green microfiber couch, a little play area for children.

An older woman behind the counter was on the phone. "I'll be right with you," she said. "Have a seat."

Melissa did. There were plenty of current magazines on the table. *Cape Cod Home*, eh? Maybe she should hire a publicist to get her in this type of magazine. She wanted to be featured in *Martha Stewart Weddings*, too. Those were just a start. She only had thirty-two thousand followers on Instagram, but she hadn't posted many wedding photos yet. Yes. A publicist. She'd have to google "celebrity publicists" when she got home.

"How can I help you?" said the receptionist.

"Melissa Spencer to see Dr. Owens," she said. Using her own last name had seemed like a good idea.

"Right this way," she said. "I'm Carol, by the way. I do everything here except the medical stuff. Step up on the scale, please."

Melissa obeyed, and after a second, the number blinked: 134.

What? She practically leaped off the scale. She'd never weighed so much in her life! Damn all that French cheese! And bread! And chocolate! She'd have to do a cleanse. Nothing but green tea, ginger extract, lemon and cabbage juice for the next week so she could get back to her ideal 123. Since France, she'd forgotten to weigh herself each morning. For heaven's sake! She should have started with a liquid-only diet the minute she stepped off the plane.

"You're in Room Two," Carol said. "Undress completely, put on this gorgeous exam robe, and Dr. Owens will be in shortly." Carol handed her a blue-and-green cotton robe.

Melissa undressed, carefully folding her clothes and placing them on one of the chairs. The robe smelled like lemon laundry detergent and was quite soft. The exam room walls were a pretty shade of blue, and there were prints on the wall. A mobile hung from the ceiling. This was, she supposed, the Cape's version of high-end medical care.

She glanced at her watch. Ophelia was in school; Bradley was in his office. She had a meeting for the arts council tonight, and she wondered what to wear. Something interesting yet classy. Oh! The black Armani dress with the keyhole front. Christian Louboutin leopard-print ankle boots and dangling Marie Mas earrings. Yes! They were funky and artistic and also damn expensive. A gift from Dennis when they'd gone to France the first year of their marriage.

Bradley wouldn't be able to afford that kind of jewelry, not on his salary. She'd been a bit shocked at how little he earned, to be honest. Then again, all his money was discretionary now. Even so, maybe she'd give him an allowance so he could step up his game. He'd grimaced at the cost of her engagement ring, and honestly, it had only cost $17,000. Lucky for him, her fingers were slender, and the rock looked bigger than it was.

She should buy Ophelia some diamond earrings. Just little ones. Half carats, maybe, so she could start exerting her own brand, her own sense of style. Maybe they'd go shopping in Boston over the weekend. The truth was, Melissa missed her a little bit. She'd been largely silent and resentful since Bradley moved in. When Dennis was alive, she'd been much livelier and more talkative. Even after he died, when it had just been the two of them, it had been kind of . . . snug. Almost-mother and almost-daughter, finding a new place in the world, eating together every night, taking walks on the beach. She'd thought they'd started bonding, but once Bradley moved in, Ophelia had regressed.

Well, the child would have to start maturing. Maybe once she hit puberty, she'd appreciate Melissa more, and they could—

There was a commotion in the hallway. Urgent voices, though Melissa couldn't make out what they were saying.

Gosh darn it. She had wanted to go to Supple Apothecary in Orleans and get an under-eye serum to get rid of those dark circles. The spa treatment in Provincetown hadn't lasted beyond a few hours.

The door opened, and a woman came in, dressed in scrubs, wearing those hideous clogs they forced nurses to wear. She looked down at the clipboard in her hands, looked up and said, "Ms. Spencer?"

Then she froze.

It took a second or two for Melissa to recognize her. Women in scrubs all looked alike, more or less. Her hair was in some kind of bun, and she wasn't wearing makeup, but yes. It was Lillie Silva.

CHAPTER 18

Lillie

O h," said the whore known as Melissa. "I . . . I thought you delivered babies." Her face flushed. "At the hospital."

My heart was stampeding like a herd of buffalo. She'd used a different last name, not Finch, not Fairchild, but here she was. My replacement. Here, in my workplace—which was definitely one of the places I loved best—fouling it with her presence.

We stared at each other, dumbstruck. Then I gave my head a little shake and remembered who I was. Lillie Silva, BSN, RN, CNM. "I do deliver babies," I said. "And I take care of the whole range of women's health." My God, that engagement ring could choke a pony. *Brad* bought that? Brad the cheapskate? He'd been so relieved there'd been a family ring I could wear so he didn't have to buy me one.

On another note, I wondered if she knew I was the "performance artist" at her wedding.

"I . . . I have an appointment with Dr. Owens," Melissa said.

"She was just called out on an emergency."

"What *kind* of an emergency?"

Clearly, the self-appointed queen of Wellfleet wasn't

used to having to change her plans. "I can't discuss other patients," I said. One of our clients had gone into premature labor—four weeks early—and Wanda was riding with her to the hospital.

"Is it a baby?" Melissa asked.

I didn't answer.

She looked away. "I guess I'll come back when Dr. Owens is free."

"Yeah, I think that would be best." I took a deep breath. "But if this is an urgent medical issue, I . . . I can examine you. I don't want you to delay getting treatment if there's something wrong." I *so* did not want to look at her lady parts. Then again, if she was here for an STD panel, it would be rather karmic.

"It's minor," said Melissa. "Something that can wait."

"Okay, then. For the record, I do work here five days a week, unless I'm at the hospital delivering a baby."

"I imagine there are other gynecologists in the area. I'll use one of them."

"Great." I paused. "But Wanda is the only one on the Outer Cape."

"That's fine. I'll go somewhere else." She hopped off the table. "The fact that I came here . . . it's covered by HIPAA?"

"It absolutely is. I can't even tell anyone that you were here."

"Good." She flipped her long blond hair over her shoulder and stood up. God, she was so slim and pretty, even in an exam robe.

Suddenly, she bent over and put her hands over her left lower abdomen. "Ouch," she gasped. "Oh, my God, that hurts."

I went to her side and put my hand on her shoulder. "Take a breath. Have you had this type of pain before?"

"No! Never."

"Let's get you back on the table." I helped her up. Her face was pale. I smeared my hands with antibacterial gel and put on gloves. I had to ask the question I dreaded. "Any chance you could be pregnant?"

"No! I'm on the pill, and I'm religious about taking it. I am *not* pregnant. I had my period last month." She paused. "The pain is fading now."

"Okay. Is it all right if I palpate your stomach?" My guess was an ovarian cyst, which could be like a knife in your stomach.

She winced again. "Um . . . yeah, okay."

God, this was *weird*. I opened her robe, exposing the perfect skin over her stomach, and pressed lightly on the left side. "Any pain or pressure there?" I asked.

"No."

"Good." I repeated the move on the other side. "How about now?"

"Oof. There it is again."

I put my hand just above her pubic bone, and there it was. The fundus, a small, firm mound.

She *was* pregnant.

All the blood in my body seemed to drain to my feet, and for a second, I felt dizzy. My heart sped up, and I could feel the pulse in my eyes.

Do your job, said my mother's voice. I took a breath, held it for a second, let it go. "Does this hurt at all?" I asked, pressing gently around the baby bump.

"Not really. It . . . Well."

"No, no, tell me. I'm a medical professional right now, not your husband's first wife." Those words popped right out, surprisingly. "Everything is confidential. I've been a nurse for almost twenty years."

She closed her eyes (did she have eyelash extensions, or was she just blessed?). "I feel some pressure, and it . . . it makes me feel like I have to pee. Badly."

"Okay. Tell me about your periods. Are they regular?"

"Yes. They're light, because I'm on the pill. Which, as I said, I *never* miss." She looked at me, and yeah, I had to hand it to God, her eyes were spectacularly pretty.

"You're sure?"

"Yeah. I don't—This is confidential? You can't tell Bradley?"

Bradley. That stupid name was worse than Brad. "I can't tell anyone except Wanda, and she can't tell anyone outside of the practice. You could sue us for a ton of money if we said anything."

"Okay." She looked up at the mobile. "I do *not* want children. So I'm really, really good about taking the pill. Which is ninety-nine percent effective, right?"

"When taken correctly, yes. Do you take them at the same time each day?"

"Yes! Absolutely."

"Every single day?"

"Yes. I mean . . . a few times, I've been maybe a couple hours late." She closed her eyes. "It's possible I could've missed one day. Oh, gosh darn it. Maybe two."

And that, ladies and gentlemen, is why nine out of one hundred women on the pill get pregnant. For that magical 99 percent efficacy rate, the pill has to be taken at the same hour of every day without fail. "Have you taken a pregnancy test?"

She closed her eyes again, and two tears slipped down her temples. "No."

"Okay. You can sit up now," I said, closing her robe. She did, wiping her eyes. "Melissa, I'm guessing you *are* pregnant," I said as gently as I could. My own feelings would have to wait, because without Wanda here, I was it. Carol wasn't an ultrasound tech. And I couldn't let a pregnant woman in pain leave, no matter who she was. "We have an ultrasound machine here, so let's see what we're dealing with, okay?"

"Do you do abortions here?" Her cheeks reddened.

"We don't. You'd have to go to Hyannis for that." I took another quiet breath. "Let's do the ultrasound first, okay?"

"What about a pregnancy test?" she asked.

"I'm pretty positive about this. You need a full bladder

for an ultrasound, so I don't want you going to the bathroom first." I paused. "Do you want to call Brad?" *Don't think about that. Focus on the patient.*

"No!" She looked at me with scared, wide eyes. "This was *not* part of the plan."

"I know this is a shock, but the more you know, the better you'll be able to . . . decide how to move forward."

And so I got the ultrasound machine and the gel we kept in a bottle warmer and asked Melissa to lie down on the exam table again. She stared at the mobile. I put the gel on her lower abdomen and pushed the transducer against her tummy.

She farted loudly, jumped and looked mortified. "Excuse me! Oh, gosh! I'm so sorry."

"Happens all the time. Don't worry about it."

In 95 percent of my cases, this was the magical part, the moment they would never forget, especially with a firsttimer. I slid the transducer down her abdomen, and there it was.

The *thwack-thwack-thwack* of the baby's heartbeat. I didn't say anything. Neither did she. I pushed in another spot, and the heartbeat took on a swishing sound. "That sound is the baby's heartbeat," I said, my voice husky. I cleared my throat. "So yes, Melissa, you're definitely pregnant."

"Oh, gosh." She looked at the screen, her eyes widening even more.

"The fetal heart rate should be between one forty and one seventy, and it's at one fifty-nine. Perfect. And here's the fetus. You can see the head." I paused, clicked the computer to take a measurement of crown to rump, the head. About twelve weeks along, a little more, maybe. There was the head, the choroid plexuses, the spine. The baby moved a little, and Melissa sucked in a breath.

"Is that its *hand*?"

"It is." Pregnancy really was a miracle. The wonder of my profession washed away the hatred I had for Melissa, at least for this second. For now, she was just a young woman with an unexpected pregnancy. We watched as the fetus moved, almost as if it was dancing. Beautiful. Miraculous that a human could form from one egg and one sperm.

"It looks like an alien," she said, and I couldn't help a smile.

"Its head takes up about half its length for now, but the body will catch up. The legs are teeny . . . see? But the eyes and nose and ears and even teeth have already started." Her eyes were glued to the screen. I moved so we could see the profile.

"Can you tell if it's a boy or a girl?" she asked.

"Not definitively. A few more weeks, and you can. According to these measurements you're . . . twelve weeks and five days." I checked the heart, the brain, the face. All normal. Four limbs, check. "Here's your placenta, which is in a great place and looks completely normal. Plenty of fluid in the sac."

"It already looks like a person," she said, wonder in her voice.

Based on this timeline, Brad had fathered a baby while he was still married to me. Just when you thought the knife couldn't twist any harder. My ex-husband would be having another child. Dylan would have a half sibling, nineteen years younger than he was. Brad would get another chance at parenthood.

Maybe. If Melissa didn't get an abortion. I barely knew her, so I couldn't guess.

I needed a nice long walk with Zeus. I needed my dad. I needed alcohol and homemade bread. I swallowed. Moved the transducer and did another measurement. Everything was normal. *Do your job, do your job, do your job.*

"Would you like me to print out some pictures?" I asked.

"Oh. Um . . . I don't know. Sure, I guess."

I took a few. "Okay, we're all set here." I turned off the ultrasound machine, wiped off Melissa's belly with a warm facecloth, suddenly feeling ninety-four years old. "You can go to the bathroom now, then get dressed and come into my office so we can talk. I'm sure you have a lot of questions," I said.

That was what I'd say to any patient. Give them a minute or two alone, then bring them out of the exam room where they'd just been given life-changing news.

"Everything okay?" Carol asked as I walked out.

"Just fine." HIPAA. I wasn't going to be able to talk to anyone about this. I was glad to be in my little office, because I needed a minute, too. Unlike Brad's office, mine was tiny and crowded with books and journals. On my desk was a photo of Dylan, taken last year. In the picture, he was standing on our dock, the water sparkling behind him, his grin so dear to my heart.

I laid the photo facedown so Melissa couldn't see it. It felt like I was protecting my son from her. My eyes were abruptly wet. Dylan might be a big brother after all. Not how I'd pictured it.

Melissa stood in the doorway. She was a lot more imposing in clothes—chic fawn-colored pants that stopped above her ankle, a sleeveless mock turtleneck sweater in exactly the same color. Looked like cashmere. Simple jewelry— gold hoops in her ears, a delicate gold necklace that probably cost more than I made in a month, and that frigging beautiful engagement ring. Her wedding ring was a diamond band. Those sparkles could hypnotize a person. I wondered how much they'd cost, and if I could steal them the next time I broke into their house.

That's a very unprofessional thought, chided my mother. "Come on in," I said. "Close the door."

She did, then glanced around the room and sat in one of the two chairs. I'm sure it was quite shabby in here, quite working class to a person like her. "What would you like to ask me?"

"I . . . I don't understand how the pill could fail. I was so careful. If I missed it, it was only by half a day."

Brad would have another child. Not me. That part of my life was over. My body wasn't getting my brain's message about being professional. I folded my hands together, fingers interlaced, to hide the shaking. Pushed the personal thoughts away. It was a necessary skill for my job. Watching a tattooed seventeen-year-old boy play games on his phone while his girlfriend pushed out their child and not smacking him. Seeing a fifteen-year-old girl who'd been raped without bursting into tears and holding her like she was my own. Telling a woman that her baby had severe congenital defects and wouldn't survive the pregnancy without bawling. I stuffed my feelings down all the time in this job. I could do it now.

"Well, no contraceptive is foolproof. If you had a few days where you took it a couple hours later than usual, that can give your ovaries the green light to produce an egg. The pill stops the hormone surge that usually causes the egg to release. If you were late taking it, an egg can be released by your ovaries. It's rare, but not unheard of."

She still looked confused. "But I had my period last month."

"You had some spotting. Not a true period."

"Dang it all," she said under her breath. Right. She didn't swear. She was too refined for all that.

"How are you feeling? Physically, I mean?"

She blinked those amazing eyelashes. How much time did she spend on looking this way, damn it?

"Well," she said, and her voice quavered. "I, uh . . . we're still covered by doctor-patient confidentiality, right?"

"Right. And we always will be."

"Okay." She twisted the aforementioned pony-choker ring. "Well, I've thrown up a few times. My breasts are sore. My skin broke out, which it never does." Of course not. "I'm a lot hungrier than usual, and I've already gained eleven pounds." She paused. "I can't seem to hold gas in." Her face flushed.

I bet she'd never farted before in her life. "Those are all normal symptoms of pregnancy. That pain you felt in the exam room is most likely the ligaments and muscles

stretching in your abdomen, making room for your expanding uterus. But if you have really bad pain or severe cramping, or *any* blood more than a few drops, call us right away."

"Gosh. There's so much going on. My pants are tight
already."

I couldn't help a petty feeling of triumph. "Are you on
any medications, either prescription or over-the-counter?"

"No. I take a multivitamin, though."

"Good. How about fatigue?"

She nodded. "Definitely. It's hard to stay up past nine. I
thought it was jet lag."

And how was *Paris?* "Mood swings?"

Another blush. "I've been a little more easily . . . irritated."

Wonderful! I hoped Brad was miserable. "Again, totally
normal. Your hormones are going wild. This may also
cause a milky vaginal discharge, so use panty liners."

"Darn it!" She let out an exasperated breath.

I reached in my drawer and pulled out a booklet, handed
it to her. "Here's some information about what's happening
in your body. If you decide to stay pregnant, you should
have a monthly checkup. If you decide not to keep the pregnancy, well, we can discuss that, too."

"Okay." She thumbed through the booklet. "It says the
baby is as big as a plum."

"Mm-hmm. There's a nutrition section in there to help
you make good food choices. No alcohol, no marijuana in
any form, no illicit substances, no smoking, and go easy on
caffeine, saturated fats and sugar. Drink at least ten eight-
ounce glasses of water a day. At *least.* I'm going to write
you a prescription for prenatal vitamins, and you need to
take one every day."

"Okay." Her voice was meek.

"I'm sure you have a lot to think about, so call the office
if you have any questions. Wanda is a fantastic doctor, but
there are also many great obstetricians and certified nurse-
midwives closer to the hospital." *Please pick one of them.*

"Thanks," she said. She stood up, her hair so straight and shiny. "Thank you, Lillie."

We looked at each other for a minute. "You're welcome," I forced myself to say. "Take care of yourself."

When she left, I held my head in my hands. What was I going to say to Dylan if she kept the baby? And what if she didn't? I'd know, and no one else. The last thing I wanted was to share a secret with my ex-husband's new wife. No, the last thing I wanted was for him to have a baby with Melissa and screw up my son's life even more.

My stomach growled, and crap, I had no food in the house. I left my office—Carol had gone home already—and locked up. I got in my car and drove to Stop & Shop in Orleans, the biggest grocery store on the Outer Cape. I'd get some . . . I don't know. Sushi. A half gallon of ice cream. A Boston coffee cake. I blasted U2 and forced myself to sing along to keep thoughts of *her* out of my mind. "In the name of love!" I bellowed at the stoplight in front of Eastham's town green. "What more in the name of love!" I didn't have it hard. MLK had it hard, and it would be good to remember that kind of thing. I cruised around the rotary—God bless the off-season—and pulled into the store's parking lot.

The second I got inside, a gorgeous smell hit me. Oh, *mommy*. Their rotisserie chicken. I don't know how they did it, but Stop & Shop had the best rotisserie chicken, and it was cheap, too. I wasn't starving anymore. I was *desperate*. I got the biggest chicken I could find, inhaled through the plastic lid and nearly swooned. At the self-checkout I added a bag of peanut M&M's, sharable size, ran my credit card and stuffed the M&M's in my purse. Didn't even use a bag for the chicken, just carried it out to my car. As I got in, it started to rain.

By the time I got back home, the chicken would be cold, its skin puckered from the steam under the plastic lid. No time like the present. I popped off the plastic top, pulled off a drumstick, and my God, it was so good. I closed my eyes, groaning in satisfaction. Oh, that fatty skin! The rain picked up, drumming on the roof of my car, and it was damn cozy in here, water streaming down the windshield. I tore a chunk of breast meat off and stuffed that in my mouth, too, my fingers greasy, some juicy deliciousness running down my chin. Did I have a napkin? I did not. A tissue? Nope. The sleeve it was. Another incredibly satisfying chunk of breast meat. *Try not to choke to death, Lillie.* I managed to chew a little bit more, then tore off the other drumstick.

Someone knocked on my window, and I jumped, screamed and nearly dropped my precious chicken.

It was Ben Hallowell. There was a very slight smile on his face.

I turned on the car and rolled down the window. "What?" I said, mouth still full.

"Just taking in the sights," he said. "Nothing like a woman tearing apart a carcass in a parking lot."

"The Cape is considering me for a tourism ad."

He gave a gruff laugh. "Everything okay?" he asked.

"I'm just hungry." I tore off another hunk. "Want some?"

"You know, I'll pass," he said. I shrugged and shoved it into my mouth. Oh, yes. Eating it hot had been the right decision.

"How are you doing these days?" he asked. Though it was raining, he didn't seem to mind. Then again, he was a fisherman.

"Good! What could possibly be wrong?" I answered.

"How's your son?"

"Great. So happy his father married Anne Boleyn."

Ben drummed his fingers on the roof of my car. "Hey, since we're both here, you want to go to the Ho and get something to eat? They have forks and everything."

The Land Ho! was a stone's throw from here, and they *did* have the best chowder in these parts. I hesitated. I could go back to my house, eat ice cream and then hide treats around the house and time Zeus to see how fast he could find them (don't judge me, it was fun). I could obsess over Bralissa and their unborn child. Or I could hang out with Ben, who, though as chatty as a barnacle, wasn't a bad person.

"I need to call my dad and ask him to feed my dog," I said.

"Let me do that. You enjoy your dinner," he said, raising an eyebrow. He stepped away and made the call. I took his advice and had a few more bites of chicken. I could still have clam chowder, I thought. Maybe a hot dog. And definitely dessert. If the Ho had apple pie, I'd get that. Their pie was killer.

"Your dad said he'll get a pizza and watch TV at your house until you come home," Ben said, coming back to my car.

"Okay. Get in, sir." I moved my bag to the back seat. There were Zeus's nose prints all over the passenger windows, since my dog liked to sit in the front, but Ben wouldn't care.

Ben got in, and I handed him my decimated chicken. "Mm-mm," he said.

I laughed a little. "Shut up. It's been a day."

As we pulled out of the parking lot, it occurred to me that the last time Ben and I had driven together, I'd wound up in a coma with several torn organs.

Had it really been that long? Twenty-four years? Crikey.

Since it was the off-season, we got a table easily, in the back near the jukebox. I went to the ladies' room, washed my greasy hands and chin and joined Ben. The Ho was famous for being famous—it wasn't anything superspecial in the culinary world, but you'd never have a bad meal here, either. The tables were small and covered in red-and-white-checked tablecloths. Newspapers hung from a wire that separated the bar from the restaurant. Signs from local businesses hung from the ceiling, and Cape-oriented license plates from various states were hung everywhere. NAUSET. CPECOD. CAPE01. WHYDAH. EXIT 12. PTOWN. It was a tourist place in the summer, a townie bar in the off-season.

"What can I get you?" asked our server, a girl of about twenty.

Ben nodded at me, still looking at the menu.

"Um . . . a cup of chowder, side of onion rings, and a Devil's Purse, please," I said. I liked drinking local beer, when I did drink beer, which was about twice a year. Usually with Brad, Dylan and Charles when we went to Fenway. There was a great Irish pub near the ballpark, and we'd go to a game every fall. Brad's father had season tickets. Vanessa would join us at the restaurant, since she hated watching sports, and we always had such fun. Such easy laughter, light teasing, affection.

This was the first year we wouldn't be doing that. Would Brad think about it? Would he miss it? Would he take his new wife and new child there?

One thing was certain—I'd never go to Fenway with the three generations of Fairchild men again. Shit. My throat was tight.

"A Reuben and a Guinness," Ben said. "Side of fries. Thanks."

We sat there, not talking, just watching the rest of the customers and staff. Several generations of the Smith family were at a big table in the back, laughing and teasing like a normal family. I waved, and they waved back, and Harlow reminded me that the book I'd ordered was in. The Sox had been rained out, and caber tossing was on ESPN, which was wicked pissah. Our beers arrived, and we sipped, still not talking. Someone came up to the jukebox, and a second later, Van Morrison's "Someone Like You" came on.

"Nice song," I said.

"Mm."

As I said, chatty as a barnacle.

"How's your daughter?" I asked. "What's her name again?"

"Reese. She's good."

"How old is she now?"

"Twenty-three. Same age as I was when she was born."

"Wow, Ben. You're old."

He grinned.

"Is she in school, or does she have a job?"

He sipped his beer.

"Come on, Ben, you're the one who wanted to eat together."

"She's in medical school. Tulane."

"Wow. Good for her!"

"Yeah." He took another sip of beer. "How does Dylan like college?"

I thought a minute. Most of his texts were checking up on me, and me checking up on him. We FaceTimed once or twice a week. "Well, aside from Brad and me, I think he's good. He loves football, of course, and he's taking mostly core classes. Not sure what he wants to do yet. I think he might have a girlfriend. A girl invited him for Thanksgiving, so . . ." So he wouldn't be home this year for the first time in his life.

"Hard when they go away."

I swallowed and nodded.

More silence. It was fine. Our food came, and we ate. Funny, all the meals I'd had with Ben, but never once just the two of us.

He had a good face, I decided, finishing my beer. It was . . . I don't know. Durable. The face of a workingman, rugged and a little plain, but nice. His mouth was expressive. The slightest pull at the corner, the faint purse of his lips before he spoke. Those lovely, dark blue eyes, so different from Brad's remarkable shade of aqua. Ben's were less remarkable, but also a little more mysterious. The way they slanted down at the corners . . . he could pass for an Aussie cowboy.

"What are you looking at?" he asked, and he gave his lopsided smile, eyes crinkling. Something stirred in me. Something . . . lustful.

"My dad's best bud," I said, remembering to answer.

Ben shrugged. "He's always been good to me."

"It's mutual. If he couldn't go out to sea, he'd go crazy."

Ben smiled again, and again, my stomach felt warm. I wondered what he looked like when he laughed. Couldn't say I'd ever seen that. It was strangely nice, sitting here with him, no agenda, little conversation. Just . . . companionship. No wonder Dad liked him.

Our server brought the check. "No hurry. Whenever you're ready," she said.

We were ready, I guessed, because Ben took out his wallet and left two twenties on the table.

"Let me get my half," I said.

"No need. You've fed me more than once."

"True," I said. "Thank you."

"You bet."

We went out into the parking lot, and I glanced at the license plates. Mostly Massachusetts, dotted with a few from Connecticut and New York. Soon, it would be dark too early, and the off-Capers would go back to their other homes, and our little peninsula would quiet under the gray winter skies.

I paused in front of a BMW with a Massachusetts vanity plate. CHSAFRM. Choose a farm? Chase a farm? I didn't think it was Capey enough to hang in the Ho. I never did understand the allure of a vanity plate. Brad's new Jaguar, courtesy of his Amber Alert wife, had one that said BTF PHD. His initials, his degree, lest anyone forget.

I drove Ben to the Stop & Shop parking lot, where his truck sat alone. "Thanks again, Ben," I said.

"You're welcome. Next time you feel the need to tear apart a chicken, call a friend." He paused, and I waited for him to . . . I don't know . . . give me his number or something.

But he didn't. Just got into his truck and drove off.

CHAPTER 19

Lillie

Three days later, I drove home from an uneventful day at work (no word from Melissa, thank God). There was my father in the driveway, leaning against his truck. Mirroring him was Ben, leaning against his own pickup. The difference was (a) thirty years and (b) Ben wasn't related to me. Otherwise, they were essentially the same person. Zeus was sitting at my father's leg, thanks to his doggy door, moaning as Dad scratched his blocklike head.

"Hi, guys," I said. "You here to be fed?"

My dog leaped over to me, crooning with joy, and my voice changed into that ridiculous voice all people used on their dogs unless they were sociopaths. "Hello, Zeusie! Hello! Yes, I love you! Do you want to be fed, too?"

"Dinner'd be a good start, Squashy," Dad said. "What's cooking?"

I kissed his scratchy cheek. "Beggars can't be choosy, Dad. Come on in. You, too, Ben." Like a good dog, Ben followed my father as Zeus ran in joyful laps around the house.

"Smells good in here!" Dad exclaimed. "Ben, you won't go hungry, not with this one. With Hannah, well, at least she'd take you out a lot."

"It's just chicken in the Crock-Pot. Some chorizo. Artichokes. I'll make a salad, too." I opened the fridge. "Actually, no salad. You want to sit on the porch before we eat?"

"I'm starving," said my father.

"Grab a bowl, then." I checked the Crock-Pot, lifesaver of working people everywhere, and breathed in the fragrant steam. Yummy. My poor son, having to eat dining hall food after growing up with food like this! It was mid-November. Well, it was November 12, which was almost mid-November. On December 19, my son would fly home. Just thirty-seven days. Eight hundred and eighty-eight hours. Not that I was counting or anything.

I set the Crock-Pot on the table, took a bottle of wine from the fridge (Cousin Silverio's finest) and got glasses. Ben filled up his with water, and we sat down to eat.

"Ben and I went to the Land Ho! the other night," I said.

"He told me. Said you were tearing apart a chicken in the parking lot of Stop and Shop like a feral raccoon."

"Hey! For one, all raccoons aren't feral, because they're *meant* to be wild. For two, I was very hungry."

My father looked at me from across the table, his face stern. "Your sister told me about your little stunt."

"What stunt?" I said, feeling immediately guilty. There were so many. Peeing in Brad's ironing water. The half-and-half in his car. Hannah suspected me about the skunk, but did she know about the shrimp?

"The one where you dressed up like a witch and stood in the mud to ruin your ex-husband's wedding."

Ben choked.

"Oh, that one," I said, unperturbed. "They deserved that." Shit. Now that I'd seen Melissa as a patient, I'd have to stop, uh, tormenting her, wouldn't I? Crap. I would.

"Rumor has it you've broken into their house a time or two—"

"Dad! Is there any proof of that whatsoever?"

"—and now you're eating with your hands in the parking lot like a crazy woman."

I glared at Ben. "Traitor."

"My first loyalty is always to your father." He lifted one eyebrow, a skill I lacked.

Dad leaned back in his chair, smiling. "Great. We're all agreed, then. Ben's moving in."

My turn to choke. "What? Uh, no. Where did you come up with that idea, gentlemen?" I looked at Ben, incredulous, but he just kept eating.

My father was still giving me the *you are not going out dressed like that* look. "Obviously, he'll live in the studio. But someone should keep an eye on you."

"No. Someone should not."

"I don't like you living out here alone," Dad said.

"I don't live alone. I have a dog now. A big, terrifying dog." Zeus rolled over onto his back and farted. "Zeus, go to your bed," I said. He did, but not before giving me the Saddest Dog in the World face.

"He'll respect your privacy," Dad said. "But you need someone. Remember that guy who disappeared around here? Matt what's-his-name?"

"Matthew Dudek. That was ten years ago, Dad, and it has nothing to do with me. And, Ben, do you have anything to say for yourself? Were you evicted or something? Bedbugs? A tree fell on your house?"

"No," he said. "Your father asked me to do him a favor."

"Besides," Dad said, "it's just for the winter."

"The wint—What? No! I'm sorry. No, thank you."

"Squashy," Dad said, leaning forward. "You jumped the rails, honey. You need to have someone around. I'd do it myself, but you said you didn't want me. And I'm busy these days."

"Busy doing what?" I asked.

"None of your business."

"Okay, well, that doesn't change the fact that I don't need a keeper."

"Think about it, Squashy. The snow, the ice. Ben has a plow."

"So do you, Pop. You can plow my driveway when it snows. You always have."

"My plow broke."

"Fix it." I glanced at Ben, who was calmly eating.

"What if you take a header down those stairs and break your leg?" Dad said, gesturing toward the pond. "What if your dog does? You gonna lug that moose up from the dock? I helped you build those stairs, don't forget."

"Okay," I admitted, "I have thought about falling down the stairs, and I have a plan for that. Ropes and a come-along."

"What if you lose power?"

"I have a generator and I'm a very capable woman, as you know, Father, since you raised me."

"What if you get sick and can't get to the doctor's and the Wi-Fi doesn't work? What if a serial killer comes along? No one will hear you out here, will they?"

"What if it's a grizzly bear?" I said. "Or a pack of wolves? Or a *zombie*. Because those are more likely to appear on my doorstep than a serial killer in Wellfleet, Dad. Come on."

"That's what everyone says until it happens," Dad said. "'Couldn't happen in my little town.' Hey. You're the one who got me hooked on true crime podcasts."

Dang it. He was right.

"You come in at all hours from that hospital, Squashy. And now there's no one here to look after you." Zeus barked from upstairs. "Except the dog," Dad added.

"I'd leave you alone, Lillie," Ben said. "Your dad says the studio is completely self-sufficient. He just wants you to have someone close by to put his mind at ease. It gets dark early out here."

I opened my mouth to protest, then shut it.

I had five neighbors within a ten-minute walk. All of them lived elsewhere in the winter. Four of the five had already left, and the Burtons would head out the week before Thanksgiving and go home to Colorado.

This would be the first winter of my life that I'd be alone. There would be nights that I'd come home at 3:00 a.m.

Times when it might be nice to have someone feed Zeus for me without asking my dad to drive over and do it.

And Dad was right. I could scream at top volume, and no one would hear me.

"Did your plow really break?" I asked Dad.

"The frame snapped on that damn pothole on 6A," he said.

"Ben? Don't you have a life? I thought you owned your own house."

"I do."

"And you're just going to abandon it while you sit in my shed like a creeper?"

"No, Lillie. I'm going to rent it out to a nice couple from Florida who don't want to live there anymore. I'll be on the *Goody Chapman* every day. I'll just sleep here." He paused. "If you don't mind. But I think your father has a point."

I didn't want him here when Dylan was home. Dylan loved the studio, and so did his friends. "You can stay with my father over Christmas when my son is home," I said.

"Speaking of that," Dad said, "I was actually thinking of staying with *you* when Dylan's home."

I set my fork down with a clatter. "Excuse me?"

"What?" Dad said. "I love my grandson. He loves me. I miss him, and I'm old."

Ben laughed, and there it was. That warmth in my stomach. His face went from stoic to . . . to . . . to dead sexy. Delighted and mischievous and yep, dead sexy. "You know he means it if he's pulling the old man card," he said to me, and I couldn't help smiling.

Not a housemate. Sort of a . . . property mate. The thought of coming home to the studio lights on, or smoke coming out of the woodstove we had in there . . . it might be kind of nice.

"We'll give it a week and see how it goes," I said.

"See? I told you she'd love the idea," Dad said, then ducked as I threw my napkin at his head.

CHAPTER 20

Melissa

If Melissa kept the baby, she'd be just another *look at my baby bump* person on Instagram. Boring! Plus, she already had Ophelia (who wasn't great about letting her take pictures that showed them having fun together, since they rarely if ever had fun together, though Ophelia's room had gotten a whole heap of comments and likes).

Plus, she'd been feeling abysmal (word of the day!). Seriously. She could not keep the gas in. The other night, it had surprised her while she was cooking, and Bradley laughed and said even her farts were adorable. (She hated the word *fart*, and she nearly stabbed Bradley—hello, mood swing.) The acid stomach. She'd vomited a couple more times, too. And the exhaustion!

Then again, she didn't mind taking a nap. It helped pass the day.

A baby. Ugh. Diapers and screaming and sleepless nights.

But *she* was in charge of the money now. She'd hire a nanny or a night nurse and get right back into shape. Maybe she'd be one of those Kate Middleton types who looked like she'd never given birth. Even if pregnancy did ruin her body, she'd get it back into shape with yoga and Pilates, just as she did now. If her lady garden got a bit droopy, there was surgery for that. Ditto breasts, but gosh golly, they were looking amazing these days. Rounder. Perkier. Bradley couldn't stop touching them.

And then there was the image of that little creature inside her. Its tiny, mysterious hand, so small but already a hand. A plum, the pamphlet had said (currently hidden in a pair of boots in her vast closet). A plum wasn't nothing.

Bradley was a good father, more or less. He had been until the divorce, from all accounts (well, from his account). He'd been a good husband to Lillie. It had been one of the things that attracted her, his ability to commit and be a loving husband; he'd told her he'd never cheated on Lillie before. Dylan would *have* to be nice to her if she was having his half sibling. It would be a sister- or brother-cousin to Ophelia.

Oh! And Melissa could name it! Wasn't she fantastic at picking out names! Granted, she would've chosen something other than Melissa for herself, but the memory of Kaitlyn calling her Missy—Kaitlyn's first word—had been too strong back then.

Melissa hoped it was a girl, because those names were much more fun. Addison? Emery? Fairchild was *such* a great last name, much better than Finch (or Cumbo, for heaven's sake . . . Kaitlyn had wanted to keep Cumbo as Ophelia's last name, but when she changed Harminee's name to Ophelia, Melissa also changed the girl's last name to Spencer). Hang on a sec! She could ask for names on Instagram and TikTok! And the baby's room would be *so* beautiful. The clothes for little girls . . . they were almost too adorable!

The nanny would watch the baby when Melissa got bored or needed her facials or a nap or yoga classes or shopping trips (she still wanted to go to New York with Ophelia, especially for Christmastime). What fun it would be to see some of the old crowd and put her hand on her adorable tummy and modestly acknowledge that yes, she was expecting. She'd have to look up some designer maternity clothes.

But she was getting ahead of herself. Did she *really* want to give the rest of her life over to some tiny, unreasonable tyrant? She could go down to Hyannis and get an abortion, and only Lillie would know.

How was that for irony? The first wife being the confidante of the second! It was kind of delicious, if Melissa was the malicious type. She had to admit, though, that Lillie had been very . . . kind . . . in the office. Melissa could see why people wanted her to deliver their babies. She'd asked all the personal questions without making Melissa feel stupid, and during the ultrasound, she'd seemed a little . . . tender.

That tiny head. The profile. Her little plum had a profile. A beating heart.

Yes. She'd keep it. It would only add to her influencer status. Melissa Fairchild, decorator, fitness expert, adoptive mother and now child-rearing expert, someone who'd show off her beautiful home, children and body but still be realistic and relatable (without being *too* real, of course . . . she wasn't going to talk about vomiting or gas, for gosh sake!).

A baby bump, glowing skin . . . she'd make a yoga-workout-for-pregnant-women video! Maybe she could get it copyrighted and start an empire. She was rich. Money made money. She could afford the marketing and publicity, right? And Bradley would be thrilled . . . he would love his new child, her fame would rub off on his book sales, and they'd become a power couple. It would be nice to have him pull his weight around here, especially if he could do it as a bestselling author.

Now, how to tell him . . . where would be most romantic? Most public? What should she wear? She'd have to schedule a professional photo shoot to show off her bump, for sure. With Ophelia, to make them look like a happy family.

Melissa made reservations at the Ice House and went over the scenario a dozen times in her head. They'd eat, the server would clear, and then she'd say, "Babe, I have some wonderful news. I'm pregnant!" He'd probably cry, then they'd kiss—hopefully, he would kneel by her chair. She'd ask the waiter to film the whole thing. Gosh, Instagram and TikTok would *love* that! It would definitely go viral. Enough of those marriage proposals. Time for something even better, even more important. Something *sacred*.

She'd hired Sophie, the nice babysitter Ophelia actually liked, and who worshipped Melissa, since she'd given her a few pairs of shoes and some last-season purses. Sophie could help get her younger viewers, so she should definitely do a video with the girl. She was pretty enough, too, and just unpretty enough not to outshine Melissa.

Currently, Sophie and Ophelia were eating the macaroni and cheese the chef had left, and even from way up here, she could smell the gorgeous, rich Boursin and cheddar. Cheese. She never stopped loving it.

She waited until Bradley was done in the shower. She liked prepping alone, and she didn't want to take the chance that he'd see her tiny baby bump and guess before she could announce the happy news.

As she stood in her silk bathrobe in front of the mirror, she peered closer. Her face looked . . . different. It looked . . . *fat*. Where were her cheekbones? What had she eaten today? A green smoothie for breakfast, some grilled chicken for lunch with a side salad . . . nothing that would make her swell! A few Lindt truffles that had somehow gotten into the pantry. One paltry chocolate chip cookie from the still-warm batch Chef Paul made for Phee. Plus, she was guzzling water and peeing incessantly. But otherwise, super healthy.

And what were those little dots on her chin? Blackheads? She didn't get blackheads! Spinning the mirror around, she took a look in the magnifying side.

They weren't blackheads. They were *pores*. When had

her pores suddenly expanded? She had flawless skin! Flawless!

"Babe? Our reservation is at seven thirty, right?"

"Right, babe," she called back, an edge of panic in her voice.

She grabbed her concealer kit and got to work. When she was finished, she looked more or less herself, but she could tell. She'd have to see a dermatologist, because she was so *not* going to have disgusting skin during this pregnancy.

An ivory wool dress with a wide neckline, clinging to her boobs. She needed a bigger bra, gosh darn it. Well, that was fine. Underwear shopping was fun, though it might require a trip to Boston or New York. She cinched her waist with a brown leather belt, but it didn't look right. Her waist was . . . thicker. She turned around. Her ass was wider, and another ripple of panic went through her. Already? Already her body was changing? What had Lillie said? Twelve weeks. Almost thirteen. If she already looked so gross, what would the rest of her pregnancy do to her body?

"Calm down, Missy," she whispered to herself. "Remember who you are." She'd consult someone about a pregnancy workout to make sure she looked fit and gorgeous. Who was that woman who'd helped the Kardashians? She'd find out.

"You look beautiful," said Bradley as she finally emerged from the bathroom.

"Thanks, babe," she said, giving him a smile. Their baby would have the most beautiful eyes, courtesy of his turquoise, almost fake-looking blue and her translucent green. Should she reach out to a modeling agency now, or wait till the baby was born?

At the Ice House, Beth gave a clipped "Hello, Melissa" and ignored Bradley. Whatever. "Would it be all right if we sat here, Beth?" Melissa asked sweetly, pausing at a table in the center of the restaurant.

"Sure." She put down the menus, said "Enjoy your dinner" and left.

"Well, *someone's* still not over our marriage," Bradley said. "She and Lillie have been friends since they were little. I hope she doesn't spit in our food. Huh huh huh. Oh, I have to tell you something. I think Lillie is *stalking* me. I saw her car in Orleans the other day? Right on Main Street. She's obsessed with me still."

"I'm sure she had other reasons for driving on Main Street, honey," Melissa said.

"She used to come by the office unannounced sometimes. With flowers in a jar or some banana bread. As if my work was so frivolous she could just stop by whenever she wanted."

"She would interrupt client sessions?"

Brad paused. "Well, no. But I'd hear her coming in the back. She'd leave stuff in the kitchen."

Yes, call the wife police. How dare she? "Well, you can be sure I won't be doing that, babe." She laughed seductively, her fingers at her neckline. "I have my hands full these days."

"You know she still won't let Dylan FaceTime me. I mean, I know he's an adult, but I'm sure she's manipulated him into not speaking to me. She's turning him against me. We were always so close, and now she's preventing him from building a new relationship with me. He probably doesn't even realize he's being used. I would have thought me telling him about her wedding stunt would show him how vengeful she is, but he hasn't called me back. And I know it's because of her."

Enough talk of Lillie, though it was hard not to think of her, given that Lillie was the one who had told her she was pregnant. "Speaking of Dylan, when is he coming home for Christmas?" Melissa asked. "I want to have his room at Stella Maris ready for him."

"I don't know! She won't even tell me how long his break is."

"Doesn't it say on the college website?"

Bradley flushed. "I guess."

"Well, we'll see him, babe, don't worry. I'm sure of it.

You've always been a wonderful father." And maybe there'd be a gorgeous new car sitting in the garage with a big bow on it. A bribe, sure. They worked. "Remember," she continued, "Dylan hasn't actually met me. Once he does, I think he'll be able to see how happy you are, and that I don't have horns and a tail."

Brad's face relaxed. "No. I've seen your ass enough to say it's perfection."

As if on cue, she farted. She jerked, shocked. She hadn't even felt the urge! They both pretended it hadn't happened, and she prayed that no one else had heard it. She'd book an appointment this week and see what could be done. In addition to the gas, her stomach was burning with acid, and she was out of Tums. She hated needing them, but they did work, at least for a while.

"Oh, guess what I heard?" Bradley said. "Lillie's renting the studio! She has a *man* living there, and she was oh so judgmental of us. Now she's—"

"Can we stop talking about her, Bradley? Please. I'd like to have a nice dinner." She took a long sip of water, then set the glass down. "She's entitled to her anger, Bradley. You cheated on her."

Brad blinked. "I mean, it wasn't cheating as much as a relationship transition."

"Whatever you call it, it happened. Let's order, babe. What looks good to you?" She looked down. Oh, yes. Tuscan-style veal with rosemary, garlic and sage. She hadn't had red meat in *years*, but her mouth watered. *Sorry, baby animal, you are too good to pass up.* And oh, golly, the clam chowder. She knew it was basically hot cream with clams and potatoes, but she suddenly had to have it. She could taste it already.

Her blood sugar must be low. She felt more gas coming and clenched.

The server, a young man with a ring in his nose, came over. "Hi, I'm Tanner. Can I get you two some drinks tonight?"

"We'd like to order everything now, if you don't mind," Melissa said, her stomach growling loudly. She pretended she didn't notice. "I'll have a Caesar salad, a cup of clam chowder and the veal, please." She also pretended not to notice Bradley's face, which was shocked. She didn't usually order so much food. He did, though. He always had three courses, at least.

"Got it. Anything to drink?"

She usually ordered a gin martini. But she couldn't drink now. She'd already soaked her little plum in French wine. Maybe she should name it after a wine! "Just club soda and lime, please," she said, gracing him with a big smile. He didn't seem to notice.

Bradley ordered a dozen Wellfleet oysters, the lobster bisque, a garden salad and the rib eye steak. "I guess we're both in the mood for red meat," he said, raising his eyebrows suggestively.

She stifled a yawn. Like the gas, they came out of nowhere. "Excuse me one second. I need to powder my nose." She went to the ladies' room, because she did have to pee. Good golly, she could pee twice an hour these days! And the fatigue . . . she could probably take a power nap on the toilet right now.

She washed her hands and looked at herself in the mirror. Still beautiful. Just . . . not as much.

On the way out, she slipped over to the waiter, who was just leaving the kitchen with two plates. "Tanner, would you mind doing me a favor?"

"Uh . . . I have to get these out."

"It'll be quick. After you clear our dinners, I'm going to surprise my husband. Would you take a movie?" She took her phone out of her purse.

"Yeah. Um . . . just put it in my apron."

She did, accidentally brushing her hand against his groin. "Thank you," she said, looking up at him.

"Yep." He raced off.

Well, that was odd. She hadn't *meant* to feel him up, but

dashing away like that was a little bit insulting, Tanner! He was probably gay, she decided. But it had been completely innocent. *Innocent, my ass,* she could almost hear Kaitlyn saying. *You're cougaring like a she-dog in heat.*

Well. Kaitlyn might not use those exact words. Maybe Melissa would call her tomorrow and tell her about the baby.

She walked back to the table and kissed Brad's cheek. "Missed you," she said.

"Missed *you.* Hey. Let's talk about Ophelia," Bradley said, and her heart warmed. He wanted so much to have the girl like him. "I was thinking summer camp would be good for her. Six weeks, eight weeks, say. We'd have the place to ourselves. Maybe we could travel some more."

They'd be changing diapers by then.

"I'm not sure it's the right time," she said. She'd thought the same thing before she'd known she was pregnant, but it rubbed her the wrong way when Bradley said it. Ophelia was not his to boss around. "I think she's made a lot of progress since coming to the Cape. Can you believe we've been here nine months? I think she feels at home, finally."

"I'm happier than I've ever been," Brad said. "Than I ever dreamed I could be."

She forced a smile. They were supposed to be talking about her niece.

Their soups came, and Tanner didn't make eye contact. "Enjoy," he said.

She tasted it, closed her eyes, and tasted it some more. Golly, it was good. But a cup wasn't what it used to be, was it, because suddenly, her chowder was halfway gone. "This is delicious," she said. "I'm hungrier than I realized."

Ooh, rolls, still warm from the oven! And the salad was amazing, so garlicky and good! Bradley's oysters came, and she looked away as he slurped them down. Her stomach gave a twinge, and she put her hand over it protectively.

When the veal came, Melissa took a bite and moaned in bliss.

"I've never seen you eat so much in my life," Bradley said, smiling at her like an idiot.

"Do I ever criticize what you eat, Bradley?" she snapped.

"Um . . . no. I just . . . I didn't realize you were so hungry, that's all."

"Well, I am." She ate her mashed potatoes defiantly, her mouth rejoicing at the flavors, the creaminess. Yes. She was going to need that pregnancy trainer. She would not be one of those cautionary tales like . . . like Jessica Simpson or Kim Kardashian, who'd looked *enormous* while pregnant.

But tonight was special, and she deserved it. When did she ever let herself eat like this? Never, that's when. And oh, the *food*. It was all she could do not to order crème brûlée.

"All finished with the oysters, sir?" Tanner asked. There were three left on the plate, the ice melted under the shells.

"No, no, leave them. It's a shame to waste even one," Brad said.

"Thank you, Tanner," Melissa said. He finally looked at her and gave a little nod. Good. A thrill of excitement tingled through her. It was time. Nope, not time. Tanner was bringing their dishes to the kitchen. Brad slurped down an oyster, and yuck, that noise. She'd had to force herself to learn to eat them, since she knew it connoted (word of the day!) a certain degree of class. The taste was fine, eventually, but they still felt like great big wads of phlegm.

Her stomach rolled. Think of something else, she told herself. She did. The ocean? No, too much movement. Um . . . brushing Ophelia's hair? No, again, too springy and unstable. The yoga mat. There. Nice and solid.

She took a breath to make sure she was fine. Breathe in serenity, breathe out nausea. Better. Okay. Tanner was standing behind one of the posts, waiting for her. "Now?" he mouthed. She nodded, and he lifted the phone, turning it horizontally. Good boy.

"Bradley. Sweetheart. I have something very exciting to tell you," she said, making sure her posture was perfect. She clasped her freshly manicured hands and leaned forward.

"Oh? Great!" he said, and he slurped down another oyster and reached for the final one. She pressed her lips together.

"Honey? I want to have your full attention."

"Okay. Sure." Brad put the oyster down. "All done. What's exciting?"

She smiled. "Well, honey, this wasn't planned, but I'm—"

Bradley, for some unknown reason, couldn't resist that last oyster. He lifted it to his mouth, slurped, swallowed, swallowed again, his throat working.

Then Melissa was vomiting. All over the table, all that food, barely chewed, gobs of veal and bits of carrot, and the *cream* from the *chowder* . . . another racking convulsion and a stream of garlic-flavored vomit from the Caesar salad.

"Jesus!" Brad yelled, leaping up and away from the table. "Honey! What the hell!" He held his fist to his own mouth and gagged.

"Ma'am? Ma'am?" someone was saying. "Do you need an ambulance?" People were grimacing, moving their chairs farther away, holding napkins to faces to ward off the smell. She gagged again.

"Babe!" Bradley barked from ten feet away, fist still at his mouth. "Is it food poisoning? What's the matter with you? A little warning next time?"

"I'm pregnant, you idiot!" she yelled. "You and your stupid oysters made me barf!"

Suddenly, she was sobbing. Oh, God! She had veal puke on her beautiful dress! And clam chowder? Why? Why had she ordered that?

Brad's face was a mask of horror. He approached (finally!) and said, "Oh, man, this mess . . ."

Then he caught a whiff of her vomit, and he threw up, too, splattering his shoes and pants. Melissa puked yet again, right into her lap, warm, garlicky spoiled cream instantly soaking through her dress to her skin.

There were people all around her, whisking away the

tablecloth and glasses, offering her napkins, asking if she needed an ambulance.

"I'm fine! I'm *fine!*" she shrieked. "Just give me some air." They were more than happy to do so. She couldn't blame them.

Brad looked at her, wary. "Honey? What did you say? Before?"

"I'm pregnant," she snapped. "Are you happy?"

"Oh, hooray!" said an older couple seated across from them, and they started clapping. For crying out loud! She was covered in vomit! This was *not* how it was supposed to be.

"This is . . . um . . . wow. Unexpected. But, but . . . you know. Great," Bradley said, dry heaving. "I'm so . . . happy." He threw up an oyster, and good golly, she'd never eat them again.

ᏨᎷ

Tanner the waiter had apparently filmed the whole thing, but on *his* phone, not hers. Then he posted it, which, according to Google's definition of copyright, he was allowed to do.

It went viral, all right. Seven million views in twelve hours. At least he didn't tag her, but it was already being shared by a few Lillie-loyal Wellfleeters, and apparently one or two of them had become Facebook friends with one or two of the New York housewives, and it was *everywhere*. Tanner had entitled it *You and Your Stupid Oysters*. The next morning, Jimmy Kimmel's people saw it, shared it, and by the afternoon of Day Two, it had been watched twenty-one million times and shared tens of thousands of times.

Melissa didn't know if she'd ever recover. She hadn't left the bedroom since she'd gotten home last night, nor spoken to Bradley, the cause of this mess. He'd left for work already, and she hoped he'd stay late. Or never come home.

Sitting in bed, tears leaking out of her eyes, Melissa watched it again.

So humiliating.

A knock came on the door. "Melissa?" It was Ophelia, backpack on, ready for school, her hair still snarled.

"Come in," she said, sitting up in bed.

"I saw the video," she said.

"Oh." Humiliation washed over her again. "Well, shoot. I wanted to tell you myself."

Ophelia bit her lip. "It's pretty funny. Sorry, but I mean, it's *hilarious*, Melissa."

"Not to me."

"So . . . how far along are you?"

"About thirteen weeks." Even Bradley didn't know that, because she'd been too mad at him to talk last night.

"So . . . springtime?"

"Yeah. April."

"How are you feeling?" Ophelia asked, fiddling with her backpack straps.

"Not great."

"I guess that's normal, right? I mean, everyone feels like garbage when they're pregnant, right?"

"Not everyone. But yeah, lots of people." She looked at her niece. "The . . . the nurse said everything looks perfect."

"That's good." There was a pause.

Ophelia's head was bowed, those snarled curls a cloud around her face. Melissa took a chance and reached to touch the back of Ophelia's hand. "What are you thinking, Phee?"

She shrugged. "I don't know. I never had a sister or brother before. But Mama lived with this guy? And he had a baby, like a year old? She could walk and talk a little. She was really cute. I liked her."

"How long did you live with them?" Melissa asked. Ophelia had never mentioned this. Nor had Kaitlyn in their infrequent phone calls.

"I don't know. But it was nice. Like a family, you know?"

It was so rare that Ophelia offered anything personal to

her. Melissa felt like she was holding a bubble, and any movement would pop it.

"Why did you leave?"

"I don't really remember. They started fighting, I guess. I was, like, four or five. I just remember the little girl. Bitty, we called her. We slept in the same room."

"Do you think . . . Well, how do you feel about me having a baby?"

She looked down at their hands, then up again at Melissa. "Guess it means we're stuck with Doofus."

"Other than that, I mean."

Another shrug. "Does it matter?"

"It does." And it did. It was surprising how much it mattered.

"It'd be nice to have a . . . I don't know. Cousin, I guess?"

"Almost like a brother or sister."

Ophelia gave her a look, warning her not to push it. "Do you know if it's a boy or a girl yet?"

"Not yet." Melissa paused. "Do you want to come to one of my appointments? You can already hear the heartbeat."

"Sure!" Then, as if embarrassed by her enthusiasm, she added, "I mean, I guess."

"Great." Melissa smiled at her.

"I gotta go to school."

"Okay. Thanks, Ophelia."

"For what?"

"I felt like a jerk because of last night. Now I feel better." She smiled at her niece again.

"Whatever. Bye."

The bubble popped. But it had been there, even so.

CHAPTER 21

Lillie

I had watched *You and Your Stupid Oysters* seventeen times, and I wasn't even a little bit ashamed. Beth had called me moments after the vomit explosion happened, then again an hour later when Tanner uploaded it.

It truly was a thing of beauty, because I knew—I *knew*—Melissa had planned the entire evening to be set up as the #MostPerfectMoment of #OurBliss #BunInTheOven #OurBabyStory. Oh, yes, I followed her on Instagram. Of course I did. It was a public page, and I'd made an account under a fake name. Just because I'd seen her as a patient didn't mean I couldn't look at her pictures. Ever since I'd learned she was Brad's mistress, I followed her, just to see how incredibly shallow she was.

Her photos had started in New York with a zillion pictures of her and her father—sorry, *husband*. Their apartment. Their vacations. Her perfect body in designer workout clothes, #selfcare #fitnessjunkie #workout. Of her beautiful face, #playingwithmakeup #chanel #skincare. Her incredible clothes. Her stunning view, NYC and Wellfleet editions. The beautiful dinner she'd made. Her beautiful closet, for God's sake. Then we moved on to Ophelia . . . #niece

#fostering #girlpower #fostercare #fosterchild #fostermom #lovemygirl. Once she moved here, it was #StellaMaris #CapeCodLiving #sunset #beachlife #SandBetweenMy-Toes, and the hashtag I hated most in her case, #blessed.

Then came engagement photos of her and Brad frolicking on the beach, in the long golden grass, Brad down on one knee. (And please, you know it was all staged. She probably had Steven Spielberg directing the whole thing.) More nauseating hashtags . . . #ISaidYes! #MyTrueLove #CapeCodJoy #InSicknessAndInHealth. Sure, lady. Wait till he gets a cold. You'll want to smother him with your $200 pillows.

The wedding photos had just appeared (minus me, alas). #MarriedMyBestFriend. #HappilyEverAfter. #Bralissa #Bride #brideandgroom #wedding #weddingday #wed-dingdress #weddingcake #weddingveil #couplegoals #cel-ebrate #celebration #cloudnine #happiness #FairchildsForever #HappilyEverFairchild.

So you could see how watching them both vomit up their dinners, hearing her screech at *Bradley* . . . Well, let's say I was quite pleased with karma today.

But my first thought had been Dylan. After Beth had called me last night to say the video was online and going viral fast, I texted Bridiot. Tell your son the news before he sees it on YouTube. Brad hadn't responded, and when I'd called Dylan this morning and then again at four, the call had gone to voice mail. He'd texted me later, saying only, Everything's fine, studying for a big test, TTYL.

Did that mean he knew already? Or was Brad going to force me to tell him before he saw the video? What if he'd already seen it?

God, I missed Dylan. Things we would have once talked about over dinner, or in the car, or sitting on the porch were now reduced to a few brief words in a text, sometimes sent hours and hours after I reached out. It was so hard, wondering if your kid was okay, not being able to tell.

In a few days, he'd be going to someone else's house for

Thanksgiving for the first time in his life. I'd have my dad over. Hannah, if she wasn't seeing the Moms, which, given Beatrice's plans to move, she probably was. Wanda, Addo and my beautiful goddaughter, Leila, always came. It wouldn't be like I was home alone all day.

Maybe I'd ask Ben, if he didn't have other plans.

Ben had been living in the studio for a week. It wasn't horrible, seeing his light on when I came home. He'd fed Zeus on Wednesday, when a labor had gone long at the hospital. He was quiet; he left early, came back after dark and didn't have much stuff. But I was wary . . . I knew he was reporting to my father. Not that I had anything to hide.

Today was my day off, and after rewatching *You and Your Stupid Oysters* four more times, I took Zeus out for a walk. The weather was raw and thick with the smell of the ocean, and I breathed in deeply as Zeus snuffled along, nose to the ground. We walked down Black Pond Road, then turned to go along the Higgins Pond loop. The leaves had fallen from the trees, and the woods had a mystery to them. A literal mystery. Ten years ago, Matthew Dudek had vanished.

It was a reflex, looking for him. Long after the police had called off the search, I'd looked for him, this stranger from the North Shore. For years, I'd hike through the deer paths and bayberry scrub, sometimes alone, sometimes with Dylan or Brad, always looking for that little flash of blue, the color of the jacket he'd worn the last time he was seen.

Obviously, we'd never found anything. Once or twice a year, I'd google his name to see if he'd shown up somewhere, but the last mentions of him were when he'd vanished.

Zeus was sniffing and snuffling away—a chipmunk hole, some deer droppings. It was nice to think he'd find poor Matthew's remains so the Dudeks could have some closure, but my dog, while sweet, was not terribly bright, and every smell, from an earthworm to a human crotch, was equally interesting to him. Plus, the police had brought in those cadaver dogs.

All these years, no answer.

When we got back to the house, I did what I usually did on my days off—tended to my house. I raked up the last of the oak leaves from the gardens, did my paltry load of laundry, cooked a big pot of chicken-pumpkin curry, which I'd then divide into smaller containers for the rest of the week. My fridge and freezer were already packed with my own work, but I loved cooking. Couldn't help myself, honestly. I'd bring some to Carol, who lived alone, or better yet, invite her over for dinner.

Time to phone a friend and shake off this melancholy. Beth was free and more than happy to come over tonight. "I had to go into Eli's room this morning, and I stepped in something sticky, Lillie! He's fourteen! I don't want to know what it was. Oh, and his laundry! My God, the smell, I can't even go upstairs without gagging. He supposedly cleaned his room this weekend, but you know he just shoved all his crap under the bed. There was half a tuna fish sandwich growing penicillin in his sock drawer. Tuna! In his sock drawer! Why? Why?"

"Here's where I get to tell you how much you'll miss it someday," I said, laughing at her horror. "Well. Not the stickiness and the mold, but the boy. See you at seven, okay?"

And then, because I knew Hannah was agonizing over Beatrice leaving, I asked her if she'd like to come over that night, too. It would be less awkward with Beth here, because she was the friendliest person on earth and could talk to a stump if need be. Called my father, but it went to voice mail. Texted him and got the response I'm busy, get a life, Squashy, love Dad.

I snorted. So you say to the daughter who loves you and feeds you. Shame on you. What are you doing?

None of your business. Go do your baby thing.

"My baby thing" was the only way Dad could talk about midwifery, since he was squeamish that way. Once, when I was thirteen, he'd seen a pair of my underwear stained with blood and had fainted. *Fainted.* I liked to taunt him by asking if he wanted to hear about a breech birth or a rectal tear.

Hannah arrived first, dressed in that effortless way our stepmother had taught her—that je ne sais quoi that my shorter, rounder frame could never manage. We were both wearing jeans and a sweater. I looked like I had just cleaned the house; Hannah looked elegant and wealthy, which I suppose she was. To be fair, Beatrice had offered to make me over thousands of times, and I had always turned her down.

"Hi," said my sister. "How are you?"

"Good. You?"

"Good." She glanced around. "The house looks nice. Oh, hi, doggy. What's his name again?"

"Zeus."

"A great name. Look at that heart on his nose. So cute." She stepped to the side to avoid Zeus's gynecological nuzzling.

"Zeus, stop," I said. "No sexually harassing our guests." I took Hannah's coat. "Um, how's your cat? Thomasina?"

"She's good. Sleepy. Old."

"Any weddings or events coming up?"

"One corporate Christmas party down in Chatham. Otherwise, it's pretty quiet."

"Mm." We looked at each other for a minute. "Sit down. I made food."

"Of course you did," she said, and I wasn't sure if it was a compliment or a mild insult. "Hey, your shed lights are on," she added.

"Oh, yeah. Ben Hallowell is staying there for a little while."

"Any particular reason?"

"Dad thought I could use a babysitter after you narc'ed on me about Bralissa's wedding."

"Well. Ben is a good guy."

"Yeah, sure. Yep." I sat down in the chair across from

her, and Zeus collapsed on his bed in front of the fireplace. "Hannah, do you remember that car accident I was in?"

"Of course I do."

"Ben was the driver."

"I know." She poured herself some red wine and swirled it in the glass, sniffed it and managed not to look like an idiot while doing so. "He pulled you out. Saved your life, didn't he?"

"I don't remember, but that *is* the story."

"Why do you bring it up?"

"I don't know. Just . . . having him here made me think about it, I guess."

I had no memory of when Ben's truck went off the road. None at all. The last thing I remembered was the smell of coffee and the cool of the window against my head . . . and then the hospital, the searing pain, the morphine fog.

Hannah leaned back and looked out the window. It was too dark to see the pond. I wondered if she ever missed it. Her own place was lovely, but it wasn't this. Even now, the forest smelled like pine needles, and the rain blew against the windows, that loveliest of sounds.

Beth came in at that moment, bringing a gust of salty air with her, and Zeus leaped out of his bed like he'd been zapped with a cattle prod. "It's getting cold out there!" Beth said. "Hi, Zeus! Who's my baby? You are! Yes, you are!" Zeus, wagging so hard he fell down, offered Beth his stomach to rub. She obliged, then came into the living room, poured herself a glass of white, stuffed a piece of chorizo in her mouth and chewed. "What did I miss?"

"Lillie was asking about the car accident with Ben." Hannah and Beth were sort of friends, too, since Hannah pitched the Ice House to a lot of her clients.

"Right! The bad boy of the bay is living with you! How is it, having him out there? Weird? Sexy? Do you watch him from the windows? Are you guys doing it? Because he's wicked hot."

"Did you forget your Adderall today?" I asked.

"I may have."

Zeus climbed up onto the couch to gaze adoringly at the food. I slipped him a piece of sausage. "In answer to your questions, no. He's practically my father's son, so it would be almost incestuous and therefore wrong."

"But so hot. Right, Hannah?"

"Sure," Hannah said. "We graduated the same year, I think. But I was in Provincetown, and he was down here at Nauset."

"Did you ever have a crush on him, Han?" Bethie asked.

"No. But he was always fun to talk to."

Was he? Not to me.

Beth sighed happily. "Remember how we'd go to the dock to watch him when we were teenagers, hoping he'd take off his shirt?"

"I remember going to the dock to see my father," I said firmly, stroking Zeus's silky head. "Not to ogle Ben."

"Liar." She raised her eyebrows and sipped some wine. "I would do him in a New York minute. Wouldn't you, Hannah?"

"I invoke my right to the Fifth Amendment," she said. She was so graceful that way . . . dodging the question, being in the conversation but also being neutral, never having much of an opinion about anything. Always completely in control. God. We were so different. "Speaking of handsome men, Beth, how is your husband?" Hannah asked with a smile.

Beth sat back on the couch with that smug smile of a happy woman. "He's okay. I'll keep him for now." She took another mini quiche and popped it in her mouth. "Let's invite Ben in. His lights are on, his truck is right there and it feels rude, not having him here."

"Isn't it girls' night?" I asked.

"What if he's lonely?" Beth asked.

"It's fine with me," Hannah said. "I haven't seen him in ages."

"Fine," I said. "And then we kick him out so we can really

talk." I pulled out my phone and dictated a text. "'Hi comma Ben comma Hannah and Beth are here and there's food period. Want to stop in question mark.' How's that?"

A minute later, there was a knock on the door, and there he was, all jeans and flannel and rugged face and disheveled hair. "Hey."

"You hungry?" I asked.

"I ate."

"Okay." Such rapier-sharp dialogue with the two of us. "Come on in anyway."

"Ben!" Beth cried, launching herself up for a hug, which, to my surprise, he returned. Then he turned to my sister. "Hannah. Gorgeous as always."

She laughed, got up and hugged him. "Nice to see you, Ben. Have a seat. Red wine, or white?" Nice of her to play hostess. I supposed it was an occupational hazard.

"Red is good, thanks. Hey, Zeus, old buddy."

"So you're my sister's bodyguard now?" Hannah asked.

"More like the dog sitter for when she's stuck at the hospital." That had happened once so far. But yes, it was convenient.

"How's life in the shed?" asked Beth, who remembered the little building from when it housed my father's tools. "Lillie, you need to call it something cooler than the studio. Rename it, and you can rent it for five hundred dollars more per week in the summer. The Studio at Herring Pond. Pitch Pine Cottage. Make that seven hundred."

"I hate houses with names on principle," I said. "Stella Maris, for example."

"Star of the Sea?" Ben asked, and I was a little surprised he knew Latin. "Should be a boat's name."

"That's where my ex-husband and his child bride now live, Benjamin," I said.

"Very pretentious."

"See? I knew we liked you," Beth said. "Ben, did you see the video of them at my restaurant the other day?"

"I'm not on social media."

"Saving your soul?" Hannah asked.

"I'm trying to stay pure," he returned, winking at her. Were they *flirting*? My sister? And Ben? It was kind of cute.

Beth grabbed my laptop from a side table. "I want you to get the full effect, Ben," she said, tapping away. "I've watched it a thousand times. Oh, Lillie, we're up to seventy-five *million* views! So glad my sweet Tanner hashtagged us. The restaurant's booked through the middle of January. I think everyone wants to see another . . . um . . . event, shall we say?"

She turned up the volume.

"Bradley. Sweetheart. I have something very exciting to tell you." Then the sound of my husband's voice. Melissa again, and then . . . then the beautiful and unmistakable sound of puking.

"Oh, God," Ben said, smiling against his will.

The yelling. The clattering of silverware. Another puke. Brad puking (my favorite part). And then, Beth and I said it in unison . . . "I'm pregnant, you idiot! You and your stupid oysters made me barf!" We dissolved into near hysterical laughter.

"Sweet baby Jesus," Hannah said. "It gets better with every viewing."

Ben looked at me. "How do you feel about that?"

Shit. A serious question. "Captain Hallowell, I'm not prepared to talk about feelings with you, sir."

"Fair enough."

"Okay," I said. "It's time for Cards Against Humanity, and then we're kicking you out, Ben, so we can talk about periods, boobs and menopause."

"My three favorite subjects," he said. "But message received."

My sister was right. Ben Hallowell was a good guy.

○～

An hour later, Ben left as promised after Hannah creamed us all in the bawdy game. Beth left, too, moments later when she got a text from her husband saying both their boys seemed to have fevers, courtesy of a virus that was making the rounds.

The rain was steadier now, a comforting thrum against the roof. I cleared up our snack and wine detritus, returned from the kitchen with a tray of oatmeal raisin cookies, which were perfect for the rainy night. I put another log on the fire, and sparks flew up the chimney, the pleasant smell of wood smoke mingling with the scent of rain and cookies. Love for my home wrapped me like a warm blanket.

For a few minutes, Hannah and I just sat. Before this year, I'd never included Hannah in a girls' night. Carol and Wanda; Jessica and Ashley, my high school friends who'd also stayed on the Cape, sure. Beth was automatically included in everything social I did, plus the nights when it was just the two of us. I'd had Jenn from the bakery over for a dessert-a-thon last winter when Brad was in "Boston." Three of the Smith sisters, Beth and I had a loosely scheduled book club that met here every once in a while.

But not my sister. She only came over for family events, and I was only invited to her place for the same. We'd never gone out just us two. We were pleasant, we loved each other more or less and we gave each other presents on birthdays and Christmas.

It would be nice to be—and have—a different kind of sister.

"So," I said, "how are you doing about Beatrice and Mom?"

Hannah looked at the fire. "I'm doing badly," she said. "I feel like an eight-year-old." She glanced at me sharply, then grimaced. Eight had been my age when she and my mom had left. I let it go.

"What does doing badly look like?" I was good at asking these questions, given my career (and my ex-husband's, I supposed).

She sighed. "I've cried more in the last few weeks than I have in the last two decades. I keep asking Beatrice why she can't stay, or move to Boston or New York. Total guilt trip.

It's not working." She paused and looked at me. "I guess you know how that feels. This is karma, biting me on the ass."

"Oh, Han," I said. "I . . . It's not that. You did what you had to do back then."

"And now Beatrice is doing what she has to do and I'm out the best friend I ever had, the best parent. My role model and mentor. All those things. I put all my eggs in the Beatrice basket, and I'm paying the price." She glanced at me, her eyes wet. "I understand if this is extremely satisfying for you to hear."

She took a napkin and wiped her eyes. I went over to sit with her. Put my arm around her shoulders, but since she was ten inches taller than I was, it was awkward. Like most things between us. No. I didn't want that to be the case anymore. I slid my arm down and linked it with hers. "It's not satisfying, Hannah. I'm sad for you."

"I'm forty-six years old," she said. "I did this to you when you were eight. Eight! I'm so sorry, Lillie. I never let myself think about how bad it would be because I . . . I didn't want to know."

That was true. Then again, she'd been horribly bullied, and I hadn't even known. What if she'd decided to kill herself, like too many teenagers had? What then, huh? I was abruptly *glad* she'd had Beatrice. "You know what? Let's blame Mom. She ruined my life by taking you, and now she's ruining yours by driving Beatrice away. Honestly, I can't believe Beatrice lasted as long as she did. She's a saint."

"Amen."

Maybe it was the wine, or the coziness of the night, but I felt some talking coming on. "I was so jealous of the three of you," I said. "I didn't want to live there, and I couldn't do that to Dad, but every time I went over, you were this merry little band of women, making all this great food and speaking in French. Like it was this constant party that I was missing. And then you learned how to dress and had your signature shade of lipstick and got all glamorous."

Hannah snorted. "Listen. That was all smoke and mirrors, Lils. I mean, it was better for me because of Beatrice, and because I was in a different school district. Suddenly, I was a lot cooler, living with an interracial lesbian couple in an amazing house on Commercial Street. But Mom and Beatrice fought *all* the time."

"What? They always seemed so . . . obnoxiously happy."

"Yeah, right," Hannah huffed. "It seemed like every day, one of them was yelling at the other, or Mom was giving us the silent treatment while Beatrice overcompensated. They also drank *way* too much. By the end of the first month there, I knew how to cook a huge pot of French onion soup so we could have it on hand. Remède contre la gueule de bois. Their hangover cure."

"They got drunk and fought? My God! I mean, I knew they could put away a few cocktails and wine, but . . ."

"More than a few." She glanced at me. "I mean, yes, I had Beatrice to be a mother to me, or at least a cool aunt, but I was still with Mom, and you know how she is. The insults that trick you by seeming like compliments until you find out she's slicing you up. The nit-picking, the perpetual disappointment, the sheer *boredom* of being a mother. I never wanted kids, and I think that's the reason why. She made it seem awful, and I was sure I'd screw it up."

"She was disappointed in *you*? You? You were the perfect child! *I* was the filthy urchin from the woods."

She looked at me and sighed. "I missed you and Dad so much, but I didn't think I was allowed to say that. So many times, I wanted to call Dad and ask him to pick me up."

"Why didn't you?"

"I did, once. Mom didn't speak to me for weeks after that. The message was received." She paused. "It's kind of terrifying to think that your mother can stop loving you. Can just . . . make you nonexistent." I handed her a tissue from the box on the coffee table. "So I learned pretty fast that I was only allowed to be funny and calm and smart. I kept that up for four years, you know? Because I skipped eighth grade."

"Oh, I remember. Mom loved to rub that in."

"Why do we put up with her?"

"I don't know," I said. "If she was my friend, I'd dump her."

Hannah laughed, and Zeus came to worm his way onto the couch to lie on her other side. "Me too. If I hadn't been such a freak back then, I would've stayed with you. I'm sorry."

"You were *never* a freak," I said fiercely.

"Sure I was. I still am. I'm all smoke and mirrors, too. Take away the cool job and the clothes and the lipstick and the makeup and the haircut, and I'm just an unattractive female having hot flashes."

"You're *not* unattractive! Come on! You saw how Ben was flirting with you."

"He's just being kind. Believe me, I can tell. I've *been* told."

"Told what?" I asked.

"That if I was prettier, or shorter, or had a better body, some guy might be interested."

"Ben said that?"

"No, of course not. He was just a sweet guy who worked for Dad and then got married." She sighed. "Other men told me. At least four or five over the years."

"You're so elegant, Han! You are!"

She rolled her eyes. "One guy walked out when he saw me in the restaurant. Another guy couldn't get it up and blamed my 'horse face,' as he so kindly put it. Toby at the vineyard told me if I was prettier, he'd ask me out. Justin Cardi? We went out once, and he said at the end, 'Hannah, you're perfect for me, I love your personality, you're so smart and funny, but I'm just not attracted to you.'"

"Justin Cardi, huh? I know him."

She laughed. "Don't shiv him on my behalf," she said. "Though I do love seeing you getting your Portuguese up."

"I thought you *wanted* to be single. I really did. You make it seem so cool."

"Nope. I wanted . . . well, not to be alone." She shrugged.

"Didn't you date a nice guy in college?"

"Yep. Steve. He broke up with me just before graduation." She sighed. "I thought I'd meet someone else, you
know? I mean, by the time I was twenty-four, I owned my
own business, and it was high-end and classy. I joined the
Cape Cod Young Professionals and networked and met
people . . . but nothing ever happened. I've had three flings
since college. The dating pool up here isn't very deep, as
you know, and most of the men I meet are engaged, married, way too old or way too young." She sighed. "I'm sorry
to be dumping all this on you."

"No! No, I think we're having a sisterly moment." I refilled her wineglass. "I insist that you stay over, so go
ahead, enjoy. It's the wine you brought, so you know it's
good."

She gave a small smile. "I never guessed Beatrice would
leave. She taught me how to dress, walk, talk, *be*. She
helped me build my business. She gives me design ideas if
I'm stuck. We go to lunch every week." She swallowed.
"Beatrice is my best friend. Kind of my only friend. And I
know it's not the same as your situation with Brad, but I
just . . . I feel for us both."

My heart squeezed. "Well, Han . . . you and I can do
better, right? I mean, we can have lunch and stuff. I can
even help with weddings." I thought a minute. "The flowers, anyway. And I can definitely eat lunch with you."

She smiled. Her lipstick was still perfect. "I'd really like
that."

"I've missed you. I'd be so happy to be close again, Han."

She burst into tears, wrapped her arms around me and
cried on my shoulder.

It felt strangely wonderful. A few tears leaked out of my
eyes, too.

"Regarding your hot flashes, come see me at the office,"
I said, patting her back. "No one should suffer through
those."

"Right? If men had them, there'd be seventeen cures,
and Nobel Prizes all around."

"You are so right." I looked at her face, now smeary from her tears. "Come on. Let's go downstairs and make macaroni and cheese."

"Okay. But only if we can talk about you now. Your idiot ex is having another kid. That must be . . . weird."

"It is," I said. "I'm mostly worried about Dylan. I *think* Brad told him, but he hasn't called me. And I've been thinking about the Fairchilds, too. I wonder if that's why they didn't . . . fight for me, I guess. Because they didn't want to be estranged if Bralissa reproduced." I hesitated, but since we were doing the sisterly bonding thing, I figured what the hell. "He tells everyone he's never been happier, and they feel compelled to report that to me."

"People who are truly happy don't walk around proclaiming how happy they are."

"You're a wise woman, Hannah Silva Chapman."

"And then there's that video showing him for the asshat he is."

"That video gives me so much joy, Hannah. So much joy." I swallowed. She'd bared her soul to me, so it was only fair that I did the same. "But his life is better now. He lives in this huge house on the water, has a hot young wife, all this money to do whatever he wants. He has a stepdaughter and a baby on the way. The Fairchilds lost me as a daughter-in-law, but they instantly got another one. Even Dylan will have a half sibling and stepsister. Everyone's family is growing, except mine. My only child is an adult now, and he's so far away."

"Well," she said. "Your big sister is here for you. I have years to make up for."

It was my turn to sob.

Which did not prevent us from making the world's best mac and cheese and eating it well after midnight.

CHAPTER 22

Melissa

Melissa had seen Dr. Owens twice since she'd first gone to Wellfleet OB/GYN. Driving to Hyannis took too long, and she didn't know anyone down there. Everyone in town said Dr. Owens (and Lillie) were the best, and she did want a blissful, calm labor (filmed, of course), maybe in a birthing pool, because the babies got an instant rinse that way and weren't covered in blood.

So she'd asked Dr. Owens if she could see *her*, and Dr. Owens said that it was only with the understanding that there might be occasions when Lillie would be the care provider, and so only if it was all right with both Lillie and Melissa. It was fine as far as Melissa was concerned. As for giving birth, Dr. Owens assured her that the hospital had many fine labor and delivery nurses, so if Wanda was handling another patient, Melissa would still be in experienced hands.

But aside from being assured that the plum-baby was perfectly fine, things weren't going as planned. First, there was that wretched video. She'd decided to post it anyway, since there was no escaping it: #hormonal #PassingOnOysters

#SomeoneHelpUs #LOL #PregnancyAnnouncementTookA-Swerve. She'd gotten a *lot* more followers, so go figure. But she didn't want to be known as the Barfing Madonna, as someone had tagged her. She wanted to be known as a tastemaker, someone celebrated for beauty and style and . . . well, beauty and style.

And then there was her body.

It was not cooperating. Thanksgiving had been a complete disaster . . . Chef Paul had made a fantastic meal for the three of them, "with plenty for leftovers," he'd said as he left. All Melissa had to do was keep things warm.

But the smells had haunted her, and she'd surreptitiously sneaked a few scoops of mashed potatoes just after he left at nine on Thanksgiving morning. An asparagus spear wrapped in prosciutto. Then another. The smell of turkey was incredible. She tried to stave off the hunger until dinner at two o'clock by making a grilled cheese sandwich. By the time she'd set the table, she was ravenous. She had thirds of everything. Thirds! While she cleaned up, she kept popping turkey and stuffing into her mouth, shooing Brad out of the kitchen so she could be alone with the food.

And then late that night, when Bradley and Ophelia were asleep, she crept down to the fridge to survey the leftovers, neatly wrapped by herself, since she'd given the housekeeper the day off. She made a turkey sandwich the likes of which she hadn't had since she was a kid at Mee-Maw's. Thick white bread, gobs of mayonnaise, stuffing, slabs of turkey breast and some dark meat, cranberry sauce (Mee-Maw's had come out of a can, and Melissa missed that . . . she and Kaitlyn had loved the slurping sound it made when Mee-Maw expelled it into the bowl).

The sandwich was so *good*. Nothing else mattered in that moment except the tastes exploding in her mouth. She heard a moaning sound similar to the one she made during sex, and yes, that was about equal. This turkey sandwich was as good as an orgasm.

And that was another thing. She couldn't get enough

sex. Normal, according to the literature. Bradley was certainly happy, but as soon as the orgasm faded, Melissa found herself increasingly irritable with her husband. He'd cut back on his hours at the practice so he could "share these months" with her.

"You can share them, of course," she'd said the first time he'd come home early. "But I know how important your patients are to you." The fact that he came home at five fifteen every day was bad enough. At least Dennis had had long hours and emergencies.

The second time he'd done it, she said, "I really love my time here alone, sweetheart, but it's so sweet of you to check in. Text me next time, okay?" Then she'd gone upstairs and taken a nap, and he was grumpy because she hadn't jumped him. Which she did later, and not to appease his mood but because he was closer than her vibrator.

The third time, when he appeared at 3:00 p.m., she said, "For the love of God, Bradley, get back to the office! You're driving me crazy!" She'd been just about to take some pictures for Instagram, and she didn't want him watching. He'd left, chuckling over his pregnant wife's mood swings, which made her want to stab him in the back of the neck.

He'd left, but he'd ruined her good energy for the photos, and she anger-ate some ice cream.

Today, a professional photographer was coming for some of those "me and my bump" shots. A few tasteful nudes, like Beyoncé or all those Victoria's Secret models. Before the photographer arrived, though, she wanted to take a good look at herself. She needed to know which angles were best for the bump reveal.

Honestly, after seeing how . . . fat . . . she looked in the video, Melissa was a little scared to take a hard look at her body. Lately, her breasts ached and were mapped by blue veins. Also, the headlights were on, as the boys in her high school used to say. All the time, rubbing against her lacy bras. She'd taken to wearing her Lululemon yoga bras, but even those were getting too small.

She said a silent prayer to the universe that a lifetime of fitness would pay off as she got ready to strip in her closet. Best light, best mirror. Of course, she was getting a little rounder. She accepted that. She walked for an hour every day, on the elliptical if it was cold. She did prenatal yoga with two other women at the studio in town. She ate well (with those few cheats, which were to be expected). Of course she'd be beautiful in pregnancy. The universe wouldn't fail her like that, would it?

Well, the moment was here. She stood in front of the huge antique mirror, slipped off her robe, took a deep breath and opened her eyes.

The universe had turned on her.

Melissa's breath left her in a rush. That couldn't be her, could it? She moved her hand just in case. It *was* her. She burst into tears. No! No! She was huge! She was hideous and huge and wide, like Jabba the Hutt! Her body was a slobby triangle with her head as its tiny point. Yes, she'd known her breasts had grown, but these things were massive, the size of hefty watermelons! She looked like . . . like . . . like one of those women on *Botched* (one of her favorite TV shows) who'd gone way too far with implants. And what had happened to her . . . areolas? They were bright red and huge. Huge! The size of a saucer or something.

Her baby bump was lost in what looked like . . . like . . . like *fat*. It didn't jut out, tight and round. In fact . . . did she even look pregnant? Or did she look . . . like pudding?

She looked like pudding. A wobbly, white pile of tapioca. Wait, what was this? Splotchy stripes of pink on her stomach. A rash? Stretch marks? No, not yet!

Now that she was full-on sobbing, she felt a liquid heat between her legs. Oh, no! Was she bleeding? She raced to the bathroom.

No blood.

It was pee. She'd just *peed* herself.

Something must be wrong. She was not supposed to

look like this. She called Dr. Owens's office and said it was an emergency.

Twenty minutes later, she sat in the exam room. Dr. Owens came in. "Hi, Melissa. What's going on?" she asked.

"Something's wrong. Look at me!"

"Any pain? Bleeding? Cramping?"

"No. But . . . this can't be right." She gestured to herself.

"What can't be right?" Dr. Owens asked.

"How I look! I'm huge!"

Dr. Owens took a step back and tilted her head. "You said this was an emergency, Melissa. That usually means miscarriage, preterm labor, bleeding, pain, severe headache . . . Are you experiencing anything like that?"

"No. But I *do* feel like something's wrong with me. The *size* of me. Could I be closer to full term than Lillie said?"

Dr. Owens sighed. "I doubt it. First, let's get you on the scale."

Melissa froze. The old woman, Caroline or something, had tried to get her weighed, but Melissa had refused.

"Now, please," the doctor said.

Melissa slid off the table and got on, closing her eyes.

"One hundred and fifty-two."

"No! That can't be right!" She started crying yet again.

"Our scale is calibrated every week." The doctor typed into the computer. "What was your pre-pregnancy weight?"

"A hundred and twenty-three," she said. "I haven't gained or lost a pound in ten years, Dr. Owens, I swear."

"Mm-hmm. Well, you're pregnant now. You're supposed to gain weight. Not this much this fast, but we'll get to that. Sit back down, please, and lie back."

The doctor was faster than Lillie had been, her movements brisk. She felt around the "bump"—it felt squashy and fat now, not the firm little bump she'd wanted. She put something against her belly, and once again, Melissa heard that otherworldly *wow-wow-wow* of the baby's heartbeat.

"You're seventeen weeks along, according to the chart," Dr. Owens said. "Do you want another ultrasound, or shall we wait for next week, when we have it scheduled? I'm getting the sense that you're mostly upset with the weight gain."

"I walk for an hour every day. Quite fast, too. I used to run, but . . . with these things, I can't." She gestured to her chest, mortified. "And I do yoga, too. Also every day. Well, at least four or five times a week."

"Mm-hmm. And how are you eating?"

"Great! Fine! Really clean!" Well, that was partially true. She did eat healthy foods. And unhealthy foods, too.

"So, here's the thing about pregnancy," Dr. Owens said, sitting down in the rolling chair. Her eyes were lovely, so big and brown, but she could use some help with makeup, that was for sure. An eyebrow tutorial for starters. "You only need to eat about three hundred and fifty calories more per day. That phrase 'eating for two'?" Melissa nodded. "It doesn't mean you should double your calories. You've already gained thirty pounds"—did she have to say that in such a loud voice?—"and you're less than halfway there. So obviously, you've been eating quite a bit more than you need."

"But I'm so hungry," Melissa said, wiping her eyes on the sleeve of the robe.

"You need to stick to the nutritional information we gave you, Melissa. But just to reiterate, three hundred and fifty calories is about half a cup of trail mix, the kind *without* the chocolate. An apple sliced up with a tablespoon of peanut butter. You can keep some hard-boiled eggs on hand for some additional protein."

Yesterday, when she'd been alone in the house, after her kale and quinoa salad, Melissa made a fluffernutter sandwich on white bread. An hour later, she'd made scrambled eggs with Kraft shredded cheese. *Lots* of cheese. Just thinking about it made her feel famished for the food of her youth. Cheetos. Twinkies. Chick-fil-A and orange pop. Mee-Maw's shoofly pie.

"We recommend about five small meals throughout the

day," Dr. Owens said, snapping her back to reality. "Lots of dark greens, like kale and spinach. Beans, broccoli, salmon, sweet potatoes, bananas . . . I can have Carol print out some recipes or recommend some good cookbooks."

"What about my face?" Melissa asked. She sounded worse than Ophelia on a whiny day. "I'm breaking out. And my . . ." She gestured to her breasts. "They're huge and weird and . . . there's hair." Her throat tightened to a whisper as tears flowed out of her eyes. "My shoes are tight. I think I have . . . I think I have cankles." She sobbed, then clenched her Kegel muscles so she wouldn't wet herself (again).

Dr. Owens covered her mouth with her hand. "Mm. Yes, your feet can spread during pregnancy. Especially with a sudden weight gain like this."

"Will I ever fit into my nice shoes again?" All those gorgeous shoes and boots that had made her legs look so fantastic . . .

"Probably not," Dr. Owens said. "Most of us go up at least half a size and don't come back down. Listen. With the holidays coming up, you'll need to be extra careful about what you eat. Be very sparing on sugar, absolutely no alcohol. You don't want to get gestational diabetes—"

"What's that?" It sounded familiar.

"It's when your blood sugar is too high during pregnancy. It often results in very big babies, which can complicate labor and delivery, and the health of both of you. High blood pressure, preeclampsia, preterm delivery, serious breathing troubles for baby . . . all sorts of things you don't want."

Melissa swallowed. Her little plum could come out looking like a fat piglet. Could be sick, too. "I understand," she said, feeling chastened. "Um, is there a way I can lose this weight now? Liposuction, maybe?"

"God, no!" Dr. Owens snapped, then corrected herself. "Listen. Your body is no longer your own, and I understand it's an adjustment. But if you want a healthy baby, there are basic things you need to take care of. Mostly, you need to eat healthfully, exercise moderately and regularly, and get a good night's sleep. I'll have Carol print you out some literature, okay? And if you go online, please go to reputable sources. Hospitals, doctors, certified nurse-midwives, okay? Don't listen to celebrities who think they have all the answers."

How bossy. And celebrities did have answers, many of them. Was not Gwyneth Paltrow a nutrition guru? Kim Kardashian had been pregnant a bunch of times, and she'd lost a *ton* of baby weight. Melissa took a breath and reminded herself of who she was. Melissa Spencer Fairchild, a wealthy and admired woman. "Of course. Thank you, Wanda. Can I call you Wanda?"

"I prefer Dr. Owens," she said. "Anything else for today?" Her face was impassive.

"No. I appreciate you seeing me on such short notice."

"We're always here for you. Have a good day."

Dr. Owens walked out of the exam room without even saying goodbye. Not super friendly or kind. Melissa almost preferred Lillie. Lillie, who was *not* statuesque, like Dr. Owens. Lillie, who obviously loved food. Who had been pregnant herself, even if it was only once. Did Dr. Owens even have kids? Melissa didn't know. Probably not, if she was so heartless.

Maybe Melissa *would* change practices, just to get a little more respect than she got from Dr. Owens. Someone who cared about cankles.

She should have stayed in New York or moved to LA, where all the good doctors were. The kind who'd do anything you asked.

But she was stuck here instead.

CHAPTER 23

Lillie

On December 19, I leaped out of the car in the pickup zone at Logan and hugged my child. "Oh, honey! It's so good to see you!" He tolerated a few kisses on his stubbly cheek. "Are you growing a beard?"

"Maybe," he said. "How are you, Mom?"

"I'm *very* happy," I said, hugging him again.

Oh, it was so wonderful to see him! To actually see him live and in person. He slung his giant duffel bag in the back and got in the passenger seat. I got in, too, and looked at him. My handsome boy. My eyes were wet with happiness.

"Okay, Mom, maybe you should start the car or something? I'd like to get home and see everyone. Do you want me to drive?"

Everyone would have to wait a day or two. "You're a sight for sore eyes, that's all." I patted his knee. "I'll drive. Traffic was murder on Route 3."

"Someday, Ma, you'll have to let me drive through Boston, you know."

"Not if I can help it, sweetie."

He grinned, and my heart grew three sizes, like the Grinch's.

"So how's everything?" I asked, finally starting the car.

"Good. Finals were okay. I think I did pretty well."

"Attaboy. When are grades posted?"

"A few weeks. But you know, you can't see them. Because I'm eighteen."

"Don't remind me. But you'll tell me, right?"

"Probably." He smiled at me, but there was definitely a . . . well, an independence. A bit of a wall. "Hey, I might have to join a gym over break. Coach wants daily workout and food updates."

"Really? Well, I guess that makes sense."

"How's the dog?"

"Very excited to meet you," I said, inching onto the highway. "He's great. Very mellow and easily trained."

When we were on Route 3 and cruising along, I asked him questions about school, Chloe, the team; told him what I was planning for dinner (roast chicken, mashed potatoes, blackened carrots and a coconut cake for dessert).

"Sounds great," he said. After a moment, he asked, "So it'll just be the two of us?"

I read into his question, his tone, wondering if he was envisioning lonely dinners with his mother, year after year after year. "Actually, I invited Pop and Hannah, too. They're dying to see you."

"Oh, awesome!" he said, sounding genuinely happy, and I was glad I'd included them.

I wanted to tell him that Hannah and I were getting closer, and that I suspected his grandfather had a girlfriend, and that I'd taken two weeks of vacation during this break so I could have as much time as possible with him. But it was hard, knowing how much to say to your almost-adult son, especially when he had so much to face here at home, thanks to Brad.

I glanced at him. "Anything you want to talk about, honey?"

He looked out his window. "Dad asked me to come over for dinner with them."

"Mm." Even though I knew this had been coming, the pain hit me in the heart.

"I kind of *have* to see him, Mom. He's still my father."

"I know, sweetheart."

"And . . . you know. The . . ."

"The baby." I kept my gaze forward.

"Yeah."

With me driving, we didn't have to make eye contact. We'd had so many conversations this way, in this very car, from him admitting in first grade that a boy bullied him on the bus to the awkward questions about puberty, and later, to whether or not he should have sex with his high school girlfriend. He never went to Brad with these issues, or if he did, Brad never told me.

"How are you feeling about that, honey?" I asked gently.

"Shitty." I waited. "That's it, Mom. Shitty. I haven't even met her, I don't *want* to meet her, but apparently I'm a stepbrother and have a half sibling in the making."

"It's a lot," I said.

"And I'm still like, 'Fuck you, Dad, you cheated on my mother,' but also . . ." His voice trailed off.

"What, Dyllie?"

He looked out his window. "Also, I . . . I miss him. I've barely even talked to him since you guys told me you were splitting up. He's texted and left messages and emailed. Then he sent me a text about becoming a big brother. And I saw the video, like everyone else in the world."

Brad had texted our son. He *texted* that news. The shithead.

"I don't know how to feel," Dylan said, sounding wretched. "But I feel like I have to see him. And then I feel like that's stabbing *you* in the back, and I hate that. I hate this whole thing. Everything's so different now, I feel like I'm gonna start bawling when I walk in the door."

"Listen, sweetheart," I said, glancing at him and taking his big hand. "It's a mess, and you get to be mad about it. And you get to miss your father, too."

"I don't know who he is anymore. He has an Instagram and a TikTok, Mom. No offense, but you guys are way too old for that."

"No, I agree," I said with an inner eye roll. I was forty-one. I wasn't too old for anything. "I don't know what to tell you, Dylan. But you don't have to worry about stabbing me in the back. You only have one father."

I doubted that Brad would *ever* stick up for me this way. Instead, he'd try to manipulate Dylan into believing that yes, Brad *did* deserve joy, and it didn't matter how that happened or how he lied and cheated, because "it takes two" and we'd "grown apart."

But I was trying to be a selfless mother. It really sucked sometimes.

Dylan wiped his eyes on his sweatshirt. "So if I do go over, you won't be mad or feel . . . I don't know. Betrayed?"

"No," I lied. "He divorced *me*, honey. Not you. He loves you, and even if he's a little . . . embarrassing right now, he's always loved you. We both have, and we both always will."

Dylan squeezed my hand. "Thanks, Mommy," he said, giving me the rare gift of using the name he'd called me the first twelve years of his life. "I really appreciate the lack of a guilt trip."

I squeezed his hand, too. "You're welcome. But I have plenty planned for the future, just in case."

He laughed at that, then let go of my hand.

"Tell me about Chloe," I said, and he did, imitating her Montana accent, telling me how she made fun of his Cape Cod vowels. Her parents' home was huge and posh, as I'd seen when we FaceTimed on Thanksgiving. She had two younger brothers who'd liked him right away. It sounded like the family was wealthy—they were well traveled, and Dylan said they owned a ranch.

"They want me to come to Spain with them this summer," he added.

"Wow! Spain!" *For how long?* I wanted to demand. My

heart clenched, and my mind calculated the cost of the plane ticket.

"I said we'll see, but if I do, she definitely has to come to the Cape. She has no idea what the East Coast is like."

"She's more than welcome anytime, honey." *Thank you, Saint Anthony.*

Zeus was almost hysterical with joy that I'd brought him a very tall, two-legged playmate. Dylan collapsed in the front hall, allowing himself to be licked, jumped on, pawed, snuzzled and licked some more.

"He's awesome, Mom," Dylan said. "Aren't you, boy? You are! You're wicked pissah, buddy! Yes, you are! Yes, you are!"

Getting a dog had been a smart move on so many levels.

Then Dylan got to his feet and looked around. His eyes got shiny. "Shit," he whispered.

"I'm so sorry, honey," I said, my own eyes stinging.

"Whatever. It's not your fault. It's just . . . weird. I expect him to come in any sec."

"Yeah." I wanted to redecorate a little, at least buy a new couch, but the literature had said to wait a bit, for Dylan's sake. Also, new couches were expensive.

With a huge sigh, Dylan shouldered his duffel bag. "This is all dirty, by the way," he said. "Sorry. The dorm washing machines were all taken."

"Of course. Don't worry about it."

"I'll do it."

"Damn right you will." There. The mood was lighter. "You want a nap before Hannah and Pop come over?"

"Maybe. Hey, is Ben coming, too?"

I had told Dylan about my recent tenant, of course. "I didn't invite him, no," I said.

"Okay. I'm sure I'll bump into him. I gotta get a good picture of this dog and text it to Chloe. Zeus! Come here, boy! Come on, buddy." My dog—or Dylan's dog, apparently— ran up the stairs on Dylan's heels.

It was so good to have my boy back in my house. For the next four weeks, I could cook for him, watch TV with him, beat him at Scrabble, take walks with him. We'd go to P-town tomorrow for Christmas shopping, because other than University of Montana gear and mugs, Dylan hadn't bought any gifts yet.

Christmas morning would be . . . different. But for Christmas Eve, I'd invited a few extra people. Wanda, Addo and Leila always came, since their families were from away, and this year, Carol would also come, because her daughter was flying out to see her own daughter in California. Ben, because how could I not? This year, Hannah had asked me to invite Manuel, her assistant, who'd recently broken up with his boyfriend and had nowhere else to go.

Hopefully, the places where Dylan's father and Fairchild grandparents used to be wouldn't be too obvious.

As I went downstairs to check on dinner, my phone chimed.

Brad.

Lillie, I was thinking we should all have Christmas dinner together. It would be a great way for Dylan to ease into this new dynamic and understand that we're all still family.

I ignored the text—did he *really* think I would have dinner at his house with his pregnant new wife, his new daughter and our son? He probably did. He was that obtuse. A moment later, this was confirmed by another text. Especially since he is going to be a brother soon.

Translation: We have something you never will.

Not for the first time, I wondered if Brad ever thought of our daughter. I remembered him sobbing in the hospital, holding her. Holding me. He slept in the hospital bed with me that night. Where had that guy gone?

Another text from my ex. BTW, we are waiting till the delivery to find out the gender. Thought you would be interested bc you are a midwife and my wife goes to your practice.

Now he was just rubbing it in.

I might need another skunk.

∼

Christmas Eve was oddly wonderful. I'd been bracing for more weeping in the closet, or that heart-punched feeling I'd had so many days after Brad left. But having Dylan home outweighed everything, I guess. And having a crowd was always fun.

Much to my surprise, the Moms showed up . . . I always invited them, and they always declined. They had declined this year as well, a fact my mother disputed for ten minutes as I was making her a martini.

"We did say yes, Liliana," she said. "It's Beatrice's last Christmas with us. Of course we were coming." I still had the text she'd sent saying no, but I let it slide. "Oh, our divorce is final, did I tell you?"

"No, Mom, you didn't." I poured her martini into a glass.

"Well. It was amicable, not like you and yours. There you are, Dylan! At last! Give your Mimi a hug, darling. Oh, you've gained weight. Was that on purpose?"

A minute later, Wanda, Addo and Leila came in through the kitchen door, bags of gifts and food in their hands.

"Brother from another mother!" Leila announced, launching herself into Dylan's arms.

"Sister from another mister!" he said. "You got taller!"

"Catching up to you, Dill Weed. I'm a famous model now, did you hear?"

"Feel free to marry each other," Wanda said, leaning on the counter. "I've always wanted you for a son, Dylan."

"And I'm already your godmother, Leila," I said, "so is mother-in-law really such a stretch?"

"Come on upstairs before they whip out a minister," Dylan said.

For once, Dad didn't seem to mind that his ex and her lover / his replacement were here. Usually, my parents were like two wet cats, circling each other with the occasional hiss. Maybe they had silently agreed not to fight at Christmas. I'd have to ask Dad how he really felt tomorrow. Wanda and Addo helped me carry appetizers and drinks upstairs to the living room.

Ben made the thirty-foot journey from the studio; Carol was in fine form, telling gruesome stories about birthing (not that she'd seen any firsthand, but still). Hannah and Beatrice sat together like they were joined with glue. The food was fabulous (of course), and we took our time eating. Ben told a funny story about my father going crazy with joy when a humpback whale breached right next to the *Goody Chapman*. Manuel got teary-eyed and thanked us for having him, and Leila and Dylan had reverted to twelve years old and kicked and snickered at their inside jokes. When we were done, we left the messy kitchen and went upstairs to the living room for dessert. Hannah had brought cookies, and I made aletria, which my dad adored—a Portuguese pudding sort of thing with angel hair pasta (weird, I know, but it's delicious), lots and lots of milk, eggs, cinnamon and lemon.

Dylan smiled the whole night. That was definitely the best part. Just before everyone left, he and Leila dutifully left cookies out for Santa. I was so glad they were still friends. With Leila's modeling, they hadn't seen each other much this summer.

It was after eleven when everyone had left. Dylan offered to help me clean up, but I sent him to bed, saying I was faster on my own.

It was only when the house quieted that I allowed my shoulders to drop and acknowledged what I'd been avoiding all day.

I missed Brad. I missed the man I'd thought he was, the guy he'd seemed to be just last year, funny and appreciative, affectionate and nerdy. I missed Vanessa *so* much. Did she think of me? They hadn't even sent me a Christmas card, though I had sent them one.

I missed our traditions . . . taking the family photo for the card, hiding the pickle ornament on the tree—Vanessa had German roots, and apparently it was a tradition. Brad and I would stuff each other's stockings with mysterious gifts, put out Dylan's gifts and, when the house was finally cleaned up, we'd have one last drink and look at the beautiful tree, tired and happy . . . and together. A team.

I folded my arms on the table, put my head down and had a little cry as Zeus licked my knee. "Thanks, buddy," I whispered. "Sometimes, I think you're the only one I can really talk to."

There was a gentle knock at the kitchen door, and I jumped. It was Ben. He opened the door and came in, bringing the cold, fresh air with him.

"Hey," he said. "I thought you could use some help cleaning up."

My mouth wobbled, and I turned my face away. A second later, I felt his arm around my shoulders.

"The first Christmas is the worst," he said, giving me a brief squeeze. "Now. I'll wash the pots and pans, because I don't know where everything goes."

"Thanks, Ben," I whispered, because my throat was tight.

He was already filling the sink with hot water. "You bet," he said, and it was so nice not to have to do this alone, and so kind of him to have recognized that. I gave him a quick hug from behind, and he laughed a little, the sound ashy and full of the old bad-boy promises he'd once been known for.

I think it was fair to say we were becoming friends.

CHAPTER 24

Lillie

Dylan went to see his father the day after Christmas. I tried not to obsess. On Christmas Day, Dylan and I had gone to the Moms' place for their annual brunch, and that had softened the lonely Christmas morning, though Dylan and I had exchanged gifts. We both cried a little—angry tears, sad tears, sentimental tears. For once, I was happy to visit my mother . . . or at least her house.

On Christmas Day, Ben had flown to New Orleans to see his daughter, and I was truly alone at my place for the first time in more than a month. It had snowed last night, and I took Zeus for a nice long walk after Dylan drove off in my car. Came home, expecting that Dylan would be there, but my car was still missing.

I hadn't expected him to be with Bralissa for so long, to be honest. To kill the time, I checked Wellfleet OB/GYN's emails for nonurgent questions. Turned down an overtime shift at the hospital. Ate some cookies. Fretted. Tried to read.

Dylan came back a few hours later.

"Hey!" I said, getting up from the couch.

"Hi."

Okay. "How was it?"

"It was fine." I waited for more. More didn't come.

"That's it?" I asked.

"The kid is nice. Ophelia."

"Yeah, I've met her." Still no details. "Anything else you want to tell me?" I asked.

"Look, Mom," he said, sounding slightly defensive. "As you said, he's still my father. I'm going to be a big brother, which is weird as f—as anything. They were bending over backwards to make me like them. Jesus. There were, like, twenty presents. Dad even said they'd buy me a *car* if I wanted and then showed me his Jag. Their garage is heated, by the way." He picked at a cuticle.

"What did you think of Melissa?" I asked.

Dylan sighed. "You want my honest answer?"

"Yes. Of course." But my toes were clenched, and anxiety sweat was already breaking out on my back.

"She's okay. Shallow, but okay. It was really awkward. I knew she wanted me to give them my blessing or whatever. But she tried, and she was . . . nice."

I swallowed the bile in my throat. "That's . . . good, I guess."

"Beats her being a bitch, right?"

"Right." But to me, she *was* a bitch, though I hated that word. She was thoughtless and cruel and self-centered and entitled. She had broken my family. She had made me a joke, the older, graying first wife, replaced with a perfect face and perfect body and now a baby in her perfect womb.

"Okay," said Dylan. "If the interrogation is over, I'm gonna FaceTime with Chloe now. Oh, and Brandon, Leila and Cassie and I are going out tonight. Movies, burgers, that kind of thing, so I won't be home till late."

"Sure. Sounds fun." *There was no interrogation,* I wanted to add, but we moms bit down on these things.

He turned to the stairs, then turned back. "Do you want me to stay home, Mom?" he asked, and his voice was very gentle.

"No, honey. Go see your friends. You'd be bored, spending every night here."

"Thanks. But um . . . well, Dad wants me to stay over one night. I don't know if I will," he added hastily. "But he did ask."

"Do what feels right to you, honey. Don't worry about me."

"Got it. Okay, I'll be on my phone." He ran upstairs, eager to talk to his girlfriend.

Don't worry about me. Why should you, Dylan? Because I raised you? Loved you? Cheered you on your entire life? Hey, it's fine. Go ahead and like your stepmother. Take a day away from me and spend it with your cheating-ass father. Don't worry, I'm *fine.* Go ahead and wipe your feet on my heart, you little shit.

Which, you know, I understood wasn't fair. But that's how I felt in the moment.

"I'm going for a walk," I called up the stairs.

"Okay," he called back. "Have fun."

Fun. I leashed up Zeus for the second time that day, and we went out for our fun.

We went past Slough Pond, past Horseleech, the sound of the ocean becoming louder as we headed toward it. My chest was aching, eyes tearing, and I felt ridiculously rejected. I took the little path toward the beach, and only when sand seeped into my hiking boots did I stop.

He thought she was *nice.*

Get over it, Lillie, I told myself. *He'll always be your son. And Brad's son, too. Those are the indisputable facts.*

I let Zeus off the leash so he could run, which he did, galloping along, a little clumsy, wicked cute. The ocean crashed and roared; the sky was slate gray.

I wondered if Matthew Dudek, the lost man of Wellfleet, had gone into the ocean and drowned. If his bones were somewhere in those woods I'd just tramped through. If he was okay in the afterlife, and if his family had made peace with his disappearance. How sad Christmas must be for them every year, that tiny ember of hope still glowing.

The wind seemed to blow away my irritability, and I inhaled steady lungfuls of the salty, clean winter air.

I would be okay. Of course I would. I was Liliana Madalena Silva, Pedro Silva's daughter, descendent of hardworking Portuguese stock. I'd always be me.

Then I whistled for my dog, chased him around a bit and we went back home.

CHAPTER 25

Melissa

Even though she'd changed her diet to be healthier, Melissa still wasn't Instagram pregnant. She was white trash pregnant, bloated and oily and disgusting. By January, she was buying the largest-size maternity clothes with more than three full months to go, resentfully eating Greek yogurt, quinoa salad and legumes. She was so gassy she couldn't walk five steps without breaking wind, and it was so embarrassing. Also, her number of followers on TikTok and Instagram hadn't gone up since *You and Your Stupid Oysters*, so she still wasn't at influencer level.

Also, this marriage thing. She may have rushed into it. Bradley wasn't as cerebral (word of the day!) as she'd thought originally, and he was mighty comfortable in her house. Completely at ease, telling Ophelia she should chew more quietly (but yeah, the kid was like a goat, all those etiquette lessons for nothing). Still, it chafed Melissa that Brad was so at home, so relaxed . . . so lazy. When *she* had married money, she'd made sure her sugar daddy never regretted his decision.

On Christmas Eve, it had been just the three of them. Vanessa and Charles stayed in Boston, which caused a fight between them and Bradley, Bradley saying they'd *never* missed Christmas Eve when he was married to *Lillie*. It didn't change their minds. The night didn't feel very festive, even though her decorator had dressed up the house with garlands and tasteful ornaments. Aside from watching Ophelia open her gifts on Christmas morning, it was a flop.

Bradley's son had finally come over to meet her, and she'd been so nervous. It was strange, because she'd never cared if Dennis's kids liked her. Dylan looked so much like Lillie, those big, wise brown eyes. Was he spying for his mother? Would he tell her his new stepmother was ugly and fat and stupid?

But he had nice manners, and thanked her politely for having him over, and for all the gifts she'd ordered. Ophelia had liked him, and she showed him around the house. Later, Melissa found them doing a puzzle together in Phee's room, Teeny sitting on his lap.

Bradley was awkward around him, hugging him too long when he first came in, crying a little, too. Over dinner, he'd talked about second chances and new adventures and how excited he was that Dylan would have a sibling and how profound those bonds could be. In other words, he sounded like an idiot. But Dylan . . . he was a nice enough boy, and she felt pathetically grateful that he didn't give her the silent treatment or call her a whore.

On New Year's Eve, they hosted a party with the same locals they'd had at their wedding—the arts council board, a few business owners, a couple of people from yoga. Melissa sipped sparkling water and wondered if her makeup was hiding the acne on her cheeks. She'd invited Hannah Chapman, who had *seemed* like a possible friend during the wedding planning, but Hannah had sent her regrets.

There was hardly anyone she really knew there, and she understood they had come out of curiosity or for the free food and booze—top of the line, of course. A jazz trio played in front of the French doors, and Melissa found that she hated jazz. Four people asked if she was having twins, and when the woman from the cute boutique asked if she was close to her due date, Melissa slipped upstairs to check on Ophelia, wishing she could stay there and watch TV with her niece and Teeny.

The holidays drained her, and she was glad for the empty weeks of January. She was too exhausted to do anything anymore, falling into bed after her one-mile waddle. (Her thighs rubbed together! For the first time in her life!) Lucia the housekeeper came every day to tidy and clean and do laundry and bring groceries. Chef Paul brought them dinner every afternoon, so all she had to do was pop it in the oven. And even so, staying awake past eight was herculean (word of the day!). Her only outings were to the doctor's office.

She might be lonely. No one except the housekeeper came to the house, and these days, Melissa was too tired to care. Also, people would see her this way, pregnant, spreading wider and wider each day, her skin a mess. She, the fitness goddess, now panted while climbing stairs. She cried for no reason, then peed because she was crying, then cried because she'd peed. She couldn't do anything she used to love doing. The prenatal yoga class? Ha. She got her workout by tying her shoes these days.

One foul-weather day in February, Chef Paul got hung up off-Cape and texted her that he was so sorry, but he wouldn't be able to get over the bridge till tomorrow. She texted a gracious note back, but being the mysterious patron of Wellfleet wasn't as much fun anymore. Maybe Wellfleet had been the wrong choice. It sure felt that way today, the eighth consecutive day of gray skies and raw temperatures.

"Can we eat early?" Ophelia said, coming into the massive living room, Teeny in her arms. "I'm starving."

"Sure, honey," Melissa said, shifting uncomfortably on the couch. On the TV, Judge Judy chastised a thirty-two-year-old son who refused to leave his parents' house. "Can you see what's in the freezer?"

Phee peered in. "Salmon, steak, chicken, green beans. All frozen solid."

"That doesn't sound very good, does it?"

"Nope. Where's Chef Paul?"

"Stuck off-Cape," Melissa said, burping. This heartburn was agonizing. She chomped on a Tums. "We'll have to make something ourselves."

Where was the frozen pizza with the rising crust from the Dollar General, huh? Yearning for the processed deliciousness of her youth made Melissa's stomach growl. The baby kicked as if agreeing. In a few more months, she'd have this baby to feed as well. Visions of organic carrot mush being flung at her filled her head. She really needed to hire a nanny ASAP, but the thought of looking through applications—and having another person living here—made her weary.

At five fifteen on the dot, Bradley walked in. Habit had Melissa get up from the couch to greet him. He took off his coat and draped it over the back of a counter stool, swung his bag onto another one, taking up too much room. Would it kill him to hang up his coat in the huge front hall closet, as she had asked him a dozen times?

"Hello, babe," she said, kissing his cheek.

"Whoo!" he said. "Busy day! I had five clients."

Five entire hours of work? Gosh golly. She wondered how he spent the rest of his workday.

"And how are you, beautiful woman with my baby in her stomach?" he said, putting his arms around her.

"Ew," said Ophelia.

"I have to agree," Melissa said with a forced smile. "Ew." He could do better. She waited.

Instead, he opened the wine fridge and took out two bottles of white. Studied them like they were the Bible, then opened one and poured himself a hefty glass, leaving the other bottle on the counter.

"I thought you gave up drinking while I was pregnant,"

she said, scooping Teeny up into her arms and kissing the dog's head.

"Did I say that?" he asked. "I don't remember." He sipped the wine without meeting her eyes.

"You did," Melissa said.

"Early Alzheimer's," Ophelia whispered loudly. Melissa smiled. This, too, was new . . . Ophelia on her side, ever since she'd found out about the baby. She was still moody, but something had shifted between them. It was still fresh, but it was there, growing like the baby inside her. The thought made her eyes tear up.

Bradley sat at the counter with his wine, now taking up three stools—one for his briefcase, one for his coat, one for his body. "When are we having dinner?"

"I don't know," she said. "Depends on what you make."

"What happened to Chef Paul?" Bradley asked.

"What happened to Chef Paul?" Ophelia echoed in a whine. Yes. Solidarity.

"He got caught off-Cape because of the weather," Melissa said.

"Hon, you should've called me. I could've picked something up on my way home."

"Or you could cook, Brad," Ophelia said. "Your wife is *pregnant*, in case you missed it. Though I don't know how you *could* miss it. No offense, Melissa."

He muttered something under his breath. "What did you say?" Melissa snapped.

He looked right at her. "Lillie cooked even more when she was pregnant. Nesting, they call it."

"And I'm sure everything was *delicious*," Melissa said.

"It really was," he said, missing the sarcasm in her voice. He picked up his phone and started scrolling. "I miss her cooking. We should go out for some good Portuguese food sometime."

"Passive-aggressive much?" Ophelia said. She took an apple from the bowl and headed back to her room.

"I don't think you truly understand what that term

means, Ophelia," Bradley said, not noticing that she wasn't here anymore. Too focused on his phone. So much for #girldad.

"Bradley," Melissa said, keeping her voice deceptively calm, "other than Lillie's cooking, what else do you miss about her?"

He glanced up fondly. "Oh, a lot of things . . . she line dried our sheets in the summer. God, what a great smell that is. Line-dried sheets. And she had the best laugh. Great sense of humor. I don't know. She really knew how to make a home."

She picked up an apple and threw it at him. It hit him on the shoulder, and he jolted out of the chair.

"Melissa! What are you doing?"

"You're talking about how much you miss your ex-wife while I'm standing here with this baby kicking me in the ribs. You don't lift a finger around here. Feel free to go back to your first wife anytime, since she was so nurturing and perfect!"

He blinked his irritatingly beautiful eyes at her. "Wow. I didn't know you felt so jealous of her," he said in that infuriating, condescending way.

"I'm not jealous!" she shouted, then burst into tears.

"Oh, babe," he said, taking her in his arms. "It's normal to have these feelings. She was here first. I understand."

"Get out of my kitchen, Bradley," she said, pushing him away. "In fact, take a night off. Go stay at Lillie's if you miss her so much. Go see a friend. If you have any, that is. Go do something productive. Work on that second book, maybe. Oh, I forgot. You're not writing one."

They hadn't really fought yet. It felt *amazing*.

"Wow," he said. "I'm sorry you're feeling so aggressive. I guess it's hormonal, and I understand the impulse to take it out on me, since you don't doubt my love. Even so, maybe you should check with your obstetrician about this sudden hostility."

She picked up another apple and cocked her arm. "Go."

"Fine," he said. "If it will make you feel better, I'll give you some space. I'll stay at my parents' house, even though it'll be cold there, since it's been closed up since October. It'll take hours to warm that place up, but if you need me to do that, I will. I'll be back in the morning so we can talk like adults."

With a martyred look on his face, he gathered his laptop and put on his coat. She only unclenched her jaw when she heard his car leaving the garage.

Then she opened the fridge and started making dinner for herself and Ophelia.

Men. No matter what, women still got stuck doing most of the work. But it was worth it. She'd have to send Bradley away more often, because the house immediately felt lighter without him. She cooked some cauliflower pasta with garlic, broccoli and tomatoes, and Ophelia even said it was good. When she asked if they could watch *Glow Up* on Netflix, even though it was a school night, Melissa said yes and made them popcorn.

"I might wanna be a makeup artist for the movies," Ophelia said, eyes glued to the giant screen as the contestants transformed faces. "It looks so cool."

"It sure does," Melissa said. The wind gusted outside, and sleet pattered against the windows, but inside, they were just two girls interested in makeup, cozy as two bugs in a rug.

Bradley came home the next morning with whole-grain carrot cake muffins from Cottage Street Bakery, still warm. He apologized profusely, and without sounding like a condescending prick this time. "I'm sorry, baby," he said. "I'll try to be more in tune with your needs."

"Thank you," she said coolly. Best if he remembered his place here. He was her *guest*. The husband part could be temporary.

Then he knelt down and lifted her shirt to kiss her stomach, his beard tickling, and after a minute or two, as he worked his way downward, she decided she'd keep him a little bit longer.

But he was on notice. If she was his boss, there'd be a note in his file.

⌒

Later in the week, Melissa lay on the white couch, scrolling through TikTok to see what cute pregnancy ideas she could steal (though, confound it, every woman seemed to have that perfect round bump, not the pregnant-all-over look she had). Teeny, who'd been sleeping in a little cinnamon bun curl next to her, suddenly leaped down and started barking.

Melissa rolled off the couch, wincing as her back twanged. She went into the foyer and looked out. There was a car in the driveway. That was odd. No one ever just stopped by.

Then the driver got out, and Melissa gasped and flung open the door. "Kaitlyn! Are you out of jail?"

Her sister rolled her eyes. "No, Missy-Jo, I'm still in it. This is just a hologram." She gestured to the house. "Done pretty good for yourself, I see. And son of a gun. You really are knocked up. The rumors were true." She looked her sister up and down. "You gonna let me come in or what?"

"Um . . . sure. Come in and warm up." Ten seconds in her sister's presence, and the hillbilly was back in her voice.

"Is Harminee here?" Kaitlyn asked once they were inside, looking around the place. "Whoo-whee! Sweet!"

"She's at school," Melissa said. "She'll be home around three thirty. And she goes by Ophelia now."

"About that," Kaitlyn said. "I'm taking her back."

Melissa froze. "What? No, you're not."

"I gotta pee. Where's the bathroom?"

"Um . . . it's down the hall on the left. Are you hungry?" she asked.

"Starving! Hey, little rat dog. You're cute."

Melissa opened the fridge and took out some cheese, grapes, the salami made with porcini mushrooms. Went into the butler's pantry and took out some organic whole wheat crackers and laid them out on a wooden cutting board. Some olives (which were too salty for her) and gherkins. If she'd had more notice, she could've done a proper charcuterie board, but . . .

Her sister was here. Her *sister*. She remembered them sleeping in the same sweaty twin bed in the summer, back when Kaitlyn was scared of thunderstorms. Making popcorn after school. Walking to school together when Katie was little enough to hold her hand. After all these years, they were together again. Kaitlyn was here.

To take Ophelia back. Well, that wasn't going to happen, and Melissa couldn't suppress the thrill of seeing her sister again. It had been so long. There was so much to talk about.

"I poked around a little, Missy. Criminy, this place is amazing! You got another sugar daddy now?"

"I'm the sugar mommy, actually," she said, smiling. She opened her arms. "Give me a hug, sissy."

Katie grinned, and though her hair was dyed black with white streaks and she wore shredded jeans and a T-shirt that read "Not today, Jesus" with a picture of Satan underneath the words, and her arms were covered in tattoos, it sure felt good to hug someone Melissa had always loved.

Both of them had tears in their eyes when they broke apart.

"Come and sit," Melissa said, glancing at the clock. They had hours before Ophelia would come home. "Tell me everything."

"Long story short, I got released for good behavior, believe it or not."

"And how was . . . jail?"

"Oh, it was great, Miss. I'm thinking of buying a timeshare so I can go visit my gals."

"But you were okay?"

"More or less." She offered her left arm for review. "See

that scar? A fight in the bathroom. She got me pretty good. I had to have stitches and stayed in the regular hospital and everything. It was a pumper, all right. Blood everywhere, then a ride in the ambulance, handcuffed to a bed."

"That sounds exciting."

Katie laughed. "It was. Hey, thanks for filling up my credit at the commissary. I was the only one who always could afford lipstick *and* hot sauce."

Melissa smiled. "You're welcome."

Katie ate a few crackers, sniffed the salami and took a bite. "Got any wine?" she asked. "Maybe a beer? I got outta jail, borrowed Angela's car and headed straight here. I haven't had a drink in five years."

Melissa didn't answer.

"It was heroin I was addicted to, Missy. Not wine."

"Okay." She heaved herself up and got a bottle of sauvignon blanc, opened it and poured her sister a glass.

"You gonna join me?"

"I'm pregnant."

"Oh. Is that how rich people do it? Mama used to brag about how she had an Old Milwaukee every night when she was pregnant. Didn't hurt us none." She flashed that mischievous grin, almost begging Melissa to correct her grammar.

"It's really good to see you," Melissa said. For the first time in . . . in years, in a *decade*, she felt something inside her relax a little. "How did you find me?"

"Oh, honey. You think your little sister ain't as smart as you? Took me about five minutes on the Google. That oyster video helped a *lot*. Had to say, it sure made me laugh. So I got the name of the restaurant, googled 'real estate transactions,' and bing bang boom, here I am."

"Good for you. I love your tattoos, by the way." She didn't, of course. They were so common. "So many of them."

"Thanks. So, you feeling okay? Pregnancy-wise? When are you due? You're big as a house."

"Late April. No, I'm not feeling okay. I cry all the time, can't stand my husband but I'm unbelievably horny. I want to eat everything that's not nailed to the floor, can't sleep for more than twenty minutes without getting uncomfortable, and I hate how I look." It was kind of wonderful, being honest. God knew it had been a long, long time.

"So . . . normal, in other words." Katie laughed and ate another piece of salami. "This shit is amazing, by the way."

"You're staying for a few days, right?"

"Sure. I'd love to sleep in one of these rooms and look out at that there ocean. Eat your good food. Meet your husband and tell him all about you."

"Kaitlyn, I . . . I don't want him knowing where I grew up. How our town was, our parents."

"Why not? Look at you now! You're loaded, you have this place, you're like Oprah or something. Good for you, I say. Really. You got everything you wanted, Missy. You should be proud of yourself."

"I married money. The first time, that is. Dennis."

"Yeah, I remember that name. Harminee was sure broken up when he died."

"He was a good guy." Tears flooded Melissa's eyes . . . pregnancy hormones and nostalgia. "He really was. Incredibly generous and even-tempered. He was a surgeon, and he was one of the best. He *adored* Ophelia. They were thick as thieves, those two."

"Why'd you leave New York? Oh, man, this wine is amazing! At least, it is to this poor jailbird junkie." It should be good, Melissa thought. It cost $300 a bottle.

She shifted before answering her sister. "I guess I wanted a change. Thought it would be good for Ophelia to grow up in a small town."

"How long you been here?"

"A year. She does well at school and takes French lessons. She said she wants to play softball in the spring." She paused. "She has friends here, Katie."

"Well, she can have friends and do all that back in Wake-ford. Mama and Daddy said they'd let us live there for free while I look for work, but I want to get my own place, you know? For me and her."

"There are French tutors in Wakeford now?"

Kaitlyn rolled her eyes, so much like Ophelia. "Probably not. But I'm her *mother*, Missy. She should be with me. Besides, you got one on the way. You don't need mine any-more."

"I'm her legal guardian," Melissa said. "She has a good life here."

"Does she? She says she can't stand your newest hus-band. Has some complaints about you, too, for that matter. She wrote to me when I was in prison, you know."

"Of course I know. I *encouraged* her to. Who do you think mailed the letters? I didn't want her to think you just abandoned her. But you can't *take* her." What were the complaints? God knew she'd given the child everything a kid could want for the past five years. Was it five? Gosh, it was! "She's been with me almost half her life."

"Well, we'll see what she thinks, won't we? Because le-gal guardian ain't no mother. Hate to break it to you."

Melissa put her hand on her stomach and took a slow, calm breath. "Obviously, we can talk more about it. But I haven't seen you in so long, Katie, and I really am so glad you're here to visit."

That might not have been the case when Dennis was alive . . . it *definitely* wouldn't have been the case when he was alive, because he'd thought she was an aspiring doctor with a first-rate education. With Bradley, she hadn't had to spin so many lies. Her money told its own story. Tragically young widow with a huge heart, raising her niece, throwing money around the community. He didn't ask many ques-tions, anyway.

Kaitlyn was right. So what if Bradley found out she was white trash? She wasn't anymore, and as Katie said, she had every right to be proud. She'd made this life for herself and for Ophelia, and it was a beautiful life at that. Sort of. It looked beautiful, anyway.

"All right," Katie said. "We'll call a truce for a couple days. I missed you, too, sissy. And I could get used to this lifestyle. Show me your closet. I bet it's stuffed to the gills."

They talked for hours, laughing, telling each other stories. Melissa let her help herself to clothes, because who knew when she'd fit back into them? Besides, she could get new stuff.

All that loneliness inside Melissa seemed to melt away. Sisters. There was no one who knew you better or loved you more.

When Ophelia came home, she dropped her backpack, saw her mother and stood there, dumbfounded.

"Hey, baby," Kaitlyn said, opening her arms.

"Mama!" Ophelia shouted, then bolted to Kaitlyn and flung herself into her mother's arms, sobbing.

"Oh, baby, I missed you so much!" Katie was crying, too, and Melissa couldn't keep her own tears from flowing, either.

It was a lovely scene. It wasn't that her sister was a bad person. But she just wasn't mother material. Ophelia was Melissa's, and there was no way in hell she'd let Kaitlyn take her. No way Melissa was going to let Ophelia Harmony Spencer Finch become Harminee Fawn Cumbo once more.

CHAPTER 26

Lillie

Dylan went back home on January 23, and I gave myself a week to be melancholy and weepy, then got my shit together. It had been a good visit. He did *not* sleep over at Bralissa's, though he had dinner there twice and informed me they had a chef bring dinner every day. Every day! He liked Ophelia and said the house was "huge and white" (which I knew from breaking and entering). Otherwise, he offered no commentary, which was mature and irritating.

He also told me about his classes, his grades (two As, an A minus and a B minus . . . pretty good, all things considered). He loved being on the football team, even when they did drills in the snow. The coach had said he might start next year if he worked on reading the plays a little better, but that his speed and defense were great. Dylan described the vast, glorious skies over Montana, and the day he and Chloe had driven to Flathead National Forest and had parked and gone for a hike, the wonder they felt when they saw a wolf not twenty feet away, staring at them. He was considering spending a summer out there, working at Yellowstone or Glacier National Park, and I couldn't blame him.

And he *would* be home for the summer, but he was also going to fly to Spain for a week with Chloe's family.

I was so happy. No. I was *joyful*. Take that, Brad! I'd always had joy, and its name was spelled D-Y-L-A-N.

But it wasn't just Dylan. I'd forced myself to be more social these past few months, since I didn't have the family I once did. After Beatrice had gone back to France, I had Hannah sleep over so she could be near Dylan and cry on my shoulder. Beth and Wanda and I did things more regularly, and I'd gone back to yoga after making sure Melissa didn't use the same place.

One morning at work a few weeks after Dylan's break ended, my cell phone rang. *Elizabeth Coughlin.* Thirty-nine weeks, four days. "Lillie Silva," I said, already smiling.

"Hi, Lillie." It was her husband, Tom. "Contractions are every seven or eight minutes, have been for a couple hours. My mom's here to take care of Willow, so we're ready to go if you give us the green light. Elizabeth says she's done laboring at home."

Because they lived in Truro and the hospital was an hour away, I said, "Sounds good to me. I'll meet you at the hospital. Don't speed, Tom!" I hung up, told Wanda that Elizabeth was in labor, and patted Carol on the head as I left.

I made it before them and stopped at the nurses' station to chat with Tonya, the admin who ran the unit.

"What have we got today, Lillie?" she asked.

"Gravida two, thirty-nine weeks and four days, steady contractions. Mama's name is Elizabeth, Daddy is Tom. No preexisting conditions, first baby came easily with no pain meds. Pregnancy has been picture-perfect, baby was head down and ready to go when we saw her Monday in the office." In other words, all signals were go.

"Another baby today," came a voice, followed by a heavy sigh, as if the birthing center produced calves or ducklings. It was, of course, Carline Schneider, ob-gyn, hater of pregnant women. She *really* needed to retire.

"Where are we putting her? I'll have to check her, I suppose."

"No, no. Please have a nap or something. We'll call you if we need you," I said. Yes, there had to be an obstetrician at the hospital 24/7 in case of an obstetrical emergency, such as an unplanned C-section or postpartum hemorrhage. No, Carline didn't need to helicopter around, telling the patient (and me) we were doing everything wrong.

Then the elevator dinged, and there they were. Elizabeth was walking slowly and a little hunched over, but she smiled when she saw me.

"The big day is upon us!" I said, hugging them both. "Let's get you to your room and we can see where you are."

"She doesn't look full term to me," Carline said. "Were the ultrasounds okay? That baby looks to be mighty small. Microcephaly, maybe?"

See? Retirement. Microcephaly was a birth defect in which the baby's head was too small, causing a wide range of health issues. And Carline said these things right in front of them! I gave her an evil look. "Elizabeth is full term, and the ultrasounds were perfect. Right this way, guys."

We got to the birthing suite, which consisted of a birthing tub, obstetrical bed that could be broken down in the middle so the mama could squat or sit, stirrups if she wanted to labor on her back, handles to adjust herself, and a birthing bar she could grab or lean against. The bathroom had an absolutely lovely shower with room enough for the partner, if that's what mama wanted.

There was the ultrasound and fetal monitoring equipment, suction, infant resuscitation table (discreetly tucked in a closet), oxygen, nitrous oxide for pain control, couch, recliner, rocking chair, labor ball, state-of-the-art music system and adjustable lighting. Even flameless candles. Give me a kitchen, and I could live here quite happily.

I scrubbed my hands, put on gloves and waited till Elizabeth was ready for me to check her cervix. "One and a half centimeters," I said, and she groaned. "Don't worry. You can dilate really fast in some cases. In the meantime, do you want to put on your music? Have Tom rub your back?" She nodded, and her husband got to work.

Birthing plans were great, if fragile. They helped the mama feel more in control of a situation that could be overwhelming. For most women, this meant deciding on their support people, knowing who'd watch their other kids if need be, making a playlist, figuring out how to pass the time if labor was slow to progress. Elizabeth and Tom had been practicing hypnobirthing, which would help her relax and give her positive affirmations and visualizations, combined with deep breathing. Tom would massage her lower back for relief during a contraction. She wanted to walk the hall while she could, sit on the labor ball and maybe try to relax in the birthing pool, but she didn't want a water birth. She'd try different positions while pushing to find the one that suited this delivery the best. After her son was born, she wanted to delay cord clamping for sixty seconds and wait a bit before he got the hep B vaccine, vitamin K to prevent clotting and eye ointment to prevent bacterial infection.

While Elizabeth wanted a medication-free labor, she was open to nitrous oxide and Demerol before she'd try an epidural. A C-section only if her life or the baby's was in danger.

A perfect plan, in my opinion. She knew how intense labor was from her first go-round, and she wasn't fixated on any one method. Well-rounded and well-thought-out. As Tom and Liz murmured to each other, I texted Ben and asked him to feed Zeus and, if possible, take him for a walk.

You got it, he texted back.

Seven hours later, Elizabeth still hadn't progressed much . . . she was at four centimeters but handling the pain well, breathing through the contractions, which were strong and steady at five minutes apart. She was currently in the birthing pool. I checked the water temperature and occasionally put a cold facecloth on her forehead or neck, but tried not to intrude, either. They were doing great . . . Tom murmuring the phrases from the hypnobirthing meditation. It was a lot like yoga—breathing deeply, consciously relaxing your muscles, picturing lovely things, telling yourself your body was strong and capable.

Elizabeth seemed completely in the zone, eyes closed, breathing fine.

"I'm going to step out a minute," I whispered to Tom. "Can I bring you something to eat from the cafeteria?"

"That'd be great," he whispered back. "A sandwich?"

"You got it. I'll only be ten minutes, and Nurse Jane is right outside if you need anything."

I filled Jane in and waved to another midwife who had her own patient in labor. Women in labor didn't usually want to eat, and in the olden days, they weren't allowed to, on the off chance that they'd need a C-section under general anesthesia. But statistics showed that the chances of aspiration were minuscule, and a lot of us in the business actually *wanted* our mamas to eat a little snack to boost their energy. In the cafeteria, I waved to Isabel, one of my favorite OBs.

"How's your mama doing?" she asked.

"Doing great. Beautiful labor so far. Are you on duty?" I hoped so, because the thought of having Carline interfere made my jaw clench.

"Afraid not. My wife and I are having dinner. It's our third anniversary. I just needed a snack. It was a long night."

"Congratulations! Have a great time." I put two slices of bread in the toaster, then spread on some strawberry jam. Some carbs and a little sugar to give Elizabeth some energy. For Tom, I got an egg and cheese sandwich with sprouts on whole wheat bread and an apple. For myself, just a smoothie.

When I got back to the birthing suite, I could hear raised voices. My patient's, in fact.

There was Carline, standing in her white coat over

Elizabeth. "I'm sorry, but these contractions are awful," Carline said, "and you're failing to progress. You need Pitocin or you're putting your baby at risk."

"Carline!" I said sharply. We did *not* use those terms anymore. "Elizabeth is doing amazingly well. She's in no pain, and the fetal heart rate is strong and steady. She doesn't need Pitocin, and it's inappropriate of you to swoop in here and order her around."

"Thank you, Lillie," said Tom, glaring at Carline. "We've never even met this woman."

"Poor maternal effort," Carline snapped, "indicates the need for Pitocin to get this baby moving. Do you want her to suffer all day?"

"She's not suffering," I said. "Or she wasn't until you came in."

"Can you get her out of here?" Elizabeth said.

"I'm a *medical* doctor," Carline said, "thank you very much, and an *obstetrician*, but if you want to stick with your woo-woo, go ahead. I'll be here for the emergency C-section."

"Out you go," I said, setting the tray on a table. I took her by the elbow and led her out of the room. "That was extremely unprofessional," I hissed once we were outside. "Do not come into this room unless you're asked to."

"You can't talk to me that way," Carline said.

"I just did." I closed the door in her face, took a cleansing breath myself, and went to my couple. "I'm so sorry about that," I said.

"Was she right?" Elizabeth asked, looking scared for the first time.

"No. Not at all," I said. "Listen." I put the doppler on her belly, and we listened to the baby's heart: 146 beats per minute. A contraction gripped Elizabeth's stomach, and the heart rate raised to 153, then dropped back to 145. "See? Perfect. There's absolutely no sign of fetal distress. You're doing beautifully with labor."

"You are, honey," Tom said. "You're amazing."

"Can you check me again?" Elizabeth asked. "See if I've progressed."

"Sure thing." I washed my hands, pulled on some gloves and did a cervix check. "Six centimeters. You're doing great."

I'd be talking to the head of obstetrics about Carline Schneider, that was for sure. Elizabeth announced she was getting pruney in the birthing tub, so she got out, pulled on a johnny coat and sat on the labor ball, Tom behind her on a stool, arms wrapped around his wife.

It was a slow labor, yes. She'd come in a bit early, but that had been her choice. She had a little one at home, and wasn't thrilled at the idea of Willow (and Tom's mother) watching her labor. But there was nothing wrong here.

Time trudged by. At 2:00 p.m., she was at eight centimeters and had been in labor for fifteen hours. I refilled the pool with warm water, and she climbed back in, naked (another thing Carline disapproved of). Tom resumed the affirmations in a low, quiet voice as gentle music played in the background . . . the umpteenth time through the playlist, but hey. Babies don't follow orders.

Around four, the contractions became more intense, and Elizabeth breathed through them, exhaling in a low groan. Tom pressed against her back. I added more warm water and stayed on the periphery. They were such a lovely couple.

"Why is this taking so long?" Elizabeth asked, her voice wobbling. "Willow was born in four hours."

"I guess this little guy wants to make an impression," I said. "You're doing so well, Elizabeth. You're mighty."

Tom grinned. "You are. You're mighty and strong. An oak tree." His voice dropped back to the soothing, repetitive phrases he'd been saying all night. "You're safe, calm and relaxed. Our baby is safe. Breathe in relaxation, exhale tension. In . . . two . . . three . . . four, out two . . . three . . . four . . . five . . . six. That's it. Your body knows just what to do."

The mind was a powerful tool.

An hour later, she gestured toward the bed. We helped her out and onto the bed, raising the back so she was sitting. Tom sat behind her so he could support her weight (and put his arms around her). Elizabeth put her feet against the birthing bar attached to the bed. I checked her, and yep, she was fully dilated. She closed her eyes and rested for a minute, breathing through the next contraction.

"Push when you feel the urge, Elizabeth, with a nice big breath in, and a long, hard exhale out." Downbreathing, we called it, and I loved it because it saved the mama's energy and let the contractions do most of the work. Could she breathe the baby out? Not exactly. But she didn't have to pop a blood vessel pushing, either.

Another contraction. Another. Another. Another. Elizabeth kept her eyes closed in concentration, breathing steadily and deeply, pushing well, not saying a word.

"That's it, honey," Tom said. "The only muscle that needs to work now is your uterus. Let everything else relax. Ride the contraction like a leaf on a river."

Woo-woo? Hey. It was clearly working.

The door opened, and I glanced back. Carline was standing there, a puss on her face. I had no time for her. Two more contractions, Elizabeth breathing deeply. No screaming, no cursing, nothing like the movies. Just the most intense concentration of Elizabeth's life. Some women called it turning inward, so much so that they forgot where they were. Carline left, sighing as she did so.

The baby's head eased down the birth canal, nice and slow. I checked the fetal heart rate—160. Perfect. I could see his dark, wet hair. "Elizabeth, the baby's head is about to crown, so bear down, sweetheart, and give him a little help."

She grabbed Tom's hand with the next contraction and pushed, and the baby's head eased toward daylight. "Okay, Elizabeth, just breathe here, and the baby's head will come out nice and slow." She whimpered. "I know, honey, but you've got this."

"He's right there. You're doing great. He's almost out," Tom said. His eyes were full of tears.

She took a huge breath on the next contraction, exhaled through pursed lips, pushing as nature told her to do. Then she made a thin, keening sound, and the baby's head slid right out with no tearing.

"Perfect. The hard part's over," I said, smiling at her. She was breathing hard and damp with sweat, but she smiled back. "Next push, and you get a baby to hold."

She took another deep breath, exhaled long and hard, and the baby was in my gloved hands. I slid him right up onto Elizabeth's chest, tears in my own eyes as he reached out a little hand.

"Hi!" she said, her eyes shining. "Oh, God, thank you! Hi, baby! Hello! Hi!"

This was the best part. The wonder. The awe at what her body had done. The beautiful, perfect infant. He opened his eyes and looked around, then opened his mouth and gave a hearty cry.

"You did it," Tom breathed. "Oh, honey, I love you so much." They stared at him, and then at each other. Elizabeth turned her head and kissed her husband, tears streaming down her face as they marveled over their miracle.

This was what I got to witness. Best job in the universe.

I covered the baby with a blanket, clamped the cord, delivered the placenta and put it aside. No stitching necessary. After we'd cut the cord and Elizabeth had held the baby for a while, Jane came in to help me check the little guy and do the necessary tasks.

"Seven pounds, ten ounces," I said. "Apgars are ten and ten." I burrito wrapped him, put a little striped cap on his head and gave him back to Elizabeth. "Congratulations, guys. I'm so happy for you. Does he have a name?"

"Silas John," Tom said. "Named after my dad."

"Oh, how lovely! Elizabeth, how do you feel, sweetheart?"

"Amazing. Oh, Lillie. Thank you. You were wonderful."

"Eh," I said. "You did all the work. I just caught him at the end."

⌒

Turned out that when I went to Dr. Barton's office later that day to lodge a complaint about Carline, I found she'd already lodged one against me.

"What?" I said, jerking back in surprise. "The baby and mother are doing great! Thirty minutes of pushing, ten on both Apgars, no stitching, no pain meds. What's to complain about?"

Dr. Barton sighed and pushed her glasses up her nose. "She doesn't like you, Lillie."

"That goes both ways. She suggested the baby might have microcephaly right in front of them! Told the mama she needed Pitocin because labor was taking too long, and it wasn't, and she didn't."

"Look, I know she's . . . old school."

"Archaic."

Dr. Barton grimaced, not contradicting me. "She's good in the OR and only has two more years here, and then she's retiring. But, Lillie . . ." She looked down at the paper in front of her and read aloud. "'Nurse Lillie Silva spoke in a hostile and unprofessional manner. In addition, she put her hands on me and dragged me out of a patient's room.'"

"I'd use the word 'escorted,'" I said. "Firmly escorted."

"But you did put your hands on her?"

"Yeah. I took her by the arm and walked her out of the room." A sense of foreboding darkened my earlier euphoria. "Shit."

"She's saying you assaulted her."

"Dr. Barton! I was protecting my patient's labor process and abiding by her choices. Dr. Schneider was intrusive, demeaning and wrong."

"Look. I understand, believe me. But she said she won't file charges if we suspend you for a week."

My mouth fell open. "Suspension?"

"I'm sorry, Lillie, but we can't have this accusation out there. Effective immediately. Do you have any patients who are due in the next few days?"

"No," I said, blinking. But what if someone had an emergency?

"So it's almost a moot point, and it'll make her feel powerful *and* we'll avoid a scandal. Imagine the *Cape Cod Times* lead story—'Midwife Assaults Elderly Doctor.' I'm so sorry to do this, but . . ."

"I get it," I said. "It's okay. Let me just check on my patient before I go, okay?"

"Are they staying overnight?"

"Yeah."

"I'll discharge them myself tomorrow morning." She gave me a kind smile.

"Wanda can take care of it. They know her."

"Okay, great," Dr. Barton said.

Carline Schneider was a *horrible* old crone. I gave myself five minutes to hate on her in the ladies' room, then substituted my irritable thoughts for the beautiful rehashing of Silas's birth. Elizabeth had been incredible. Tom had been amazing. And that baby was so *stinking* cute. I checked Elizabeth, saw that Silas was already nursing, gave Willow a blue sticker proclaiming her a big sister, and told them I'd see them in the office. Then I headed home.

Zeus greeted me at the door as if I'd been deployed overseas for years. "Hello, you beautiful boy! Hello!" I kissed his head and scratched behind his ears. Went downstairs to the kitchen and found a note on the island. *Zeus had a very happy day on board the Goody Chapman. He's had his dinner. —Ben.*

"Did you go out to sea?" I asked my wonderpup. "You did? You are the captain now, eh? You are?" He wagged, then collapsed and offered me his belly. Yeah, he did smell a bit fishy. "But what an adventure, right?" I said. He yawned.

The dog had a point. Fishy or not, he was a great cuddler,

and the bed warmed up a lot faster with him on it. I pulled off my clothes, took a shower and fell into bed.

What a great feeling.

It took me till the next morning to realize I'd barely thought about Brad and Melissa all day.

CHAPTER 27

Lillie

Being suspended gave me a little bit of celebrity, I found. Wanda fully supported my action and filed a protest on my behalf to go in with the complaint (for HR purposes). Tom and Elizabeth had been glowing when she checked them the day after the birth. She also told me to take the week off, because I'd be pulling double duty when she went to Jamaica to visit her parents at the end of the month.

So. An unexpected vacation week. I checked ticket prices to Missoula, but they were ridiculous—ski season, I guessed. Instead, I sent out a group text to Dylan, Dad, Hannah and Mom, giving them a summary, saying I had a one-week suspension and was therefore free if anyone wanted to do anything fun (though there wasn't much to do on the Cape in the winter). My father told me he was surprised I hadn't decked Carline Schneider, and Hannah said I had done the right thing. Dylan even FaceTimed to tell me how proud he was, and what could be better than your kid saying he was proud of you? Nothing.

Mom didn't respond, though the message had been delivered. I shouldn't have included her. I don't know why I still tried. If I left her to her own devices, she would probably forget she had a second daughter.

The first day off, I cleaned the house and baked cookies to FedEx to Dylan. Asked Hannah, Carol, Wanda and Beth if they were free for dinner and a movie, and so we had a fabulous meal at CShore and then got the world's best popcorn at Wellfleet Cinemas.

The second day off, I went grocery shopping, did laundry, took a long walk. That used up the entire morning. I made and ate a heavy, delicious lunch and took a nap. That brought me to 3:00 p.m.

I was itchy and scratchy. What to do, what to do.

I texted Ben. Want to go to the Ho tonight? My treat as thanks for taking Zeus on his first boat ride.

He didn't answer right away . . . out to sea, I supposed, or just busy. I started a book called *How to Marry Keanu Reeves in 90 Days*, only to find out it was, alas, fiction and not an instruction manual. But it was funny and smart, and I read until dark.

Finally, my phone dinged. Sure. Pick you up at 7?

Sounds good! I answered.

I hadn't seen much of Ben in January, since I'd had Dylan to focus on. Not much this month, either. Maybe he was seeing someone, because his truck didn't pull in till late some nights. Or maybe he was just going to his own house, if the renters had left, that is.

The truth was, I liked having Ben in the studio. It wasn't just that he was a good friend to Zeus, or my father's best buddy. Seeing his light on, knowing he was awake when I got home, definitely took the edge off my loneliness. As did having a dog. As did seeing my sister more. As did knowing Dylan would be home for a good part of the summer, and that was just a couple of months from now.

But the surprising truth was that somewhere over the past six months, I had found that I liked living alone.

Go figure.

⌒

Later, the Land Ho! was crowded and festive as always, being one of the few affordable restaurants that was open year-round on the Outer Cape. We got the table under the "Mr. Speaker" sign (for Saint Tip O'Neill, our illustrious congressman from way back when) and ordered piles of fried food—scallops for me, clams for Ben—and drank Outermost IPA.

I told him about my recent dustup at the hospital, and he clinked his glass against mine. He described Zeus's glee on the boat, sitting like a good dog on the bow, ears flapping, barking at the seals and leaving the scallops alone.

"Was my dad with you?" I asked.

"No. He hasn't been coming out as often."

"But the *Goody Chapman* is his truest love," I said.

"I know." Ben scratched his forehead. "I think he has a girlfriend."

"I think so, too! He's been weirdly evasive when I ask where he is. Tells me it's none of my business, which is the first time in my life he's kept a secret." I ate another scallop. "Supporting the local fleet," I said, and he grinned that crooked smile that showed the crow's-feet around his blue eyes. Nice. "So who do you think it is?"

"No clue. But he asked me if there were any florists around the other day."

"Really!"

"Yep."

"Well, *I* didn't get any flowers, and I'm pretty sure *Hannah* didn't get any flowers . . ."

"The plot thickens," Ben said.

"In all the years since the divorce, I don't think he's *ever* had a girlfriend. Or he's a secretive old bastard and hasn't told me." I took a sip of beer. "How about you, Ben? You seeing anyone?"

He gave me the side-eye. "None of your business."

I laughed. "So it's a yes."

"Actually, it's a no. I'm too busy babysitting a recently divorced woman with a tendency to trap wild animals and release them in people's houses."

I laughed around my beer. "Who told you that? Not that I'm confirming such a *preposterous* story."

"Hannah mentioned it."

"Traitor. I still admit nothing. Hey, there's a woman for you, Ben. My sister."

He ate a french fry. "Nah. We're just friends. Have been for too long to mess it up by dating."

I remembered what Hannah had said about men telling her she wasn't pretty enough. "But you think she's attractive, right?"

"Sure. I like a tall woman." He looked at me and winked, since I was short, and I kicked him under the table.

"So you never said anything to her, did you? About dating her?"

"No, I just told you. We're friends, more or less. I saw a lot of her when she lived in Provincetown. She'd bring her friends down to the wharf and say hi to your dad. She's good people, Hannah."

The image of her visiting our father warmed my heart. I always assumed she ignored Dad as much as possible, since it fit the "us versus them" narrative I'd spun. But back to the current subject. "So why wouldn't you date her? Friendship is a nice place to start, isn't it?"

He frowned. "You fixing me up with your sister?"

"Just . . . a fishing expedition. See what I did there?"

He rolled his eyes. "I like Hannah. I have never had a negative thought about Hannah. I do not wish to date Hannah for the simple reason that, for one, the idea never crossed my mind until you shoved it in there tonight, and for two, I doubt I'm her type. Never got the vibe that she was interested, you know?"

I *didn't* know. I thought everyone got the vibe from Ben.

Those crinkly blue eyes, the hair that always seemed in need of a trim, the slow, bad-boy smile and ashy laugh.

I realized I was still looking at him and hadn't answered.

"Hey, how was everything?" our server asked, and I jumped a little.

"Great," Ben said. "What do you have for dessert?"

"Apple pie, blueberry pie, New York cheesecake, chocolate lava cake—"

"That one!" I said. "Please."

"And you, sir?"

"I'll just share hers," he said.

"The hell you will," I said. "Two chocolate lava cakes, please."

The dessert was orgasmically fantastic, and by the time I was done, I was thinking about unbuttoning my jeans and/or ordering another one. Instead, I wrestled Ben for the check.

"I asked you," I said. "Consider it your babysitting fee."

"It's Valentine's Day. Let me get this."

"How sexist of you." I paused. "Is it really Valentine's Day?"

"Yes, Lillie." He looked at me patiently.

"Huh. That explains all the hearts in the hospital cafeteria."

"You're so observant."

"Shut up. Well. Happy Valentine's Day." With that, I snatched the check triumphantly and held on to it until the waitress came and took my credit card.

"Thank you, Lillie," Ben said.

"You're very welcome. Thanks for hanging out with me."

Outside it was snowing a little, and it looked so pretty that Ben and I stopped to watch the flakes. Suddenly, a BMW sedan going way too fast pulled into a space, nearly grazing us. The license plate said CHSAFRM. I'd seen that before, hadn't I? Something about farms . . .

The door opened, and Chase Freeman got out.

The boy who had tried to rape me.

I froze. In all the years since that night, I had not seen Chase Freeman. I'd spent the rest of the school year in the hospital and my summer had been consumed with physical therapy. He graduated, I started my senior year, and though we both went to school in Boston, Harvard and Emmanuel weren't exactly in the same circles. It had been years and years since I'd thought of him.

But here he was. The license plate spelled his name. No farm involved.

I was suddenly very glad Ben was with me.

"You might want to slow down, buddy," Ben said easily.

"You might want to mind your own business," Chase said. He'd put on about fifty pounds since high school, and his face was bloated and red from drinking. He glanced at me and did a double take.

"Lillie Silva. Well, well, well. It's been a long time."

I didn't answer. I *couldn't* answer. But I was shaking, I realized, and not because of the cold. Chase didn't notice. "Oh, and hey. It's Ben . . . Ben something, right? Soccer championship at Nauset High?"

Ben didn't answer, either. He was looking at me.

"Whatever," Chase said, snapping the collar of his coat. He looked me up and down slowly. "Luscious Lillie. Good to see you remember me."

"Lillie?" Ben murmured.

My eyes were locked on Chase. I swallowed, dimly aware that this was fear, and even though it had been so long, I was terrified, I was crouching in the reeds, covered in mud, teeth chattering.

"Call me sometime," Chase said. "I'm living in Eastham again. We can pick up where we left off." He grinned, that smug, entitled, rich-boy smile, and my vision started to gray. Then he was opening the door to the restaurant, and he was gone.

"Lillie. Hey. Are you okay?" Ben said, taking my arm.

"Um . . ." I looked inside the Ho's window.

"Let's get in the truck," Ben said. "It's cold out here."

"Okay," I whispered.

The truck felt safe and dark. "What's going on?" Ben asked. "You have history with that guy?"

"Can . . . can we just go home, please?"

He looked at me a minute, then started the truck. We didn't talk on the ride home, but as we passed Governor Prence Road, which led to Chase's family home, I shuddered.

At home, Ben walked me to the door. "I'm coming in, if that's okay," he said.

"Sure." My voice still sounded odd.

Zeus greeted us with his super-wags and crooning, but even his adoration didn't break through the shock that wrapped me in cold. I took off my coat and hung it on the hook, and Ben did the same.

My house suddenly felt very exposed, all these windows and doors and glass. All this darkness.

"Want me to make a fire?" he asked as I stood there.

"Yeah." I gave myself a mental shake, then went downstairs to the kitchen, calling my dog so I wouldn't be there alone.

It would be easy for someone to break into the house. I checked the sliding glass door to the porch . . . it was unlocked. Of course it was unlocked! This was Cape Cod. We didn't *need* to lock our doors. I locked it now, but the porch just required a knife to cut through the screens. Someone could wait out there until I was home. Someone could smash the glass on the slider. The kitchen door out to the patio? I could kick it in myself. What about the door in the guest room? Also glass.

I'd get an alarm system. Yes. That wasn't just a reaction to seeing . . . him. It was smart. I was a woman living alone on a remote dirt road.

"You good down there?" Ben called.

"Yep! Be right up."

Should I make coffee? No. Bourbon. I poured some into two glasses, automatically checked the cookie jar—I had some spare snickerdoodles that hadn't fit into the package I'd sent Dylan yesterday. I put them on a plate, set everything on a tray with a couple of napkins and took a deep breath.

Chase Freeman was back in town.

I suddenly bolted for the guest bathroom and threw up.

I had not thought of him, or that night, in a very, very long time. That night had become a blank spot, dominated by the car accident. But the body remembers, doesn't it? I vomited again, caught my breath and flushed. Stood up and splashed some cold water on my face. I brushed my teeth, gargled, brushed again and went back to the kitchen, and carried the tray upstairs. Set it on the coffee table, sat on the couch and took a hearty sip of bourbon. It burned at first, then settled in my now-empty stomach with a much-needed warmth.

Ben had the fire going pretty good now. God, I was glad he was here. Zeus jumped onto the couch next to me and put his head on my lap. "I'm glad you're here, too, buddy," I told him, touching the heart on his nose. "Very glad."

Ben sat in the chair across from me and eyed the tray. "So . . . something happened back there. Want to tell me about it?"

My hand found Zeus's silky head, and I took another sip of my drink.

I had never told *anyone* about what happened that night. Not even Beth. It had all been overshadowed by my many injuries. Sometimes, though not so much in the past decade, I'd jolt awake from a nightmare of being chased (God, the double entendre), being lost, unable to run fast enough, hiding in a place where I knew I'd be found . . .

"Lillie?" Ben asked.

I took another sip of bourbon. "Remember . . . uh, that night? Of the accident?"

"Of course I do."

"Remember how I was muddy and . . . alone?"

He leaned forward. Nodded.

"Chase had a party that night, and I got . . . drunk and stoned and . . . he . . . he tried to rape me."

Ben's jaw turned to granite and his eyes narrowed. Otherwise, he didn't move or speak.

Another big breath for me. "Yeah. So. I got away and ran. Hid in the salt marsh on Town Cove, because I wasn't thinking clearly, and . . . and they came looking for me." Suddenly, I was crying. "With flashlights, and I just stayed where I was and didn't even breathe, just hid in the reeds. When the house was finally dark . . ." I grabbed a napkin and scrubbed it across my eyes. "I ran down to Route 6 and started walking home. And then you picked me up."

He rubbed a hand across his face, then came over to sit next to me. He put his arm around me and pulled me a little closer, and with Zeus on one side and Ben on the other, it was impossible to not cry. All that . . . kindness.

"Did you ever tell anyone about it? File charges?" he asked, his chin on my hair.

"No. I was drunk *and* high, I went to his room willingly, a zillion people saw me. And then . . . well, then there was the accident." I wiped my eyes, blew my nose and stuffed the tissue in my pocket.

Ben was silent, and the only sound was the fire, snapping and hissing. I had never even told *Brad* about that night. About the accident, sure. But about Chase Freeman's party? No. I didn't want him to think of me as a stupid girl, even if I had been only seventeen. That sense of superiority he had, that faint disapproval when someone did something not entirely smart. I hadn't wanted a lecture about something I'd learned the hard way.

Ben, on the other hand, said nothing, and nothing seemed like the right choice.

"Will you tell me about the accident?" I asked, my voice nearly a whisper.

His chest lifted with each breath. "You sure you want to know?"

I thought a minute. "I was there. It feels like I should."

He got up and once again sat across from me. Took a drink of bourbon, then gave me a little smile. "Liquid courage." He leaned back in the chair and sighed. "What do you remember?" he asked.

"I remember you picking me up in your truck." The smell of coffee, and mud. "You asked me a couple questions. I remember feeling . . . safe. Your truck smelled like my dad's. And that's about it. I think I fell asleep, or . . . or I just blocked out the rest."

He nodded. "Yep. Well, when I saw you walking, I figured something happened to you. It didn't take a genius to tell you'd had a rough night. I thought maybe you'd—" He shook his head. "I thought maybe you'd crashed your car."

"How's that for irony?" I said, curling up so Zeus could have more room.

Ben looked out the window. "So we were driving along, and you were quiet. And . . ." It was clearly hard for him to revisit this night as well. I wondered if he'd had anyone to talk to. My father, maybe. "I was speeding. Doing about sixty, sixty-five."

That was twenty miles an hour above the speed limit. Easy to imagine that late at night, when no one else was on the road.

"Then the tire blew, and we swerved across the westbound lane. I tried straightening us out, but I was going too fast. The truck went through the guardrail at Blackfish Creek." He stopped for a minute and turned his eyes to me. He took a drink, then another. "You doing okay, hearing this?"

I nodded.

"Tell me to stop if it gets to be too much."

"Keep going."

He gave a slight nod. "We hit the marsh and the truck rolled. It was weird . . . it felt like I had all the time in the world to think. 'Oh, shit, this will be bad, all this noise, are we ever gonna stop, is Lillie okay, what is all this shit flying around.' That kind of thing. If the tide had been higher, we would've hit the water and probably would've been better off. But the tide was about halfway in, so there was still plenty of land for us to hit, which is why we rolled."

I knew the spot well, of course. Passed it nearly every day. Blackfish Creek was more of a marsh with a tidal river in it. It boasted an unfettered view toward the bay, utterly breathtaking, a spot beloved by photographers and artists.

Ben took a deep breath and continued. "So we finally come to a stop, and we're on the roof of the truck, which was completely smashed in, and the dashboard . . . it didn't even look like a dashboard. It was just wires and twisted metal and plastic. But I was hanging upside down, so I knew I was still buckled in. Then the truck flopped down on the passenger side. Your side."

His voice broke a little, and I did what I always did when people were struggling . . . I offered him food. "Here. Snickerdoodles make life better." My hands were shaking, but only a little.

Ben gave a short huff of a laugh, took the cookie and set it on his napkin. Zeus lifted his head, offended that Ben got a cookie when he was lying *right there*, so I gave him one, too, which he chewed delicately, then let his big head fall back into my lap.

"So, uh, it was so . . . quiet after all that noise, and I was kind of trapped, with the steering wheel being in my lap, and the roof knocked in. I had no idea where my phone was, so I couldn't call for help. I asked you if you were okay, and you didn't answer, and then I . . . I realized how bad it was. My door didn't open, so I kicked out the windshield, which was shattered, undid my seat belt, climbed out and fell right in the water, because the tide was coming in hard and fast. And you were . . . shit. Give me a minute."

He got up abruptly and went out the front door. No outside lights were on; I could only see him in silhouette. He leaned forward, hands on his knees, as if he'd just finished a long run, his breath fogging in the cold air. After a minute or two, he came back in, added a log to the fire, and took his seat once again.

"Your side of the truck was in the water a good few inches. And I thought, in this weird, calm way, 'She's gonna drown, so get her out of there right now.' I had to put something—a box from the back of my truck—under your head to keep it out of the water. I couldn't tell if you were even alive." He took an unsteady breath. "And while this one part of me could see the technical problems of getting you out, the other was . . . I was screaming for help. Calling your name."

He paused and wiped his eyes with his fingers and thumb, and it was only then that I saw the tears in his eyes. "I couldn't get you out through the windshield, because you were stuck, or pinned. I just kept pulling on the hood of the truck, trying to make a little room, thinking this wasn't working, and I needed a crowbar. Which I didn't have. Then, finally, something gave. I tried to pull you out again, and this time, I . . . I got you out. I think I might've made things worse, but I knew if you stayed in there, you'd have drowned." His voice broke again. "I still didn't know if you were alive, because there was so much blood everywhere, and you were . . . limp."

"Oh, Ben," I whispered. "You poor thing."

"Me? You were the poor thing, Lillie. Jesus."

We sat there in the quiet for a few minutes, the snow falling faster and heavier outside.

"Ben," I began.

"Let me finish, okay?" he asked, his voice rough. "I carried you to the road, and someone was there, and she helped me get you up to the shoulder. She'd already called 911, and she took off her jacket and held it against your stomach, because it was . . . it was ripped open, Lillie. You were bleeding so much. We could already hear the sirens, but my God, it seemed to take them hours to get there. Then they packed you up into the ambulance, and . . . and that was it. The lady let me use her phone, and I called your dad." He leaned forward, elbows on his knees, and held his head in his hands.

All these years of blaming him for my scarred insides, the months of pain I endured, my lost baby. I had never fully considered the trauma he'd suffered that night. I'd been too consumed with getting better, and the fact that he was physically unharmed had been enough.

I got up, went over to him and pulled his hands away from his head. Sat on his lap and put my arms around him, pulling his head against my chest. It took a second, but then he put his arms around me, too.

"I'm so sorry, Lillie." And it was exactly what he'd said all those years ago when he held a jar of daffodils in his hand.

"Sounds to me like you saved my life."

"I caused the accident. Going too fast, shitty tires on the truck, no airbags . . ."

"It was bad luck, that's all. But yes, the speed limit exists for a reason."

He chuffed another laugh, then looked at me with those gentle blue eyes. "You're a very forgiving woman," he said.

"Oh, I've been mad at you for years, not to worry."

He smiled a little at that, eyes sad. "You were hurt so bad . . . I could barely look at you, I felt so guilty."

I thought of my injuries, my missing spleen, my torn uterus that had miraculously grown Dylan. My badly broken leg, the crutches for six months, my wired jaw and the bruises that took weeks to fade. My tiny daughter, so still and white.

Nature could be cruel, and no one knew that better than a midwife.

"Well," I whispered, "I got better."

Because I had. I'd never tell him why I miscarried. I'd never describe the doctor telling me the placenta had tried to attach to the section of my uterus that had been scarred. He didn't need that burden on top of what he already carried.

Then I kissed him, and his mouth was warm and lovely

against mine, and when his hands went to my head, his fingers threaded through my hair.

As I'd always imagined, Ben Hallowell knew how to kiss, and my whole body seemed to flush with a delicious warmth as his mouth moved gently against mine, our lips fitting together perfectly. We needed this kiss, Ben and I. Two survivors. His shoulders and arms were hard and muscled under my hands, and it was so gentle, this moment, soft as the falling snow.

It was a long kiss. A really, really *good* kiss. I pulled away eventually, though I wasn't sure why. Common sense, probably.

The clock on the mantel showed it to be 12:40 a.m.

"It's after midnight," I said.

He nodded, not looking away from my face.

"You should go back to the studio."

Another nod, then he stood, lifting me with him, and gave me a brief kiss. "Happy Valentine's Day," he said, and I burst out laughing. Yeah.

Valentine's Day. I was on suspension, had run into my would-be rapist and learned the details of the accident that I'd never been able to face before, and still ended up snogging someone. Yay, me. I bent over, clutching his shirt, laughing till I just squeaked.

"Happy Valentine's Day," I managed, wiping my eyes.

"We'll do better next year," Ben said, and, grinning at me, he pulled on his coat.

I watched through the window until he was at the studio, and the light going on inside was the warmest, safest, coziest sight I'd ever seen.

CHAPTER 28

Melissa

Her sister had already stolen a few things, Melissa knew. A bottle of Jo Malone perfume. A necklace, one of her pairs of diamond studs and her recently purchased soft leather boots.

She and Kaitlyn had agreed not to talk about Ophelia's future for a few days and give Kaitlyn a chance to catch up with her daughter before bringing up the idea of moving back to Ohio.

The thought of Phee leaving . . . and leaving for *Wakeford* . . . made Melissa's chest ache. She cried all the time these days, but now it wasn't just pregnancy. Ophelia deserved more. She had a fairy godmother in Melissa, and Melissa was determined to keep it that way. She lied to Kaitlyn, telling her she had to go get some pregnancy tests, and talked to a family lawyer about Kaitlyn's rights.

The news wasn't great. If Kaitlyn wasn't using anymore, the lawyer said it would be hard for Melissa to keep custody of Ophelia.

"But I can give her so much more!" Melissa said. "And she's been mine since she was seven!"

"Money can't buy children," the lawyer said. "Your sister

has done her time so far as the law is concerned. As long as she's not using, abusive or neglectful, it's going to be very hard to win this."

Melissa sobbed all the way home.

There was something wrong with the way Kaitlyn looked at Ophelia, she thought. Something . . . hard. She'd called Phee "Miss Fancy-Pants" and told her she sounded like a "snooty college kid." Ophelia had looked so hurt in that moment.

"Smart, you mean?" Melissa said.

"Sure. Smart," Kaitlyn said. "You'll blow the kids in Wakeford out of the water. Valedictorian, maybe."

Phee glanced at Melissa but said nothing.

"She can't take her back to Ohio," Melissa whispered to Bradley the fourth night of her sister's visit. They were in bed, and Melissa had pillows under her knees while Bradley was stroking her stomach, irritating her. "If you want to feel the baby move, just leave your hand still," she snapped. "But I'm trying to tell you that Ophelia would suffer, Bradley. She needs to stay with us."

"Which I would absolutely love," he said. "She's a very unique girl with a bright future, no matter where she ends up. Kids are adaptable, Melissa. Kaitlyn loves her and has a right to raise her daughter."

"No, she doesn't! She's a junkie! Sorry, substance abuse disorder sufferer or whatever the heck you people call it. She just hasn't relapsed yet. And she will, Bradley. She's been on drugs since she was thirteen years old. Wakeford has *nothing* for Ophelia. Nothing except easy access to heroin."

"Well, you know, the Cape has its drug issues, too," Bradley said. "Lillie and I were vigilant with Dylan and the kids he hung out with. We talked very openly to him and his friends about drug and alcohol abuse. And sex. Oh, God, Lillie was so funny! There was no escaping her talks about teenage pregnancy. Every one of Dylan's friends got lectured about STDs and condoms, consent, ovulation, everything." He smiled fondly.

"Oh, for criminy's sake, Bradley, do you have to talk about Lillie again? Can you just focus on my problem here?" The twang was in her voice . . . unavoidable when Katie was so close by.

"Honey. Sweetheart. I know this is very hard. But the fact is, Kaitlyn will probably get custody. You know that. It's hard to accept, but we'll adjust."

She tried to turn on her side, away from Bradley's too-kind face, but rolling was not her strong suit these days. "Give me a shove," she said, and he pushed her back until she made it. She stuffed another pillow under her stomach, and the baby rolled and kicked against her. Maybe it was upset, too. Tears leaked into her pillow, and she belched. Grabbed the Tums she now had to keep on the night table.

"You okay, honey?" Bradley asked.

"No," she said. "I hate being pregnant, and I'm about to lose Ophelia." She sobbed, burped again, and let her husband put his arms around her.

It didn't help.

⁓

The next day, when Bradley had gone to work and Phee was at school, Melissa asked Kaitlyn to sit down with her. They went into the den, which was cozier than the vast, echoing living room, and because there was a huge photo of the three of them on the wedding day—Melissa beautiful in that amazing dress (would her waist ever be that small again? Would her breasts ever come back to human size?), Bradley gorgeous in his suit, and Ophelia smiling brightly, delighted by the "witch" who'd stood out there on the sand (who'd been photoshopped out, obviously). But Kaitlyn didn't need to know the backstory. She could just see her daughter beaming, their little family so perfect.

"Helluva dress," Kaitlyn said, studying the picture.

"Thank you," Melissa said. "Let's talk about Ophelia."

"Actually, I want to talk about *Harminee*," Katie said, narrowing her eyes.

"Sit down. Make yourself comfortable," Melissa said.

It was snowing hard outside, big wet flakes. Under other circumstances, it would've been snug, sitting here with her sister. When they were kids and the snow would come to the mountains, she'd make Katie a cup of cocoa by melting down a chocolate bar she'd swiped from the Dollar General and adding sweetened condensed milk.

That was a lifetime ago. She wished they could go back in time, so she could save Kaitlyn somehow. Save her from drugs, from jail, from a pregnancy she didn't plan and a baby she couldn't raise, from the pain of all those things.

"Right. Well, Katie, we took her in when you asked, and I'm so glad we did. I've been able to give her a good life. She's had every advantage since she's been with me, and—"

"You mean money. She's had a ton of money thrown at her. I get it. You're rich, I'm poor. But I'm still her mother, and now that you got a bun in the oven, you can probably tell how much that matters. I gave birth to her, raised her till she was seven—"

"Except for the years when her grandparents had her, because you were using. And then you got arrested. I'm sorry, Katie, but it's true. You're not . . . reliable."

"Fuck you, Missy-Jo. I changed."

"Really? Where's my perfume? My necklace with the pearl on it? The diamond earrings? Those brown leather ankle boots?"

"You told me your feet were swolled up. I'm doing you a favor, taking them off your hands."

"You're stealing from me. I could report you. I doubt your parole officer would like that."

"I'm borrowing a few nice things from my beloved sister while I'm visiting her. You said to make myself at home, and that's what I'm doing. You gave me all them clothes. Who's to say I'm stealin'? I ain't even left your house yet."

Melissa shifted and tried to breathe in calm, exhale fear, but the baby's head was pressing against her lungs. "Katie, do you really think your daughter would be better off with you, or do you think she'd be better off with me? She's getting a great education. She has a father figure. She's taking piano and French. I can afford college for her. Don't those things matter?"

"What about a mother's love? Don't you think *that* matters, Missy? I ain't had her for five years. I want her back. She's mine. And your snooty-ass husband barely pays attention to her, no matter what he says on social media."

Oh, this wasn't how it was supposed to be at all! Kaitlyn was supposed to be grateful and stay far away, and *Melissa* was supposed to be the *real* mother no matter who'd given birth to Ophelia. Melissa wasn't supposed to be having another baby, and she wasn't supposed to be faced with losing Ophelia! They'd gone through so much together . . . adjusting to New York, Dennis's death, the move out here. The pregnancy had brought them closer than they'd ever been. Having a baby without Ophelia to be a big sister . . . it felt unbearable.

"I'll fight for her in court," Melissa said quietly. "I've already spoken to a lawyer."

"Yeah, well, you'll lose. I got papers saying I've been sober for five years. You don't got a leg to stand on, Missy-Jo. Besides, you'll have your own baby soon enough. Is it a girl? I'm bettin' it's a girl, from the way you spread out. Girls take their mother's beauty, they say. So get ready to say goodbye, because I ain't doing nothing that's illegal, and I'm getting mighty sick of your so-called hospitality. I'm telling Harminee that we're going back home when she gets outta school today."

"Don't," said Melissa. "At least . . . at least wait till the weekend."

"Nope. She's my daughter, and I'm itching to get home. I've had enough of your rich-bitch lifestyle, Missy-Jo. Mama and Daddy would be ashamed of you."

Fury rushed through Melissa, turning her cheeks hot, prickling her skin. "Ashamed of *me*? I made something of myself! Look around, Kaitlyn! I'm winning, and you're still a loser."

"Well, suck on this, princess. You're losing Harminee. Get used to it."

ᕳᕲ

When Ophelia got home from school, her tangled curls were coated in a layer of melting snow.

"They already called a snow day for tomorrow," she announced. "Mama, you want to go sledding? We know a great hill at the golf course!"

Kaitlyn said, "Come on up to my room, kid. I gotta tell you something."

Ophelia shot a look to Melissa.

"Don't look at her," Kaitlyn said. "*I'm* your mother."

"Let's talk to her together," Melissa said. "Please, Katie."

"Not your business," Kaitlyn said.

"Mama, can't you say it in front of her?" Ophelia asked, her eyes worried. She picked up Teeny and held her close.

"Fine. Let's get this over with," Kaitlyn said. "Have a seat, Harminee."

They sat at the dining room table, and Ophelia's face was pale with worry. Melissa squeezed her hand, ignoring the evil look Kaitlyn gave her.

"Honey," Melissa began.

"Let me do the talking, Missy," Kaitlyn said. "Since she's my daughter. Harminee, we're going home. Back to Ohio, back to Mee-Maw and Pop-Pop and Granny and Gramps and all your friends from before. You and me will be living with Mee-Maw for a little while till we get our own place. We'll be leaving Friday after school. Exciting, isn't it?"

"I . . . We're leaving? Forever?" Ophelia asked, and Melissa couldn't stop the tears from rolling down her cheeks.

"Yes, honey," Kaitlyn said. "Your aunt Missy has done

a great job taking care of you while I was away, but we don't need her anymore."

"Melissa?" The poor kid sounded five years old. Teeny trembled in sympathy.

"I want you to stay," Melissa said, her voice breaking. "Very much."

"But she's not your mother, so she can't make that decision. It's best for you to be with me, sugar. Maybe Aunt Melissa can visit sometime." She paused. "You love your mama, don't you? We've stayed in touch all these years, and I know you've had your share of complaints about living with Miss High-and-Mighty here. Two stepfathers in five years, that's been hard, I know it."

Ophelia looked at the table and bit her lip.

"What do *you* want, Ophelia?" Melissa asked.

"Don't you put her in the middle like that!" Kaitlyn snapped. "She's a minor child. She's coming with her mother, because that's how God and nature intended it to be. Her and me have been apart long enough, right, Harminee? We *want* to be together."

"Can I go to my room?" Ophelia asked.

"You need a minute?" Melissa asked.

"Yes, you may go to your room," Kaitlyn said. "Because your mama said you could."

Ophelia slipped away from the table, still holding the dog, and picked up her backpack and coat from the back of the stool. They heard her footsteps on the stairs.

"Did you have to make that so hard?" Kaitlyn demanded. "You know you don't have a chance in hell at keeping her. Why'd you have to tell her to make a choice? You think you can bribe my daughter into staying? Is that it?"

"Well, you sure as hell didn't mind me taking her when you were in jail, Kaitlyn. Don't go blaming me for wanting what's best for her. How many times have you relapsed in your life, huh? What kind of life can you give her? What kind of job do you see yourself getting? What kind of place can you afford?"

"If you care so much, give us a nice fat check, Missy-Jo. You want your niece to live in a pretty house? Buy us one."

"I thought you were above all that. Money doesn't matter, it's what God intended! You're not getting a penny from me."

It took more than an hour before either of them realized Ophelia was gone.

CHAPTER 29

Lillie

On the fourth day of my suspension, I installed a home security system. It was just the smart thing to do, since I'd be living alone for the rest of my days. Ben couldn't stay in the studio forever, and . . . well, one kiss did not a commitment mean.

Which didn't mean I was ruling out future kisses. But the smart part of me realized I wasn't ready for a relationship yet. Maybe some casual company. I wouldn't be averse to making out a few times a week.

It was snowing pretty hard, a thick, wet snow, but my guess was that it wasn't sticking on the roads. On a whim, I decided to visit my dad, who'd been oddly scarce lately. Also, I had some kale soup that was taking up too much room in the fridge, and Dad was a terrible cook. I texted him that I was coming over and asked if he needed anything. He didn't answer. Old people and technology. I knew he wouldn't be out on the water in this weather. Ben, unlike Dad in the olden days, always erred on the safe side. Of course, Ben's father had drowned at sea, so his caution made sense.

I wondered how he felt about his father. There was a lot more to Ben Hallowell than I'd ever thought.

I headed up to Truro, where Dad had lived in a condo since he sold us the house. The building had once been a two-level motel, but as Cape Cod became more of a second-home market, a lot of motels and hotels on Shore Road had been converted to make perfect, tiny condos. Dad had bought the model unit, completely furnished, forks, plates, bath mats, sheets and all. It wasn't supposed to be a year-round condo (hence the affordability of the units back then), but try moving out a crusty old fourth-generation fisherman. The town had given him an exception.

I parked my trusty Honda next to Dad's truck. There were no other cars except a Mercedes at the other end of the lot, since Dad was the only year-rounder. I went up the stairs and knocked. No answer. Maybe he was taking a walk. Or sleeping. The man did love his naps.

I unlocked the door with my key and went in. "Dad?" I said, setting the soup on the counter. "Daddy?" No answer, but I did hear music.

Was that . . . Beyoncé? It *was*. Dad knew who Beyoncé was? I mean, *I* did, of course. We were the same age. (God, how awful. I needed to up my skin care game.) *Keep me coming, keep me humming, keep me coming . . .*

Yeah, okay, he'd obviously left the radio on and was sleeping, because this song was *filthy* (and yes, I knew all the words). "Dad?" Still nothing.

Could something have happened? Could he have . . . died? No, no, he was healthy as an ox. But still. As Queen Bey asked about eating Skittles (which were not Skittles at all), I opened the door to my dad's bedroom and saw something so horrible my brain couldn't process it, which didn't stop me from screaming at the top of my lungs.

My mother screamed as well.

"What?" Dad said, looking up at me from where he was . . . where he was . . . lying. On his back.

I staggered out, managing to close the door.

Keep me coming, keep me going, keep me coming . . . I could hear my parents' terse voices inside the bedroom.

Oh, sweet and pure angelic baby Jesus, please erase that image from my head, I prayed, sliding to the floor.

But no. My parents were having adventure sex.

"We were just . . . we were just having a nap," Dad called. "An angry nap."

"Oh, for heaven's sake, Pedro," my mother said. "She knows what we were doing. Get out of those handcuffs and come talk to your daughter."

A minute later, they both came out, Mom in Dad's tatty flannel bathrobe, my father in jeans and a University of Montana sweatshirt, a Christmas gift from Dylan, now forever tainted.

"An 'angry nap'?" I asked. "Also, you guys hate each other."

"That's only partially true," Mom said, sitting on the couch and crossing her legs like she owned the place. "I realize you're just as repressed as your Portuguese grandparents, Liliana, but not everyone shares your Catholic sensibilities about sex."

"Please stop talking," I said.

"Squashy," Dad began.

"Nope. No pet names. What the . . . I . . . Okay, that song is porn, for one."

"It could've been Megan Thee Stallion and Cardi B," Dad said.

"You don't know that song, Father! No! I don't care if you do. You don't."

"It has a nice rhythm," Dad said.

"Shush! Do you have any booze, Dad, because I need a stiff drink."

"I also need something else stiff," Mom muttered.

"Mom! I heard that! Haven't you scarred me enough in your life?" Dad poured me a shot of whiskey, which I tossed back. "Are you guys together now?" I demanded.

"Well . . . wouldn't that make you happy?" Dad asked.

"No!" I screeched. "Hannah will stab you both when she finds out about this." A thought occurred to me. "Is this why Beatrice left? Because you cheated on her with *Dad*?"

"I can't speak for her motives," Mom said.

"Yes," said Dad at the same time.

"It's rather poetic, isn't it?" Mom said, smiling at my father. "What goes around, comes around."

"Then Dad should've cheated with *Beatrice*," I said. "Call Hannah. I'm not keeping this to myself."

They exchanged a glance. "You do it," Mom said.

Half an hour later, my sister sat in Dad's tiny living room, a look of horror on her face. "You made Beatrice leave," she said to them both. "The best parent of the three of you, and you drove her away to another *continent*. Dad, I'd expect this of Mom, but you?"

"Hannah, really," Mom said, looking bored. "Is that kind of passive-aggressive insult necessary?"

"I learned it at your knee, Mother," she snapped. "Dad? Explain yourself."

Dad was looking increasingly uncomfortable. Good. I felt a little betrayed myself, given that he'd crossed enemy lines. "Okay, girls, settle down," he said. "Obviously, your mother and I have a . . . bond."

"No, you don't," I said. "You can barely stay in the same room together."

"I think we clearly proved you wrong on that point, Liliana," Mom said.

"Gross! Stop it!"

"Anyway," Dad said, "um . . . well, we, uh . . ."

"We ran into each other on the street a few months ago," Mom said. "I told him he looked good. We started talking. The sparks were undeniable. Your father may be a Luddite, but he exudes animal magnetism."

Hannah and I shuddered simultaneously. "Please," I said. "Let *something* be sacred from our childhood, and let that be the hatred between the two of you."

"'Hate' is such a strong word," Mom said. "We don't

exactly love each other, or even like each other, to be honest. Am I right, Pedro?"

"You are, Officer." He raised an eyebrow at my mother.

"There were handcuffs, Hannah," I said. "She was wearing a state trooper's hat."

"Don't tell me these things!" Hannah said. "God, I need a bleach shower after this."

"I can't carry this alone," I said. "And I'm taking a bleach shower right after you're done."

"Girls, stop acting like wounded tweens," Mom said, and if she'd had a cigarette, she would've blown a stream of smoke into the air. "The sexual attraction between your father and me has never faded. We gave in to it."

"And you broke Beatrice's heart," Hannah said. "You never deserved her, Mom. She could've done so much better."

"And now she's free to do so," Mom said, ever unmoved where her daughters' emotions were concerned.

"Hannah, let's get out of here," I said.

"Yeah."

"Tomato," Dad said to Hannah, pulling his best sad-dad face, "don't be mad at your old man. I might not have many years left."

"Because I might strangle you if you don't stop talking," Hannah said.

"Call me, Lillie," Dad said, shifting his puppy eyes to me.

"No! I'm not going to!" I would, and probably tomorrow, but I had to show some solidarity with Hannah.

We left. Her hands were shaking, and her face was pale.

"Let's see if the Mews has a table for us," I said. "Your treat. I'll drive so you can drink."

A half hour later, we were seated on the lower level of the Mews, looking out over the choppy bay, the dark clouds hanging low on the horizon. Hannah was gulping down a martini with two kinds of vodka in it. I ordered us some food, since Hannah was shell-shocked and furious. Lots of food, because I was starving.

I took a sip of my water. "So . . . thoughts?"

"I want to kill them both. They put us through so much, Lils! They've been divorced for thirty-four years, never a civil word between them. Remember when you had to have them over in shifts on Dylan's birthdays? Or when we'd have to make sure they didn't sit within earshot of each other at his football games? All those miserable back-and-forth trips between the two houses, and now suddenly they're screwing?"

"I know," I said.

"Poor Beatrice," she whispered, and tears slid down her cheeks. "I'm going to call her right now."

"Maybe wait till tomorrow," I suggested. "It's late there, right?"

"Oh, yeah. Right." She looked so miserable. "I can't believe they were both . . . complicit. I mean, Mom is basically a reptile when it comes to morals, but Dad? Dad? Sleeping with a married woman?"

I winced. "Well, a married woman he was once married to . . . who cheated on him . . . with Beatrice . . ."

"No, Lillie! Save his defense for later."

"Roger that."

Our food arrived—I had ordered a bunch of appetizers and salad for both of us, since Hannah was in no state to think, and I got to work eating all this deliciousness Hannah was paying for.

"Here we are, in our forties, and our parents are still torturing us," she said.

"I hate that Mom always comes out on top. Shit. Bad choice of words." Because yes, Mom had been . . . Never mind. I shuddered.

"She's like Voldemort, except there's no Harry Potter," Hannah said, her voice forlorn.

"You know what?" I said. "There is. You need a Dylan fix. Let me call him." I pulled out my phone. "And obviously, say nothing about this. Let him cling to his innocence a little longer."

There. I got her to smile. And fortunately, my wonderful son answered. "Hey, Mom!"

"Hi, honey, how are you?"

"I'm fine. Just laying around. What's up?"

"Your auntie Hannah is having a rough day. We're out at the Mews, drowning her sorrows. Want to say hi?"

"Of course."

I passed the phone to my sister, and she brightened. "Hi, sweetheart. Oh, no, it's . . . nothing." She gave a slight dry heave. "What's new with you? How much snow do you have?"

They chatted in their easy way, and I felt something move in my heart. Hannah and I might not have been close for many years, but she'd always been great to Dylan, taking him to Fenway, always giving him the best presents, swapping inside jokes (about me, probably, but hey). I was glad they had each other.

When she hung up, her eyes were wet. "Thank you," she said.

"Thank *you*," I said. "You're paying. You gonna eat, or what? We need our strength."

My sister smiled at me reluctantly. "I love you, Lillie," she said.

I stopped chewing. "I love you, too, Han. Now order another drink, because yours is gone, and you have a designated driver. Maybe we should go see Filipe at the Crown and Anchor. Nothing like a drag show to cheer a person up."

"He doesn't perform in the winter."

"Damn. Well. Another time, sis. We'll make a date of it, how's that?"

"Yes, Nurse," she said. "Whatever you say."

I asked Hannah to sleep over, but she had to give Thomasina some medicine and wanted to sleep in her own bed. She asked me if I'd like to stay there, but the snow was sticking now, and I figured I should get home. It would be a snug night, and I'd make a fire, have a glass of wine, curl up with my dog and google "hypnosis to erase traumatic images."

The studio lights were off—Ben was in Boston, visiting his daughter, who'd come in for a friend's wedding. I was glad he had another chance to see her. He didn't talk about Reese much, but when he did, his face softened, and the pride and love were evident.

The snow was deep and heavy and would be a bear to shovel tomorrow. I made my way up the steps from the driveway and gave a start.

Ophelia sat on my steps, dressed in a parka and carrying a backpack. "Hi," she said. "Can I hang out here for a little while?"

CHAPTER 30

Lillie

"Hey!" I said. "What are you doing here, honey?"

"I took a walk."

Pretty long walk, especially in the snow and dark. "Well, come on in. Have you been here long?"

"About an hour," she said, brushing snow from the top of her parka.

"You must be freezing."

A thousand questions ran through my mind, but first things first. Get the kid warmed up and settled. Zeus greeted her with utter delight that Mommy had brought home a friend.

"Teeny's in my backpack," Ophelia said. "Will your dog eat her?"

"No. Zeus loves all living creatures. Even mice."

She reached into her canvas backpack and withdrew her Chihuahua, wrapped in a blanket and wearing a plaid sweater. She presented the bundle to Zeus, who began licking Teeny's head with great excitement. Teeny wagged her little tail and smiled, and they were in love. Ophelia put the dog down, and Teeny trotted around the house, Zeus following like a gracious host.

"How about some cocoa?" I asked as I turned on lights. She didn't have gloves on.

"Sure. Your house is way cool."

"Make yourself at home. Why don't you change, sweetie . . . your pants are soaked through. I've got some sweats or scrubs that would fit you. Do you need a hot shower?"

"No, I'm good. The dry clothes will be great, though."

"Right in there," I said, pointing to my bedroom. "Wear whatever you want. Nice warm socks in the top drawer. I'll start the cocoa, so come down when you've changed."

How had she gotten here? How had she found my place? Well, that was easy enough . . . the town hall website had everyone's address, if she was savvy enough to figure that out (which she probably was). Plus, she lived with Brad, who may have told her where he used to live. Maybe Dylan told her at Christmas.

I got out the milk and cream and heated them up, then added the Danish chocolate Dylan had given me for Christmas. Stirred in some sugar and vanilla and inhaled the comforting smell of cocoa. As I was pouring the hot chocolate into heavy mugs, Ophelia came down, dressed in a pair of flannel pajama bottoms and an oversized sweatshirt that read "Helltown, Massachusetts, established 1620."

"Where's Helltown?" she asked.

"It's the nickname for Provincetown," I said. "Because of the carousing and gambling and drinking and fun. The Puritans didn't like it." I put some buttery scones on a plate.

"So it was always the coolest place on the Cape, then?"

I smiled. "You got it."

We sat across from each other at the table. She took a sip of cocoa. "Oh, wow, this is so good! It's like drinking a melted chocolate bar."

"Thanks." I sipped my own, waited till she ate a scone, and then lifted my eyebrows, inviting her to speak.

"Right," she said, dropping her eyes to her plate. "Well, I guess I technically ran away from home."

"Okay. I'm gonna need to call your mother. Melissa, I mean."

"Do you have to?"

"I'm afraid so." I glanced out at the darkness, the heavy snow illuminated by the back door light. "I think you'll have to sleep over, though. I barely made it down the road."

"That would be awesome." She pulled out her phone and showed me Melissa's number. "My battery's way low." I plugged in Ophelia's phone, then called Melissa on mine, putting her on speaker so Ophelia could hear.

"Hello? Phee? Is that you?" Her voice was high-pitched and terrified.

"Melissa, it's Lillie Silva," I said. "Ophelia is here at my house, safe and sound."

"Oh, thank God! She's safe. She's safe and at Lillie's!" she called to someone. Brad, probably. "What's she doing there? We had no idea where she went! This weather is awful. Did she walk? She didn't hitchhike, did she?"

Melissa was, what . . . seven months pregnant? A little more? "She's fine, so take a breath, okay?" I said in my kindly midwife voice. "We don't need you to get too upset, though I understand how worrying this has been. Kids, right?" I winked at Ophelia.

"I can't believe she . . ." Melissa was crying.

"She walked here. She's fine . . . she's drinking cocoa right now, but the roads are pretty bad, so I think she should stay overnight. Is that okay with you?"

"Yes. Yes, that's fine. Um . . . I could come get her."

"I live on a dirt road. No plowing. You probably need to rest and drink a lot of water, have a good meal, Melissa. Ophelia is welcome here. I'll make her dinner, and she can sleep in the guest room. I'll bring her home tomorrow on my way to work."

"How do you even know her? How does she know *you*?"

"We've run into each other here and there," I said, opting not to mention my foray under Bralissa's bed. "And of course, she's Dylan's stepsister."

"Right. Right." She sounded calmer now. "Are you sure this is okay? We could have the police come and get her."

"No, let's not make this a bigger drama than it is already."

"Good idea. You're—"

Suddenly, her voice was replaced with Brad's. "What did you do, Lillie? What did you say to our *daughter* so that she felt she could run away to your house? Are you trying to ruin my life? I understand that you're vengeful and filled with hate and anger, but this is—"

I hung up. "Think about calling Melissa in a little while. She was really worried."

"Yeah, I could tell. The thing is, my real mom is over there, and she wants to take me back to Ohio, and they were yelling at each other and I just didn't want to deal with it. So I found your address and came over. You said to call if I wanted to talk."

"But you didn't call, did you?"

She looked down again. "I was afraid you'd say no, but I figured you'd let me stay here if I just showed up."

"Smart girl." I paused. "How is it, seeing your mother again?" I asked.

She shrugged. "Great, I guess. I mean, I do love her." She broke a scone in half and didn't say more. The furnace kicked on, humming companionably.

"Well, I just ate, but I'm gonna feed you. You've had dessert . . . how about some dinner?"

"Sure. Thanks."

I made her what I'd always made Dylan when he was blue—tomato soup and grilled cheese. The bread was sourdough; I used four kinds of cheese, whipped up the tomato soup using canned tomatoes and cream, and set it all in front of Ophelia. She fell upon it like a starving coyote.

"This is amazing," she said around a bite of the gooey cheese sandwich. "I can't believe you did this in, like, twenty minutes."

"It's a gift," I said. I tidied up while she ate. It was awfully nice to have a kid back in my house. Someone to take care of.

When she was finished, she very politely brought her dishes to the counter and set them in the sink.

"Let's go upstairs and make a fire," I said. "Perfect night for it."

"I love your house," she said, trailing after me. "It's so . . . funky, you know? Like this chimney up to the balcony? Wicked."

"Thanks. It was my grandparents' house, and then my dad's. I grew up here."

"Seriously? You lived here all your life?"

"Yep. Except for college, that is."

"Didn't you ever want to live anywhere else?"

I paused. "Not really. I mean, I like traveling, but I love the Cape." I paused. "Do you?"

"Sort of. I mean, our house isn't as cozy as yours. It echoes. My room is, like, super fussy, because Melissa decorated it more for Instagram than for me. We have to eat at the dining room table every night, and Brad makes us say grace first."

I snorted. "Really."

"Yeah. We go to church now. We didn't have to in New York."

Brad in church. That was rich. He had to be forced to attend when he'd been married to me, and he'd only go for the big holidays.

"Anyway, your mother is visiting. That must be . . ."

"It's great." She didn't sound convinced. "I mean . . . I barely saw her growing up. Back in Ohio, I mean. My bio-dad's parents took care of me, and Mom . . . she's got a drug problem, and a crime problem, and money problems, so . . ." She sighed and pushed back her tangled blond curls. "So anyway, my gran had a stroke, and Mom was heading for jail again, so she called Melissa and asked if I could live with her. And Melissa came out and got me and changed my name and put me in all these classes in New York and paraded me around like her charity project, which I guess I was." She slurped her soup. "But it was . . . it was okay, because I mean, I did have a nice place to live, and there was always enough food, and I didn't have to wear hand-me-downs or shop at Goodwill or eat Hamburger Helper."

"And there was Dennis."

"Exactly. And Melissa, she wasn't awful or anything. She wasn't mean. I just felt like she didn't really care about me, you know? Like I could've been any kid from anywhere, and she would've been . . . what's that thing you say when someone's trying to show how good they are?"

"Oh. Um . . . virtue signaling?"

"Yeah. That. But lately . . ." Her voice trailed off, and she didn't finish the thought.

Ophelia was smart, and observant. "How long have you lived with Melissa?"

"Almost six years, I guess."

"And now your mom wants to bring you back to Ohio?" She nodded.

"Is that what you want?"

She grabbed Teeny from where she lay between Zeus's giant paws, and held the wee rat against her shoulder. "I don't know," she said. "Not really? But I do love my mom. I just . . . I don't trust her."

Then she was crying, quietly, trying not to sob, the poor baby. Adults and their stupid lives, always messing up children. I sat next to her and pulled her head onto my shoulder. "I'm sorry, sweetheart," I said.

"I wish I could live with you," she said, and I closed my eyes. I wished so, too. For a second, the longing to have a daughter—my daughter, or anyone's daughter—washed over me.

But Ophelia wasn't mine, and I knew better than to make a hollow promise. "Come on," I said. "Let's go into the den and watch a funny movie. It's the perfect night for it. I'm sure schools will be shut tomorrow, so we can stay up late and eat popcorn and ice cream. Sound like a plan?"

She gave a half smile. "Sounds like a plan."

We were halfway through *Spy* when my new motion-sensor lights went on and my phone flashed with a warning from the security system that someone was approaching my house. Ben? Zeus gave a deep bark, and Teeny scrambled to the door. I turned on the outdoor lights and peered out.

It was a woman dressed in high boots, a fur coat, fur hat and fur gloves. It was either Lara from *Doctor Zhivago* or Melissa. Sadly, it was not Lara.

"Is she sleeping?" she said, slipping a bit on the patio. I reached out and grabbed her arm.

"You shouldn't have come out in this weather, Melissa." Where was Brad? He'd let her drive in this snow, preggers? "She's awake. Come on in."

She did, taking off her snow-encrusted boots and handing me her coat and hat, since apparently I was the butler. Then she swooped onto Ophelia. "Oh, honey! I was so worried! You can never do that again! Do you hear me? What if you got lost in the snow?"

"I wouldn't get *lost*, Melissa," Ophelia said, wriggling away, a bored sort of scorn dripping from her voice. "I'm not an *idiot*." Where was the nice kid who'd been with me for the past two hours?

"People get lost," Melissa said. "You could've frozen to death!"

"People don't get lost. Don't be such a drama queen."

"Actually," I said, "people do get lost. A guy disappeared around here about ten years ago. He was never found. They dragged the ponds and had hundreds of people look for him, but he was gone without a trace."

"Seriously? You're on her side now?" Ophelia asked.

"Google it. Matthew Dudek."

Melissa sat on the couch next to Ophelia. "Your mother and Bradley are also very upset," she said. "We were all so worried."

"Well, maybe you two shouldn't screech about who's gonna get custody of me while I'm in the house." She stared at the paused image of Jude Law. "Did you walk here?"

"Um . . . well, my car got stuck a ways back. I walked from there."

"Is Mama in the car?"

Melissa glanced at me, then back at Ophelia. "No, she stayed home. Uh, let me call her and Bradley, if you don't mind."

I gestured her into the living room and closed the den door, not wanting to overhear their cooing or Brad's psychobabble.

The other woman was in my house. In my living room, seeing pictures of my son, my family. It was unsettling . . . but at the same time, I would've walked through the deep snow for my kid, too.

"Leave it to her to ruin the happiest night I've had all year," Ophelia muttered.

"Hey," I said. "She came out in a snowstorm, seven months pregnant, to make sure you were okay. She didn't have to do that."

"I wish she didn't."

"But she did." And Ophelia's mother had not. Nor had Brad, who was the best equipped to drive in the snow down these winding, bumpy roads. Melissa had come by herself, and walked in the dark, snowy woods, pregnant belly and all.

I hated to admit it, but I kind of admired that.

Melissa knocked at the door and peeked in. "Can I . . . can I sit down?"

"Sure." I glanced at her stomach. "How's the baby?"

"Fine. Normal." She looked embarrassed.

"How many weeks are you?"

"Thirty."

"Well, there's no way in hell I'm letting you go home tonight, Melissa, so you can have Dylan's room, because Princess Ophelia has already claimed the guest room. I'm gonna get you some soup and a big glass of water."

"Oh, no, I don't want to make a fuss."

"You already have. Sit down in the recliner and put your feet up." My voice may have been a wee bit hard, but did it stop me from feeding her? It did not.

By the time the movie was over, my brain had had it. I gave each of my guests a toothbrush from the stash I kept for Dylan's friends, waited for them to get settled, and then turned out the lights. As I did, Ben's truck pulled into the driveway. I let Zeus out and went to greet Ben at the studio door. The snow was tapering off, but it sure was pretty out here. So quiet.

"Hey," he said.

"Hi. How's your daughter?"

He smiled. "She's great. Really happy. We had a nice dinner. Nice to see them both."

"Both?"

"Oh. Cara, too. The three of us."

I had heard of amicable divorces . . . or at least, cases of parents who could get along in each other's company. Couldn't picture Brad and Dylan and me sitting down for a pleasant dinner, but . . .

"I passed a BMW stuck on the road back there," he said. "You got company?"

"Yes, I do. I'm having a sleepover. Melissa Fairchild and her niece. Ophelia ran away and came here, and Melissa drove over to check on her, got stuck and walked the rest of the way."

"That's a good mile back."

"Eesh. Well, with the weather being so dangerous, and her being great with child, I invited them to stay."

He raised his eyebrow. "Very generous of you."

"Thanks. I know. I'm a saint."

He smiled. "You're not bad, I'll give you that."

"Oh, and I found out who my father's girlfriend is," I said.

"Really?"

"Brace yourself. It's my mother."

"Holy shit," he said. "Are you sure?"

"I caught them in the act, Ben."

His face contorted. "Oh, man. I'm so sorry."

"Thank you for your much-needed sympathy. It was horrible. Hannah is especially traumatized."

"I can imagine."

I looked at him, snow falling on his shaggy hair. The clouds were faintly pink, and the quiet wrapped us like a secret. I wanted to say something profound, or . . . something, just to make this moment last.

"I'm gonna go to bed, Ben." Dang it. Not what I meant to say.

"Yeah. Quite a day for you."

"Understatement of the year."

"Well. Sleep tight."

I didn't move. "You can kiss me if you want." There. That's what I wanted to say.

He gave that wonderful, smoky laugh, and pulled me close and kissed me, long and slow and warm. "Good night, Lillie. Love your pajamas."

I looked down. Cartoon sharks carrying human legs in their mouths. "Limited edition," I said. "Just like me."

I was smiling as I got into bed and hugged Zeus tight. Weird, to feel so happy after one of the strangest days of my life, but here I was. I'd done the right thing tonight. By Hannah, by Ophelia, by Melissa. And Ben was out there, willing to kiss me.

It was a good feeling.

CHAPTER 31

Melissa

Lillie had made them oatmeal with dried fruit and cream for breakfast. Of course she had.

Melissa was exhausted . . . sleeping on a strange mattress, her brain still buzzing with all the things that could've happened to Ophelia. Hit by a car on Route 6! Twisted her ankle and fallen in the snow. Taken by some pervert and . . . But she was safe, thank heavens.

Typical, that she'd come to Lillie. *Everyone* loved Lillie. The fact that Ophelia even knew what Lillie looked like, let alone where she lived, was a shock. The house was nothing like Bradley had described—crowded, dark, poorly laid out. It was adorable. Homey. All the photos of Dylan and Lillie's father, her sister, her friends. All the strange little touches. The collection of Portuguese chickens lined up on the windowsill in the bathroom. The sturdy, colorful plates on the kitchen shelves. A framed piece of artwork from Dylan's school days. His little handprint preserved in clay, hanging in the kitchen.

Totally not Melissa's style, but not ugly, either. She'd pictured Lillie's house as dirtier, less . . . lovely. It was the epitome of the type of home Melissa herself had wanted to grow up in, the smell of baked goods and coffee in the air, rather than cigarettes and cheap beer. She found herself strangely choked up when, upon awakening, she'd noticed a little slip of paper taped next to Dylan's bed. *Mommy loves you!* it said, and she could tell it had been there a long, long time. Imagine that. Imagine an eighteen-year-old boy keeping a little note from his mother.

Is that what she'd have to do for hers? As if in answer, the baby rolled and kicked, and she grunted a little, putting her hand on her stomach.

"Baby kicking?" Lillie asked, her voice mild.

"Mm-hmm."

"Always a good sign. Finish your breakfast, and try to get enough rest today. You probably overdid it last night, slogging through the snow."

"It was beautiful, though." Melissa stopped, blushing. It felt weird to be chatting with *her*, the woman whose husband Melissa had seduced and married so easily.

"It is pretty out here." Lillie didn't seem to be that angry.

Ophelia had left the table, allegedly to gather up Teeny, but she was throwing a ball upstairs, laughing as both dogs barked and played. The child had come somewhere safe yesterday. At least there was that.

Lillie drove them to the car, then got behind the BMW's wheel and efficiently backed it out and turned it around. She got out, hugged Ophelia, said, "Use that phone next time," and got into her car.

"Thank you again," Melissa called.

Lillie waved in response, then drove off.

"You look ridiculous in that fur getup," Ophelia said.

"It's the warmest thing I have."

"Well, buy something from L.L.Bean like everyone else out here," she snapped, flinging herself down in the passenger seat.

Melissa got in as well and inched the car toward Route 6, following someone's tire tracks. "Ophelia, you can't just run away like that," she said when they were on dry pavement.

"But I did."

"Please don't ever do it again. You worried us all, and you know better. You're going to have to be punished."

"What will you do? Take away my friends? Guess what? I don't have any."

Melissa looked at her. "Me neither." She sighed. "Why don't you think of something? For your punishment. What do you think is fair?"

Ophelia shrugged. "I don't know."

"Write a letter saying that you're sorry?"

"But I'm not sorry. Lillie's *normal*. She's actually interested in me, Melissa, not like you and Bridiot."

God, it was tiring, dealing with this kind of attitude all the time. "I'm interested in you, Ophelia."

"Sure. That's why you're letting my mom take me away. Because I'm so much fun to have around. Send me back to wherever. I don't care. I belong there. I'm a loser wherever I go."

Melissa slammed on the brakes and pulled into the parking lot of First Congregational Church. She turned to Ophelia. "No, you're not!" she shouted, surprising herself. "You are not a loser, Ophelia! You *could* have been, left in that godforsaken place without anyone to believe in a decent future for you! You could've been like me, having to turn yourself inside out to be someone different just to have some security in the world. But you didn't! I came for you. I made sure you knew how to talk and eat and read. People will look at you and say, 'That kid is going somewhere. Look how smart she is! How tough and resilient she is.' Even if your mother takes you home, you'll still have six years of . . . of advantage."

"Well, I didn't have love," Ophelia said, twisting the knife the way only a tween could. "Maybe I know which fork to use and have a closet full of snotty-ass clothes, but ever since Dennis died, no one has given a shit about me."

"Really." Melissa started the car again. "Well, *someone* walked a mile through the snow in the dark to make sure you were okay last night. I call that giving a shit."

Once home, Melissa sent Ophelia to her room with instructions to clean it from floor to ceiling, and then the bathroom as well.

Kaitlyn rolled her eyes at the decree and said only, "Glad to have you back, nugget."

Bradley wasn't even home. Seemed like he was always around except when she needed him.

I hate everyone, Melissa thought. The ungrateful, sullen child. The sly sister who was running some kind of game. The husband who knocked her up and only thought of himself, acting as if *he* was the one who'd earned this house, this lifestyle. His parents disapproved of her, and other than Lucia the housekeeper, she didn't have a single friend.

Had she ever?

"Come into the study," she told Kaitlyn, chomping on some Tums. Her stomach was churning with acid. Allegedly, that meant the baby would be born with a lot of hair. She wished it was bald.

"Sleeping with the enemy last night, huh?" Kaitlyn said. "So what's she like, this ex-wife?"

"How much, Kaitlyn?" Melissa asked, sitting heavily behind the desk. She pulled out her leather-bound checkbook.

"How much for what?"

"For giving me custody of Ophelia."

Kaitlyn's eyes narrowed. "You think I'm gonna sell my kid to you?"

"Yep. Let's be honest. That's why you're here. You know you can't take her back to Ohio. You'd be ruining her life. She barely knows you. With me, she has stability and security."

"Yeah, right, until you get tired of your middle-aged boy toy and trade him in for a younger model," Kaitlyn said.

"Oh, so that means you're giving up men until she goes to college?"

"Maybe. Or maybe Harminee needs a real father figure in her life. Not that pretentious asshat parading around in a teenager's jeans and a stupid shirt."

"And where in Wakeford are you going to find this upstanding citizen who's dying to settle down with a felon, her history of drug abuse and her twelve-year-old child?"

"Fuck you, Missy Jolene. You're just as much of a hillbilly as I am. You fake being high-class, but everyone can tell what you are. A gold digger who got lucky. A whole lotta nothing."

"How about a million dollars, Katie? Sign custody over to me, and you'll walk away with enough money for a lifetime."

Kaitlyn leaned back in her chair and folded her arms.

Melissa folded hers, too. "Two million."

"Is that all my baby's worth to you?" Kaitlyn asked, her voice like the snake's in the Garden of Eden. "You're sittin' on a fortune, Missy-Jo. This house has gotta be worth at least a few mil. And that dead doctor of yours . . . I read about his practice down in New York City. I bet you got a lot more than two million when he died."

Oh, Dennis. He'd been so good to her and Ophelia. If only he hadn't died. Melissa swallowed. "Five. That's life-changing money, Katie. You could do a lot with that. Get an education, travel, buy a house."

"If you're offering five mil, I bet you can get up to ten," Kaitlyn said in the snake whisper.

"We used to love each other," Melissa blurted. "You and me. You were my only . . . person. I wanted you to come with me, to . . . to get away with me. I loved you, Katie. You're the only thing I ever missed from my old life. I could've erased you from Ophelia's life, but I didn't. I let her call you and write to you because I remembered who you used to be. My friend. My smart, funny little sister."

Kaitlyn just raised one eyebrow, waiting.

"How about this, Katie? You stay clean for a year. I'll rent you a place in town, and you do a urine test every week, and after a year, you can come live with us, here, in this house. You can have the apartment over the garage, or . . . or I'll buy you your own place. You'll be right here, part of her life."

For a second, she thought she saw the shine of tears in her sister's eyes. Then Kaitlyn looked out the window toward the bay.

So she knew, then. Kaitlyn knew she wouldn't be able to stay sober, or be the kind of mother Ophelia needed. "Let's settle on seven," Katie said. "You give me the money, and you'll get the kid."

Melissa heard a small noise in the hall. She didn't turn her head or acknowledge it. *Please be Teeny,* she thought. "Okay. I'll call a lawyer."

⌒

Kaitlyn left five days later. She hugged Ophelia, told her she'd see her soon, flipped Melissa the bird and got into her car and drove away. Ophelia didn't say much, just went to her room and didn't emerge for a day. Melissa left a tray of cinnamon toast and tea outside her door.

Bradley was upset, too. He felt that she should have "consulted" him because, he said, "giving away that amount of money impacts both our futures, and our unborn child's." He was currently attempting a regal disappointment. Money-grubber. Also, he was sleeping in one of the guest rooms, because her snoring had gotten worse, and she soaked the pillows with drool. Oh, and she rubbed her legs against the sheets, because it felt like they were covered with spiders, and it irritated him.

As for sex, that window had slammed shut the last time they'd done it, because parts of her . . . lady garden . . . hurt. He'd better be an incredible father, or she was ditching him. His WASPy charm, his soft voice, his ability to make it seem like he was so much smarter than everyone else . . . if she had a nickel for every time he'd said "Well, actually, that's not *quite* true" when she tried to make conversation about current events. He used to find her fascinating. He was basically *paid* to find her fascinating, the jerk.

She was too tired to care, honestly. She had Ophelia, and the adoption was locked tight, and yes, her net worth had taken a punch.

Two nights after her sister left, Melissa knocked on Ophelia's door. It was after ten, and though she was tired, Melissa wanted to see her niece. Her *daughter* now.

Ophelia was curled on her side, looking like she was six years old. Her eyes were closed, lashes resting on her cheeks like an angel's, a halo of tangled blond curls around her face. Melissa lay down on the covers as slowly as she could manage and put her arm around Ophelia. Took a throw pillow and stuffed it under her stomach. The baby rolled and pressed against Phee's back, and Ophelia stirred.

She lifted her head and glanced at Melissa. "You okay?" she whispered.

"Yep. Are *you* okay?" Melissa whispered back.

"Yeah." They looked at each other for a minute, then Ophelia put her head back on her pillow. Melissa couldn't help it—she reached out and stroked her niece's—daughter's—hair.

"Thanks for buying me," Ophelia whispered. She took a shaky breath, and Melissa knew she was crying, and hugged her close.

"I can feel the baby," Ophelia said after a minute.

"She can feel you, too," Melissa answered.

"Is it a girl, then?"

"I don't know for sure, but I think so."

The wind blew against the window. "A little sister. That'd be nice."

A few hot tears slid out of Melissa's eyes, but this time, they didn't feel like those uncontrollable pregnancy tears. This time, they felt good. Like they were sealing the deal.

CHAPTER 32

Lillie

March was soggy and gray, but the wind carried the scents of spring like a promise. The wind still howled, but the smells of dirt and rain were in the air.

I went to the hospital one Tuesday to catch a baby—seriously, I almost missed it, because the mother dilated eight centimeters in two hours and only needed one push to birth her child into the world. After we got the mama settled and the baby tucked in against her, and I'd taken a hundred or so pictures for them, I went to fill out the necessary reports.

"Hey," said Tonya, the admin. "Got a little news for you. Dr. Schneider's taking early retirement."

My head jerked up from the keyboard. "Say again now?"

Tonya lowered her voice. "Patient complaint. One of yours. You didn't see it? Hang on a sec. You were cc'd. And there's a viral video!"

She printed out two sheets of paper and handed them to me.

During my labor, I was calmly breathing through my contractions in the birthing pool when certified nurse-midwife Lillie Silva stepped out to get some food for my husband and me.

For no reason we could determine, Dr. Carline Schneider interrupted without knocking. Without even examining me, she decided I wasn't giving birth fast enough, was not progressing well, informed me that I was giving "poor maternal effort," needed medical intervention and that I was endangering my baby's life.

Fortunately, Nurse Silva intervened and escorted her from the room even as Dr. Schneider told me I would need an emergency cesarean.

She was wrong. A couple hours later, I joyfully gave birth to a very healthy baby, thanks to my midwife, who encouraged and helped me during this natural process. I could not have wished for a better birth experience except for the rudeness and inaccurate, outdated information from Dr. Schneider.

It was from Elizabeth and Tom.

"There's a video, too," Tonya said. "Elizabeth holding her baby, telling her birth story. Some of the big pregnancy blogs picked it up and are using it as an example of things not to say to a woman in labor and how outdated some OBs are."

"Whoa," I said. I blinked a few times. Tonya handed me an iPad, and I watched as Elizabeth, looking utterly gorgeous holding her little sweetheart, told it like it was.

"Everyone on the floor has watched it," Tonya whispered. "We're not exactly heartbroken that the old shrew is leaving." She glanced over my shoulder. "So yeah, definitely Taco Heaven over Sam Diego's," she said loudly. "Can't beat their guacamole."

I turned. Carline Schneider, in the flesh.

"Well, if it isn't Nurse Jenny Lee," she said to me. "God forbid we actually use modern medicine to ensure the health of a mother and child as long as they can post their birth stories online. I hope you're happy."

"I'm *so* happy, Carline," I said. "For one, *Call the Midwife* is my favorite show." Tonya snickered. "For two, I did everything I was supposed to do as a midwife. You inter-rupted a perfectly beautiful labor, tried to intimidate my patient and misinformed her about the threat to the baby. And then you threw me under the bus, attacked my reputa-tion, accused me of assault and got me suspended. So yes, I'm glad you're leaving." I put the complaint down. "Now. I have a new mama to see."

Sometimes, you get those moments. Sometimes, the perfect words just roll off your tongue. Sometimes, you get to be right and have the last word. Not often, but some-times.

⌒

Winter, in one last gasp to show who was boss, dumped six inches of snow on the Outer Cape, followed by freezing rain that made the snow impossible to walk on. The Heart-break Storm, I always called it, because just when spring had finally arrived and the little crocuses and snowdrops were poking out of the ground, Mother Nature got that look in her eye. Every year. Zeus and I slipped and slid on the hard ice, barely able to make it to the beach so he could run. Tonight, it was supposed to be ten degrees out. Ten degrees! Bitter cold, and with a wind out of the north. I hoped my little daffodil buds would survive the cold. I'd planted hun-dreds over the years, and every spring, it was such a glorious surprise to see them pop, little balls of sunshine on stems.

This summer, I'd be renting the studio out at tourist rates. Ben told me he'd move out by April 15, just two weeks from now. With the amount of debt I had, I knew I should rent out my house, too, but where would Dylan and I stay? I wanted my son to have his home this summer, because soon enough, he wouldn't *have* a summer vacation. I wanted that glimpse of life as it had been, at least one more time. This past summer had been so fraught, so off balance and distressing that I hadn't been able to enjoy it.

"First world problems, Lillie," I reminded myself, zip-ping up my parka. Even so, owing more than $300,000, without the income to make a dent into it, made my knees wobble in fear. If I kept the house, I'd go under. If I sold the house, I'd rip my heart in two, let alone what it would do to Dylan. This house was his legacy, and whether or not he settled here as an adult, the plan had always been that he'd inherit it.

I'd just have to figure it out.

Ben had not only plowed on his way out, he'd scraped my car clean of snow. As I made my way into work, I decided to invite him over for dinner. Without Dad this time. Just him and me. Almost like a date. Maybe an actual date, in fact. I knew I wasn't ready for a real relationship. But a friendship with chemistry . . . that might be nice. I mean, we'd kissed twice. Three times, actually.

When I got to work, Wanda's car wasn't in its usual space. "She's running late," Carol announced as I walked in. "Shoveling her driveway as we speak."

"Not a problem. Who've we got?"

"Karen Henderson is back, surprise, surprise. Another UTI. Sex addict," Carol said, smiling. "Melissa Fairchild in for her eight-month checkup." Carol scrunched up her cute little face. "Can I tell her we made a mistake and she's actually due in August?"

"No, you cannot," I said with a smile.

I hadn't seen Melissa since our inadvertent sleepover (seeing her in my son's pajama bottoms and one of his T-shirts stretched tight against her enormous, fertile boobs had compelled me to toss those items).

Ophelia had texted me that she'd be staying in Wellfleet and that her mother had left. When I asked if she was okay with that, she answered, Totally.

Wellfleet OB/GYN had a policy that pregnant women were prioritized over more routine patients, so I called Melissa in. Weighed her, didn't comment on the seven-pound gain (because I was a kind person) and had her sit on the exam table.

"First, do you have any questions, Melissa?"

"I wanted to thank you again," she said. "Things . . . things are better. Ophelia's staying with me. My sister signed away her parental rights." She flushed. "Ophelia's legally my daughter now."

Wow. "Um, great. I really like Ophelia."

Her eyes welled. "Me too."

Was Brad now Ophelia's adoptive father? If so, he didn't deserve that kid. She was special. But I didn't ask.

"Any questions about how you're feeling or where the baby is, growth-wise?"

The tears spilled out of her sea-glass-green eyes. "I have a beard now," she whispered. "I shave every day."

Yes, and she'd missed a patch. On the left side of her mouth was some significant fuzz. "That's actually a good sign," I said. "Your hormones are working. That's the androgen, which contains testosterone. The new hair should fall out after you give birth."

"Can I do anything about . . . leakage?" she asked.

"Kegels. But don't hold in your pee. You don't want a UTI."

"What about these?" she asked, gesturing to her chest. "This isn't normal, is it?"

I couldn't suppress a laugh. "Totally normal. Just your body getting ready to feed the baby."

"I'm not going to *nurse*!" she said.

"Well, you may change your mind. I'll give you some information about it."

"You nursed, I suppose." There was a little resentment in that statement.

"I did."

"Bradley loves to tell me what a perfect mother you are. It's like he's telling me to be more like you."

"How irritating for us both," I said, and I swear, she shot me a glance of . . . of gratitude.

Strange, to feel a pang of sympathy for the other woman. "Let's check your blood pressure and see if the baby is head down yet."

Her BP was fine, the baby's heart rate was perfect, the

fundus was just as big as it was supposed to be, and yes, the baby was head down. I checked her hands and feet for swelling—she did have cankles, but it was more from her sixty-three-pound weight gain than retained fluids. I asked if she had headaches—pregnancy headaches can be a harbinger of preeclampsia or HELLP syndrome, but she had no signs of either. I reminded her to eat well and drink lots of water and told her the difference between Braxton-Hicks and real contractions.

"You don't . . . you don't schedule cesareans, do you?" she asked.

"Not unless there's a reason to," I said. "If the baby's breech and we can't get it to turn, we do, or if the baby is so big that we're concerned it won't make it past the pubic bone. Otherwise, it's for emergencies only. Both mother and baby do best that way in almost every case."

She nodded glumly.

"Are you taking childbirth classes at the hospital?"

"No."

"Why not?"

"Because . . . because I think the whole thing is absolutely disgusting, and I don't want to know more than I have to, and . . . and because I'm . . . scared." Those green eyes welled again.

Again, my heart squeezed in sympathy. "I think you'd be less scared and less grossed out if you knew more, Melissa. It's the most amazing process a body can experience."

"I've seen some videos on YouTube," she said, wiping her eyes. "It's horrifying."

Those were the videos I watched to feel good about humanity. "Come on, now. It's nature at its finest," I said. "Don't worry. You'll do fine. Your body will know what to do." I hesitated, then added, "You have my number."

"I do?"

"I called you when Ophelia was at my house."

"Oh, right."

"Call me or Wanda if you have questions, okay? We're

always available. You can get dressed now." I gave her a professional smile and turned to the door.

"Do you hate me?" she asked suddenly.

I froze. Turned around and looked at her.

"I did," I answered. "Sure. But it's hard for me to hate a pregnant woman."

"If we weren't in this office, and I wasn't pregnant, you would hate me, though?"

I sighed. "I don't know, Melissa. Last year at this time, I thought my family was rock solid. You and Brad . . . you broke that. The three of us will never be together the same way again. All of our family traditions, not to mention the future we'd planned. My son has to deal with this huge swerve. I loved Brad's parents like they were my own. More than my own. Neither of you cared about that. Obviously, I have feelings about it."

She nodded and swallowed. "When my sister came to take Ophelia back, I was . . . terrified. I didn't really know how much I loved Phee till I thought she'd be taken away from me. So . . . I guess I can relate."

"Ophelia seems glad to be staying here," I said.

Melissa looked down, her silky blond hair (not quite so blond, now that she couldn't color it) swinging forward. "It probably doesn't mean much," she whispered, "but I'm sorry."

We looked at each other a minute. She really was beautiful, even with the blotchy skin, red eyes and double chin. "Thank you for that," I said. "Good luck with the rest of your pregnancy. I'll make sure Wanda sees your notes." I opened the door, then looked back. "You can do this, Melissa. Give birth. Take care of a baby. You know more than you think."

And then I left, hoping never to see her in the office again.

Wanda came in a half hour later, her cheeks glowing from exertion, and I updated her on Melissa. "You're a better woman than I am," she said. "Second time seeing your husband's pregnant wife? Carol, let's find a medal to give Lillie, okay?"

"I'm actually fine with martinis," I said.

"Carol, schedule drinks this week for the three of us," Wanda amended, flashing her smile. "Make it dinner. Someone's birthday is next week."

"I know, I know," I said. "Forty-two."

"What a sexy age," said Carol. "Forty-two. Enjoy it before you hit menopause, Lillie."

The rest of the day was fast and busy and satisfying. We'd seen thirteen patients by the end of the day, and Wanda and Carol and I sat in the waiting room for a few minutes, talking about who would need what in the coming week. No babies were due this week or next, so we didn't expect any late-night calls, which was convenient, because my family was taking me out for an early birthday dinner, since Hannah would be at a wedding planners' conference on my actual day.

My birthday was one of the traditions Melissa and Brad had broken—we'd always had a big dinner at Vanessa and Charles's house in Orleans, which made my mother seethe (not that she offered, mind you). It would be the first birthday in twenty years without Brad and his parents, the first birthday dinner Dylan wouldn't be able to attend, the first birthday without Beatrice. I'd written her a letter last week, missing her a bit. It was nice to be able to tell her that. Maybe Beatrice and I had more of a bond than I'd ever admitted before.

ᐁ

I went home, showered and put on some makeup, including some red lipstick Beatrice had given me for Christmas. Wow. It was red, all right. She had a point about it . . . I looked rather fabulous, like a 1940s pinup girl. What the heck. I managed a cat's eye on the third try and put my hair up in a funky twist. I had a white dress with red polka dots somewhere in the back of my closet, and yes, even a pair of black heels. Maybe a black belt? Why not?

When I stepped back and looked at myself in the mirror,

I smiled. I'd never be as sleek and sophisticated as Hannah, and I sure would never be as gorgeous as Melissa, but there I was, and I liked me. Maybe I looked a little bit like Minnie Mouse, but she *was* a fashion icon, was she not?

"Wow," said Ben when he knocked at my door. His blue eyes drifted slowly down and up, pausing at the V of my dress, and when he met my eyes again, he was a little . . . flushed. "Okay if I mess up your lipstick?" he asked.

"Definitely okay," I said, and he kissed me, a deep, hot kiss that lit up my insides and made my knees feel deliciously weak. When we disentangled, his mouth was smeared with my signature red.

"Go clean up or my dad will clobber you for kissing his little angel," I said, laughing as I went back into my room to do the same.

We'd chosen Pepe's for the coconut cake, and as Ben and I drove up, I realized I hadn't eaten here since Brad had dumped me the night before graduation. Shit. But you know what? I'd loved Pepe's long before I loved Bradley Fairchild, and I wasn't going to let him ruin my favorite restaurant.

Mom, Dad and Hannah were already there, and the maître d' led us to our table, gabbing and chatting. Given the time of year, it wasn't that crowded. Only a few other tables were occupied, and—

And there was Chase Freeman, sitting with a young woman. A teenager.

"Lillie, where do you want to sit?" asked Hannah, but once again, I was frozen at the sight of the boy who'd tried to rape me.

"Lillie?" said Ben. Then he saw Chase, too, and I swore he growled.

"Uh . . . I'll be right there," I said. I looked at Ben and said, "Go sit down. I've got this."

"I'll come with you," he said, his face locked and hard.

"An old classmate," I said to my family. "I'm gonna say hi." They sat down, Mom muttering something about my sense of timing.

The table was just two away from ours, but Chase still hadn't seen me yet. He seemed to be arguing with the girl, and he jumped as I pulled out a chair and sat down. "Hi," I said. Ben stood next to me, his arms crossed over his chest.

"Jesus! Lillie . . . I—I'm having dinner with my daughter," Chase said.

"Yes, she looks just like you," I said. I extended my hand to the girl. "Lillie Silva," I said. "I went to high school with your father."

"Nice to meet you," she said. "Brielle Freeman."

"Pretty name," I said. "Oh, you got the coconut cake. My favorite."

"Lillie," Chase said, his eyes darting between Ben and me. "I—I—Can you . . . Maybe this isn't the right—"

"Let her talk," Ben said, and his voice was Clint Eastwood scary.

"Guess what I do, Brielle?" I asked. "I'm a midwife."

"Um . . . cool," she said, clearly confused about why I was here.

"Yeah, it is cool. But you know, I take care of any kind of women's health issues. How old are you?"

"Sixteen," she said.

"Uh-huh. Well, is it okay if I give you some information?"

She glanced at her father, who remained mute. "Uh, yeah? Sure, I guess."

"Brielle, one of the things that girls your age often face is date rape," I said, and Chase flinched as if I'd stuck him with a hot poker. "It's unfortunately common. You find yourself at a party, maybe drinking or smoking weed for the first time. Maybe you're on a date with a guy who seems nice. But then all of a sudden, you might find that he thinks you're going to have sex with him."

"Why are you—" she began.

"It's just part of my job. Educating young people about the risks out there. Consent is something that has to be given. Every time. There should never be any doubt that you are consenting. But a lot of boys don't want to listen."

My voice was hard. "A lot of them feel entitled to sex. Maybe they're used to getting what they want. Maybe they're stronger than you are. You can get into a situation you don't want to be in very quickly."

I turned my eyes to Chase, who was staring at his plate, his face burning red. Then I looked back at his daughter, who was silent and listening, her mouth a little open. Ben stood by my side like a piece of granite. "A certain type of boy, Brielle, just assumes he'll get sex. Some of them might try to force you, or tell you that you want it. But even if you were kissing or groping or whatever, you have every right to stop. Every right. You get to say no. No one has the right to put hands on you when you say no. Right, Chase?"

He looked halfway up but was unable to look at his daughter. "Right," he managed, his voice strangled.

"And if that boy won't let you go or gives you a hard time in any way, you punch him in the throat, Brielle. Hard. You call the police. You tell your parents. Because rape is no joking matter. It is a terrifying, life-threatening act of violence."

"I know," she said. "I do know."

"Right, Chase?" I said. "You wouldn't want anyone to hold your daughter down and tell her she wanted sex when she was trying to get away, would you?"

He didn't look up, but a tear dropped onto his napkin.

"Chase?" I demanded.

"No," he whispered. "I would never, ever want that." Of course he wouldn't. But Chase was one of those assholes who only cared about something when it happened in his little circle.

I sat back. "Sorry for the lecture, Brielle, but I try to take every opportunity to tell girls about consent. And boys. Boys need to hear it even more. Do you have a brother?"

"Yeah. He's nine. We . . . we live in Boston with my mom."

Aha. So Chase was divorced. Good. I hoped his wife got everything. "Be a good sister and talk to him about this when the time comes." I stood up. "Well! Good talk! Enjoy your dessert." I went back to my table. Ben stood a second longer, eyes on Chase, then came with me.

"Why did a stranger just lecture me on date rape, Dad?" I heard Brielle ask, and there was something in her voice that told me she knew . . . and it wasn't exactly a surprise. No, there was steel in that voice. "Why would she come to *your* table and launch into that speech?"

I didn't pay attention to his fumbling, stumbling words. A second later, they left, Brielle saying, "Dad? Explain what just happened. Dad!"

"Everything good?" my father asked. My mother's eyes were narrowed and fixed on me like a laser.

"Everything is great," I said. I sat in between Hannah and Ben, across from my parents.

"Everything doesn't seem great," my mother said. "Do you want to tell us something, Liliana?"

I hesitated. But, just as Ben never needed to know the accident caused me to lose a baby, my parents and sister didn't need to know about something that had happened a quarter of a century ago. I was over it. I was *finally* over it.

All these years, and I'd only talked about my near rape a few weeks ago. All these years of buried fear and rage and shame. The assault—because that's what it had been, no matter that I'd gotten away, no matter that I'd willingly stumbled into his bedroom—had been secondary to the car accident and my injuries, I'd always told myself.

I never focused on *why* I'd been in Ben's truck.

I hadn't realized that, by burying that night so deep that I never spoke about it, I'd created some kind of . . . link to Chase Freeman. I'd given him power over me, let my fear from that event prevent me from dating for *years* afterward. No wonder I'd picked Brad, who'd seemed so gentle—who *had* been so gentle—so unintimidating. The kind of guy who'd never give me trouble, never physically scare me. We used to joke that I was stronger than he was, because it was true. Brad had been the kind of guy I could beat in a fight. Who would always follow my lead in bed and in life (until he didn't anymore). He was not a strong man in any sense of the word, and maybe that was exactly why I'd picked him.

"The only thing I want to tell you," I said, "is that I'm very happy to be with my family."

"Hmm," my mother said. Dad stared at me, and thankfully, the waitress brought me a martini.

"I ordered that for you," Hannah said. "Same kind I drink, so you know it's top of the line." She smiled and squeezed my hand. "Oh, hang on, before we toast Lillie, just one second." She pulled out her phone, tapped it a few times, and my son's face appeared via FaceTime.

"Dylan!" I said, my eyes filling with happy tears. "Hi, baby!"

"Hi, Mom! Happy birthday!"

How sweet that Hannah had thought of this! How adorable was my son? We chatted and laughed, and I was toasted, and we sipped our drinks, Dylan drinking Gatorade and saying he loved me before hanging up.

And all through this, from the moment he'd sat next to me, Ben Hallowell held my hand. It wasn't until dinner was served that he let go. Then, when Dad was cutting into his steak, my father said, "When are the two of you gonna tell us you're dating?"

"What?" Mom yelped. "Oh, my God, Lillie, a fisherman?"

"Marry your father, they say," Hannah murmured. "Whoops. Too soon to mention the M word. Sorry."

Ben and I looked at each other. He shrugged. I smiled, and Ben looked at my dad. "Your daughter's not quite ready for dating," he said, giving me a wink. "But when she is, I'll be first in line."

Dad looked up from his beef. "About damn time," he said. "About damn time."

CHAPTER 33

Lillie

It was not my plan to be Melissa's midwife, but God had the last laugh. Wanda had gone to Jamaica for an uncle's funeral, and Melissa called after her water broke, panic in her voice, Brad yelling in the background.

That was thirty-seven hours ago. Way too much time with my ex-husband. He was rather . . . useless, fluttering around, getting in the way, just the way he'd been whenever Dylan was sick as a child. At one point, a mere fifteen minutes after they'd arrived, he told Melissa, "Just breathe the baby out," which earned him a smack in the face with her flailing hand. But it wasn't until he said, "I don't remember *you* making such a fuss, Lillie," that Melissa and I both agreed that Brad needed to take a long walk outside. Over the course of the day, he'd taken several. Unfortunately, he was back now, and Melissa was at the pushing stage, though she was exhausted and wrung out.

"That's it, Melissa, you're doing so well," I said, smiling at her. (I know. It was weird for me, too.) "Great job. Take a couple deep breaths, and give me a nice, strong push."

She did, gripping the pull bar and heaving herself forward,

grunting. "I can't do it," she said. "Lillie, if I die, will you raise Ophelia and my baby?"

"Sounds good to me," Ophelia said from the corner where she'd been hiding.

"You're not going to die, Melissa," I said, almost fondly. "Okay, another contraction. Relax your shoulders, relax your legs and just bear down, really strong. Good girl."

Then I checked to see where the baby was in the birth canal.

Shit.

"I can see the head!" Brad said, sticking his face down near mine. "Babe! The head is coming!"

"Brad, I need you to step back," I said firmly. "Melissa?" She lay back, panting. "The baby is breech, honey. That means it's coming butt first."

"No," said Brad. "I just *saw* the head, Lillie."

"It wasn't the *head*, Bridiot. Brad. Sorry. Go stand with Ophelia." I pushed the help button on the bed. "It's gonna be okay, Melissa. Hang in there."

"Is my baby okay?" she asked, and her voice was so small.

"Absolutely." I held the doppler on her abdomen, and there was the heartbeat, nice and strong. Out of the corner of my eye, I saw a movement, and then Ophelia was standing next to Melissa.

"It'll be okay, Missy," she said, biting her bottom lip.

Melissa clutched her hand and tried to smile, but another contraction gripped her and she pushed. The baby came a few centimeters closer. "No need to rush this, Melissa. Take a little rest in between contractions, honey."

Jane opened the door. "I'm here."

"We have a frank breech here. Can you assist?" I asked.

"Yep. I'll get Isabel," Jane said. "Back in a flash."

"I thought the head was down," Melissa said, panting. "You said it was down!"

"Sometimes, the baby turns at the last minute. It's not a problem, Melissa. You can do this."

"You got this, Missy," Ophelia said.

It would just be harder. Another contraction, and the baby came closer. Brad was hovering behind me. "That *is* the butt," he said, since I obviously needed male confirmation of this fact.

Jane and Isabel came in. "We're just here to watch," Jane said. "Looks like you're doing an amazing job."

"Total champion," Isabel agreed. But they were here just in case.

"Jesus, she's stretched out," Brad muttered. "It doesn't even look like a vag—"

"You're doing great, Melissa. Nice push here," I said as the baby's butt emerged. The trick with breech was to let nature do the work and not pull the baby. Melissa was whimpering in pain. "Just breathe. Take a deep breath and hold it, then let it out nice and slow." Brad was supposed to be helping with breathing, but . . .

"Nice and slow," Ophelia repeated. "Doing great, Missy." She looked at me and made a face of horror. Well, this would keep her from having sex too young, that was for sure.

Another contraction, a few more centimeters. It was a girl, I could see. Her legs were still tucked up, so I gently slid my finger under her left knee and bent it, and it popped out.

"Jesus!" Brad said.

"Dad, why don't you step aside?" Isabel said as I swept the other leg out. Nice and chunky, those legs. Now Melissa had the lower half of the baby pretty much dangling out of her. "Easy, now, Melissa," I said. "You're amazing. Almost there. Don't push right now . . . just let your uterus do the work. You're doing great."

Gently, slowly, I rotated the baby and slid one finger in to help the shoulder deliver. "Nice job," Isabel murmured. Another slow rotation to the other side, and the other shoulder delivered smoothly. All that was left was the head.

"My baby," Melissa said. "Oh, my God, my baby."

"Nice size, too," Isabel said. "You're a hero, Melissa."

"I am never getting pregnant," Ophelia said.

Now was the hardest part. Because the head was the biggest part of the baby, and it was coming last, it wouldn't be molded, the way a headfirst baby's would after such a long labor. Melissa would need help here. "Nice big push, Melissa," I said, and she did, full of renewed energy. When the baby's neck and hairline appeared, I slid my forearm under the baby, positioning my index finger against her right cheek, my middle finger against her left. Then I rested my other hand on the baby's back, my forefinger and ring finger over each shoulder, my middle finger at the base of the baby's skull.

"I'm gonna give a tiny bit of help here," Isabel said. "Just going to put some pressure on your belly, Melissa." She looked down at me. "Ready?"

"Yep. Give us a nice push, Melissa! Last one!"

She pushed, keening. Isabel pressed down, and I pressed my fingers on the baby's cheeks, angled my arms up to maneuver the head, and just like that, she was born.

"It's a girl!" I said, putting her on Melissa's chest.

"My baby! Oh, my God, my baby is here! Hi, baby!"

"A girl?" Brad said from somewhere behind me. "Oh, wow, babe!" I felt him move closer to me to look between Melissa's legs. "Holy God," he muttered, because yes, she was a little gory at the moment. She'd just given birth, and that baby was not small! "Will she ever be normal again?"

"Sir? Let's have you sit down over here," Jane said as he wobbled.

"I'll clean her up," Isabel murmured, and I stood up, my lower legs asleep from having been down there so long, and went to Melissa's free side.

"You did it," I said, and she lifted her shining face to look at me. "That was really something, Melissa. I'm proud of you."

"Thank you, Lillie," she said. Tears were streaming down her face. "That means so much to me."

Ophelia was looking at the baby quizzically. "Guess I'm the pretty one," she said. "Hey, there, baby. I'm your sister."

"What's her name?" I asked.

"Orialis Melody Spencer Fairchild," Melissa announced.

"Oh, God, Missy," Ophelia said. "Orialis? It sounds like a medication." I couldn't help snorting.

"It goes with Ophelia," Melissa said. "And her middle name is Melody. Yours is Harmony. Get it?"

"I get it," Ophelia said, rolling her eyes, but she was smiling, too.

Orialis was . . . well, all babies are beautiful, right? She had very thick hair, but also a receding hairline, a hooked nose and puffy lips, and . . . well . . . hey! She'd been being squished by contractions for a day and a half. She'd pretty up.

"She looks like Nicolas Cage," Ophelia pronounced. "And she looks like she could beat me in a fight."

"Oh, stop," said Melissa. "She's beautiful." She was drunk on hormones, adrenaline and exhaustion.

Orialis Melody Spencer Fairchild weighed nine pounds, three ounces and was twenty-two inches long. With her genes, she would turn gorgeous, I had no doubt. Still, there was a wee bit of pleasure in handing her to Brad after I'd swaddled her and watching a look of confusion come over his face.

"She *does* look like Nicolas Cage," he said. "After a bender."

"I think she looks exactly like you," I said, keeping my tone warm.

"She's huge," he said. "Is this normal?"

"She's on the larger side, which makes Melissa's delivery even more heroic, but she seems perfectly healthy," I said. "Family picture?"

"Not . . . not right now," Melissa said. She glanced at *Bradley*. "Maybe just of Orialis, Ophelia and me," she said, reaching to hold her child. "Hashtag girl-power."

"There's still time to rethink the name," Ophelia said. "Another Shakespeare name? Goneril, maybe? Cressida? Anything would be better than Orialis."

I sure did like that kid. I winked at her, and she grinned back.

"It goes with Ophelia quite nicely," Melissa said, staring at her daughter. "Ophelia, come get in this picture. Bradley? Can you take a few?"

After fifteen minutes, I offered to take a picture of the four of them, and they accepted. But I could read Brad's body language, and with Nic Cage's face staring up from an infant's body, I had a feeling that Brad wasn't going to make the best girl dad to Orialis.

⌣

Sure enough, a month after he became a father for the second time, my ex-husband knocked on my door, suitcase in hand. It was nearly a year to the day after he'd told me he wanted a divorce.

"Are you here to tell me about the church of the Latter-day Saints, or are you selling essential oils?" I asked, not opening the door.

"Lillie. How are you?"

"Fine," I said. I didn't open the door. Zeus stood at my side, wagging, the dopey dog. "Attack," I whispered. He looked at me and smiled his doggy smile.

"Can I come in?" Brad asked. "I have a lot to say."

"You can say it from there," I said.

"I guess I deserve that," he said, looking up at me from beneath a furrowed brow, his freaky blue eyes penitent. "Lillie, there are no excuses for what I did, but there are reasons."

I rolled my eyes.

"I'd like to apologize," he said. "I've been doing a lot of thinking, and, well . . . I don't think Melissa and I are going to work out."

"You're leaving your wife a month after she gave birth?" I asked.

"It was a mutual agreement," he said.

"So she kicked you out."

"I like to think of it as coming home to my *true* wife. I had a breakdown, Lillie. I haven't been myself. I've always loved you. I miss our family. I want to live with you and Dylan again. Share the holidays again. My parents miss you so much, and I . . . I've learned so much about myself."

I looked at my watch. "You done?" I asked.

"So can we try again? Please? Twenty years is worth a second chance, as you said."

Looking at his familiar, handsome face, I did remember the now-distant longing for the past. I thought I'd done such a great job creating our life, our home, our family. I remembered feeling so special because Brad Fairchild of the amazing blue eyes and classic bone structure, this son of Beacon Hill, had chosen me, the down-to-earth daughter of a hardworking fisherman.

"You never deserved me, Brad," I said. "And you know what? You didn't deserve Melissa, either. I'm glad she dumped you."

"But you hate her!" he said.

"Nah. Not anymore," I answered. "As for you, I'm sorry, Brad. You're just not worth it." I smiled. "But we'll always be Dylan's parents."

"Well, where am I supposed to go?" Brad asked. "Can I at least rent the studio from you?"

"The prenup was that good, huh? I'm guessing you can't *afford* to rent the studio, and even if you could, I wouldn't have you here. Go home to your mommy," I told him. "Now. You're on Silva property, and you're trespassing. Time for you to go."

With a disappointed sigh and a tragic face, Brad turned around and trudged back to his Jaguar.

Later, I would learn that Brad did indeed get nothing other than the gifts his second wife had given him. The car, some clothes, his expensive watch. He could visit the baby for twenty-four hours each week, but after a month of living with his parents in Orleans, he moved to Brooklyn to start over and find joy there, I guess.

Meanwhile, I'd taken an advisory position two days a week at Brigham and Women's Hospital for the summer, overseeing their nurse-midwife training. Wanda had recommended me, and it would be extra money. The drive was long, but I listened to audiobooks and tried not to flip off too many fellow Masshole drivers. And . . . well, it got me off-Cape and opened the world a little more for me, and I didn't think that was a bad thing. It would be a little less time with Dylan, but it would help pay off my debt, too.

Except one day, when I checked on how much I still owed, I found the balance was zero. I drove to Seamen's Bank immediately, still in my scrubs. "Something happened with my mortgage," I said. "It's listed as nothing, but I owe at least three hundred grand."

The bank manager, Mark, looked me up. "Oh, yes," he said. "That was paid off. Not by you, I'm guessing?"

"No! I don't . . . Not by me."

He clicked on the keyboard. "Well, it *is* paid off."

"Does it say by whom?"

More clicks. "I'm afraid it doesn't. A money order was sent in with no return address."

"So some rich person just swooped in and paid off my mortgage?" I asked.

"It appears so."

"I . . . That doesn't seem legal. How would someone else know what I owed?"

"Well, what's really private these days? Someone knew your account number and that we held your mortgage. It's legal." He smiled. "Congratulations."

I went home in a state of utter confusion. Dad didn't have the money. Neither did Ben, plus he had a daughter in med school. If he had extra money, he'd give it to her, as he should. Hannah? Possibly, but I couldn't imagine her doing that without asking me first. I did have my pride, after all. Too much of it, probably.

Melissa? She was the only one I knew with that much money. If it was Melissa, I couldn't take it for many reasons, not the least of which was I'd been her midwife. But even at her richest, I still couldn't imagine her just giving away three hundred grand and change.

But my mortgage *was* paid off.

It couldn't have been Brad. The Fairchilds, in a fit of guilt? Hell, they hadn't given us much when I was in the family, let alone now. It wasn't their style. A family vacation, sure. College tuition? That was the parents' job.

I grilled my father and Hannah, then Wanda to see if we had, I don't know, a millionaire drug-dealing patient who needed to unload some cash. I asked Dylan if his grandparents had said anything about money lately. They had not. Chase Freeman, out of guilt? But he'd just declared bankruptcy, having lost his job more than a year ago, according to Beth.

For now, it would remain a mystery.

Dylan came home for the summer, and it was wonderful. He went to meet his baby sister, pronounced her "durable" and said she was pretty cute. Because even though his father had ditched both his kids, my son, my wonderful boy, would never turn his back on his family. He was a Silva, after all, no matter what his last name was.

Then, one day en route back from the hospital, I stopped in Orleans to hit up the gorgeous produce at Friends' Marketplace, since I was making dinner for my parents, Hannah, Dylan and Ben. I meandered through the aisle, sniffing tomatoes and fondling eggplants, then rounded the corner and jolted to a stop.

There was my former mother-in-law.

"Lillie!" she cried. "Oh, Lillie, how *are* you?" She came in to hug me, and I stepped back behind my cart, avoiding her arms. "Oh," she said, her expression crashing to the floor.

I just looked at her. She had aged, finally—her face had suddenly realized it was well past seventy and had dropped an inch in the last year. She looked . . . tired.

"Well, of course you're entitled to be angry," she said. "Of course you are." I still said nothing. "We're closing the

Cape office of Fairchild Properties, did you know? And we sold our house here. It just . . . It didn't seem . . . anyway. You look wonderful, Lillie."

I searched my heart for something to say and came up empty. If she had been the mysterious benefactor, she could tell me. Even if she had been—which I doubted—it wouldn't undo the past year.

For two decades, this woman had been better than a mother. She'd been so woven into my life I used to pray that she'd live to be a hundred and ten.

Now, she was a stranger. She had loved me, I did know that. But she had abandoned me, too. I didn't hate her, of course. But I had already mourned her, and I wasn't going to do it again.

"Take care of yourself, Vanessa," I said gently. "Take good care."

Then I turned my cart and headed for the checkout.

Ben was sitting on the steps when I got home, waiting for me, Zeus at his side. His face lit up—well, both their faces lit up.

"Hi, boys," I said as Ben relieved me of the groceries.

"How was your day?" he asked.

"Pretty great," I said. "And yours?"

"Pretty great, too. Especially now." He gave me his bad-boy look, full of promises and fun, and opened the front door. Just then, a bird swooped over our heads, right into the nest behind the light fixture.

"The swallows!" I said. "They're back! Hi, Mama Swallow!" She looked at me with her bright black eyes, then fluttered away to get more mud for her nest.

God, it was good to see her. My eyes were wet with happy tears.

Ben and I carried the groceries down to the kitchen, Zeus sniffing helpfully.

"Put me to work, Chef," Ben said.

Ben and I were a thing. We hadn't slept together yet, though dang, I was looking forward to that day. "When you get your shit together," he'd said fondly, after we'd made out at his place for an hour and a half and I was so weak with lust I could barely stand. "When your head is clear."

My head was feeling very clear these days.

I gave Ben three onions to chop and got to work on the garlic, clams and butter. God, I loved cooking for my family. Dylan, Mom and Dad, Hannah and Ben. Our little circle. Once, I'd dreaded my family getting together. I'd thrown myself into being as much a Fairchild as I'd ever been a Silva. And in this past year, I'd found that the Fairchilds were not what I'd thought they were.

My parents and Hannah came in, Mom and Dad arguing about something. Hannah went straight to the fridge and poured a big glass of wine. "Hey, Ben, hey, Lils," she said. "Remind me never to drive Mom anywhere ever again."

"So reminded," I said. "Want to help? You can slice this eggplant."

"Where's Dylan?" she asked.

"I think he's out in the kayak," I said, jerking my chin in the direction of the pond.

"Good. Ben, could you run interference with our parents for a few?" Hannah asked. "I need to talk to Lillie."

"You got it, gorgeous," he said, giving her that look.

"He's so hot," Hannah said as he walked up the stairs.

"She's got a point," he called, and I laughed as I nudged minced garlic in the frying pan.

"So I have some news," Hannah said. "I hope it won't upset you, Lils."

"What? Are you sick?" I blurted.

"No, no. I'm perfectly healthy," she said. "But . . . I'm . . ." She half grimaced, half smiled. "Well, things are . . . It's just . . ."

"Hannah! Just rip the Band-Aid off," I said, putting down my spatula.

She looked at me. "I'm moving to France, Lillie. I miss Beatrice so much, and this wedding business is getting . . . exhausting. She has a contact in event planning for Chanel, and . . . well, I guess I want more in my life. More adventure, you know?" She looked out over the pond, her eyes filled with tears. "I think it's time to try something else."

I closed my mouth, wanting to protest. We'd just started getting closer after all these years. Why would she want to leave now? It wasn't fair.

No. It was. It was perfect for her. "The Cape was never big enough for you, Hannah," I said. "You belong in Paris." I hugged her, my eyes filling. "As long as you come back to visit at least twice a year."

"And as long as you promise to visit me twice a year, too," she said. "The worst part of this is leaving you."

"But the best part is, you don't have to see Mom and Dad playing footsie with each other."

She wiped her eyes. "Tell me about it. Jeez Louise, you just can't predict anything."

"We can still talk all the time," I said. "We're both having new adventures, all that good stuff. Oh, my God, I can't wait to meet your much younger French lover," I added. "Jean-Paul, you think? Or Claude-Philippe?"

She laughed and hugged me, my big sister, and for a minute, it was just like when we were kids and I felt safe and special because of her. Hannah, who'd come back to me after all this time.

"Are you sure you didn't pay off my loan?" I asked.

"I told you, no. I wish I had. But no, it wasn't me."

"What are you girls talking about? How abused you were as children?" Mom came into the kitchen. "Do tell." She looked at us. "Are you crying? You really *were* talking about me, weren't you?"

"Believe it or not, we weren't," I said.

"I'm moving to Paris," Hannah said.

Mom raised her eyebrows. "How very exciting. I'm sure Beatrice will be thrilled. Go tell your father. He, on the other hand, will be heartbroken."

Hannah went upstairs, and Mom looked at me critically. "Does it ever get old, channeling your dead grandmother, sweating over the stove and martyring yourself?" she asked.

I laughed out loud. "No, Mom. It never gets old."

"You are a mystery," she said, sipping her wine.

I turned down the heat and looked at her. Yep. There it was, a little twinkle. "Thanks for paying off my mortgage," I said.

"I have no idea what you're talking about," she answered.

"Mm-hmm. Thank you anyway."

"Well, Liliana, if you're going to stay in this ridiculous, dank little house, you may as well own it free and clear. When are we eating? I'm famished."

And that was that. Nevertheless, I took off my apron, came around the island and hugged her.

"Okay," she said. "That's enough." She patted me on the shoulder, as a person who feared dogs would pet a Great Dane. "Always so sentimental, Liliana. It's a wonder you can make it through the day."

Maybe paying off the mortgage was an apology. Maybe it was simply a gift. Probably, it was love. You never could tell with Mom.

Dad took Hannah's news harder and cried a little, but told her he was proud and yes, he'd visit. Dylan was psyched that he'd have a place to crash in Paris (!), and Ben told her it was fantastic.

Life would be so different in the next year. I'd be working in Boston, Hannah would be on another continent, and my parents were talking about living together at Mom's house on Commercial Street. Dylan had a job lined up in Yellowstone next summer, and as for me . . . well, I had a really nice guy who I think probably loved me.

"I think you probably love me," I told him later, after Dylan had gone out with his pals and the family had left and we were alone on the porch, listening to the birds.

"I think you probably love me, too," he said easily.

"Oh, no. You go first."

He looked at the ceiling. "You got me. I've loved you since you were seventeen and all busted up and broken and brave."

"Wow. That's a long time not to make a move," I said.

"I didn't know you'd run off and get married." He glanced at me. "Or if you'd want to marry some smelly fisherman like your dad."

"Smelly fishermen are my favorite," I said. "Ask me in a year or two."

"Will do."

Sometimes, your life shatters when you least expect it. Car accidents, lost pregnancies, divorce, loneliness. People you loved could disappoint you, and other people came through when you never expected it.

And sometimes, happiness just rains down on you out of the clear blue sky.

Acknowledgments

A thousand thanks to Carin Tripodina, PhD, for sharing her knowledge, and for putting me in touch with Michelle Killingsworth, CNM, who walked me through the details of midwifery. A thousand thanks, Michelle! Without the firsthand information and wisdom of these two, I would not have been able to write this book. Any mistakes or exaggerations are mine.

Thanks also to Rachel of Daylynn Designs, for helping me envision the fascinating, gorgeous world of high-end event planning. I'm so glad your couples are not like Hannah's.

To Stephanie Sykes, program and outreach coordinator at the Cape Cod Commercial Fishermen's Alliance, thanks for giving me such great information on scallop fishing. I will think of you and the fleet every time I order my favorite seafood.

To Maria Carvainis, thank you for hand-holding supreme during a difficult year and being such a good friend. To the entire team at Berkley, thank you for the innumerable things you do for me.

Thanks also to Mary Ellen Pettit and Robyn Carr for so many wonderful conversations and laughs. Hilary Higgins Murray, Joss Dey and Jennifer Iszkiewicz, when you look up "best friends" in the dictionary, there you are, you gorgeous creatures! Hilary, extra points for being the world's best sister. Thanks to my sainted mother for always thinking my ideas are great.

This book is, in many ways, about parenthood. When I started writing my first book, my kids were adorable toddlers who took long naps and went to bed at seven o'clock. Today, they're adults and have lives of their own, and every day, I think about how wonderful they are and how lucky I am. To the Princess and Dearest Son, and also the World's Best Son-in-Law, thank you for being the absolute best. I'm so proud of you, I have so much fun with you, and I love you all so much.

Terence Keenan, you are the love of my life. Marrying you was the smartest, best, happiest thing I've ever done.

Finally, thank you, readers, for spending your time with this book. Thank you from the bottom of my heart.

Out of the Clear Blue Sky

Kristan Higgins

READERS GUIDE

Discussion Questions

1. It's not uncommon for a marriage to fall apart just as children leave home as young adults. More than one person has been told the week or even day of their youngest child's graduation from high school that their partner is leaving them. Why do you think that happens? Do you think men initiate a breakup more than women?

2. Why do you think Lillie married Brad? She thought they had a strong marriage, but in hindsight, she sees things she didn't before. Was it all bad, or did Brad change?

3. When Brad tells Lillie he's leaving her, she keeps eating the coconut cake. Why do you think she does that? And in the middle of their fight, she and Brad both pause to joke about a song they both love. Why do you think that happens?

4. They say revenge is a dish best served cold. Lillie disagrees and takes bitter delight in some of her actions while Brad is still living at home and after he moves in with Melissa. What did you think about her ways of leaving her mark, so to speak? Was she justified in these actions, or did you think she was being petty?

5. Melissa is a woman who seems to have no remorse about moving in on another woman's husband. She's completely confident that she'll get Brad, and she's right. Have you ever known someone like Melissa, who dismisses other people's feelings in order to get what she wants? Which of Melissa's qualities did you admire, if any, and why?

6. Motherhood is a recurring theme in this book. Lillie is well aware that her son is moving away from her both geographically and emotionally—as it should be, she says, but which is a painful experience nonetheless. Her own mother seemed to barely tolerate her. Melissa uses Ophelia almost as a prop, but their relationship changes as well. Hannah has Beatrice, and Lillie adores her mother-in-law. There are so many different mother-child relationships in this book. Which do you think are best and worst, and why?

7. Lillie's anger at Brad for leaving her is based on her feeling that the divorce would destroy their family, and the family's future. So many people deal with this changed dynamic after a divorce, from the former in-laws to the kids and grandkids. Did you relate to Lillie's protectiveness of her family and its future? Could you stay after infidelity to preserve your family? Do you know a couple who's stayed friends after a divorce?

8. How did the various Cape settings play a role in the book and affect the characters? Lillie never wanted to live anywhere else; her mother hated the house on Herring Pond and moved to the more glamorous place in Provincetown. Hannah makes a healthy living as a Cape Cod wedding planner; Beatrice leaves after thirty years there. Melissa moves to Wellfleet because she thinks she can stand out more. What did their various views say about the women in this book?

9. Lillie survives an attempted sexual assault but feels powerless to turn Chase in or even tell anyone about it. With the Me Too movement, so many similar stories have come to light. Do you think things have changed in our culture since Lillie was a teen so that girls feel more empowered to report?

10. Discuss the way Melissa uses people—her college boyfriend, Dennis, Ophelia, Brad and others. What were some other choices she could have made, given her background? Does she have more than her looks, despite what she thinks? What does she learn in hindsight, if anything? How does her relationship with Ophelia and Kaitlyn grow during the book? Did you have any sympathy for Kaitlyn?

11. Brad repeatedly asserts that he deserves joy at the expense of all other considerations, which enrages Lillie. What do you think Brad means by that? Do you think he is entitled to leave the marriage for this reason? Is he more than a cliché of a middle-aged man? Was Lillie as good a partner as she thought?

12. Why do you think Lillie's parents got married? How did their marriage affect Lillie's choice in life and marriage? How do you think it affected Hannah?

13. Lillie assumes Hannah is perfectly content with her life but finds out that's not quite true. Have you ever learned something about your sibling or close friend that shocked you?

14. Lillie and Melissa's relationship changed a lot over the course of the book. By the end, do you think they were friends, or could become friends? Have you ever known a situation where the first spouse becomes friends with the second?

15. Later in the novel, Lillie says she likes living alone, which surprises her. What do you think she enjoys? What does she still struggle with? Have you ever lived alone, either by choice or because of someone else's choice? How did you feel?

16. The author leads us to believe Lillie will develop a true romantic partnership with Ben after the story ends. But does she need that to be happy? Do you think the novel ends happily for her as it is?

17. Many characters in this book do things that anger other characters, but most of them are forgiven by the end in one way or another. What about Melissa and her sister, Kaitlyn? In the end, though Melissa loves her, she does not forgive her or find a way to have an ongoing relationship with her. Why do you think that happened? Do you think there are some people you just can't mend fences with? Why?

Keep reading for a preview of

A Little Ray of Sunshine

Coming soon from Berkley!

Harlow

I didn't ask for this," I said. "Why are you tormenting me, Addie?"

"It's a lunch date," my sister said. "Don't be such a gutless wonder."

"Cancel him." I continued placing books on the new releases table of Open Book, the store I owned with my grandfather. It was the second week of June, and Cape Cod's tourism season was just about to explode. "I'm very busy."

"Addison, stunning shoes," said Destiny, the one employee not related to me and our resident fashionista. I glanced at my sister's shoes . . . pink leather ankle boots with snake-skin straps. Tacky, if you asked me, but I tended to wear Converse most of the time.

"Gucci," Addison said proudly. "Fifteen hundred dollars. Anyway, Harlow, he's already on his way to the Ice House. It's too late to back out. I'm doing you a favor. You want what I have. Everyone does."

Destiny gave me a pained look and went to the back to get more boxes of books. "Goggy?" asked Imogen, my two-year-old niece. "Goggy!" She was strapped in her stroller more securely than an astronaut about to take off. Her pudgy little hands reached toward my dog. Ollie was our resident literary mascot (full name: Oliver Twist), a little black-and-tan mutt I'd rescued. He whined, rightfully wary of my niece.

"Doggy is dirty, Imogen," Addie said. "Dirty dog. Nasty."

"Oliver is *not* dirty," I said, slicing open another box. Oh, yay, the new Susan Elizabeth Phillips book. "He's afraid of your demon child."

"She's an angel," Addie lied cheerfully. "Harlow, I'm happily married, have two beautiful daughters and live in a stunning home."

"Yay for you."

"You're dying of envy. You, too, Cynthia," she said to our cousin, the third partner of Open Book. Cynthia hissed in response. For once, I agreed with her. "You need to take action to fulfill your dreams," Addie continued. "Put on some lipstick." She pulled out a tube and offered it to me. "You can't stand him up. What would that do to his ego?"

"For one, I hate lipstick. For two, why would I care about his ego? You go. Explain that you're a pushy, irritating sister who thinks she found the secret to happiness."

"I have, though."

I sighed. However, I *was* starving, and the Ice House had the best burgers on the East Coast.

"Go," said Addison. "I can hear your stomach growling. You can eat and maybe meet your future husband."

"Some of us are happily single, Addie. Right, Cynthia?"

"I prefer not to discuss my private life, but yes, I'm fine with my own company." My brother had suggested that Cynthia ate her first husband, praying mantis–style.

My stomach growled again. The image of a massive, juicy burger tipped the scales. "Okay. But he's normal, right?"

"He seemed normal enough on his profile. If he's a serial killer, he hid it well."

"They *all* hide it well," I said. "That's the reason they're serial killers."

"You read too much," said my sister.

"I own a bookstore, and it's hardly a character flaw."

Cynthia stomped past. "That baby is chewing on a sixty-five-dollar book," she said. Imogen had wriggled a shoulder free and was laying waste to a book on photography.

"She's very advanced," Addie said. "Aren't you, Imogen?"

"Is she rich, though?" I asked. "Can she afford what she's eating?" My niece smiled at me, then spit out some paper.

"Did I hear someone say I had a date for lunch?" Grandpop asked, wandering in from the back room. "Wonderful!"

"Can you all just go?" Cynthia asked. "This is hardly a professional discussion. And try not to take too long. The rest of us are also entitled to a lunch break."

"Go ahead," said Destiny, coming back into the room with a box in her arms. She set it down with a thud. "Hardcover James Patterson," she said.

"Wish Auntie Harlow luck, Imogen," Addie said. "Tell her not to bite the nice man."

"Pay for that book," I told my sister, grabbing my backpack from under the counter.

"I love lunch!" Grandpop said merrily. "And I'm *famished*! What should I have?"

"A cheeseburger," I said.

"Too much fat and salt," Cynthia said.

"So? He's ninety," I said, pushing the door open. Grandpop could eat whatever he wanted. My grandmother had been gone for three years now, and if a cheeseburger killed Grandpop, well, was there a better way to go? "Come on, Grandpop."

The screen door banged behind us. Open Book was that store people dreamed of owning. Housed in the three-story Victorian that had been in the family since 1843, the store had been founded in the 1980s by my grandmother. Inside, the store was cheery and snug with lots of alcoves and cozy corners, a fireplace and places to sit, a little coffee bar and gift area. The children's section was in the sunny, enclosed front porch.

I slid my arm through my grandfather's, since he tended to wander. Grandpop was my favorite person, and it truly was a beautiful day to be out—clear blue sky, a breeze off the water. Main Street was in peak form . . . pink, red and white rhododendrons just now coming into full glory, the crooked old buildings awash in character and charm.

Wellfleet was my hometown, and my three sisters and brother all lived in the area. Our parents owned Long Pond Arts, a well-respected gallery that featured Mom's work. Addison was a stay-at-home mom, Winnie an event planner. Lark was doing her residency at Hyannis Hospital and Robbie was a boat mechanic. We five Smith kids knew everyone.

I was the quiet one. The eldest. The responsible one. For the past ten years, I'd lived in an apartment over the bookstore, kept an eye on Grandpop and was happily turning into the clichéd bookish spinster. It was a good, quiet life, and I planned to keep it that way.

"Speaking of dates," Grandpop said, "I think I want to get married again. I do! Yesterday, I took a nap under the porch for two hours, and no one even missed me."

"I wondered where you'd gone," I said. "Why under the porch?"

"It looked *very* cozy."

I nodded, understanding the allure. Dark, private, cool . . . I might have to give it a try.

"Will you help me find someone?" he asked.

"Sure! What are you looking for in a person?" I asked.

"Someone who can talk loud enough for me to hear, first of all."

"If you wore your hearing aids, we could widen the net," I said. He chuckled. "You're serious about this, Grandpop?"

"Why not? Life is short! Actually, life is horribly long, Harlow! I thought I'd be dead and buried at least twenty years ago!"

"Well, I'm glad you're not," I said.

"Did you know," Grandpop said, "last week, I went for a drive and forgot where I was!" He announced it as if it were a delightful surprise. "I got lunch somewhere . . . Orleans, maybe? That crowded place with all the signs?"

"The Land Ho! probably," I said.

"Yes! That one! Anyway, after I ate, I was feeling a little sleepy, so I got in my car and took a nap. But it turns out it wasn't my car! The owners were very nice, though. A little surprised to find me, but they were very friendly."

"Didn't we talk about you not driving anymore, Grandpop?" I asked. "Cynthia and I can take you wherever you want to go."

"We did talk about it," he said. "I just felt like taking a spin. Gosh, it's a lovely day, isn't it?" Grandpop asked. "I love August."

"Me too," I said. "But it's June."

"Is that right? Goodness. Time flies." He smiled at me, making me glad he was coming along.

We got to the Ice House, and Beth, the owner and a member of my book club, waved to me. "Just you and your handsome grandfather today, Harlow?" she asked.

"Oh, aren't you a *charmer*, Beth," Grandpop said. "Are you making a pass at me? I *am* looking to get married again."

"Are you?" Beth said, grinning. "Well, if my husband leaves me, you'd be my first choice. Where would you two like to sit?"

"Actually, I'm meeting someone," I said, grimacing. "Grandpop, would you like to sit at the bar and flirt with Beth here?"

"I would *love* that!" Grandpop exclaimed. "I so enjoy talking to pretty girls!"

"And *I* love talking to charming older men," Beth answered. "Sit wherever you want, Harlow, and Tanner will be over in a few."

I took a seat facing the door so I could see . . . oh, shoot. I didn't know his name. I took out my phone to text Addison, but she'd beat me to it.

Pete Schultz, data analyst, divorced, no kids, likes fishing, boating, the Patriots. He knows you have four incredibly attractive siblings and dropped out of law school. Should be worth a second date.

We'd see about that. Thus far in my adult life, I had not had a meaningful, committed relationship. I wasn't averse to one, but I wasn't looking, either. If, say, Keanu Reeves dropped into the bookstore one day and begged me to marry him, I would definitely consider it.

Tanner, Beth's nephew and my server, came over with menus. I ordered a glass of prosecco to make this meeting more pleasant and the cheeseburger du jour. No need to wait for my, uh, companion. My stomach growled with appreciation.

"Got it," he said.

Destiny texted me. Anything to report?

He's not here, I texted back. Praying for a no-show. Only in this for the cheeseburger.

Ah. My parents had just walked in, holding hands. I waved. They didn't wave back but walked right past me. "Hello, Mother, Father," I said. Mom jumped.

"Oh! Harlow. We didn't see you there," Mom said.

"Hello, honey," Dad said. "Having lunch?"

"Yes," I said. "And you?"

"Also lunch." We smiled at each other.

"Well. Have a good time," Mom said, and off they went to a table in the back where they could play footsies and coo at each other. They were *the* happily married couple of Wellfleet, and while it was nice, it could also be a bit icky. That time they were trying for a quickie in the coatroom at church, for example, just before Esme's baptism, for example.

An average-looking man came into the restaurant. Khaki pants, blue button-down, Nikes. His hair was light brown. He'd make a *great* serial killer, I decided, going with my original instinct. No one would be able to remember that face. "Pete?" I called. "Hi." I gave a little wave.

"Hey!" he said. "Pete Schultz. Great to meet you, Harper!"

"It's Harlow, actually, but hi. Nice to meet you, too."

"Harlow, right, right," he said. "How are you?"

"Doing fine. How are you?" My brain emptied of small talk, something I was quite good at behind the counter of my store.

"I'm good. Cool place." He looked around appreciatively. "Was it once actually an ice house?"

"Yes. Mm-hmm." The building's history was printed on the menu. Pete could read it himself. From the corner, I heard my mom give a sultry laugh at something Dad had said.

"This was indeed an ice house, young man," said my grandfather, walking over. "Back in the day, the ponds on the Cape would have ten or twelve inches of ice come winter. The ice man would cut great chunks of it and store them here, then put them on a cart and go around town. The ladies of the house would leave a number in their windows, letting him know how many pounds of ice they needed! Isn't that interesting?"

"I guess," said Pete, scratching his head, then examining his fingernails. He flicked a little scalp out of his ring fingernail. Nasty. Unfortunately, my burger awaited.

"This is my grandfather," I said. "He's a whiz with history. You should see him at trivia night." Yes, yes, I was that dork who loved trivia nights. We'd been All-Cape champs last year, though we'd lost our strongest science guy to a Florida retirement. But Grady Byrne, a marine biologist and a former classmate, had replaced him in January. I was confident we would win the trophy (again).

"Here's a dating tip, Harlow," Grandpop continued.

"Talk about topics of general interest. Stay away from money, politics and sexual preferences."

"Good advice. Thanks, Grandpop," I said, accustomed to these little tidbits. Beth called him back to the bar, and Grandpop tipped an imaginary hat and left us.

"Your grandfather's a little . . . unfiltered," Pete said.

"My grandfather is *perfect*."

Luckily, Tanner arrived with my cheeseburger. I took an enormous bite and moaned in pleasure, eyes closed. "Uh, I'll have a salad," Pete said. Boring. I took another heavenly bite. "So you own a bookstore?" Pete asked as he watched me eat. "It said so in your profile."

"Mm-hmm," I said, wiping my mouth with my napkin. "Open Book."

"Great name."

"Thanks." I swallowed. "Um, do you like your job, Pete?"

The next fifteen minutes were filled with Pete's description of data integrity. I tried. I did. Not too hard, because that burger was way more interesting, but I gave it a shot. "I'm kind of known for statistical inference," he told me, a fleck of carrot stuck to the left side of his lip. "Not to brag, but I'm kind of famous in my world. My predictive modeling is world-class."

"Wow," I said.

"I know." He smiled proudly.

We chewed in silence. Well, I did, anyway. He sounded like a horse. Ten more minutes? Sadly, Pete wasn't ready to call time of death just yet. "What do you do for fun?" he asked.

"I kayak and paddle board," I said. "Almost every day. I have a dog. Trivia night, as I said. And of course, I read a lot."

He didn't answer, just kept chomping on the salad. "How about you?" I asked. "What do you like to read?"

"I'm not much a reader," he said. So he was dead inside. Got it. "But I do write."

"Most writers I know love to read."

"I dabble in poetry."

Unexpected. "Who are some of your favorites?"

"Gosh. Hard to say." He offered a shy smile.

"I love Mary Oliver," I said. "Amanda Gorman, Robert Frost. I'm on a Rumi kick these days."

Pete tilted his head. "I guess I'd have to say *I'm* my favorite poet, to be honest."

"Oh. Um . . . that's great." From behind me, my parents' murmured sweet talk stopped as they began eavesdropping (or kissing). Grandpop had just left—I imagined he forgot to pay, as was his habit, so I'd have to check with Beth. I ate a french fry.

"Can I read you something I wrote?" Pete asked. "I'd love to have your take on it, since you're in the business."

"We just sell books." You'd be amazed at how many people thought I could help them get published. And yes, we did occasionally sell self-published books by local authors, but it wasn't like we could make anyone a national sensation. "I'm not involved with publishing."

"Sure you are," Pete said. "Let's see if you think this is something your customers would enjoy. Maybe I could do a reading at your store." He lifted his eyebrows suggestively.

Not gonna happen, pal. "Fire away." I drained my prosecco.

Pete reached into his pocket and pulled out a worn-looking piece of paper. "I call this one 'Despair.' "

"Catchy," I said. The date had suddenly gotten more interesting.

"It's about my ex," he said.

Did I have time to fish out my phone and record this? Rosie, my best friend, would love this. "Go for it," I said.

Pete cleared his throat. "'You ruined my life. I thought you'd be my forever wife.' "

Definitely should've asked to record it.

"But you brought me strife. Like a sharp and hacking knife. Cutting through my heart. Instead of cherishing it like a piece of art. And pierced it like a dart." He glanced at me to see if I was paying attention. I was. "You are still in my head. But now I dream of you dead."

The serial killer odds skyrocketed. He put the paper away and looked at me expectantly.

"Tanner? Check, please!" I called. "Very powerful, Pete. And terrifying. You might want to reconsider that last line."

"Too harsh?" he said.

"I'd get a restraining order if I were in her shoes."

"But what about the rhyming? It took me a really long time to find words that rhyme."

"It does rhyme. You are correct about that. Tanner? We're all set here."

Pete shrugged. "I guess it doesn't matter," he said. "My ex, I mean. She'll be super jealous that I've moved on. When do you want kids, by the way? I'm totally ready. I'd like us to get pregnant within the year. That would really chap her ass."

"Sorry. We're not really a good match, Pete," I said. "I don't want kids."

"Shit," he said. "Think you could've said that in your profile?"

"My sister wrote it. I don't even know what's in it, to be honest."

"Great. Thanks for totally wasting my time." He tossed a ten down on the table and stomped off.

"My time was also totally wasted," I called. "And your salad cost sixteen dollars." He didn't pause.

My parents were instantly at my side, wheezing with laughter. "We won't let you marry an awful poet," Mom managed. "You can do better."

They were already disinterested. "Ellie," Dad said, "what do you say we skip dessert and head home for a nap?"

"I love naps," she said coyly. "Even more than dessert."

"Okay, kids," I said. "There are children present. Me. I'm your child."

They left the restaurant, laughing, arms around each

other. I settled up with Beth, paying for Grandpop's lunch, too. Still single, I thought as I walked home. Which was far better than being with a homicidal poet. Besides, I had an arrangement with a guy named James, who taught cello and violin in Harwich. Once or twice a month, I'd drive to his place so we could fool around. We had no pretenses. He served a purpose, and so did I. It wasn't the worst scenario in the world.

My only life goals were to make Open Book the best bookstore on the Cape and win every trivia game I ever entered. I couldn't see myself married at this point. Kids? Out of the question.

My phone started blowing up with texts from my siblings, since the parents had clearly updated the troops. Sorry, said Addison. He seemed normal, but what do I know? I'm gay. She included a rainbow flag emoji in case I'd forgotten.

Finding a spouse is almost impossible after 30, and you're 35. It's not Addison's fault. This from Nicole, Addie's wife. No sense of humor.

At least he didn't write a crappy poem about YOU. ☺ This from Lark. Not yet, anyway. ☺ <3 <3 <3

You don't HAVE to be with someone. Winnie. But if this is your kink, you do you.

I fail to see the problem here, Robbie said. Sounds like you were perfect for each other.

I texted an emoji of a laughing face and a middle finger to Robbie and left the rest for later.

"I already heard," Destiny said as I walked in. "But you can tell me all the details later."

"News travels fast," I said, bending to pet Oliver's silky fur and gaze into his beautiful eyes. "I don't need anyone but you, Ollie," I said, kissing his perfect head.

"Am I the only person who works here full-time?" Cynthia snapped.

Destiny and I exchanged a look. Some people had resting bitch face. Cynthia had resting bitch soul.

A woman was in the back, perusing our teeny tiny erotica

selection. "Hi, Ms. Henderson!" I called. "Looking for something new?"

"Just browsing. Getting inspiration," she said. She picked up a book called *Super Sex After Sixty* and thumbed through it. "Heh. I could've written this one."

"Oh, we got a new book in," Destiny said. "It's not in your usual BDSM vein, but I think you'll love it." Hand-selling like a champ, our Destiny. She knew how things worked, and sure enough, Karen bought Destiny's recommendation, plus two more. I rang her up and told her to have a great day. I saw that Grady Byrne had ordered another marine biology book. This one cost $204. Good on you, Grady, I thought, and sent him a quick text thanking him for using us. See you Friday! I added. Trivia night.

Father's Day was coming, so I went through the store, grabbing books for the window display. Red Sox triumphs. World War II. James Patterson and Michael Connelly. The most recent Colson Whitehead novel. Some Robert Bly poetry. *This Old House* how-to manuals. Cookbooks that featured meat, beer and fire.

Outside, the June day beckoned. I'd probably take my paddle board to Marconi Beach after work, since it didn't get dark until almost ten o'clock.

The window display could use a little something else. "Do we have any manly objects lying around?" I asked.

"You're asking the wrong person," Destiny said, giving a little twirl so her dress swirled around her. I smiled, went to the back closet and rummaged around. Ah. A baseball mitt. A hammer. My Red Sox cap. I could raid Grandpop's place later for other masculine touches, like his Panama hat and a shaving brush.

The bell over the door rang. I looked up to see two men—one in his forties or early fifties, and his son, I assumed, who wore droopy jeans and a hoodie. The man had salt-and-pepper hair and a solid build. He picked up a book and said something to the boy, and the boy smiled. I couldn't quite see their faces, because the light was behind them.

I started to say hello, then stopped. A weird, prickling feeling started in my knees, almost painful. The air seemed to change and grow too thick to breathe.

The older man turned, and I saw his profile. I *knew* him. Sure, I knew many customers. But he wasn't a regular. No. My mind skipped like a stone on the water. I knew him. Once, I'd known him very well, but my mind wasn't letting me place him.

Then younger one turned, and I saw more of his face. My stomach dropped like I was in an express elevator.

He was about five-ten. Lanky. Unkempt, curly dark hair. He glanced at me surreptitiously, not long enough for me to see his face clearly, then looked down at the book he'd grabbed off the shelf. *The Enduring Shore.* He was holding it upside down.

My heart was banging against my ribs like it wanted to burst out and run down the street, and yet my brain couldn't gather a single coherent thought.

Then the boy moved away from the window, and I could see his face now, and once again, he looked at me. Our eyes met. He smiled, and the floor dropped away

I took a step forward, but my knees were made of water, and I staggered. The older man looked up. I reached out to steady myself on a table, missed, and took another wobbling, unsure step. "Are you all right?" said the older man, starting toward me. He was Indian. Oh, yes, I *knew* him.

"Harlow?" said Destiny.

"Oh, crap," said the boy, his smile fading. I was falling and my vision was shutting down.

He looked so much like my brother with his dark curly hair and brown eyes . . . he looked like Robbie because he was related to Robbie. He . . . he was . . . Robbie's nephew.

In other words, he was my son.